BROKEN SINS

A REVERSE HAREM DARK MAFIA ROMANCE
(VOLKOV BRATVA BOOK 3)

NICOLE FOX

Created with Vellum

MAILING LIST

Sign up to my mailing list!
New subscribers receive a FREE steamy bad boy romance novel.

Click the link below to join.
https://sendfox.com/nicolefox

ALSO BY NICOLE FOX

Belluci Mafia Trilogy

Corrupted Angel (Book 1)

Corrupted Queen (Book 2)

Corrupted Empire (Book 3)

De Maggio Mafia Duet

Devil in a Suit (Book 1)

Devil at the Altar (Book 2)

Kornilov Bratva Duet

Married to the Don (Book 1)

Til Death Do Us Part (Book 2)

Heirs to the Bratva Empire

**Can be read in any order*

Kostya

Maksim

Andrei

Tsezar Bratva

Nightfall (Book 1)

Daybreak (Book 2)

Russian Crime Brotherhood

**Can be read in any order*

Owned by the Mob Boss

Unprotected with the Mob Boss

Knocked Up by the Mob Boss

Sold to the Mob Boss

Stolen by the Mob Boss

Trapped with the Mob Boss

Volkov Bratva

Broken Vows (Book 1)

Broken Hope (Book 2)

Broken Sins *(standalone)*

Other Standalones

Vin: A Mafia Romance

Box Sets

Bratva Mob Bosses (Russian Crime Brotherhood Books 1-6)

Tsezar Bratva (Tsezar Bratva Duet Books 1-2)

Heirs to the Bratva Empire

BROKEN SINS

A REVERSE HAREM DARK MAFIA ROMANCE (VOLKOV BRATVA BOOK 3)

My father's enemies have claimed me for revenge.

Life as Luka Volkov's daughter is hell.

I live in a gilded cage.

I want out.

But not like this.

His enemies came for me in the night.

Four of them.

Vito, Mateo, Leo, Dante.

Each is darker and more savage than the last.

The Bianci brothers plan to use me for their vengeance.

But not before they use me for their pleasure.

In their hands, I will be bent. Broken.

And after each midnight session, they promise me this...

By the time it's all over, I'll be begging for more.

PROLOGUE: MILAYA

I'm running for my life.

My lungs are screaming at me. They're filled with fire, acid, lightning. My body wants me to stop. It's practically begging at this point. I don't know how long I've been running. I don't know how much longer I'll have to run if I want to escape. I don't know if escape is even an option anymore.

The men pursuing me want me so they can break me.

They've come close to doing that already. All the days and nights I've been under lock and key in their fucked-up mansion of shadows and secrets have pushed me close to the edge. This is my last chance to get away before they finish what they've started.

They told me I'm their princess. They said that *they* serve *me*.

What a load of fucking bullshit.

For a while, they almost had me fooled. As whips turned to caresses and cruelty turned to kisses, I started to believe the lies they were feeding me. *You're safer with us. We want what is best for you. We are on your side.*

Lies, lies, and damned lies. I've been a pawn since the beginning.

I almost preferred the way things were at first, on those first few nights after they kidnapped me. Back then, I could understand their hatred for me. I could understand why they wanted to make me scream until my throat was raw and my voice gave out.

We were enemies, plain and simple.

But nothing is plain and simple anymore.

One thought runs through my head on repeat, a broken record: *Don't stop. Don't stop. Don't stop.* If I stop, I die. Simple as that. There are no second chances in this game I was born into. The men on my trail will kill me with their bare hands.

And the sickest thing of all is that part of me believes I deserve it.

Maybe I didn't choose to become an expendable piece on their chessboard. It was just my birthright. The blood in my veins is what brought me here.

But I've made all my own choices since then—that is, if choosing between death or captivity can even be considered a choice. So perhaps I've earned this ending. Perhaps I brought it all upon myself in some sick, twisted way.

The alley is long, damp with rain, cloaked with shadows. My feet pound the pavement. I don't have much longer before my body simply quits on me. It has been through so much already. I have been stretched and bent and broken during my nights in the Bianci Castle. Who knows how much fight I have left in my bones.

I can hear the breathing of the men behind me. Their footsteps are heavy and pounding. Four men, almost one thousand pounds of hot muscle and seething rage, have spread themselves out in the night to encircle and ensnare me.

Getting this far was a miracle.

And, as I'm beginning to realize, getting any farther will soon be an impossibility.

I go left, then right, winding through the labyrinth of interconnected alleyways. I run until I'm aware that suddenly, I don't hear my pursuers anymore.

There is a rectangle of light at the end of the alleyway I've found myself in. I go towards it. My bare feet splash through puddles, crunch broken glass, step past rats and cockroaches skittering around the dark concrete. I'm bleeding, crying, sweating—but I can't slow down.

I reach the mouth of the alley, burst out onto the street, and race halfway across without even bothering to check for oncoming traffic. I don't care anymore. If I die smeared across the grill of a taxi—well, so be it. Just another cruel twist of fate from an uncaring universe.

The night around me is silent and oppressive. It feels like the very air itself wants to suffocate me with its weight. Humidity and darkness combined are like a hand pressing against my chest, stopping me from drawing in a full breath. Time—brief, precious seconds—meanders past at the pace of a predatory shark trawling dark ocean waters.

I don't have much of it left.

I freeze in the middle of the road. There is a streetlight at the intersection fifty yards to my left. The lamp casts a cone of orange light that looks far too warm and friendly for what's happening to me right now. I think, with the same dark sarcasm that has stuck with me throughout this entire nightmare, that whoever designed this world fucked up. That light should be a cold, vicious blue. Fluorescent. The kind that exposes everything.

The first night I woke up in the castle, that was what greeted me. Harsh light. Illuminating faces that looked just as cruel, all sharp angles and deep shadows around the eyes—but God, those faces were beautiful, too. They made me understand why angels chose to follow Satan. Darkness can be beautiful. Tempting. It can swallow you whole and make you love every second of it.

The cone of light is empty. It reveals bare sidewalk, nothing more.

Then I blink.

A man steps into the light.

He is almost impossibly tall, with shoulders as wide as a doorframe. He is too far away to make out much of his face. But I don't need to be close to know what he looks like. I have seen it plenty. Up close and personal, just inches away from mine. How many nights have I seen that face? Too many to count. In real life, in my dreams—it won't leave me alone. That aquiline nose. Those verdant green eyes, like an ancient forest underneath the canopy of thick, dark eyebrows.

This can't be real. I'm dreaming. I have to wake up.

But I know I'm not.

How many times over the last few weeks have I tried to pretend I was Dorothy in Oz? How many times did I click my heels together and say, "There's no place like home"? Too many to count.

But here's the other thing I've learned:

Home isn't heaven, either.

Home might even be worse than this hell I've found myself in. At least, in this messed-up nightmare, the demons announce themselves as such. They don't hide who they are and what they want.

Home ... home is where the devils dress up as angels and say they're here to save you. Home is a thicket of lies.

Funny that I should be thinking of home right now. Because the man standing underneath the light is the one who ripped back the curtain and showed me the ugly underbelly of everything I once knew and loved.

He sees me now. I can tell he does, though he doesn't move or acknowledge me at all. He simply stands under the light, awash in orange. He's wearing a dark navy suit over a crisp white shirt. Both are torn to shreds and stained with blood. One of his hands is bloody, too. It drips from his fingertips and puddles on the sidewalk beneath him.

His other hand is holding a gun.

I freeze like a deer caught in the headlights. He won't fire. At least, I don't think he will. But there are no rules left to be followed. The game has been broken wide open. Up is down and left is right. The good guys are the bad guys and the bad guys are—fuck, I don't know what they are. Or who they are. Or what they want.

As I watch, another man materializes next to the first. Just as tall, just as broad. His hair is shaggier, hanging almost down to his shoulders. I can see the glint of an ear piercing. I know from firsthand experience that the rest of his body is similarly riddled with piercings and tattoos. The angle of the streetlight throws his five-o'clock shadow into sharp relief. He looks dirty, savage, like a wild beast merely pretending to be a man.

I didn't know it was possible, but at the sight of him, my heart sinks even lower.

I knew that he was with his brothers, of course. They were all after me, moving as one, as a pack of wolves. But somehow, seeing him here and now, in the dead of the night, is even more haunting than it was the first night I woke up.

He was the first one of them I saw. He sat in the corner of the room they held me in. I heard him before I saw him, actually. The sound of a blade sliding against a whetstone, again and again.

When I opened my drug-addled eyes, I saw him there, casually leaning backwards on a stool propped against the stone wall. Like sharpening his knife and looking at a bound, captive girl was no big deal. Just another day in the life.

I knew instantly that he was unhinged. His eyes told the whole story. Pain swam in them like molten lava. He had honey-colored irises—if honey had a lethal aftertaste.

I see now that he is holding that same knife. His hands, like his brother's, are stained with blood.

I start to back away. I want to be anywhere but here.

As I watch, a third man steps into the light. He is jaw-droppingly beautiful. Even now, in the midst of all this whatever-you'd-call-it—chaos? nightmare? hellscape?—I sense his beauty and let out a soft sigh. His jaw is sharp enough to slice you wide open. His lips can say and do such beautiful things to me. I know this because he's said them. He's done them. Hell, I asked for it. I *begged* him to trace his lips down the curve of my neck, between my breasts, past the hollows in my hips, and down ... I wanted it so badly. And he gave it to me—in a manner of speaking. But like an evil genie, the wish he granted was somehow everything I wanted and nothing of the sort, all at the same time.

The third man's eyes are cold, blue, and clear. Right now, they betray nothing. A mountain lake, undisturbed by even the tiniest ripple. Like the first man, he is wearing a suit. The slacks, at least. The jacket must have been lost somewhere in the mayhem that all of us left behind. His white dress shirt is crisply ironed, the first few buttons rakishly undone. Somehow, he made it through everything with only one drop of blood staining the collar.

I count the men again. One, two, three. Green eyes, blue eyes, honey eyes.

But the fourth is missing.

The one who started it all.

The one whose voice, whose touch, whose very essence is seared into my soul like a cattle brand.

Where is Vito Bianci?

I turn and find out immediately.

Vito's chest is as solid as granite when I turn and collide into him. How he snuck up behind me without making a sound, I'll never know. There are many things I'll never know about Vito. He is like an ocean of oil, hiding so many secrets beneath his surface.

But I have seen some of them. There is a beating heart behind that chest. It is buried underneath pain, but I have seen it in one beautiful, unforgettable glimpse. He may regret showing it to me. In fact, I know he does. It makes what he has to do next so much harder.

I take a deep breath and swallow past the knot in my throat. It's over for me now. I am back in the brothers' possession. Perhaps it was foolish to think I ever had a chance of becoming free again. That shattered hope is stabbing me in the heart right now like shards of glass that once made up a delicate sculpture. I shouldn't have ever hoped. It will make the ending that much worse.

I look up at Vito. He is not as tall as his younger brothers, but he is the most muscular. He has the same nose that they all do. Strong, straight as an arrow, leading up into a proud forehead. Those eyes—I used to swear they were black all the way through, pupil and iris alike. I don't know anymore. I don't know anything anymore. What's real, what's fake, what's a lie, what's true?

Who the fuck knows?

"We have found you, Milaya Volkov," he growls in a voice deeper than sound, rasping like a metal edge on stone. "You cannot run anymore."

I don't say anything. There's nothing to say. He's right—I can't run anymore.

We stand there and stare at each other for a few long moments. My breath has slowed from short, sharp gasps to a soft inhale, exhale, inhale, exhale. He doesn't blink, doesn't move, doesn't say anything else.

Is it insane that I notice his smell? Blood and sweat and cologne all mixed together. It's as intoxicating as it was the very first time. I must be deranged. My time in their castle drove me mad. Stockholm Syndrome doesn't even begin to cover it.

Maybe I was wrong about being near the breaking point.

Maybe the truth is that I broke a long, long time ago.

I can sense the others drawing close around me. They step in and join me in a circle of darkness. I am surrounded now by a wall of men. They all have a similar smell. The same blood and sweat as Vito. But each brother bears a unique musk that is entirely his own.

Like a ballerina figurine in a toy box, I do a slow pivot and drink in the sight of them. Even now, I can see that my killers are gorgeous. Sculpted by the hands of angels.

Mateo, the wise one, green-eyed.

Leo, the beautiful, blue-eyed.

Dante, the wild, honey-eyed.

And back to the front, to the beginning, to Vito, the leader, black-eyed.

They're waiting for me to do something.

I swallow again. It hurts. Christ, everything hurts, from the bottoms of my bleeding feet to the hair on my scalp, the same hair that each of these men has wound their hands through and tugged back on to make me moan and scream and beg in turns.

I didn't expect the end of my life to hurt this badly.

"Well?" I say with a voice cockier than I truly feel. I haven't made this easy on them since the night they took me. I don't plan on starting now. "You found me. Now what?"

"Now," Dante answers, "we are going to finish what we started."

1

MILAYA

ONE MONTH EARLIER

I'm walking underneath the awning of the strip mall on Westwood, right down the road from the Equinox by campus, when I see them.

Crap.

I feel exposed, even though I'm wearing baggy gray sweats over my tight spandex booty shorts and a white tank top over my neon pink sports bra. My hair is pulled back into a no-nonsense ponytail, but I'm still wearing makeup because I had a coffee meeting with a professor on campus this morning to discuss my proposal for an upcoming assignment.

I don't have long to act. I think about what I should do next.

I've got a duffel bag slung over one shoulder that holds all of my gym gear. I rifle through the contents with my free hand real quick, trying to come up with a game plan.

My fingerless padded boxing gloves won't help much. That'll just make my punches that much less threatening. At five-foot-four, one hundred and twenty pounds, I'm petite enough already that there are very few people on earth who are scared of my punches as it is.

Jump rope? I could swing it like Indiana Jones' bullwhip. Or, wait, maybe I can hide behind a pillar until one of the two bald Mafia goon-looking guys who are hunting me down gets too close. Then I'll jump out to strangle him. It's not a great plan, but it's the best I've got …

Until my fingers close around the gun my dad gave me before I left for school.

I forgot I'd stashed it in here. The feel of the cold metal against my palm gives me goose bumps. I don't like guns. It took Dad almost two weeks of arguing to get me to accept it. But he wouldn't take no for an answer. He never does.

He just wants what's best for me, of course. What father doesn't want his daughter to be safe while she's attending college across the country? He's no different than any other dad in America. But his overprotective streak has lasted twenty-two years. I'm fed up with it. I'm an adult now. I don't need Daddy keeping me safe.

I let the gun drop back into the bottom of the bag and pick up my pace a little bit.

The door to the fitness studio is about thirty yards away. Glancing over my shoulder, I see one of the two suited men prowling through the parking lot, trying to see where I'm going. The other must be …

Shit!

I dive behind a parked car right as the second man rounds the corner ahead of me. His head was turned, so I don't think he saw me, but I hold my breath and stay crouched low.

Easy, girl, I whisper in my head. *Wait for your chance.*

I changed buses three times to slip these guys and get here. I'm still not sure how they found me, but it's kind of a moot point now. They're here. Safety, though, is just a ten-second sprint away from me. I can see the door. *Big Fist Kickboxing Gym, Los Angeles, CA,* is embossed on the frosted glass. Even from where I'm squatting behind a gleaming new Range Rover with a Starbucks cup abandoned in the center console—how freaking original—I can hear the sound of padded fists striking the bags and the huffed breath of UCLA's fit-chick population trying to sweat off another five pounds before the weekend hits. Although, to be fair, I'm about to go join them, so maybe I should bite my tongue and not be so condescending.

The second man, the one who rounded the corner, is checking the windows of each of the shops in the strip mall as he strides slowly down the covered walkway. I duck lower and watch his feet move from my vantage point below the Range Rover. He's wearing leather shoes with an athletic rubber sole fixed on. Some aftermarket upgrades, no doubt. All the better to chase down twenty-something females who don't want to be caught by a big, burly guy with such a nasty gleam in his eyes.

My gaze moves up a few inches to the bulge hiding at the side of his calf.

That's a gun in an ankle holster.

I swallow hard. In the distance, I hear the first guy interrogating some innocent shopper about where I've gone. "Have you seen a girl?" he asks the unlucky victim. "Dark brown hair, about this tall, wearing ..." The rest of what he's saying is lost behind the sound of a nearby car engine coughing to life.

I keep my eyes fixed on the man nearest to me. He's close now, hardly a stone's throw away and narrowing the distance with each step. He moves toe, heel, toe, heel, like he's trained in how to walk without making a peep. Probably because he *has* been trained. He's been trained in other things, too. Like enhanced interrogation techniques, which I usually understand to mean breaking people's fingers until they tell him what he wants to know.

He's almost even with me now. It's time to make my move. Slowly, I creep around the back of the car in rhythm with him, keeping the vehicle between us so he can't see me. I stay crouched low to the ground and move the way he does. My sneakers—gleaming white, a twenty-second birthday gift from Mom last week—are as sneaky as their name suggests. Normally, I don't stay up on the latest haute couture trends like some of the other girls I'm friends with, but I gotta admit, I'm a sucker for the nineties nostalgia throwback wave that's been sweeping LA fashion lately, including the big, chunky white dad sneakers that everybody and their freaking grandma seem to like. It just so happens that they're coming in handy right now.

We're moving around the car in a weird lockstep dance now. Both of us are sliding counterclockwise. He's at eleven o'clock right now versus my four o'clock. He goes to ten, I go to three. He goes to nine ...

And I run.

My timing is exquisite. Someone is opening up the door to the kickboxing studio right as I approach it. I dive through into the air-conditioned interior and immediately fall to the floor, gasping from my all-out sprint effort.

It takes me a minute or two of breathing in a sweaty lump on the ground before I regain my sense of my surroundings. I get to my hands and knees and feel eyes on me.

"Uhh ... are you okay?" asks the middle-aged woman who inadvertently held the door open for me to make my great escape. She's classic LA—Botoxed until her face looks like petrified wood, with fake tits and clothes that cost more than my monthly apartment rent. Her nails are gleaming freshly done, and she's at least forty-five, but her lips are plumper than a baby's bottom. Whatever—I resolve to save the judgment for another day. For right now, she's my freaking hero.

"Fine," I say with as innocent a smile as I can muster. "Thanks for holding the door open for me."

"Sure ..." she says, still suspicious.

I give her a little waggle of the fingers as she walks away, throwing one final glance over her shoulder that might as well say, *Maybe we shouldn't let crazy people in here.*

She doesn't even know the half of it.

"Milly!" comes a familiar voice from the back half of the building. Anastasia bounces over. She's got her hair braided into fishtails and she looks as cute and sexy as ever. I still don't understand how she manages to capture both those looks at the same time. She's got a real "bang me all night long then cook me breakfast" vibe to her, which makes me insanely jealous.

My sexual vibe is more along the lines of "Uh, well, I guess." It's not that I have low confidence. With the right makeup and clothes, I can hang with the best of them. Or at least, that's what I tell myself. But I don't hold a candle to Anastasia. She gets hit on all the time.

Guys tend to be more, like, afraid of me, sorta. Anastasia usually says that I just need to be more approachable. "You always look like you're hiding state secrets," she's said to me more than once.

Oh boy, I inevitably want to say back, *if only you knew.*

Like the name she uses for me, "Milly." I've been using it since I started high school, but there's still a part of me that cringes every time. I've gotten used to it, kind of. I just don't think it'll ever be truly me. But with parents like mine, I didn't really have a choice. Dad, after all, is not the negotiating type. When he handed me a driver's license and a passport that read "Milly van Der Graaf," I just took it and didn't ask questions. Life with him is easier when you learn which subjects not to press him on.

"Hey, girl," I say to her. I'm still a little out of breath, though I'm trying my best to pull myself together. "What's up?"

"Was that you who just came flying in the door like a freaking Olympian?"

I blush and stammer, "Uhh, no. I mean, yes, it was. But I, um—I tripped."

"You tripped?"

"Yeah. You know me. Major klutz when my head is in the clouds."

She wrinkles her brow and tilts her head to the side. "Mm, okay. Anyways," she says, clapping her hands, "let's go get our spots before those witches from Theta come and steal them. Danny is teaching today and lemme tell you, my form needs some *extremely* hands-on correcting." She grins wickedly. I can't help but laugh.

Danny the Kickboxing Instructor has been a recurring theme in our conversations for a while now. It's not a serious thing; he's just a cute, ripped guy who has a penchant for helping the pretty females in the class with some cues that tend to border on—well, *handsy* is one way to put it. *Uber creepy* is more how I would describe it personally. But I do have to admit that he is very easy on the eyes. Tall, with a deep SoCal surfer's tan, and curly blond hair that he ties up in a man bun. If that's your kind of thing—and it is absolutely Anastasia's kind of thing—then you'll probably be a Dan Fan, just like her.

She's my best friend though. So even if I don't normally go for the "What's up, brah?" airhead surfer types, then I'll still come along for the ride as moral support. Plus, no matter how much I mock some of the moms and coeds who are in here doing booty-building exercises just so they can impress some lame Hollywood producer at an overcrowded cocktail party tonight, I could use a little exercise, too. It's been a grueling semester.

I drop my duffel off in the cubbies and bring my water bottle and boxing gloves over to my punching bag. The rest of the women attending today's class shuffle around and find their spots as well.

Anastasia and I chitchat about our respective weeks while we wait for class to get started. She's been dodging some frat guy named Carlos who wants badly to profess his undying love for her.

"Wait, Carlos the one you were in love with, like, last month?"

She flips her long blonde hair over one shoulder and sighs dramatically. "Ugh, that was a lifetime ago. He's a total creep now. He sent flowers to my dorm! Who does that?"

I bite back my answer, which would've been something along the lines of *"a reasonable guy who likes you"* and instead just nod my head and agree with her. Luckily, the infamous Dan comes bursting into the room from the back office moments later, saving me from having to hear more.

Dan is shirtless today. He kicks off class with some has-to-be-made-up story about spilling coffee on his only work shirt this morning. I roll my eyes, but none of the other girls in the class seem to mind his abs being on display for the next sixty minutes. Guess it's just me, then.

We get underway shortly after that lovely opening spiel. Jabs first, mixed with a circuit of jumping rope, crunches, and burpees, which I despise with an unholy fury.

In between rounds, Anastasia starts talking about a party she wants me to come to this weekend.

"... so it's not an *official* Chi Omega bash; they're not allowed to throw those anymore since the last incident. That's why it's off-site at the Ritz. But it's gonna be lit. I saw the budget and it's truly, like, mind-blowingly insane."

I'm a little too out of breath to respond. School has been kicking my butt lately, which is why I've missed the last few weeks of Dan's classes. But I gotta do what I gotta do. The end of the semester is coming up, which means exams and papers galore. It's important to me to get good grades. My parents think I'm doing it to make them happy, but that's only part of it. The real answer is that I'm doing it so I can finally be a real freaking adult. My whole life, I've been under their thumb. It's like being in a gilded cage. I don't *want* to have everything handed to me on a silver platter. I don't want to be given a gun before going away to college. I just want to be normal, like Anastasia, worried only about which guy I want to talk to at the party tonight. She's so carefree.

I've never been carefree.

Speaking of carefree, I hear "Good jab, girl!" from a voice that is both way too chill for the current EDM soundtrack blasting through the speakers at deafening volume and way too close to my left ear. I turn my head a quarter inch and see Dan taking up my whole field of vision. He's got a blindingly white smile. Definitely has one of those teeth whitener things I see on Instagram ads all the time, the one the celebs use when they're also wearing waist trainers and electronic booty-blaster machines. He's also got a dimple in his chin like Superman.

Maybe my issue with him is that he looks *too* perfect. As if he walked off the page of a GQ spread and right into this kickboxing classroom. No one is supposed to be that perfect. It unsettles me.

"Er, thanks," I tell him, flashing a grin that's supposed to say, *"I don't need any hands-on coaching, please."*

But he clearly doesn't read the signals I'm giving off, because he stations himself behind me with his hips flush against my ass and takes hold of my elbows. "But try loading this hip more. If you squeeze your butt back here and rotate"—he pivots me accordingly, which has the no-doubt-unintended effect of pulling my torso closer into his embrace—"then you'll get way more power out of your punch."

"Thanks," I say again, shaking myself loose and stepping away in a hurry. I pretend to be fixing my hair. "I'll keep that in mind."

His grin falters for just a second. He's clearly not used to being pushed away like that. Judging by the googly eyes that four or five of the girls have been throwing his way constantly, this class is more like shooting fish in a barrel for him, sexually speaking.

But that's not my game at all. I don't want perfect, I don't want flawless.

I don't want anything, actually.

I just want to be normal.

I'm drenched in sweat by the time the class ends forty-five minutes later. I'm sure I look like a troll who just rolled around the floor of a hair salon, but when I glance over at Anastasia as we're packing up our stuff, she still looks runway ready.

Bitch. Good thing I love her.

"So you're gonna come to the party?" she asks brightly.

I take a glug of water from my bottle and eye the windows. If the bald men are still around, I'm going to have to find the rear exit. Better delay my departure for the time being until I figure out a feasible plan.

"Um, maybe," I tell her.

"Oh, come on, Milly!" she squeals. "You're always ducking out on this stuff. College isn't about class, you know. It's about fun."

"Says the communications major."

She swats me with her towel as I laugh and duck away. "Don't be a bitch. I'm not the one who told you to sign up for bio. You're coming, mandatory. My place for pre-game and getting ready, got it?"

I sigh. She's relentless when she thinks she's got me hooked. Like dealing with my father, it's way easier to just give in sometimes. "Fine," I answer. "Pencil me in as a firm maybe."

"I'll take that as a yes."

"Is that what I said?"

"It's what I heard."

"You're batting your eyelashes at me. You know that only works on dudes like Carlos, right?"

"*Ugh,*" she whines. "Don't remind me. He just texted me, actually."

I watch as she opens the text, reads it so that Carlos gets the read receipt and knows she saw it, then closes it without replying. I can only shake my head and laugh. This girl blows my mind.

We both look up when we hear a woman in the corner laughing way too loudly. She's talking to Dan and standing in extremely close proximity to him. Next to me, I hear Anastasia sigh like a movie starlet. "Think batting my eyelashes would work on him?" she asks wistfully.

"You can do way better than that greasy man bun," I tell her. "Even Chi Omega douchebags are a step up from there."

"Maybe you should talk to him!" she suggests, brightening up like it's the most brilliant idea of all time. "I saw how you were getting all up on him. *Get your power from your back hip,* he says. That's hot."

I resist the urge to roll my eyes. Mom always says they're going to get stuck in my head if I keep the habit up. She's not wrong. "*He* was all up on *me,*" I correct, "not the other way around. Besides, not my type."

"What *is* your type, Mil?" Anastasia asks.

"Tall, dark, and handsome," I say with a grin. "And mysterious."

Just then, I hear the doorbell tinkle. I glance up and see two bald men in suits enter the studio.

My heart plummets. *Shit.* I thought I lost them.

I'm vaguely aware of Anastasia next to me, saying something about how starving she is. "Ooh, ding ding ding, let's go get those matcha pancakes from Café Chez. Those things are to die for."

"I, uh, I gotta go, Ana," I tell her. I'm trying not to look like I'm totally freaking out, but the bile rising in my throat is making that a little harder than anticipated. "Rain check on the matcha."

She frowns. "What's the big rush?"

"Just, uh. You know, nothing. School. Work. Or whatever."

"Wait, which one is it?"

"None. I mean, all of them. I gotta go. I'll text you later. I love you. Stay out of trouble, don't break any boys' hearts. 'Kay?" I kiss her on the cheek and head towards the door.

The two bald men are like a wall of beefy male as I approach. Neither one of them smiles. I'm about a yard away when I mutter to them under my breath, "Outside. Parking lot. Now." Right when I'm about to plow into them, they part ways like a double door opening inward, allowing me through. I don't break stride, just keep on walking, out of the studio, away from the strip mall, into the bright Los Angeles sunshine.

I'm halfway into a rant. "How many times do I have to tell you morons that I just want a little privacy sometimes?" But it's like yelling at a brick wall.

The two bald men, Anton and Matvei, don't blink or move. They're twins. It took me forever to learn how to tell them apart. Turns out Anton is a little squintier. But, since they're both wearing wraparound sunglasses right now, I'm not sure which one is which. It doesn't really matter, I suppose. I'm equally pissed off at both.

When they see that I'm out of things to bitch about for a second, the one on the left—I'm pretty sure it's Anton—speaks up. "I am sorry, Miss Volkov, but your father has given us very strict instructions not to leave you unaccompanied at any time. You were not supposed to separate from us today."

I hold up a hand to cut him off. "Keep your voice down!" I hiss. I glance around to make sure no one heard him call me by my real last name. "First things first, let's get this clear: I don't give a *shit* what my father told you. I'm a grown woman. I don't need babysitters."

"We are bodyguards," says probably-Matvei, "not babysitters."

"What is there to protect me from?" I screech. I want to tear my hair out. They may be trained killers, but they are dumb as rocks sometimes. Like fricking robots, programmed to do one thing and one thing only: whatever Luka Volkov tells them to do.

"Your father has many enemies," Anton answers firmly.

I look around the parking lot. Palm trees wave overhead, the sky is impossibly blue, and the sun is heating the air to a balmy but breezy seventy-five degrees. "What enemies?" I say. "Look around you. There's no one here who even knows who I am, much less gives a damn about me. Just let. Me. Live. My. Life."

Matvei starts to say something else, but I sigh for the billionth time since this infuriating conversation began and turn away. There's no point in continuing it. We've done this whole song-and-dance way too many times and it always ends the same way: whatever my father wants, my father gets.

Speaking of the devil, my phone starts to vibrate where I have it tucked in my sports bra. Dad's ears must have been burning. I retrieve it and answer with an irritated, "What?"

"That's no way to greet your father," he chuckles.

"Not the time, Dad. Your shaved monkeys are getting on my nerves today."

I can hear him frowning through the phone. "Are you giving Anton and Matvei a hard time? They're good men, Milaya. They're there to protect you."

"Protect me from—you know what, never mind. It's not even worth it."

"Good." I sense that he feels like that settles things, which irritates me even more. But I decide to drop it for the time being. "How are you?"

"I'm good. School's hard. Professor Mills is a pain in my ass."

"Stefano Mills?"

"I don't even want to know why you know his first name, Dad."

"It's my job to know things, *lubimaya*." That's his pet name for me. It means *my love*. I'm not feeling the love right now, though. At the moment, he feels more like my prison warden than he does my father. "Do you want me to—hold on, your mother wants to talk to you."

"Hey, baby," Mom says after the phone is exchanged. "How's your paper coming?"

"Hey, Mom. It's almost done. I spent a few hours in the library yesterday cranking on it."

"Good. Doing anything fun this weekend?"

"Not sure. Anastasia wants me to go to some frat thingamajig. I'll probably go there if I can't dream up a good excuse."

"Having some fun is good too, you know. As long as you're being safe."

I hear Dad in the background, grumbling something about "... she's going to a frat party?"

"Yes, honey," Eve scolds him, muffling the phone away from her mouth with one hand. "She's a twenty-two-year-old girl. That's what twenty-two-year-olds do."

"I don't like it," Dad answers.

I just laugh bitterly and shake my head. Like yelling at Anton and Matvei, this is a ritual I've been through a thousand times before. Mom wants me to have fun, Dad wants me to stay locked away like Rapunzel in the castle, and I just want everybody to leave me alone. In the end, nobody gets what they want, and we all agree to argue about it some more next time around. Hip-hip-freaking-hooray, I love my life.

Mom and I chatter for a while about all the things going on in each of our lives before Dad gets back on the phone. "Milaya," he says in that stern voice of his, "this professor ..."

"Professor Mills?"

"That one. Do you need me to do anything? I can handle anything you need. If he is giving you trouble ..."

"No, no, no," I say hurriedly. There's a dark, ominous undertone to his voice that I want to steer far away from. He is Luka Volkov. When he says he'll "handle someone," there is no telling what that means. "He's just being a hardass. It just means I have to work harder. That's all. No need for anyone to handle anything."

"If you're sure."

"I'm sure. Listen, Dad, I have to go. I've got class in an hour and I still have to shower."

"Okay," he says. "I love you, *lubimaya*."

"I love you too, Dad. Tell Mom I said bye."

I hang up the phone and turn to the bodyguards, who have been standing at attention a respectful distance away while I talked on the phone. "Let's go, Tweedledee and Tweedledumbass."

Dad's voice echoes in my head the whole way home. *I can handle anything you need ...* he said. I shudder again.

I know just how seriously he means that.

2

VITO

I fucking hate this picture.

I look at it every single day.

It is like torturing myself. Why do I do it again and again? I cannot stop. It is an addiction. It is breaking me. I cannot stop.

If I were a lesser man, a weaker man, I would feel something when I pull the photo from its resting place in the false drawer hidden within my bedside table. I would feel regret, perhaps, for the things I did not or could not do back then. Sadness, for what it shows that I no longer have.

I am not a weak man though. So mostly, I feel nothing. Nothing but the same cold rage that has driven me for as long as I can remember. I wake up with it. I go to sleep with it. I feel it all the hours in between.

Only when I dream am I free of it.

I close my eyes and rest my head against the headboard of my bed. The wood is cold to the touch. Our home, the Bianci Castle, is always cold. It is an ancient structure high in the hills of Southern California. The sun seems to fail to reach here. Even now, when I look out my window, I do not see the breezy palms and crystalline skies that most people think of when they imagine Los Angeles. It is like we are in a realm removed from the world around us.

I prefer it that way.

We have high iron gates and thick stone walls to keep the rabble out. I stay here as often as I can. I only descend into the city when my work demands it of me.

As it will tonight.

I know what my father will ask of us at the council meeting tonight. Already, I dread it. It is wrongheaded and foolish. Rash. Once upon a time, my father would have known better than to let blind anger guide his decision-making. That time has long since passed though. The feared leader of the Bianci Mafia has devolved into little more than a lunatic, frothing at the mouth as he denounces his enemies.

Few fear him anymore.

But I have feared my father since the second my life began. That is no accident. He cultivates fear. Brandishes it like a weapon. Fear is equal to power, in his eyes. Even his children were taught to fear him. His moods roil like hurricane clouds. There is no telling when and where he will lash out.

"It shouldn't have been you," I murmur under my breath as I pass my thumb over the face of the girl in the picture. If I had a heart, it would be aching. But my heart has been beaten out of me by thirty-two years as my father's son.

"If you are to ever inherit my throne," he has hissed at me countless times, *"then you cannot be a slave to your pitiful fucking weaknesses. Either they perish, or you do. There are no other options."*

I remember the six-year-old Vito hearing those things from his father's mouth for the first time. I remember him crushing a butterfly before my eyes, just to show me that beauty cannot last. I remember how, when the family dog died, he locked me in a room with its corpse.

Love nothing. Want nothing. Keep nothing.

The mantra of a broken man.

But I cannot deny that we have what we have because of him. This castle, our riches, our legions of loyal soldiers—they follow the Bianci flag because they know that the man who holds it will do whatever it takes to get what he wants.

He has taught each of his sons that. As the oldest, I took the brunt of his wrath. He wanted to download his essence into me. Maybe he hopes to live longer in that way. As if he can consume me entirely and in doing so, save himself from death.

I don't fucking know. I've spent a lifetime analyzing the man. The depths of his sins are still a mystery to me in so many ways.

Like the sin I am holding in my hands. This picture and the bloodstained story behind it was the first time I saw clearly how wrong my father could be. But at least in those days he was tempered by logic.

Now, there is nothing holding him back.

The grandfather clock tolls in the corner of my bedroom. I sigh, bring the picture to my lips, and kiss it softly before I return it to its hidden resting place.

I grab my gun, my knife, my watch. Then I descend into the depths of the castle.

It is time for the meeting.

"Two decades of this shit! Twenty fucking years! I will not tolerate another goddamn second of those pig-fuck Russians infringing on my territory. Do you understand?"

My father is frothing at the mouth, literally. When he says "pig-fuck," his spit flies across the cool, dank air and lands with a spatter on the flagstones that make up the floor.

My gaze rakes around the room. There are thirteen of us here. My father, myself, my four brothers, and his seven lieutenants. I occupy myself during my father's rant by imagining how many men we have slaughtered in total. The number is astronomical. We could build another castle with the bodies and fill a moat around its perimeter with their blood.

The eyes of each man here look the same. Furtive, in that they glance into the corners of the room again and again, constantly assessing for threats. But also steady, steely, in the way that only the eyes of a man who has killed a person with his bare hands can be.

As my father's eldest and heir apparent, I am seated directly to his right. I have put on a stoic face while he rants and raves. It is best not to betray any inclination whatsoever as to what I might be thinking. My father's lieutenants are loyal and battle-tested, of course, or else they would not be in here. But there is nothing like proximity to power to build a taste for it. I know damn well that, when my time comes, I will have to prove my right to the Bianci throne.

Fortunately, I am well-prepared for that.

My eyes settle on Dante, seated directly across the circle from me. He is slouched low in his seat, picking at his fingernails with a knife blade that he should not have brought into the council room. Technically, weapons are forbidden in here. But Dante has never been one for rules. His hair is long and shaggy, and the piercings in his lip and eyebrow reflect the light from the candles that sit in wall sconces on all sides. He clearly isn't paying a lick of attention to

Father's speech. I have no doubt that his insolence will draw Father's fury soon enough.

As if he heard me thinking, my father swivels towards Dante. He has to lean heavily on his cane these days. One bad leg from an assassination attempt has left him with a pronounced limp. But his fire has not diminished even a bit.

"Dante!" he roars.

Dante doesn't even flinch. Nor does he look up. That is a mistake. If there is one thing my father cannot stand, it is disrespect.

With a flash of movement faster than any of us expected from him, Father unsheathes the knife he keeps at his side and leaps to Dante. The knife flies through the air and stops only when its tip is pressed up against the soft underside of Dante's chin. He digs it in deep enough that, even from here, I can see a bejeweled bead of blood slide down the blade.

Dante still has not moved a muscle.

Finally, he looks up into my father's face, held just inches from his and roiling with the kind of tempestuous fury that only Giovanni Bianci is capable of. "Stab me, Father," he says lazily. "I'd prefer that to hearing any more of this bullshit fucking meeting."

A few of the stupider men chuckle. The wise ones say nothing, do nothing. I see the lines of tension in my father's hands and neck. He knows that Dante does not respond to threats. Dante, of all the killers in this room, is the least afraid of death. He welcomes it with open arms. Something broke in him when Mother died. There is not much sanity left behind his amber eyes.

"Father," mutters Sergio, seated to Dante's left. The two of them are twins, physically identical in every way, other than that Sergio's eyes are a shocking violet. But in terms of their temperament, the two couldn't be farther apart. Whereas Dante is wild, reckless, unhinged, Sergio is the exact opposite. He is calm and composed no matter what he faces. Of all of the Bianci brothers, I know that Father loves Sergio the most. I may be the oldest, but Sergio is the one Father would choose to take his place if he could.

"Do not get involved," Father snaps to Sergio. He hasn't moved the knife from Dante's neck.

As we watch in frozen silence, Dante leans forward and grabs Father's hand. He pulls the knife closer to his throat, leaving a red slice in its wake. The drop of blood turns into a small but steady trickle.

"Do it," he hisses. His eyes are wild. "Cut my fucking throat right here."

"Father," Sergio says again. He reaches across and puts his hand on top of Dante's, which is resting on top of my father's, still gripping the handle of the knife. "Let it go."

Silence. The chamber seems to hold its breath, as if the castle around us were a living organism.

Then Father growls and rips the knife away from both of them. He sheathes it again and staggers back to his seat, leaning heavily on his cane. Settling back into his seat with a flourish, he looks again around the room.

And just like that, it is as if nothing ever happened. No outburst. No knife drawn on his own son.

Nothing.

It is time to restore some semblance of order to this meeting, which has been utterly derailed by Father's short temper. That responsibility falls to me.

"If I may," I begin. I look to Father, who inclines his head perhaps just a degree. "The dominance of the Bratva on the East Coast has been unchallenged for over two decades now. But only recently have they begun to extend their influence to our side of the country. Make no mistake—these are dangerous men, led by a dangerous man. We would be foolish to take them lightly."

"No one is taking them lightly, brother," interrupts Mateo. He has been silent since the beginning of the meeting, brooding as he always does. I have no doubt that he has been war-gaming in his head, running through endless permutations of the potential outcomes. He has always brandished his intellect like a weapon. Even when we were young, he took to chess over brawling in the yard. Mother encouraged his reading, even his piano playing.

But he was taught to kill, just the same as the rest of us. My father didn't care how smart each of us was or wasn't. We were the Bianci children. And that meant it was our birthright to be baptized in blood.

Mateo continues, "Three stash houses struck in the last four months. A dozen good men killed. Even the blindest among us understands that the Russians are here with malicious intentions, and they will not be leaving anytime soon. They are capable of doing what they threaten. Ask the LeClerc Cartel. They tried to hurt the Volkovs. It did not end well for them."

I can see Sergio nodding. Dante has gone back to cleaning his nails with his knife. Leo is gazing absentmindedly into the middle distance. Probably daydreaming about whatever piece of pussy he has waiting for him up in his bedroom. The rest of the lieutenants also seem to be in agreement.

I nod slowly too. Mateo is right. The Volkov Bratva demands our full attention—and our caution.

But my father does not agree. He slams the metal tip of his cane against the stones. It echoes throughout the chamber. "Fuck that," he growls. "I will not sit back and let some Russian pigs rub their slime over everything I've built with my bare fucking hands."

"No one is saying that—" I start to argue, but when he whirls on me with a crazed gleam in his eyes, I fall silent and sigh.

"*We* take the fight to *them*," he snarls. "We don't wait. They don't get to decide what happens next. I do. That's why I'm Giovanni Bianci, and they are mangy Russian dogs."

I draw in a deep breath. The air in here is cold and damp. I feel it seeping into my lungs, my bloodstream, like I am molding from the inside out. I shudder. I hate this fucking room.

"I don't think that is wise, Father," I say after a long pause.

"What do you think is wise then, son?" he replies. His voice is thick with sarcasm.

I must tread lightly here, or else I will just piss him off further. "We need to see what they have in mind. If they want to nibble at the northern edges of our territory, fine. Who cares? Little will be lost. If they have grander ambitions—well, then we respond accordingly."

"No." His answer is quick and brutally efficient, like a knife swipe across the throat. "You are the eldest. You will take your brothers and your men and you will strike at them tonight. Kill every Bratva bastard in the fucking county."

"But Father, don't you think—"

"That's an order."

I fall silent once again, brooding. My mind flashes back to the picture of the girl in my bedside table. Another monument to his cruelty. He has not changed who he is in the years since that sin. He has only become more himself.

This time, it might kill us all.

"As you wish, Father," I tell him. I only say that to appease him for now.

I have no intention of doing what he wants.

"*As you wish, Father,*" Dante mimics in a high-pitched voice. "You coward."

"Watch your fucking tongue, brother, or I will cut it out and nail it to the wall so we can all watch it for you."

"Quit bickering like little schoolgirls," Mateo sighs. He is rubbing the bridge of his nose between his thumb and forefinger as he sinks into one of the overstuffed armchairs scattered around the upstairs library.

All five of us have retreated here and shut the door behind us. This is the room we use to talk about plans that we don't want to come to Father's attention. From up here, we can hear anyone climbing up the stairs long before they are close enough to make out our conversation.

I am seated by the fire, stirring it with a poker. Dante is playing five-finger fillet on the desk, over and over again, jabbing between his spread fingers with the tip of his knife in rapid-fire fashion. Leo is sprawled on the bearskin rug, lazily flipping a coin between his knuckles. Sergio is leaning against the doorframe, deep in thought.

"Don't piss me off," I warn Mateo. I can't fucking stand when he tries to act all holier-than-thou. He already got on my nerves when he interrupted me in the meeting. Of course I'm not taking the Volkov threat lightly. What kind of moron does he think I am? But no, in Mateo's world, he is the philosopher-king, and everyone else is just a stupid little pauper who should be worshipping at the feet of his great intellect.

Leo props himself up on one elbow. He is no doubt irritated that I called us into this meeting instead of letting him go back to his room to play grab-ass with some whore. But he is needed here, just like the rest of us, so we can figure out what the hell we are going to do about this suicide mission that Father has thrown at our feet.

"What if we just do what he wants, bring him back a few Russian scalps, and call it a day?"

"Idiot," Mateo groans.

"I like it," chimes Dante.

I can only roll my eyes.

Sergio is the last to react. I turn to look at him. He's the youngest of us—born two minutes after his twin—but he carries himself with a gravitas far beyond his years. I'm the oldest, but even I like to get Sergio's counsel before making my own decisions.

"He won't take no for an answer," Sergio remarks carefully. "We have to be smart about how we play this."

"Tell me you don't think we should just fucking charge into the Russian stronghold, guns blazing, and hope it all just works out for us," I drawl.

"Of course not," he answers smoothly. His violet eyes flash in the firelight. "I don't want a bullet between my eyes any more than you all do."

"I'd welcome it," Dante butts in. "It'd save me from anymore of this god-awful conversation."

Leo flicks the coin at Dante's head in irritation. Moving with the speed of a jungle cat, Dante snags the projectile out of the air, brings it to his teeth, and bites down on it, hard. He removes the bent coin from his mouth, grinning wildly. "Better luck next time," he taunts with a smirk.

"You are in rare form tonight, little brother," Mateo tells him.

I laugh bitterly. "I'd rather he be in *silent* form."

"Don't we all," adds Leo.

"Quiet," interrupts Sergio. He has an ear pressed against the door. He must've heard someone coming up the stairs.

We all sit for a long minute without uttering a peep. The only noise is the fire crackling and the howl of wind outside. This high in the hills, the wind sometimes screeches through the tree branches with a fury. As with everything else about the Bianci Castle, it is completely removed from the pleasant California world that lies at its feet.

A few slow breaths later, Sergio relaxes. Whatever he heard must be gone now.

"As I was saying," he continues, "we have to be smart about this. I think, for now, we stall."

"Stall?"

"Tell Father we are preparing. Scouting, that kind of thing. It'll buy us time to come up with something better."

I lean against the hearth. The fire is hot tonight, but I like the heat. It helps me think. I bask in it and keep shifting the metal poker in the heart of the flames, where the logs glow.

"Stall," I mutter to myself. "It is not the worst thing we could do."

"It is the *only* thing we can do," Sergio says.

I turn to Mateo. "What do you think?"

He rubs his neatly groomed beard as he thinks. Finally, he admits, "I don't have any brilliant conclusions yet. I need more time to think. And we need to learn more about our new Russian friends."

"Friends?" snorts Dante. "They aren't exactly coming to have afternoon tea with us, Matty."

"But we don't know for sure why they're coming at all, do we?"

"They want to kill us and take everything we have. Why is that so hard for your massive brain to understand?"

"Nothing is certain." Mateo eyes Dante warily. "First, we learn. Then, we act. That means, for now ... we stall."

"Stall," Leo repeats again. "Sounds good to me. But if we keep stalling this meeting any longer, I'm going to blow my fucking brains out." He clambers to his feet. "So, if it is acceptable to you, my brethren, I will take my leave now, so I can retreat to my quarters where a fine lass awaits me in the nude. Then I'll blow *her* fucking brains out—metaphorically speaking."

"Jesus," I say, "do you ever think with anything besides your cock?"

"It's led me this far," he says with an impish smile. "Why stop listening now?" With that, he opens the door and disappears down the shadowy staircase.

"Time for me to go, too," Dante says once the sound of Leo's footsteps has faded away. "It's been a real privilege, let me tell you. Until next time, *fratelli*." Then he is gone as well.

Mateo is still rubbing his beard as he, Sergio, and I sit in silence. I can always tell when his head is somewhere else. He gets a faraway look in his eyes, like he's not seeing anything in front of him. When he was a little boy, it was the dreamy look of a bookworm. Now that he has aged and his lanky frame has filled out with muscle, it has a more sinister undertone to it. I think to myself, not for the first time, that I am glad he is on my side.

"I need to learn more about these Russians," he says after a while. "How they operate, how they move. Know thine enemy and all that."

"Go, then," I tell him. "Report back."

He nods and departs.

Then, it is just Sergio and me. My youngest brother is paler than the rest of us. Along with his gaunt, high cheekbones, it makes those purple eyes look almost supernatural. He is not just an old soul; he is an ancient. Solemn since the day he was born, or so the stories go.

Even our maids and wet nurses were afraid of him. Mother thought she had given birth to a demon.

But Father knew better. Father knew that Sergio was born for the Mafia life.

"This won't end well," I say to him. The wind outside the window has picked up some. It looks as though it might storm tonight. The fire burns lower but with greater intensity. It casts flickering shadows across the bookshelves.

"I am afraid that I agree with you," he answers without looking back at me. Like Mateo, he, too, is lost in thought, gazing everywhere and nowhere at the same time.

"Father's rage is going to get the best of him."

At that, he looks up at me. "You think he is too angry."

"He is too *everything*," I correct. "Too angry, too vicious, too feared. He thinks it makes him stronger. But it just isolates him. We have no allies. Only this ..." I wave a hand around as I look for the right words. "Cult of personality."

Sergio is still staring at me. He hasn't blinked. "We can't show weakness, though. Father understands that. If we show the Russians we are afraid, they will come through the doors like the Visigoths sacking Rome."

"I am not weak," I snap.

"No, brother, you are not."

He taps his fingers against his jaw, an old tic he's had for as long as I can remember. It means he is deep in thought.

"You fear Father, don't you?" he asks me suddenly.

Rage surges through me. I clench the fire poker in my hand until my knuckles show white. "I don't fear a fucking thing in this world," I tell him.

"Then you hate him."

I say nothing.

"He took something precious from you. I was young, but I still remember."

Still, I say nothing.

He shakes his head and snaps himself out of his trance. "Forgive me. I spoke out of turn. I meant nothing by it." He bows, strangely enough, like we're knights in the Middle Ages, instead of trained Mafia killers in the twenty-first century. Then he leaves without another word, following in the footsteps of all our brothers before him.

I stay in the study for a long time after he is gone, tending to the fire with the weapon in my hand and thinking about what Sergio said to me.

You fear Father, don't you ...

Then you hate him?

I fear him. I hate him. I serve him.

Fuck.

3

VITO

TWO DAYS LATER

Two nights after the council meeting, we're sitting in the VIP booth at a night club. For a change, everyone is in a relatively good mood. Even Dante. He's got two bottle girls in his lap. One is licking at his neck, the other has her hand buried between his legs. Good for him. That angry bastard could use a good fuck.

I look to my right. Mateo and Leo are similarly engaged.

But beyond them, seated in the shadows, Sergio is alone and brooding.

I take to my feet with a long sigh, grab two glasses and a bottle of vodka from the table, and stroll over to him.

"Brother," I say in greeting, collapsing onto the couch next to him. "Drink with me."

He waves a hand at me. "None for me tonight."

I pour a glass for him anyway. "Drink the fucking vodka," I tell him. "What is troubling you?"

"What else? The Russians."

"Ah." I frown. I've had my hands full with normal business the last few days. I haven't thought much about the Russian problem since the meeting. Thus far, the stalling tactic has worked, and Father has yet to bring up the topic again. I think we have all been secretly hoping that his rage will burn itself out and it won't be an issue again. Sergio does not seem so certain. "You think the stalling won't work much longer."

"I think we are at the end of that particular rope, Vito."

"Says who?" I wave my arms around to take in the whole nightclub. "We are rich. We are the kings of this city. Let the Russians play in the valley. Everything that matters is ours."

"For now," he murmurs under his breath.

My frown deepens. "What kind of talk is that, Sergio?"

He turns his gaze to me. "It is honest talk," he replies evenly.

"You sound like Father."

He laughs. "You don't even know the half of it."

"What is that supposed to mean?" I snap.

"Nothing," he mutters, staring into the depths of the vodka swishing around his glass tumbler. "Nothing at all."

We fall into an uneasy silence.

It is broken only when I hear a ruckus from down below. Our booth is seated at the top of a spire inside the nightclub, only accessible from a spiral staircase cut into the rising structure. We like this spot for the ease with which we can control all who wish to access us.

But someone is coming now who doesn't give a damn about what we think we control.

"Get the fuck out of my way," snarls an ugly, familiar voice.

Father emerges at the top of the staircase, eyes wild, hair mussed. His cane clicks menacingly on the glass floor. To his left and his right stand his lieutenants and bodyguards, a veritable army of them.

"If it isn't my worthless fucking sons," he grimaces when he sees us standing there.

I rise to my feet and look at the bottle girls. "Go," I say. They all slither away down the stairs at once. They know the rules here. They know that they don't want to stick around for whatever happens next.

"Father ..." I begin, tilting my head in greeting.

He glares at me. "Don't say a fucking word, Vito."

His eyes sweep around to look at each of us in turn. Mateo, Leo, Dante, Sergio, and I all look back at him, even and measured. We don't show fear. We don't show anger. We've been trained better than that.

"Tell me something, sons: why do I hear that there are Russians still living and breathing in my fucking city?" He punctuates these last three words with slams of his cane down onto the glass floor. It cracks under the power of the third blow, spiderwebbing outward from the point of impact.

"We are studying the situation," Mateo answers coolly.

Father spits on the floor. "Bullshit."

"Father, it's not wise for us to rush into the enemy's hands like that," I say. I try to keep my voice calm and reasonable. But as soon as the words are out of my mouth, I know that he doesn't give a flying fuck about calm or reason tonight.

He just wants blood.

"It's not wise, you say?" He clicks his way towards me. His bad leg drags slightly on the ground behind him. His eyes, though, are alive and glistening, reflecting the whirling overhead black lights. He looks ghostly. "You don't want to *rush*?"

I know he is mocking me, trying to get a rise out of me. If he were anyone else, I would strike him down where he stands.

But he is my father. He is the only man in this entire fucking Mafia who gets to talk to me like that.

So, as much as I despise it, I have to stand there and take it. It is better for me to do this. Mateo would retreat inwards, Leo would blow him off, Dante would stab him in the throat. I am the only one who knows how to deal with Father's anger.

"Let me tell you something, Vito," he drawls. "I was a young man when I came into this life. I built everything we have from nothing. From fucking nothing. And along the way, I learned that there are two types of men in this world. There are men you can trust, and men you cannot. What you are telling me right now is that I cannot trust you—none of you—to carry out a simple fucking order. I told you to exterminate the Russians. If you do not do that, you are saying I can't trust you. And if I can't trust you, then you are not my son. You are merely an obstacle in my way."

He breathes in my face. It smells like whiskey. He has been drinking, despite the doctors' orders to the contrary.

"Do you know what I do to obstacles in my way, Vito? I annihilate them. I eradicate them like goddamn tumors. I will ask you one more time—*ask* you, because you are my son and my heir, and because I am nothing if not a reasonable man—to go kill the Russians like I want. I don't have to threaten you. I don't have to command you. Because you already know full fucking well what will happen if you disobey me."

He leers in my face even closer. The whiskey stench is overpowering. "I will slit your throat with my own two hands." He leans back and smiles. "Now then. Shall we go?"

There is silence in the booth. In the corner of my vision, I can see my brothers looking at each other. Sergio gives an imperceptible nod of his head. They all rise to their feet. Father's smile widens. We follow him down the stairs and out of the club.

I just hope we are not following him to our deaths.

The castle armory is a cornucopia of guns, ammunition, and explosives. We operate in silence as we prepare for the raid. Each of us has changed into all-black tactical gear and begun stocking up.

I sling a shotgun over my back, stuff a pair of pistols into holsters on each hip, and wrap a belt of grenades around another shoulder. To my left and my right, each of my brothers is doing the same. Only Dante sits back, sharpening his knife again and again. The sound is irritating.

Shhhhhink.

Shhhhhink.

"I think it is sharp enough now," I snap.

Dante laughs. "It is never sharp enough, Vito," he replies. "It never will be. Not until I can make the air bleed." He swings it through the damp air in the room, testing the heft. It must satisfy him, because he smiles wickedly.

"Come," Sergio says, clapping a hand on my shoulder. "It is best not to delay this any longer."

I sigh and turn my back to Dante as I finish loading up my duffel bag with the rest of my tools for the night.

We pile into the SUVs waiting for us in the driveway at the front of the castle. My father and his lieutenants are in one. My brothers and I are in the second. We have an address, a warehouse in an industrial park outside of the city.

God only knows what we will find there.

The scant intel that we have available suggests a forward contingent of Bratva troops is using the warehouse as a staging area. Beyond that, we know virtually nothing. We don't know how many men they have, or what is the layout of the building. We don't know how heavily they are armed, if backup is nearby, if they are aware that we are coming. We are flying completely blind.

My father doesn't care. He wants only blood. He doesn't realize that this could end us all.

I feel the anxiety gnawing away in my chest. I don't like any of this. My whole life has been about learning to control the variables. This, though, is uncontrollable. This is rage-driven. It is not warfare—it is suicide, plain and simple.

I don't say a word as we cruise down the highway. Soon, we have left downtown Los Angeles behind. The industrial park looms in the distance. It grows larger as we drive farther into the night, a pit of darkness and blocky shadows.

I brood. It is too late to turn back now, I know that much. Father would kill us all with his bare hands before he let us abandon this foolhardy mission.

But how else are we supposed to get out of this alive? This chaotic approach goes against every tactic I've ever learned. Every tactic Father has ever taught me, as a matter of fact. What happened to Giovanni Bianci, the master tactician, the Sun Tzu of the Mafia world? He is a raving lunatic now, off to spill blood over some perceived threat that may not even prove to matter.

Christ, I hope that is the case.

At least I have the reassuring heft of a gun in my hand. I look around at my brothers in the car. Mateo is driving. Leo and Sergio are checking their weapons, loading in fresh clips, tightening the straps and buckles of their tactical gear. Dante is still sharpening that fucking knife. I drown out the noise, though it grates on me like nails on a chalkboard.

Focus, Vito, I growl in my head. *This is not the time to be getting distracted by petty grievances.*

Instead, I lose myself in a memory.

I heard footsteps. Then a voice. "Get up."

It was my father's voice hissing in my ear. I was dead asleep, like most seventeen-year-olds would be at two in the morning. What was he doing in my room?

"Da—uh, Father?"

"Get up, Vito."

I did as he said. I had learned long ago to do as he said if I wanted to avoid his wrath. I sat up, rubbing the sleep from my eyes. He was wearing a suit, I noticed. That was not so strange. Father always conducted business at all hours of the night.

What was *strange was that his hands were soaked with blood.*

"Father?" I said again.

"Come with me." He ignored the unspoken question in my voice.

Still bare-chested and wearing only a pair of shorts, I followed him down the hallway. The Bianci Castle was dark and quiet this time of night. It was dark and quiet at all hours, actually, day or night. But the nighttime had a special kind of silence all to itself. Deeper, denser somehow. Like it wanted to choke you. It was a silence that crept down your throat and strangled you from the inside out. I shivered.

Dad was walking fast. It had been a long day of training, so my muscles were weary, but I had no choice but to match his speed.

We went down a hallway I never went down, to a door I had been warned never to come near. Reaching into his jacket, Father pulled out a massive silver key. It was an old-school key, full of furls and twirls, the kind that looked like it was meant to unlock a treasure chest.

This was the exact fucking opposite.

He opened the door and let it swing inwards.

I saw the blood first. I heard the pained moans second.

My jaw threatened to drop, but I knew better than to display such weakness in front of my father. I turned to look at him and swallowed hard. I could feel my Adam's apple ride up and down in my throat with the effort. "What is this, Father?" I asked.

He nodded solemnly. "It's time for you to cut your weaknesses loose, Vito. Now step in and finish the job."

He put a crudely made shiv in my hand, pushed me forward, and shut the door behind me.

"Vito," says Leo from the driver's seat. "We're here. What do you want to do?"

It takes me a moment to drag myself away from the strength of the memory. That room ... those moans ... the blood ... I shudder. It is best to pretend that whole night never happened.

I look up. All of my brothers are looking at me with expectant eyes. How many times have we trained for circumstances like these? Midnight attack, locked and loaded, hungry for the blood of the enemy? I have been taught what to do. My brothers know that I am in charge here.

"We stay put for now," I order. "First, I consult with Father."

I pull out my phone and type out a text to him. *In position. Awaiting instructions.*

His reply is immediate. *Kill them all. Leave none behind. Burn the building when you're finished.*

That didn't take long.

Fuck.

I lean forward and peer through the windshield. It is difficult to make out much in the night. "Goggles," I say. Sergio places a pair of night-vision goggles into my hand. I pull them in place over my head and look once again.

Still, there is not much. The warehouse in question is long and wide open, with two wings flaring off towards the east and the west, respectively, at the far end, forming a massive T-shape with us near the base. The entire structure is maybe a quarter-mile long and sixty to seventy yards wide. The end facing us has a huge garage door that is inexplicably rolled up. Why that would be, I have no idea. But it makes me uneasy.

We are approximately two hundred yards south of the opening. Our two vehicles are parked behind a large concrete structure, some sort of embankment that runs in a ring around the entire property. One way in, one way out. Any sentries stationed within the warehouse itself would not be able to see us, though there is no telling what other posts the Russians might have set up around the industrial park. Manned or electronic, it makes no difference—there is a reasonable chance they have already noted our arrival and are prepping accordingly.

I don't like any of this.

A straight-on charge leaves us vulnerable to enemy fire from the rafters or from deeper within the warehouse. There is no way to flank the location, either, due to the wide swathes of empty concrete expanse that surround the warehouse like an asphalt moat on both sides. I have to congratulate the Russians on that, at least—it is a well-chosen fortress. Innocuous in the daytime, impenetrable under the cover of darkness.

There is only one possibility.

"All right, listen up. We have limited options here. We have to go in the front, as much as I don't like that. We detonate flash-bangs and throw smoke bombs as soon as we're in range. I'll arrange Father's lieutenants as supporting fire along the ridge of the embankment we're parked behind here, but we're going to have to lead the charge. We spread out, ten-foot separation between each of us, and sweep through. As soon as we're in, we break left and look for cover. There's no telling what is waiting for us, so await further instructions once we're able to establish some kind of sweep pattern. Understood?"

The clack of guns is my only answer.

I send a quick text to Father and his lieutenants, outlining the plan. I don't wait for a response. They know how this is meant to go.

"Then let's move out."

I open the door and step out into the night. The air is warm and sticky. Not a peep breaks the stillness. The unease that has been gnawing at my stomach since Father first proposed this foolish assault is building higher. But I have been trained far too well to let those types of things actually affect my behavior.

On my signal, my brothers and I spread out into a V with me at the head. We stay low as we sprint across the sea of concrete separating our parking spots from the mouth of the warehouse. I stay braced, waiting for the deadly whine of a sniper's bullet to greet our arrival.

But there is nothing. Only silence on top of silence.

We reach the left-hand side of the garage door entrance and lean against the wall to catch our breath. I inhale slowly and force myself to hold it, to let my heart rate come back down after the sprint. When I am satisfied, I look to my brothers. They all hold up a fist in response, letting me know that they are ready to proceed.

Then, it is showtime.

I unclip a flash-bang from my belt, pull the pin, and lean around to hurl it into the yawning darkness of the warehouse without exposing myself to any enemies who may have noticed our approach. Each of my brothers does the same.

Silence—thick, heavy, unrelenting—as it soars through the air ...

Until it hits the concrete, skitters once, twice, then explodes. I have earplugs in and my hands clapped over my ears, but I still wince as the sound pierces deep into my skull.

There is no time to wait though. "Move, move, move!" I roar.

We fan out into the warehouse, guns at the ready, maintaining our spacing as we sweep ten, twenty, thirty yards into the building, ready to fire at the drop of a hat. Each of us is looking through a night-vision scope, scanning the rafters and the towering stacks of shipping pallets for enemies.

But there is no one.

The place is empty.

Still, we do not relax yet. The five of us huddle behind one of the pallet stacks and reconvene.

"What the fuck is going on?" Leo drawls.

"Shut up. Listen to me. Leo and Dante, move down the left side. Sergio, Mateo, and myself will take the right. Check everywhere. We meet up at the intersection with the wings. Something about this isn't right."

"Maybe they just aren't here, *fratello,*" Dante suggests. He looks almost mournful. He must've been looking forward to slicing some Russian throats.

"We don't know that until we look," I snap back. "Orders understood?"

Everyone nods.

"Good. Let's go."

We split up into our two groups. With Sergio and Mateo at my sides, I race over to the other side of the warehouse and we sweep our way down. I'm expecting Russians to be waiting behind every barrel, every stack, every garbage can. But all we find is nothing. No trace that they were ever even here.

It takes us, by my watch, six minutes and thirty-five seconds to survey the entirety of the warehouse. At the end of it, where the wings split off to the east and the west, I see Leo and Dante emerge from behind the stacks that line the opposite wall of the warehouse. We reconvene in the middle.

"Nothing?" I ask.

"Nothing."

"Fuck."

"Perhaps it is not such a bad thing, brother," Sergio says. "Father will be sated for the time being. No blood is spilled."

"No," I answer, shaking my head with gritted teeth. "This doesn't make any sense."

"Then let us return to the vehicles," he urges. "Father's lieutenants are no good for covering fire if we delve further into the wings. We should regroup at the cars and circle around."

I don't want this mission to take any longer than it has to, but Sergio is right. The embankment doesn't offer any good view into the wings, meaning Father's lieutenants will be useless. Better to meet up and find a new angle of entry to the final remaining areas of the warehouse.

"Agreed. Fall back to the vehicles and await further instructions."

Dante offers me a sloppy, mocking salute before we all turn and run the entirety of the way back through the warehouse and back to the cars.

Father is irate when we return.

"What the fuck are you doing back here?" he snarls from his perch stationed behind his lieutenants on the concrete embankment. "I want Russian scalps." He's still wearing a suit, I notice, though the rest of us are dressed up for a gunfight.

"The main warehouse is empty," I explain. "We need to move our covering fire to a different vantage point before we can safely sweep the wings."

"*Safely sweep?*" he mocks in disbelief. "Do you think you're getting a goddamn lollipop when this shit is over, Vito? This isn't a fucking Boy Scout mission. I told you to go kill Russians. They're in there somewhere. Go find them, kill them, bring me their heads on spikes. What part of that don't you understand?"

"Father, I—"

"Oh, shut the fuck up. Fine. Back in the cars, we'll drive around so we can drop you off right at the front like it's your first day of school. Is that what you want, my fearless warrior son? Jesus Christ almighty, my children are pussies."

Again, the bile of anger rises to my mouth like it did when he first spoke like that to me back in the nightclub. One of these days, he will go too far and I will cut him down where he stands. But now is neither the time nor the place. We are in danger here. I want to get us out of this place while we still have the option. Fortunately, Father is out of vitriol for the time being.

We all back down off the embankment, pile into the cars, and stick to the very perimeter of the warehouse lot as we drive slowly, lights off, around to the western wing. I keep a window cracked open to listen for any sounds. I hear nothing.

If Father is right and there are in fact Russians in there, then either they are in hiding, hoping we just leave without a fight.

Or ...

"Look out!" I roar at the top of my lungs to Leo.

But I am too late.

The flash of gunfire, like a shooting star in the night. The explosion of sound, just a half-beat later.

Then a sniper's slug turns the windshield into pixie dust and pierces Leo in the shoulder.

He bellows in pain. His foot depresses the accelerator. We rev up, collide into the embankment to our left, and the car flips.

We hang in the air for what feels like forever, though it can't be longer than a second or two at the most.

Then we crash, and my world explodes.

Fire, gunshots, shattering glass, the growl of an angry, gutted engine.

I'm out of the car as fast as I can punch through the broken window and crawl out. The shards rip through my thigh, but I don't stop.

If you stop, you die—the first lesson a Bianci mafioso learns.

In front of me, I can see that Father's car has come under attack, too. There are shooters spread out all in the night. Some on top of the warehouse roof, some scattered around the ridge of the embankment that encircles the entire property.

More bullets pummel the roof of the car as I drag myself around behind it. Mateo and Dante meet me on the safe side, dragging the injured Leo between them.

"Where is Sergio?" I shout. I glance in the car before either of them can answer and see him struggling. His leg is pinned between the seats.

Wrenching open the door with brute force, I reach in and start to help pry him loose.

"Careful!" he grits out. His leg must be punctured or broken. I see blood from a thousand tiny cuts on his face, courtesy of the glass exploding inwards when the car flipped.

But we don't have time for careful. Seizing a knife from my belt, I stab it into the leather seats and saw away. Eventually, I get to the metal frame that's keeping him captive. I take a deep breath, clench it between my two hands, and bellow like a wild beast as I bend the bar away from my little brother's trapped limb.

Slowly, it gives way, until there's just enough room for Sergio to extricate himself and climb out of the top side of the car.

He throws himself to the ground next to Mateo and Dante. Leo, too, has joined us. He is bleeding badly from the shot he took to the shoulder, though it doesn't look to be life-threatening. Mateo is applying a tourniquet to stanch the bleeding.

"Fuck, fuck, fuck!"

I slap myself across the face to regain focus. *If you stop, you die.*

"We have to move," I snarl.

"Move where?" Dante asks. "In case you didn't notice, they're everywhere. We waltzed right into a fucking trap!"

"Anywhere but here! If we stay put, they'll come kill us soon enough. If we stop, we die."

Dante grimaces and nods. I don't like our options any better than he does, but I'm speaking the truth. We need to leave. This car is trashed though.

That means one thing: we have to get to the other vehicle.

"Mateo," I say. He looks up at me. "Stay here with Leo. Dante and I will go get the other car. Be ready to go—when we come back around, we won't have long to stop."

He nods and turns back to fixing Leo's tourniquet.

"Dante, you're with me. Sergio—stay here and provide cover fire."

"No," he insists. "I'm coming with you."

"Your leg is a mess. Stay put."

"No." He shakes his head again. "I am hurt, not dead. I will help."

I grit my teeth. We don't have time to argue. If he wants to come, fine. Let him fucking come.

"Ready?" I ask.

Mateo, Leo, Sergio, and Dante all grunt affirmatively.

"Then let's go," I mutter to myself.

Re-gripping my pistol, I take a deep breath ... Then I take off running.

Father's car is about twenty yards forward. Bullets whine and ricochet on all sides as Dante, Sergio, and I sprint for our lives. I can hear Sergio roaring in agony as he forces his shattered leg to bear his weight. One shot grazes my ear, tearing away part of the lobe. Pain lances outwards in every direction.

If you stop, you die.

So I keep running.

When we're close enough, Dante and I dive forwards. We hit the concrete and roll to a stop behind the SUV. It's a pool of blood over here. I count one, two, three dead lieutenants on this side alone. "Goddammit," I curse under my breath. These were good men. Proven men. Loyal men.

And now, their loyalty to my lunatic father has gotten these three killed. Perhaps the rest of them, too. The windows of the car are tinted, so I can't see inward, but there must be at least one or two others who sit dead in their seats.

I hear groaning and look over to see my father slumped up against the concrete embankment. It looks as though he has taken a shot to the knee. That leg was already ruined from a long-ago brush with a cartel when he was just a young man though, so it is not such a great loss. His eyes—flecked with pain and fury in equal measures—fixate on me.

"What are you doing?" he roars. "Go kill them!"

I don't even bother to respond. There are at least two dozen shooters spread throughout the darkness, maybe more. If Father truly expects me to go full Rambo and try to take on a well-armed, well-prepared Bratva army from an unfavorable position with my bare hands, then he's even more insane than I thought he was.

I turn to the car. Staying low so no stray gunfire can come lancing through a window and take me out, I slide towards the driver's seat. I pull it open and discard the body of the man who had previously occupied the seat. In my head, I offer his soul a silent apology. But there is no time for decorum here. Not if we want to survive.

The engine is still running. That is one small stroke of luck in a night that has been utterly bereft of it so far.

Over my shoulder, I call to Dante, "Get Father in the car." He and Sergio move over to where our father is seated. Each of them loops a hand under his arm and picks him up. His limp feet drag over the concrete, trailing blood like the slime of a snail, as they move him towards the vehicle. I open the rear door in time for them to shuffle him inwards.

The whole time, he is ranting and raving. "Put me down! Go kill those fucking bastards! What the fuck are you doing?"

"Ignore him," I tell my brothers, though I know they don't need the reminder. Dante stopped listening to Father long ago. And Sergio ... well, there's no telling what Sergio is thinking.

When Father is situated, I tell Sergio and Dante to climb into the back and shoot out the glass section of the trunk so they can provide covering fire from the rear. They nod and jump into position, as I move back around to the driver's seat.

The gunfire continues to rain down on us like deadly hail. I hear the intermittent burst of Mateo and Leo offering up some token return fire, but it does little to stem the tide of enemy bullets. We need to get out of here, right fucking now, or we will never have the chance to do so again. The longer we sit, the closer the Bratva troops can approach, pinning us against the concrete embankment.

If you stop, you die.

So it is go time. Now or never.

I stay hunched over as I jerk the gear shift into drive, floor the accelerator, and yank the wheel as hard as I can clockwise. The tires squeal and burn on the concrete, and there is a half-second delay between the RPMs increase and the car finally engages.

We take off like a rocket. *Thump-thump-thump*—sniper fire lights up the side of the car, though there are brief lulls as Sergio and Dante in the trunk manage to find targets in the night and take them out. It is too little and too late, but at least it is something.

I peek over the dashboard and see where Mateo and Leo are cooped up behind the burning remnants of our vehicle. I slow down. They see me and rise to get in. It all goes so impossibly fucking fast—Dante throws the door open from within, Mateo throws Leo into the back seat and jumps in after him ...

Then Father bellows, opens his own door, and goes tumbling out of the car, shooting in any and every direction.

My eyes go wide. "What the fuck are you—"

Crack. Crack. Crack.

We all watch in horror as our father, the unkillable Giovanni Bianci, powerful don of the Bianci Mafia, king of the Los Angeles underworld, the most feared and hated man in the entire western United States, takes three large caliber slugs in the torso.

He manages to keep to his feet for a moment before a fourth bullet right between the shoulder blades sends him face-planting onto the concrete.

He is dead.

That much is obvious.

If you stop, you die.

I press down on the accelerator again, trying desperately to escape through the last sliver of the window of time we have left ...

Just as Sergio dives out after Father.

"We can't leave him!" he bellows. "We have to get his body!"

"Sergio, no!" I cry, but he is already out of the vehicle. I watch in the rear-view mirror as he hits the ground, tucks into a sloppy combat roll, and comes up running. His lower leg is a mess of blood and tattered fabric, and yet he keeps going, closing the distance, just ten feet until he's at Father's side, then eight, then six, then he's there and I'm fishtailing the car back around so we can save my little brother before he meets the same fate my father just did, and—

Mateo's hand clamps down on the steering wheel and forces it straight. "Drive!" he commands in a voice that sounds like God's coming down from the heavens. "If you go back, we all die."

He won't let go of the wheel.

The car stays straight.

We go screaming out of the parking lot. Behind us, all the gunfire has come to a halt. Silence resumes. The darkness swallows up the silhouettes of my father and my youngest brother.

They are gone.

4

VITO

We pull into an abandoned gas station fifteen miles down the road. I put the car into park and sit.

Around us, the metal groans. It has been twisted and bent, but it has carried us to safety.

Most of us, that is.

The bodies of two of my father's lieutenants are stacked in the trunk. Dante, Mateo, Leo, and I are the only survivors.

Everyone else is dead.

None of us say a word. What the fuck are we supposed to say? Our father whipped us all like disobedient cattle until we went where he wanted us to go—right into the eye of the storm. It claimed the lives of so many men. The Bianci organization has been decimated. Why? That is all I can think to ask.

There was no good reason for this. It was foolhardy from the beginning. I tried to tell him. I tried to change his mind. But he would have none of it. Now, look where it has gotten us. Our brother dead. Our father dead. The highest ranks of our organization, dead.

There are just four of us left.

I turn in my seat and look into the eyes of my brothers. Each of us is staring into the middle distance, trying to process what just happened.

"I swear this to you right now, my brothers," I say in a rasping voice. "The Volkov Bratva will pay for what they've done."

Though it is dark in the car, I can see the whites of my brothers' eyes. We nod in unison.

Blood will be spilled for this. Lives will be lost for this. War will be waged for this.

By right, I am now the don of the Bianci Mafia. And I say this: we will not rest until we have our vengeance.

No one says anything for a while after my oath. It hangs in the air between us like fog. Eventually, Mateo speaks up. "Listen to me," he tells us. "I have a plan."

5

MILAYA

FRIDAY NIGHT

"Eeeee!"

There is about a 0.2 second gap between me opening the door to Anastasia's apartment and getting yanked inside. I'm instantly bombarded with high-pitched girl squeals that cut through the booming pop music. Anastasia jumps up and throws her legs around me as she plants wet, sloppy smooches all over my face and neck. "Ahhh, I'm so glad you're here!"

"Wait!" I yelp. "Wait, you're gonna make me—"

Fall, is what I was going to say. But I don't have time to get the last word out before we tumble over and hit the ground. Somehow, Anastasia lands on top of me. Even though she's petite, that's still a hundred-something pounds dropping straight onto my rib cage. The air rushes out of my lungs with a harsh *oomph* and I immediately see stars.

Anastasia is cackling like a madwoman. She must've started drinking without me. Rude.

From my vantage point on the ground, I can vaguely see three uncorked wine bottles sitting on her kitchen counter. Wait, actually, there's only one, it's just that I'm seeing triple from smacking my head against the hardwood floor.

To add insult to injury, her little Pomeranian, Rosco, comes sprinting up from the back room and starts humping my leg.

"Anastasia ..." I wheeze. "Get your little rat dog off me, please."

She takes a brief pause from giggling hysterically to scoop her dog up into her arms. "He's just excited to see you, isn't he?" she coos. "Just like his momma!" She kisses him between the ears.

"A little help?" I say.

"Oh! Yeah, sorry." She extends a hand down and pulls me to my feet. Then, keeping my hand squeezed in hers, she leads me over to the kitchen. "Lemme get you some wine!"

She's got her long blonde hair half straightened already, with the other half still held back by a pink hair clip until she gets to it. Pretty much her entire body is on display, since she's only wearing a lacy blue bralette and a leather black skirt that barely covers her ass.

"Tell me that's not what you're wearing," I say with a motherly sigh that's way beyond my years.

She points the wineglass in her hand at me. "Stop it right now, missy," she warns. "I want Fun Milly out tonight. Save your moralizing for a weekday."

"It's Friday," I point out. "That is a weekday."

"Doesn't count! Friday is for fun. That's why they both start with F."

I can't say that her logic is exactly airtight, but her irrepressible energy is awfully hard to resist. Better to just go with the flow.

I sigh again, drop my bag to the ground, and collapse into a footstool. "School is kicking my ass," I whine.

"None of that either." She sets an alarmingly full wineglass down in front of me.

"Then what am I going to talk about?"

She doesn't hesitate to answer. "Fun! Parties! Boys! Drinking! Drugs! Music! You know, normal people stuff."

"I can't decide which one of those sounds least fun."

She gives me the finger as she disappears into the bathroom of her small apartment. I hear the blow dryer kick on. A moment later, she yells, "Can you turn up the music?"

Still sulking a little bit, I go over to the speakers and turn the music up, even though it's already loud enough for me to feel my teeth rattling every time the bass hits. I turn back around and eye my wineglass.

I'm at a little bit of a crossroads here. I can either be normal Milly, and bitch and moan about everything all night long.

Or I can do what Anastasia wants me to do: cut loose, have fun, forget about my cares for a while.

My mom's voice from our phone call earlier is playing in my head. *She's a twenty-two-year-old girl. That's what twenty-two-year-olds do.*

Maybe, for just one night, I can relax.

I grab the wineglass and chug the whole thing in one go.

Fun Milly. Yeah, I can do that.

Two hours later, I'm way past drunk and charting a crash course for wasted. We're in an elevator on our way up to a hotel room at the Ritz. At least I'm pretty sure it's the Ritz. Maybe it's the Four Seasons? I don't know. Doesn't really matter. Hotel, shmotel.

Anton and Matvei have been blowing up my phone with texts at regular thirty-minute intervals. They've been following me around from party to party all night, though they're staying parked outside, per my strict orders. But that was as good of a compromise as I could wrangle out of them. They said that if I don't respond to every single one of their every-thirty-minutes texts promptly, they'll come kick the door down. *Yeah, yeah, yeah,* I told them, *whatever, sounds good.*

I hit "Send" on a text to Anton that says "I'mj hyere i'am safey don't wrry bout me xx." Boom, flawless.

"Milly!" Anastasia squeals. She pulls me close in a tight hug and presses her cheek against mine. "C'mere, you bad bitch, let's take a selfie." The elevator we're in is mirrored on all sides. Anastasia aims her phone at the ceiling, at the wall, at the floor, and we take a billion selfies from every angle.

"Ew," I say as we review them. "I look like a sausage."

"You look like a fucking *queen*!" Anastasia corrects.

After I threw back the glass of wine at her place, it was pretty much the Anastasia Show. She dressed me up in black leather pants that lace up the sides all the way from ankle to hip, so it is immediately obvious to anyone who cares to look that I'm not wearing any underwear. For a top, she tied something about the size of a white bandana around my neck. It barely covers my nipples, but according to her, that's by design. My makeup is dark, smoky, alluring. It's a lot, but even I have to admit that it's expertly done.

All in all, I don't look like Milly van der Graaf, nerdy bio major. I look like exactly what Anastasia called me: a queen, a bad bitch, ready to crush men's hearts with the merest shimmy of my hips.

The elevator dings and the doors open. We come stumbling out, laughing drunkenly. Three hefty glasses of wine and a shot of tequila will do that to a girl, especially one like me, who drinks less often than she gets her period. There's a fratty-looking guy standing in the hallway on his phone—ripped black jeans, a white button-down shirt, expensive leather boots, immaculately groomed hair. He sees Anastasia and his eyes light up.

"Nastya!" he says, a nickname of hers.

"Kyle!" she chirps. She bounces over to him and hugs him around the waist. Then she turns and ushers me over. "Kyle, this is Milly," she says. "She's hot and she's single and she's here to have a badass time with us tonight, so be good to her, yeah? She's my fucking soul sister."

"Milly," Kyle repeats. His eyes rake over me from head to toe as he shakes my hand. He nods approvingly. His fingers linger a little too long on mine.

I swallow past the knot in my throat. On a normal day, I wouldn't give this guy a second look. Campus is swarming with dudes like him—rich, good-looking guys in frats who can get any sorostitute they want with the snap of their fingers.

But right now, I'm no better than the sorostitutes. And it sure seems like they know how to have fun, if the first few hours of the night have been anything to go by. Everything is a little blurrier and hazier than normal, sure, but I'm laughing more than I've laughed in ages, I feel *hot*, and I'm ready to keep the party rolling. Maybe they've been onto something this whole time.

"C'mere," he says to us, turning down the hallway. "We're in 1402. Right over here." We follow him into a hotel room.

Inside is chaos. There are four other fratty guys just like Kyle in there. They're all swigging directly from big handles of vodka, their voices booming over the rap music blaring from the speakers as they throw punches and jokes and taunts back and forth. When they see us, everybody explodes in a greeting and tries to introduce themselves at the same time.

"Hey, I'm—"

"The name is—"

"This is—"

"Whoa, whoa, whoa," I blurt, holding up my hands. "I'm way too drunk to keep track of everybody's names. Let's start over." I point to each of them in turn. "You're Frat Star #1. You're Frat Star #2. You're #3, you're #4."

They all bust up laughing. "Nastya, you brought a fun friend this time!" Frat Star 3 chortles. "It's good to meet you, Milly. Shots?"

The party erupts from there. We're taking shots, playing drinking games, taking long drags from the watermelon-flavored hookah they have set up on the balcony. The music thuds into my soul, but I let it. Fun Milly is out in full force. I even let Frat Stars #4 and #1 take a body shot off my abdomen.

At one point, somebody brings out a baggie of cocaine and starts chopping up lines on the coffee table. That's a step too far for me though. When Frat Star #2 offers me the straw, I shake my head and decline.

"Not for me," I say shyly. "Not my style."

"C'mon!" he implores. He's blond, tan, flawless, very Malibu Ken-looking. "First time is the best time!"

"Yeah, I'm sure."

"Leave her alone, man," says #3. He's got dark, curly hair and intense eyes, like a more muscular Timothée Chalamet. "This isn't a fucking D.A.R.E. commercial. If she doesn't want it, she doesn't have to have it." He gives me a wink, and I'm silently grateful for his intervention. There's Fun Milly and then there's Felon Milly. I plan on staying on the right side of that line tonight, no matter how drunk I may be.

#2 shrugs and turns his attention back to the drugs lined up on the table. I sag back on the couch and look up to the ceiling. I see patterns swimming and moving in the popcorn studding, though that's almost certainly just a testament to how much I've had to drink tonight. Better to just close my eyes and breathe for a second, try to regain control.

But when I open my eyes and focus back on the room, I'm suddenly aware that Anastasia is gone. She was by my side a second ago; now she's nowhere to be seen. Kyle is gone, too.

"Hey," I say, tapping Frat Star #2 on the shoulder. "Where's my friend?"

He grins slyly. "I think she and Kyle left to go, uh, you know ..."

"Fuck each other," interrupts #1, completing the sentence.

Sure enough, I hear muffled moans and thudding coming from the connected hotel room next door. I blush immediately. Don't ask me why, but being so open about sex like that still gives me the heebie-jeebies. I'm not a virgin—I have my high school boyfriend to thank for that—but my body count is definitely not anywhere near Anastasia's.

"What's the matter, Li'l Milly?" says #4. He's leering at me with a drunken smile on his face. "Are you a little shy about the ol' bang-bang?"

"*The ol' bang-bang*?" I echo sarcastically. "What're you, Barney Rubble?"

But the joke falls flat. No one laughs.

And all of a sudden, I feel like I'm too drunk. It's like someone switched the atmosphere in the room. Two seconds ago, we were all partying together, having fun, everybody being nice and friendly and respectful.

Now, though, the air is cold, and Frat Stars #1 through #4 are staring at me with an unfamiliar hunger in their eyes.

"Are you a virgin?" blurts #3.

"That's not ... that's none of your business," I say weakly.

"How do you like to fuck?" asks #2.

#4 chimes in, "I bet she likes it facedown. Pull her hair, slap her ass 'til it's black-and-blue."

"Naw," interrupts #1, "she looks more like the type that you throat-fuck until she can't handle any more."

I try to protest. "Leave me alone!" But without Kyle and Anastasia here to defend me, I'm exposed. Vulnerable. The tone of their voices is biting.

Are they moving closer, or am I just imagining things? It feels like they're scooting towards me, boxing me in ...

Four men. Four big, strong, sexually amped-up men, with drugs and alcohol coursing through their system at maximum levels. My only potential savior is currently having drunk, raunchy sex in the next room. The thought of these guys pinning me down is overwhelming. That and the alcohol and the hookah—it's all too much.

I'm dizzy. The room is spinning. Everything is going wrong at once.

I start to scream, "Anasta—!" But before I can finish getting the words out, #1's hand clamps over my mouth and then #2 and #3 are throwing me backwards onto one of the hotel beds and #4 is tugging at the zipper of my leather pants and the music is so loud that I can't think and my head is spinning ...

Then someone pounds on the door.

I'm saved. I remember suddenly—I haven't texted Anton and Matvei back in a while. They're coming up here to rescue me. I can't wait to see them, those stupid, beautiful bald men with their stupid, beautiful, unblinking eyes. I might actually cry when they walk in here and whoop the asses of these would-be-rapist frat guys.

My joy lasts all of three seconds before I hear a booming voice at the door.

"Police! Open up!"

6

MILAYA

Everybody is frozen.

The person at the door repeats himself louder. "Police! Open the door now!"

I'm lying on the bed. Frat Star #4 is still between my legs, his hips pressing close to mine. I can feel his body heat on my thighs. #1 has let his nasty, sweaty hand fall from my mouth, thank the fucking Lord, although I can still smell his stench lingering where he touched me.

Swimming in my vision, I see all of them looking back and forth between each other. They don't look threatening anymore. They look like scared little kids.

"Fuck, fuck, fuck," mutters one of them. "What are we going to do?"

"If we get busted with this shit ..."

Everybody's eyes sweep to the coffee table, where neat little rows of cocaine are still arranged across the lacquered wood like a freshly plowed field. There's enough drugs there to put someone away for an ugly stint in prison. These frat boys wouldn't last a day locked up. I wouldn't mind seeing them end up on the receiving end of the treatment they were about to give me, though.

I don't hear the sounds of Kyle and Anastasia having sex next door anymore. Did they hear the police and hunker down, or did they go somewhere else ...

The pounding at the door strikes up again. "This is the police! I'm not going to ask again! Open the door or we'll break it down!"

The boys are bickering between themselves. "I can't get in trouble again, man. My parents will fucking disown me. I'd be dead ..." They've forgotten about me, but I haven't forgotten what they were just about to do. They were trying to rape me. Only this unexpected intervention has saved me from an abrupt and sickening end to my night.

Out of nowhere, my dad's voice plays in my head. *I can handle anything you need ...*

What I need is to get the fuck out of here.

And just like that, I get an idea.

"I'll take it," I announce. They're all still arguing back and forth, so nobody hears me. I repeat myself, louder. "I'll take it. I'll take the fall."

Frat Star #3, the one who made his friend ease up on the peer pressure to snort a line of coke, fixes me with a cold glare. "What'd you just say?"

"I'll take the fall for the drugs. I'll say it was mine. All of it."

"Are you joking?" He turns to his friends. "She's joking, right? Is this bitch for real?"

Clumsily, I take to my feet and rearrange my shirt to cover my chest as best as I can. It leaves a lot to be desired, but it will have to do for now. "I'm serious. I'll take it."

"If she wants to take it, let her take it, man! Are you stupid?" hisses #1. He's beefy and redheaded with green eyes, like an overgrown leprechaun on steroids.

"Fine," shrugs #3. "She can take it. Just ..." The knocking sounds again and he whirls towards the hotel door with a panic. "Just act fucking normal, quick!" He shoves me towards the door as they all scatter in different directions and try to look as innocuous as they can.

The room is still spinning, even worse than it was before. I glance up at the popcorn ceiling. It's spelling out words in a language I can't read, in letters that appear and shift shape and then disappear before I can get a grasp on what it's trying to tell me. Or maybe I'm just wasted and scared and running on powerful adrenaline after the assault.

I can handle anything you need ...

The cops will get me out of here, and then my dad will get me away from the cops. It's not a perfect plan, but it's a hell of a lot better than staying in this locked room, with no allies, only a quartet of rapists for company. Once I'm away from this hotel and a little bit sobered up, I can use my phone call to talk to my father, and he will fix everything.

Then I'll—I don't know, join a nunnery or something. I'm never drinking again, that's for damn sure. I wonder vaguely where Anastasia and her beau went. I hope to God she's safe and it's all consensual. After what happened to me, I have my doubts. She's a tough girl though, way tougher than me. She'll be fine. I pray.

The walk to the door seems like it's endless and instantaneous all at once. I blink and I'm standing in front of it. I can hear the shuffling of a group of men outside. A fist smashes against the wood and that voice roars again, "Last chance! Open the goddamn door!"

Breathe, I tell myself. *These are your saviors. This is your escape route. Sober up, dial in, and get out of here.*

I open the door.

There are four men on the other side. My first thought, which makes absolutely no sense whatsoever, is that they are all stunningly gorgeous. They are massive, for starters. Each of them is well over six feet. They fill out their uniforms well, all burly in blue. I scan their badges, forcing my eyes to make sense of the letters. Mueller, O'Shaughnessy, Rodriguez, and ... I think the one in the back says Underwood, but I'm not totally sure.

I make eye contact with the officer in front, the one who was knocking. As soon as he sees me, he freezes. It's the strangest thing. I swear I see a glimmer of something akin to recognition in his eyes, although I'm positive I've never met this man before in my life. He looks—scared, almost? I don't know how to describe it.

Then, as fast as it appeared, the shock is gone, and a mask of determination clicks back into place in his face. He's got such dark eyes, I notice, like they're all pupil, no iris whatsoever. A real serious expression on his face, too. All of them look fairly serious actually, now that I'm taking note. Except for the one in the very back, who has a borderline maniacal gleam in his eye, like kicking down doors and arresting college students is how he gets his kicks. He's got awfully shaggy hair for a cop. Aren't they all supposed to get matching crew cuts or something?

"Ma'am," barks the one in front, pulling my eyes back up to his. "We received reports of illicit activity taking place in this room." He's forcing his way into the room, I notice suddenly, though it's in a subtle enough fashion that we're already backed up. I feel a chill run through me. Did someone mess with the A/C? My skin—so much of it is visible; I'm ridiculously near-naked and I can feel the gaze of each of the four cops raking down over me—prickles up in goose bumps.

"Oh," I stammer stupidly. "I, uh—well, we were just, um ..."

Whatever stupid thing I was going to make up falls from my lips. In the face of the officers' intensity, my plan seems stupid. Maybe the frat guys were harmless by comparison. These cops are huge, brooding, and anger is radiating off them like heat waves. I've never felt so intimidated by officers of the law before. Something about them is—*off*, somehow. I'm way too drunk to process that feeling, but there's just a sense of wrongness churning beneath the surface.

I have a sudden urge to try to backtrack. I'll figure out my own way out of here. I don't want to go with them anymore. "No, there's nothing—"

"We need to come in." This time, he doesn't wait for an answer. He pushes through, and two of his colleagues follow him, though the shaggy-haired one merely takes a step forward to block off the whole doorway. They all have their peaked caps pulled low over their faces, but I could swear that he has piercings in his eyebrows. That can't be right. Shaggy hair is one thing, but surely no cop is allowed to have facial jewelry?

Breathe, Milly, I tell myself for the second time in as many minutes. *These are police officers. They're going to get you away from here. That's a good thing. You're just drunk and imagining stuff that's not true. LA is a progressive city; maybe cops here can have piercings if they want to. They're the good guys, remember?*

As the daughter of Luka Volkov, maybe I don't fully believe that all cops are good guys, but in this scenario, I think they're better than the alternative group of men who are still seated around the room like nothing notable is happening at all. I press myself up against the wall. I don't want to expose my back to the long-haired pierced officer who is blocking the doorway. But nor do I want to keep a blind eye to what's happening further within the hotel room.

I gulp and listen. "Is this yours, son?" the lead officer is asking, pointing with his Mag-Lite flashlight towards the cocaine-laden coffee table.

"No—no, sir," stutters one of the Frat Stars. I can't see which it is behind the bulk of the second officer. Right then, he turns and looks at me. His eyes are piercingly green, set under bushy eyebrows that are arrowed down with an almost sorrowful expression.

I'm breathing faster now, I realize. My pulse is climbing. And no matter how many times I keep telling myself to breathe and relax, I just can't shake the feeling of utter wrongness.

"No, sir," agrees another of the Frat Stars. "It's hers." He points at me. Everyone turns to look.

All four cops are staring at me now with searing, blazing, impossibly intense expressions on their faces. I feel skewered. Cornered. I want out. I want to click my heels three times and wake up in Kansas with my little dog Toto and forget all of this ever happened.

But when I swallow and blink, nothing changes.

I'm still standing in a sweat-drenched hotel room, burning under the gaze of four sinfully sexy police officers and four fratty would-be rapists. They want me to say something.

Say something! I yell at myself. *This was your stupid plan! So say something!*

Somehow, I find my voice. But it doesn't sound like it's coming from me. Is this what having an out-of-body experience is like? I feel like I'm hovering over myself and listening to a tiny, scared little voice that doesn't belong to me as I say, "Yes."

"Yes what?" growls the third officer. O'Shaughnessy, according to his badge, though he looks way more Italian than Irish.

"Yes, sir," I correct. Why do I feel heat bloom in my cheeks at the command? It feels like he yanked that "sir" out of somewhere deep and dark inside me. And as it emerged from my lips, I felt—*something.* Something I've never felt before. It scares me as much as anything else has scared me this entire night.

The cops all look at each other and nod imperceptibly. I stand still against the wall, arms folded over my chest, trying to shrink until I completely disappear.

"Then you need to come with us, ma'am," orders the lead officer, the one with the dark eyes. He jerks his head towards the second and third officers, who come up to me and lay their hands on my shoulders. They spin me around, firmly but not quite roughly, and push me in the small of the back until I'm flush against the wall.

"Hands on the wall," purrs the third officer. He is emanating a musky, woodsy smell, like a very masculine cologne. All the things going on right now and I'm noticing my arresting officer's cologne? Good Lord, my brain really is broken.

Trembling, I raise my hands up and press them on the wall.

"Higher."

I slide them higher. I've never felt more naked. My nipples are just barely covered by the white top Anastasia dressed me in, but almost the entirety of my back is exposed. I feel a cupping sensation by my ankles, and when I look down, I see that the two officers are patting me down.

What. The. Fuck?

They move slowly, almost sensually, each working on one leg. Bit by bit, they slide their hands up. My outfit makes it pretty damn clear that I'm not hiding even a credit card on my person, much less a weapon of some kind. But the officers don't seem to care. They go up from ankle to calf, to knee, to lower thigh, to ...

"Whoa," I mutter before I can stop myself.

I feel the glare of the first officer lance through me. "Shut up," he snarls.

Again, that bloom of heat in my cheeks as I fall silent immediately at his command. Why does this feel more like foreplay than a legal pat down? The pair of officers are moving their palms up past my knees, to my outer thighs ...

Then, suddenly, one of them palms my ass, hard and aggressive, at the exact same moment that the other one puts his hand flat between my legs.

I hiss a sharp intake of breath. Immediately, the dark-eyed officer is in my face. "I thought I just told you to shut up," he repeats in a menacing tone.

"I—just—I ..."

"Shut the fuck up. Stand still. Don't say anything else." He backs away, though I can still feel him staring me down. The two officers resume their pat down. Their hands are on my abdomen now, leaving little trails of fire in the wake of their fingertips. There is no reason to linger there, and yet linger they do, tracing up my rib cage, up and over my shoulders, through the nape of my neck.

I am so exposed. I want Anastasia, I want my dad, I want to be alone.

But I'm here instead. Pressed up against a wall while these four police officers practically finger me. And there's not a damn thing I can do about it.

For the billionth time, I tell myself to breathe. Better to leave with them than stay with the rapists. My dad will fix this.

The pat down ends as abruptly and weirdly as it started. "She's clean," the cologne-wearing officer announces, though there's a hint of a bitter laugh at the edge of his voice that I can't quite decipher.

"Cuff her."

My hands are wrenched behind my back and I feel the cold metal of handcuffs tighten around my wrists. Then one of them grabs me and steers me out of the door. Someone pulls it shut, and then it's just the five of us walking at a faster and faster pace down the plush carpet. We pass the elevators and go to the stairwell, weirdly enough.

Whoever is directing me—I can't see which one it is—pushes me down the stairs and grits his teeth in irritation whenever I stumble over a step.

Soon enough, we're at the bottom, and walking out the side exit door into the warm night. There is a white, unmarked van parked in the fire lane, just out of the perimeter of the light coming down from the security floodlight attached to the side of the hotel.

I'm safe. This will all be over soon. One call to Dad, and it's going to be fixed up perfectly fine. I'll get back to my life and try to forget about everything that happened tonight.

A thought occurs to me that hasn't occurred since the police first knocked on the door: where the hell are Anton and Matvei? Surely they are around here somewhere ...

Then the lead officer wrenches open the back door of the van and I get my answer.

Anton and Matvei are lying on the floor of the back area.

They're dead.

Their hands are tied behind their backs and their eyes are wide open in horror. I see a little bit of blood at the rims of their noses and the corners of their lips. They're so pale, even paler than normal.

The drunkenness has faded away enough that I can feel the full weight of the horror that lands on me like a ton of bricks.

"What—" I start to say, but I don't have time to even finish the thought before the lead officer pulls a syringe from his belt, walks up to me, and plunges it into my neck.

"Good night, Milaya Volkov," he says as the world fades to black at an alarming speed. I slump into the arms of whichever cop—though I now realize they are definitely not real police officers—is holding me.

I can feel them pick me up and lay me along the bench on one side of the van. The last thing I see before everything disappears completely is the leering face of the shaggy-haired, pierced cop. He shoves his face in mine and winks. “Sleep tight, sweetheart,” he says with a chuckle. “Your nightmare is just getting started.”

7

VITO

The ride back to the Bianci Castle is silent. Most of our rides have been silent, ever since the night of the raid catastrophe. None of us know what to say. When that is the case, it is better not to say anything at all.

Our world has been upended. But I swore an oath, one that I intend to spend every second for the rest of my life upholding: the Bratva will pay for what they've done to my family.

The execution of tonight's extraction couldn't have gone any better. This plan was put into motion as we sat in the parking lot of the abandoned gas station two nights ago, still dripping blood, sweat, and tears, only minutes removed from witnessing our father and brother mowed down in a blaze of Russian gunfire.

Mateo's research steered us well. The leader of the Russian Bratva, Luka Volkov, had a daughter. And she just so happened to be in our city. From there, it was easy work to track her down and select a time to strike. The idiot girl made things so simple for us. Abandoning her guards? Sequestering herself in a hotel room? It was child's play to don police uniforms and march her out in cuffs.

But I didn't expect tonight's twist.

She looks like Audrey.

My mind flashes back to the photo in my nightstand. They have the same dark hair, the same vivid eyes.

No. Now is not the time for weakness, Vito, I grit internally. *If you stop, you die. So keep moving. Keep executing the plan.*

We arrive at the rear entrance to the castle, the one normally used for bulk deliveries. It has direct access to the basement. I put the car in park and sit for a moment, savoring the silence. My bones are weary already, and yet we still have a long way to go before my oath is completed. Tonight was a success, yes, but only the first of many. The first domino in the line. Soon enough, the big one will fall and I will have Luka Volkov's blood puddling at my feet.

"She's a hot little thing," Leo comments, looking over his shoulder to where the drugged Milaya is sprawled on the bench seat. She is dressed up like a party girl in leather pants and a scrap of white thing for a shirt. I don't deny that my cock stirred at the sight of her, but it is hardly the time for trivial pleasures like that. Besides, she is the spawn of our enemy. I wouldn't touch her with a Russian's dick.

"Maybe we oughta have a little fun before we do what's next," Dante suggests with a wild smile.

"No," I bark at once. "Bring her to the basement."

So much for enjoying the silence.

I pull the keys out of the ignition, throw open the door, and swing myself out. I take the ramp down and find the spiral staircase that leads the rest of the way to the basement. The air gets damper and cooler as I descend. After the hot, cramped hotel room that we took Milaya from, it is a welcome relief.

At the bottom of the staircase, I step out into a cavernous room. At the far end is an archway, sealed shut by a thick iron gate. That way leads to the council chambers, where my father first laid out the plan that got him killed. It can stay locked for the rest of time, as far as I am concerned.

Between the locked archway and the little cutout from which I have emerged is a panoply of leather and steel devices. Riding crops, fire pokers, blades of every size and heft imaginable. There are chains bolted into the walls and the ceiling, and gas lamps that burn dimly in sconces set along the walls. Between each pair of sconces to my left and to my right, a cell has been cut into the stone, with thick steel doors to muffle the sounds of our inmates on those occasions when the cells are occupied. They have all been empty for some time now. Until tonight.

It is a torture cave, plain and simple. If I sniff closely, I can sense the tang of old blood that has seeped into the rock. The foot soldiers of the Bianci Mafia trade stories about what they have heard taking place down here. It is a place far from the eyes of the law, where we bring our enemies when they refuse to cooperate.

For the next however-long-it-takes, it will house Milaya Volkov, unwilling princess of the Volkov Bratva.

I hear steps coming down the iron staircase. Dante emerges, carrying Milaya's limp body in his arms like she weighs nothing. She is a petite little thing. Like a fawn, all long limbs and delicate eyes. The barbiturate I injected her with will keep her unconscious for a while yet. I made sure that the dose was strong enough to incapacitate her entirely. The last thing we needed was for her to cause a scene as we took her from the hotel.

But in the grips of the drug, she is limp. Practically dead. Strange thing that I feel a surge of something unexpected when I see the pallor of her face. Surely that is not empathy I am feeling. It can't be compassion. Those emotions are rusty and unused in me.

I have to remind myself of the facts of the matter: she is the daughter of my enemy and the key to our revenge. That ought to be enough to quiet any misgivings I have about what we are doing.

Remember who she is. Kill your weaknesses. I tell myself that again and again as I squeeze my fingernails into my palm until I feel the warm trickle of blood. Only then can I breathe easily.

"Put her there," I tell Dante, gesturing towards a long metal table that rests in the center of the torture room. He carries her over and lays her on the table. I notice he does it gently, carefully, like she is a prized possession and not simply some whore with Russian blood rushing through her veins. That concerns me and I make a note of it. I felt a twinge of weakness. Could Dante feel the same? Dante, who has always been unhinged? Dante, twin to our lost Sergio? Of course not. Dante is cut from a different cloth. He has no capacity for feelings. The man operates on bloodlust alone.

Still, there is an undeniable tenderness to his motions. He even cradles her head to its resting place on the table and tucks a strand of hair back behind her ear.

"What the fuck are you doing?" I snarl.

He says nothing. Doesn't even look at me, the bastard.

"I asked you a question, Dante."

Nothing.

As I watch, his finger lingers on the side of her forehead. Slowly, he traces it down the line of her jaw, the swan-like curve of her neck, past her collarbone, circling around to her exposed ribs. It is not sexual—it is more of a tender caress.

This is wrong. Something has broken in him. I march over and snatch his hand away.

"I asked what the fuck you are doing."

He turns to stare at me balefully. In the low light of the gas lamps surrounding us, his eyes look like petrified amber, with the tiny speck of his pupil captured like some ancient insect in the midst of it. "I lost a brother too, Vito," he says softly, in a voice I have never heard from him before. "Do not think that you are the only one with something to avenge."

I don't know what to say to that. I don't even know what he means. All I know is that I don't like it.

"Just don't touch the fucking girl any more than you have to. Understood?"

He looks at me, then down to the Volkov girl, then back to me. "What is she to you?" he asks suddenly.

His tone irks me. "She is a pawn. What does it matter?"

He just nods in response, like he heard more in my reply than I intended to share. A moment later, the light shifts, and all the strange shadows I thought I saw in him seem to vanish at once. He is the old Dante again, full of sharp, unexpected edges. Wild. Feral. Reckless. A crazed smile splits his lips. "Just a pawn. As it should be." I watch his finger trail along Milaya's leather-clad hip. "Perhaps we ought to fuck her then? Break her in, yeah?"

Inexplicably, rage blossoms in me. Roaring wordlessly, I grab him by the throat, turn, and hurl him up against the wall. My face is mere inches from his as I hiss, "Do not lay a finger on her. Do you hear me? Not a single goddamn finger."

I'm breathing heavily. He just laughs, a bitter sound. It sounds like the broken-glass laugh of our father. That sends a chill racing down my spine. But I don't let Dante know that.

Suddenly, I am aware of a presence behind me. I relinquish my grip on Dante's neck and turn to see Leo and Mateo standing at the mouth of the stairwell, staring at me with an expectant gaze.

They want me to explain myself. I am the don now and yet here I am, attacking my own brother, my own right-hand man, all because he laid a teasing finger on a girl who ought to mean nothing to me. It looks as wrong as it feels. *All* of this looks as wrong as it feels. This wasn't how things were meant to go. Fuck, fuck, fuck.

I can only double down. Retreating would send a bad message, and now is not the time to look weak in front of my brothers. I need to reassure them that I have control of the situation, that everything is going according to plan.

"*None* of you are to lay a finger on her," I order in the low, acid tone I heard my father use on his lieutenants too many times to count. "Or I will flay you to within an inch of your life. Is that clear?"

No one says a word. My voice echoes around the stones of the room and fades away, until all I can hear is the sound of my own labored breathing. Mateo blinks. Leo cracks his neck.

The walls feel like they're closing in around me. I want out of this foul room. Growling, I stride towards Mateo and Leo and shove them aside. I resist the temptation to take one last look at Milaya before I sweep up the stairs and she disappears from sight.

I slam the door to my bedroom and sink to a seat on the floor behind it. The tiny slice in my hand is tenuously scabbed over now. I examine it. The knotted, dried blood is crimson against my pale skin.

Milaya looked so pale. Not like every other female in Los Angeles, all tanned and olive-complected. She was like a dish of cream, untarnished, untouched even by the sun ...

"Fuck!" I bellow, open my hand, and slap myself across the face as hard as I can once, twice, three times. The pain is hot and relieving. It brings me back into the present. I jerk upright, snatch the glass decanter of whiskey that I keep on the bar cart in one corner of my quarters, and storm into the bathroom.

My shoes clack on the marble floor as I whirl and face the mirror. I look like a fucking mess. My hair is mussed from the policeman's cap, my eyes are whirling and wild. I have a sudden and irrepressible urge to be free of this stupid costume. I take a swig of whiskey and slap myself in the face once more, then begin stripping my clothes away. I can't get them off fast enough. I kick off the shoes, rip the buttons of the shirt wide open and tear it off me, unbuckle my belt and let it fall to the floor. Only when I am completely bared do I feel even the tiniest measure of relief.

I can't stop thinking about the moment when she first opened the door to the hotel. I froze, like an idiot. I damn near ruined everything right then. I just didn't expect her to look the way she did ...

My skin is burning hot to the touch. I grab the whiskey decanter and draw another long drink from it. It tumbles into my stomach and adds to the heat I feel. Finally, when I can drink no more, I turn and hurl the decanter against the far wall. It collides and shatters into a million pieces instantly. The thing once belonged to my great-grandfather. Now it belongs to the trash can.

Fuck tradition. I am the don now. I will destroy whatever history I please.

When I am drunk and naked, I turn back to the mirror and look at myself. "You fucking weakling," I snarl at my reflection. "Look at what you are doing. You are riddled with weakness. Rotting from the inside out. You couldn't save them. You can't even avenge them. Pathetic. You are fucking pathetic."

My words seem to dissipate like steam in the bathroom, as if the walls are swallowing them up before they get a chance to reverberate. I sigh, crack my knuckles, and retreat back into the coolness of my bedroom.

What next? Do I slice my wrists open? Bash my head into the stone walls? How much penance must I perform for my moment of weakness in the basement chambers?

Breathe, I counsel myself. *Now is not the time to lose your head.*

I stand and count to one hundred until I feel myself regaining control. Only then do I open my eyes and take in the room once again.

My mahogany four-poster bed consumes the bulk of the space, though the high arched ceilings overhead make it feel like there is still room aplenty. I pad over to where the nightstand occupies one side. With hands that I notice have begun to tremble, I pull open the drawer, remove the false bottom, and reach within to grab the only thing I keep in there.

The Polaroid picture hasn't faded much, though it has been nearly two decades since it was taken. Audrey looks the same as always. Raven-dark hair, buttermilk skin, hazel eyes that glimmer and seem to change shade if I turn the picture to one side or the other. She has a soft, enigmatic smile, that Mona Lisa quality where I am never sure if she is laughing with me or at me. She was young here, seventeen or eighteen by my count.

I lean against the poster of the bed and stare at her unblinking for so long that the picture starts to blur and fade. As my eyes struggle to focus, I notice that I am no longer seeing Audrey. Now, it is Milaya in the photo. The same dark hair, the same pale, creamy skin, the same kind of taunting, bewitching smile ...

No, I say in my head.

"No," I hiss out loud.

This is all fucked up. This is all so goddamn wrong. Why is my father dead? Why is my brother dead? Why is all of this happening?

"No!" I say again. The rage bubbles up for the umpteenth time tonight. I am filled with it and keep erupting at unexpected moments like a volcano that has been disturbed. Before I can stop myself, I take the picture in two hands and tear it in half. Taking the two halves, I lay them on top of each other and tear again. Then again, and once more, until the tattered shards of the only thing I ever loved go fluttering to the stone floor, carried to and fro by the faint drafts that seep in between the stones of the castle. I have never been so furious in my entire life. Not even on the night when she was taken from me.

She is downstairs. Not her, exactly, but a girl just like her. I think of Milaya's terrified face when we entered the room. For the briefest of moments when she opened the door for us, she looked relieved. Like we were there to rescue her. How quickly that changed. How quickly everything has changed.

My cock stiffens at the thought of her bared abdomen as she lay unconscious on the table below. Dante's teasing finger tracing along the bottom curve of her ribs—that makes the anger flare again. She looked like a butterfly pinned in a shadow box, too beautiful and fragile to be contained by something so sharp and cruel.

Before I know what is happening, my hand has found my hard cock and is pumping furiously. I am instantly on the edge of coming.

Milaya, Audrey, Audrey, Milaya ...

That skin ...

Those eyes ...

That fucking, goddamn, cursed smile ...

I come explosively, the final eruption of wrongness in a night—no, a week—full of it.

After I am finished, it takes me a long time to catch my breath again. Only then do I look down and see the torn pieces of photograph. This, too, was wrong. All of it. I shouldn't have these thoughts of the Volkov girl. She is collateral, nothing more. But Audrey ... Audrey was something special. I have tried to destroy her memory.

Falling to my knees hard enough that they scrape the stone floor and draw blood, I hunt frantically for the pieces of the picture. I pile them together. Only when I'm sure that I have every piece of it collected can I breathe again. Carefully, I pick up the stack and place it delicately back in its hiding place. I will fix it in the morning.

For now, I fall face-first onto my mattress and sleep the sleep of the dead.

8

MILAYA

My head has never hurt worse in my entire life. My mouth is drier than a desert, my neck aches, my feet hurt. What happened?

I remember my very first hangover. I'd gone to a sleepover at my friend Crystal Simmons' house with a half-empty fifth of Dad's favorite vodka tucked into my backpack. She and I waited until her parents fell asleep, then snuck up into her attic and took turns passing the bottle back and forth until it was gone. I can still close my eyes and vividly recall the taste—like battery acid going down your throat—and how you could feel it even after it was in your belly, swishing around with a weird and somehow prickly warmth. We both got giggly and then sleepy in quick succession, and fell asleep in the attic after playing Twister or tag or something silly like that, I can't exactly remember.

What I do remember is waking up in the early hours of the dawn. Crystal and I were still in the attic, and the gray morning light was filtering in through the tiny gaps between the roof and its supporting structure. I'd fallen asleep funny, so my neck was aching like I'd been stabbed, exactly the way it is aching now. It took me a long time to find my bearings and recall what happened, how we ended up there.

"That was stupid," I said back then. I swore to myself that I would never drink again.

I wish I'd kept that promise.

The light overhead is low and flickering, but it still hurts my eyes when I crack them open a tiny sliver. They feel gummed together, and it's hard to separate my eyelids. I take a deep breath and decide to keep them closed for the time being.

Step one is to breathe and do a quick self-assessment.

My thoughts are fuzzy, like a radio tuned to a frequency in between stations. My memories are gauzy, too. All I can remember is showing up to Anastasia's apartment and her tackling me at the door, then her dog licking me ... after that is a distorted blur. Faces I don't recognize, places I don't remember arriving at or leaving from.

I resolve to come back to that. Physical things first.

I wiggle my toe. It's bare, which is strange. I don't think I'm in a bed, judging by how cold and hard the surface below me feels. But if I'm barefoot and not in a bed, where am I? Did I pass out somewhere strange? That's not like me at all. Then again, nothing that happened last night is like me. The whole thing was a mistake from the beginning.

The arches of my feet ache just as badly as the rest of me. I'm pretty sure that's from the high heels Anastasia forced upon me. I should've fought her harder on that front.

Moving up, I expect to be able to still feel the sticky, squelchy leather of the pants I was wearing.

But instead I feel ... nothing.

Bare skin on metal.

Am I ... naked?

Okay, cutting this blind exam short. I'm going to open my eyes and figure out what the hell is happening.

I draw in one more breath, then force myself to open my eyes and look down, no matter how bad my head throbs when I do.

But what I see is somehow both scarier and more reassuring than anything else thus far.

I've been stripped naked by ... somebody? And cuffed by my wrists and ankles to a cold metal table. I'm stretched out, facing the stone ceiling, as if I'm about to be probed by an alien.

I'm scared because, duh, that's a horrifying thing to wake up and discover.

I'm reassured because this is obviously just a nightmare.

Any second now, I'm going to wake up on the couch at Anastasia's apartment, hungover as all hell but still giggling about the night before. We'll go get breakfast together, maybe those matcha pancakes she loves so much from Café Chez, and I'll consume enough coffee to stun an elephant, and then somehow I'll drag myself back home to start putting my life back together while simultaneously swearing that never again will a single drop of alcohol pass my lips.

That makes me smile. This scene can't be real, so why even worry about it?

A metallic *shhhhink!* sound prods into my ear like an ice pick. I'm suddenly aware of a deep rumble coming from the same direction. It sounds like breathing.

I turn my head, wincing as I do because every inch of my body hurts so freaking badly.

What I see makes my blood run cold.

It makes me realize, with the sudden vivid shock of a car crash, that this isn't a dream. This is very, very real and I am in a great deal of trouble.

A man is sitting on a stool in the corner, leaning back against the stone walls. He is sharpening a knife. That explains the metallic noise. As I watch, he does it again, and again, slowly and carefully like he is preparing it for something. I make myself promise not to think about how sharp that knife is by now. He's obviously done this before, quite a few times, judging by the calm and confident way he draws the edge of the blade along the whetstone and examines it for minute imperfections.

If I think about that knife, I'm going to hurl my guts up immediately. I might puke even if I don't think about the knife, though, because when I look at the man's face, I realize that I recognize him. And just like that, the rest of last night's memories come rushing back to me.

The hotel room, the drinking, the hookah, the Frat Stars, the almost-rape—*those fuckers tried to rape me!* Anastasia and Kyle leaving me on my own, the police pounding on the door, me opening it up, seeing their faces, that feeling that something was wrong, but not having any other choices. Going with them, but we took the back stairs, not the elevator—why did we do that? Why not go out the front door? What were we hiding from? The white van, unmarked, the doors swinging open, Anton and Matvei—*oh shit oh shit oh shit, they're dead, they're freaking dead*—and then the lead cop turning to me with that flash of a needle in his hand, that one quick motion, the feeling of the shadows in the night all swallowing me up.

Then nothing ... until now.

I remember his face. The guy with the whetstone was the "cop" with the piercings and the tattoos peeking out from beneath the cuff of his uniform, the one with the hair that was way too shaggy and long for a real policeman.

I remember his eyes. Honey-colored, teasing, taunting, crazed. They're the same eyes that are flashing in the lamplight as he passes that knife over the whetstone again, again, again. The scrape of metal on rock is grating on me, wearing my nerves thin as though he is flaying me open, even though he hasn't moved from the stool he's perched on, hasn't even realized I'm awake yet.

I must make a noise—a groan of pain or a whimper of fear—because he turns his face up to me, lazy and laconic, like a lion at rest. A smile steals across his face. It's not a nice smile. I can't see much of the room we're in because of how I'm chained to this table, but the air feels cold and damp and somehow threatening. Are we even still in LA? I haven't felt air this cold since the day I first set foot on campus.

"You're awake," he comments casually.

I try to say something, but my throat is too dry. Nothing comes out but a wordless croak. I lick my lips, work up some spit to swallow, and try again. "Where am I?"

The man chuckles. It sounds like gravel tossed down a garbage disposal. "Nowhere you want to be. That much is certain." He laughs again, and I wince.

My head is pounding so hard. I'm still hazy, though the clouds in my head are beginning to part somewhat. I fumble for what to say next. I have a billion questions floating through my mind, but none of them are fully formed. They're more like the intention to ask a question than the actual words of the question itself. It's like, *What ...? Why ...? Who ...?* without the rest of the words filling in.

I know immediately that I won't get any answers from this man, though. He looks like the kind of hunter who plays with his food before he kills it.

"Am I still in LA?" I rasp.

"Yes and no."

"What does that mean?"

"Nothing you want it to mean," he laughs again. I wish he would stop sharpening that knife. It's not helping my headache at all.

"Am I a prisoner?"

"In a manner of speaking."

"Am I *your* prisoner?"

"In some ways."

"Are you going to give me any straight answers?"

He tuts. "So many tough questions from such an innocent little girl. Or maybe ... not so innocent. Maybe not so innocent at all."

He rises to his feet, keeping that knife gripped in one hand. He is absurdly tall, or maybe it's just the way I'm lying down. But he is tall and broad, broad enough to fill the whole room. All I can see is that knife he's holding. Slowly, he struts across the five or six yards between us. He doesn't make any noise when he walks, like a cat prowling in the night.

He stops just a few inches short of the table I'm lying on. I can't see the knife anymore from this angle, though I know it's still dangling down there, waiting to be put to use. I focus on his face instead. If I keep thinking about the knife, I'll puke. If I keep thinking about the fact that I'm chained to a table, I'll puke. And if I keep thinking about how naked I am and how ridiculously, inexplicably handsome this beast is, I'll definitely puke. Pretty much no matter what happens next, I'm going to puke. So I just hold my breath and wait.

Maybe he's going to kill me now. That knife is sharp enough to do the job in one quick swipe. It'll be over fast, assuming he goes for the throat. If he goes for fingers or toes first, though, I could be here writhing in agony for a long time. That thing is scalpel-sharp now, the kind of sharp that splits you open long before your skin even realizes that anything has happened to it. And, given how naked I am, he has a lot of skin to choose from.

I start to ask, "Are you going to kill me—?" But the man lays a gloved finger over my lips. I can taste the flavor of raw leather emanating from it.

"Shh," he says. "Now is not the moment to be asking so many questions, princess. All will be revealed in time."

My eyes are wide with fear now. It has become unbearably clear that this is not a dream. I am truly naked, truly chained to a cold metal table in some fucked-up dungeon, truly being shushed in a not-unkind way by a man holding an insanely sharp knife.

I want my dad.

That was how I ended up here in the first place, wasn't it? I wanted to get out of that hotel room, away from the Frat Stars, and I thought that going with the cops was my best route away. That is turning out to be a mistake of epic, maybe even deadly, proportions. I hopped out of the frying pan and into the fire. This is much worse than anything a UCLA frat douche could dream up.

This is a horror show.

And where is my father? Thousands of miles away, on the other side of the country, without the slightest hint that his daughter is about to be violated, murdered, chopped up, whatever the hell else this sicko and his friends plan on doing to me. My dad could stop this, if only he knew. But how could he know?

I haven't even gotten to the "Why me?" part yet, though that's an obvious next step. Nobody knows who I am in this city. To all those I've met, I am Milly van der Graaf, biology major, quiet, studious, innocent. Why would anyone kidnap a girl like that and chain her to a table?

Breathe. Breathe or you're going to die, idiot.

I need to think of a way out. That plan will definitely involve sticking to my assumed identity. Under no circumstances can I admit who I really am, even as a threat. If anything, telling them I am my father's daughter just makes me a valuable hostage. It is best to convince these guys that they have kidnapped the wrong girl.

That's the only chance I have.

"You cost me everything, princess," the man mutters. I'm not sure whether he's talking to me or to himself. Either way, that's a scary sentence.

"I—I think you have the wrong person," I whimper. "I'm a nobody. You don't want me here."

He laughs again, that horrible grating sound, and shakes his head. "No, I think you are exactly who we want here. You are the key to it all."

"The key to what?" I ask, but he just lays that leather-gloved finger over my lips once more. Bringing his other hand above the table into my line of sight, he lays the tip of his knife delicately against my exposed throat.

My breath quickens. So it'll be a fast death, then. If he so much as sneezes, he's going to sever every major artery that connects my brain to the rest of me. At this point, death is looking like my best way out, though. It'd be practically merciful. The alternatives are far more nauseating.

Keeping a careful grip on the knife, the man begins to move it down my body. His touch is light enough to just graze without slicing, which seems like a miracle, given how masterfully he was sharpening the knife before walking over to me. I feel the cold metal, like the pinprick of a needle, move from my throat, tracing down the length of my collarbone. He stops at my shoulder and reverses course, taking it instead between my breasts. There, he pauses for a moment. Grinning wickedly at me, he picks up the knife and taps it teasingly, once on each nipple. They're already rock-hard from the horrible and strange combination of things assaulting my brain: the drugs I was injected with, how insanely good-looking this tattooed freak is, how naked I am, the chill in the air. Arousal and fear course through my bloodstream. I can feel my pulse behind my eyes. I try to close them, but the man grips my chin and shakes my head.

"Look at me," he orders, and when he says it in that growly baritone, I have no choice but to obey. Hell, I *want* to obey. I want to make him happy. Not just because he can kill me at a moment's notice, but because something in me responds to that subtle note in his voice. The tone that says, "I own you now."

I open my eyes and stare into his. He puts the tip of the blade back on my chest, right between my breasts, and resumes dragging it downwards. He passes my belly button, passes my bikini tan line, headed for where my legs meet.

I try to squirm and squeeze my thighs together, but the chains tighten on the table and prevent me from getting anywhere.

"Nuh-uh," he admonishes, still smiling. "I never told you you could move."

I am hot and cold all at once. I am scared and turned on all at once. I don't know what's happening, but I can't look away from the man's vicious honey eyes.

The knife starts to move again, further south, it's almost at my ...

"Dante!"

The voice cuts in from somewhere behind my head. I can't see who spoke. But I can hear the pounding footsteps of a massive man striding forward quickly and shoving the knife-bearer—Dante, he called him—hard in the chest. Dante stumbles backwards as this new man moves into my field of vision.

I recognize him too, in the quick glimpse of his face I get before he pushes Dante up against a wall. This is the lead cop, the one who drugged me. The two men start arguing back and forth in a flowing foreign language. I think it's Italian they're speaking, though I'm not sure. I am only familiar with the icy spikes of my father's native Russian. My mother refused to teach me Italian. She said that she and I were both Volkov women now. Italian was merely a relic of her past.

I wish I knew it now, though, so I could understand what these devils are saying to each other. It's clearly a heated argument of some sort. I can only make out random words here and there amidst the fast-paced flow.

Until I hear, clear as day in the midst of it—*Milaya Volkov.*

They said my name.

That means they know who I am.

As soon as the words leave Dante's lips, the two men freeze. They both turn to look at me as one. They know right away what I heard, what I understood. The new man turns to look at Dante. He doesn't bother with Italian anymore. All he says is, "You fucking fool." Dante merely scowls and plops himself back onto the stool he was sitting on when I first woke up.

The new man sighs and rubs the bridge of his nose. He looks exhausted, with dark purple rings under his eyes. "I told you not to touch her," he snaps. "I come down and what do I find you doing? Playing with that stupid knife."

"She had questions, Vito," the tattooed man replies. "I was merely answering them for her. In a manner of speaking."

"We agreed that—"

"Where am I?" I interrupt. I'm shivering with cold and pain and fear, but the questions in my head are still burning. Who are these men? What do they want from me?

Vito turns to fix me with another cold glare. He has a sharp nose—"aquiline" is a word I remember from one of my mandatory history classes freshman year. It was the Roman ideal, back in the old days. He, too, is as beautiful as Dante. They must be brothers, I realize. I don't know how I didn't see it last night in the hotel room—maybe because I was far too drunk. But they have the same nose, the same high cheekbones, the same dark hair, though Dante wears his far longer and messier.

Also like his brother, Vito doesn't seem at all interested in answering my questions. "I cannot tell you anything yet. Only this: if you cooperate with us, you won't be harmed."

"And if I don't?" I fire back, sounding far bolder than I feel.

"If you don't ..." He shrugs tiredly. "I can make no promises about what will happen if you don't."

I swallow past a throat that is still so dry and pained. "Will you hurt me?"

He hesitates, searching my face. For what, I don't know. I don't know whether he finds what he's looking for or not, either. In the end, he just shrugs once more. "If you don't cooperate willingly, I will do what I have to do until you change your mind and give me what I want."

"What is it that you want?" I ask.

He shakes his head. "That will come later. Dante, let's go." Dante unfolds himself from the stool. The two men march away.

"Wait!" I cry after them, though I can't turn my head to see anything but the ceiling once they've walked past me. "Wait!"

But they don't stop or reply. They just keep walking, their footsteps growing fainter and fainter, until the loud metallic clang of a door swinging shut and a lock sliding into place sounds.

Then, I am alone.

9

MILAYA

I have no idea what time it is, whether it is day or night, when someone comes in and puts a blanket over me. It's one of the men, the fake cops, though the lamps have been turned down so far that I can't tell which one. They all look the same anyway. Huge shoulders, angular faces, dark hair. They've each come in over the last however-long to look at me for a while, keeping watch from the stool in the corner, then leaving without saying a word. I've given up on asking questions. They don't seem keen on giving me answers, or even replies of any kind.

But they gave me a blanket. Why, I don't know, and I don't intend to ask. I'm not sure if I appreciate it more for its warmth or for covering me up to hide my nakedness from their eyes. What a dehumanizing thing it is to be stripped bare and chained in place. My shoulders are crying out for relief, as is the back of my head.

Whoever brings the blanket doesn't linger. He spreads it over me from behind, not allowing me to see his face, then disappears the way he came without another word.

I manage to wriggle the blanket up and shove one corner underneath me so I have a kind of makeshift pillow. After hours on cold, hard metal, it is an indescribable relief.

No one has touched me since Dante ran his knife down my torso. Even the blanket-bringer was careful not to graze so much as a fingertip against my bare skin. Their leader, Vito, must have given them strict orders. I wonder why they all follow his lead. He is the oldest, I assume. He carries himself that way. Proud. Serious. Stick-up-his-ass kind of guy.

Hours pass. I drift in and out of sleep. I don't dream, not even once. My brain has just given up on nightmares. What could it invent that is scarier than the things that are actually happening to me?

The sound of the steel door slamming shut wakes me from another restless sleep. Whoever has entered this time must be turning the line to the gas lamps up, because I see the shadows retreat as the lights grow brighter. Then, the stomping of boots over towards me. The man comes to stand at my feet.

I look up at him. In the brighter light, I can make out some of his features. His hair isn't shaggy and I don't see any piercings, so it's not Dante. I can see some color in his eyes—either blue or green, I'm not sure which yet—so it's not Vito. That means it's one of the other two.

His eyes stare holes through me. Even though I'm covered by the blanket, I feel as naked as I was before they brought it to me. Something about this man oozes sexuality. His fingers, tapping on the metal table by my feet, are lithe and playful. He doesn't look quite as hard or menacing as the others, either. There's a sensual softness to him. Those lips are kissable, touchable, beautiful.

"What's your name?" I ask quietly.

"I am Leo Bianci," he answers to my surprise, matching my hushed volume.

Leo Bianci. The name rolls off his tongue gracefully. When he shifts his weight from one foot to the other, the light catches his face differently.

I can see now that his eyes are bright blue. I associate the name and the color at once. *Leo. Blue eyes.* That's how I am learning to tell these men apart. They all have the same face, albeit with different souls animating them. Leo's presence feels comforting somehow, like a cat that has chosen to sit by your side for a while, though he may leave at a moment's notice. Against all reason, I find myself wanting him to stay.

"You all are brothers," I guess.

He nods. "Yes."

"And you know my name."

"Yes."

"What do you want from me?"

He shakes his head. "Not now."

"Why won't you tell me anything?"

He doesn't say anything this time. Just stares at me more.

What is it about this one that makes me feel more comfortable? When the others are around, I am fearful, trying to cower away from whichever corner of the room they choose to inhabit. But Leo ... I want his touch. I want his lips.

Maybe captivity is driving me insane.

"Does anyone know I'm here?"

One corner of his lips twitches upwards in a facsimile of a smile. His eyes don't change with it. They stay placid and undisturbed. "Funny you should ask," he says smoothly. "You have a guest."

I blink. I don't have any idea what he means by that.

Leo stares at me for a moment longer before he turns his attention to the thick eye-hook by my feet that is keeping me locked to this table.

He retrieves a key from a string around his neck and leans forward to free the heavy-duty lock. It lets the chain loose, but he is quick to reattach it so that my ankles are still bound together by a few feet of thick metal links.

He circles around to do the same to my hands and I realize instantly —this is a chance to escape.

Time slows down. I have to pick my moment right. There will be a split second where my hand is free. If I time everything perfectly, I can swing it around and hit him in the face with the loose chain. With any luck, I'll knock him out for long enough to figure out my next move.

I hold my breath and wait.

The chain shifts subtly on the table as he engages the lock and frees it.

Three, two, one ...

"If you are thinking of trying to escape, I would caution against it."

I freeze. He sounds so calm. Am I that obvious? What about this man lets him see right through me without any apparent effort? I feel, if anything, even nakeder than before. All the fight whistles out of me, and my muscles go slack.

I can sense Leo smiling, maybe even laughing under his breath, as he finishes undoing the locks and cuffing my hands together in front of me.

"Sit up," he tells me. His hand presses against the middle of my back as he helps me into an upright position. My head is swimming. I'm aware of his touch and his scent. He was the one wearing cologne the night I was arrested, whenever that was. It invades my nostrils now, overwhelming me. Shifting positions after so much time spent supine and being drugged, his smell, the lights, the fear, the nausea—all of it catches up to me at once and I start to fall over.

Leo catches me. His grip is strong and reassuring.

I look into his eyes. "I'm dizzy," I tell him.

"Breathe."

I take his advice and close my eyes to inhale. The cold air rushes into my lungs. I sit there for a moment, trying to calm my beating heart. Leo arranges the blanket around me like a cloak. I'm grateful for its warmth, though I'm still left wondering why he cares if I'm comfortable. And who is this "guest" he is talking about? Is my father here?

I open my eyes when I feel the vertigo recede a little.

"Better?"

"Yes," I answer timidly.

"Then come with me. Your guest is waiting." He offers a hand to help me off the table. I take it, squeezing his fingers, and struggle to my feet. We start to walk—slowly, since the chain around my ankles is forcing me to take smaller steps than I normally would.

He leads me to a door I hadn't seen before. Unlocking that with another key from a string looped around his neck, he opens it for me and helps me through.

A corridor awaits within. It, too, is lit by gas lamps. This passageway feels small and cramped, like the walls are going to cave in at any moment.

"This way," he says, leading me again.

We go down the hall maybe halfway before he turns to another door. This one is already open, as if it was waiting for me.

He jerks his head, telling me to go in. I raise an eyebrow, hoping for something more from him, but he just waits for me to follow his instructions.

So I go in.

He shuts the door behind me and locks it. His feet retreat just a few steps away, then stop, so I know he is still in the corridor. Waiting for something, or standing guard, perhaps.

My eyes slowly adjust to the dim light within. There is a gas lamp set above me, just out of reach. When I can see, I do a slow spin to look at the room he has let me into.

It is cramped and square, a little bit wider than my wingspan in each direction if I were able to extend my arms. Three walls are stone, like the rest of the corridor, but the fourth wall is made of a dense wood, with a mesh screen set in the middle of it. It looks like a confessional booth in a Catholic church, weirdly enough.

When my breathing slows down, I hear muffled crying on the other side of the mesh-and-wood partition.

I recognize those tears.

"Anastasia?" I gasp. My throat is hoarse from inactivity, so the words coming out of my mouth have unusual jagged edges.

"Milly?" she whispers tearfully. "Oh my fucking God, Milly!"

I touch the mesh screen and feel her press her hand up against the other side. That tiny bit of friendly human contact is enough to make me cry. And when the tears start, they don't stop for a while. In between sobs, I can hear Anastasia crying, too. We're both wailing like widows at a funeral.

I have a sudden flashback to watching *Titanic* in her apartment sophomore year. We both bawled our eyes out back then. Pretty sure we used a whole box of tissues. That doesn't hold a candle to the crying we do now.

It takes a long time for me to calm down. I don't move my hand even once. Neither does Anastasia. I need to feel her warmth through the screen, no matter how pitiful that seems. It's the only thing letting me know that I'm still alive.

After we have both calmed down, I don't know what to say. Anastasia must not know either, because she has stayed just as quiet.

A million thoughts are racing through my head. They must've captured her, too. Why, though? If they know who I am and who my father is, what good is Anastasia? Is she hiding secrets like I was? Why are they letting us see each other?

"Are you okay?" I ask her.

"Yeah, I'm okay," she whimpers. "Are you?"

"I've been better."

She laughs at that, the kind of snotty laugh you do after you've been crying heavily. "Did they hurt you?"

I think about it. In so many ways, the answer is yes. I feel like I've been beaten into a thin sheet of tin. "No," I decide to answer. If she is locked in here with me, she needs me to be strong for her. Just like I need her to be strong for me. "Did they hurt you?"

"No," she says at once. She says it kind of strangely. Then again, this whole situation is strange, so maybe I'm reading too much into it. "Milly, I'm sorry."

I'm sure she's talking about running off with Kyle and leaving me alone on this whole nightmarish ordeal. Or maybe it's just an "I'm sorry" like "I'm sorry you've been drugged and kidnapped by sexy murderers." That would make sense too.

"It's okay," I tell her, even though of course it's not, because none of this is. "Kyle's hot, I get it." I'm doing my damndest to make light of the whole situation. How else can I stay sane? Sarcasm has always been my coping method.

"No," she corrects immediately. "That's not what I'm talking about."

"What are you talking about?"

"I'm sorry for doing this to you."

My blood runs cold. "What? What do you mean?"

She starts to babble, the kind of nervous Anastasia chatter that I've only seen her do a few times. It's like a little kid telling a story but she doesn't know where the story is supposed to start or end or how a story is even supposed to go. But each and every word adds another layer to the chill consuming me.

"They came and found me, I don't even know how ... made me promise I'd bring you out—I didn't even know what they wanted—said I could either take their money or they'd hurt me, it was my choice—made me give them the hotel and everything, I had to text them when we got there so they could—shit, Milly, I'm so sorry, I'm so fucking sorry, I didn't know any of this was going to happen."

I'm dumbfounded. "You gave me to them."

"I didn't have a choice! They said they were going to kill my parents if I—Jesus, I'm so sorry."

She's crying again, but I don't join her this time. I pull my hand away from the mesh and take a slow step backwards, though there isn't far to go before I bump into the opposite wall. I'm cold all the way down to my bones now. I try to wrap the blanket tighter around me to wring some more warmth of it, but it feels like the chill is coming from within.

"You sold me out," I say again in a numb, hollow voice.

I've never felt more alone.

This was all planned, long in advance. This wasn't a mistake. These men singled me out. They chose me. Not just because my father is rich, but because he is Luka Volkov.

That means I'm not just a young girl kidnapped by some pretty bad dudes.

I'm a Bratva princess who has been snatched up by the worst men alive.

I have to get the hell out of here.

"Okay," I say to her. I don't know what else to say. It's a lot to process.

My own supposed best friend sold me out to mobsters. I guess I can't blame her. She doesn't know about this side of my life, the underworld I was born and raised in. I don't even know that much about it, to be honest. My father told me only what I needed to know and tried to shelter me from the rest of it. But I see now that that was a mistake. Because I'm trapped in the lion's den with no knowledge of why or how or what to do next. I'm helpless, and I can't stand that.

I'll have to figure this out myself. I make a solemn promise to myself: I will not die in here. I don't care if I have to fight all the brothers to the death with my bare hands.

I will either free myself or die trying.

The door to my side of the compartment swings open again before Anastasia can respond. Leo is standing there, swinging the keychain in his hands.

"Time's up," he purrs.

I stand up and shuffle towards him. My ankle chain drags across the stone, rasping into the silence. I start to go down the hallway, back towards where we came from, but he puts a hand on my shoulder to stop me.

"Wait."

He goes over to the other half of the compartment and opens the door. Anastasia stumbles out. Her face is streaked with tears and ruined makeup, but she is dressed normally and I don't see any cuffs on her. So they really did offer her a deal. Give me up and they'd spare her. Part of me wants to pity the girl. She could've had a happy life if she'd never been friends with me.

Look what my family name has cost her.

Everything.

"I'm sorry," she wails again, and she throws herself at me, wrapping me up in a hug. It's a sick replay of the hug she greeted me with when I walked into her apartment before the party. I can smell her, feel the softness of her hair. She's crying with her face pressed against my neck. I have no tears left, though. She did what she had to do. I'm about to do what I have to do.

I reach a hand up to the back of her head as I hug her back. "It's okay," I mutter, weaving my fingers through her hair to hold her close. "It's okay."

"Enough," Leo says a moment later.

Reluctantly, Anastasia extricates herself from me and takes a step back. She gives me one last long, mournful look before she turns to look at Leo.

"That way," he says, pointing the other way down the corridor. "Your ride is waiting for you."

She nods, swallows, then steps around me and disappears into the darkness.

When she is gone, Leo leads me back towards the rectangle of light that we entered through. We walk through, back into the vast, empty chamber. I see now that it is brimming with sinister-looking blades, wooden crosses, leather tie-downs, all kinds of weapons and torture devices. Bad things have happened here, I can tell. The air itself is humming with it.

Instead of taking me back to the table, Leo guides me towards one of the cells carved into the far wall. He opens the thick metal door made of corrugated steel and ushers me in. Inside, there is a thin mattress, the kind you'd see on a cot, along with a bucket. There is a tiny window cut high into one wall that lets in a sliver of moonlight. Everything else is cold, bare stone.

I step in and turn to look at him. He keeps his ice-blue eyes locked on mine until the very last moment, when the door swings between us and slams shut. The stones reverberate with the sound. I sink to a seat on the floor and pull the blanket tighter around myself.

Leo's footsteps are faint, but they disappear. I hear the slamming of a second door. So he is gone now.

I count up to five hundred, then back down, just to be sure.

Only then do I pull out the bobby pin I stole from Anastasia's hair and start trying to pick the locks on my wrists and ankles.

10

VITO

Leo slinks upstairs in that way of his. So feline. Balletic. I might call him a fairy if I hadn't seen a hundred times over what he can do to an enemy with a KA-BAR knife and a little bit of rage. Women certainly love his aura though. Ever since we were young, scarcely teenagers, and I found out that Leo was fucking the nanny twice a week, I have known that he has a way with the opposite sex.

We're sitting in the den. It is a massive room with cathedral-esque ceilings. High, dark, drafty as hell. The room is centered around a huge hearth, in which a fire burns. Each of us are seated in one of the five high-backed armchairs scattered around the thick Persian rug. I am drinking whiskey, as is Dante. As I watch, Leo uncorks a bottle of wine from the bar area off to one side and fills a glass for himself.

"Bring the bottle," Mateo mutters. Leo brings it over and hands it off before taking a seat of his own.

"I've never understood how it's always cold in this fucking castle," Dante growls, half to us and half to himself. "We live in California."

Mateo starts to say something about the wind in the hills and pockets of air pressure, but Dante just growls again wordlessly and we all fall silent once more.

We've been doing a lot of that in the days since Father's death. Just sitting in silence. I can't decide which I hate more: being with other people or being alone. No one will leave me to my own devices. I suppose I am the don now, though the official swearing-in ceremony has yet to take place. I don't know when it will happen and I don't give a shit.

This wasn't how things were supposed to go.

Still, my feelings don't matter. I have a Mafia to run and revenge to pursue. It requires my full attention. I can't simply retreat to my room and stare idly at the picture of Audrey for hours. I taped it together carefully the morning after my indiscretion. I damn near cried while I did it. These weaknesses are worsening. Every time I close my eyes, I think of Audrey and Milaya. They have begun to blur into one person. The fact that they look exactly the same doesn't help. But there is more to it than that. They have some essence, some aspect of their soul that is just as similar. In just the few scant seconds I spoke to the Volkov girl, I glimpsed it.

It frightened me.

I know what Audrey did to me. What she is *still* doing to me. I have spent years waging a war against the caverns she opened up in my heart. If I let the Volkov girl anywhere near me, the entire structure of who I am will collapse like a cave-in. It will be an ugly wreckage. I cannot allow that to happen. Certainly not while there is still Bratva blood yet to be spilled.

These are my thoughts of late. Idle and repetitive and feckless. Around and around like a cursed carousel at the fair, full of disturbing images that I cannot shake. I want off this ride. That means I need to move, to act, to do something, to feel my enemies' bones break beneath my hands. That's the only way to cleanse myself of the impurities that are haunting me. To kill my weaknesses.

I clear my throat. "We need to talk about the girl," I say in a low voice. The fire crackles.

"Indeed," Mateo intones without looking up.

I resist the urge to roll my eyes. I can see his own thoughts whirring behind his eyes. He does not think like I do, all dark waters filled with churning chum and hints of blood. Rather, he thinks like an ancient clock, full of gears that take their time to wind and click. It can be irritatingly slow, but I cannot deny that his conclusions are invariably trustworthy.

I need his counsel now, if only to forestall Dante. If I thought my inner workings were a mess, then his are something far nastier. Sergio's death has broken whatever little restraint Dante had over himself. I see it in the idle moments when he thinks no one is looking at him. He stares into the distance like he's picturing the moment we lost our brother and father, again and again and again. His fingers tap dance on his thigh and he sharpens that knife constantly, even more than before. If he had his way, he would go downstairs and slice the Volkov princess wide open right now, just to see her blood. That would render her useless to us. It would also start a war that I still hope we can find a way to avoid. Retaliation—yes, of course. But full-on war with the Volkov Bratva? It would cost us a great deal.

Leo couldn't care one way or the other. Well, perhaps that is not fair. He cares about what happened to Sergio and Father, of course, every bit as much as the rest of us. But he doesn't show it. Those panther eyes betray nothing, not a single drop of emotion. He buries everything so deep inside himself that it never sees the light of day. I envy his self-control. I feel at all hours of the day now like I am about to explode and engulf the Bianci Castle in an inferno of rage and guilt and decades of pent-up frustration.

My thoughts drift back in time as I stare into the fire ...

I was in the closing minutes of combat training under the watchful eye of the Bianci master-at-arms, Antoni. "Again!" he barked, clacking his wooden staff against the ground. My sparring partner and I had been at it for hours already, and I was slick with sweat, my legs leaden, my arms impossibly heavy. I wanted so badly to quit, to go jump into the coolness of the pool and rest my weary muscles.

But then I saw Father watching from the shadows lining one edge of the courtyard, and I knew that I did not have a choice.

The man squaring up across from me, Roberto, was nearly two decades my senior. He was a decorated soldier in the Bianci organization. Today, it was his duty to beat me into the dirt as best he could. Both our shirts were off, so I could see the veins cording in his neck and shoulders, along with the slitted scars along one shoulder; scars that were given to our troops who proved themselves in the field.

He raised his fists, a pained grimace on his face, and began to creep across the dirt ring towards where I stood. After God-only-knows how many rounds, the last thing he wanted was to go again. But like me, Roberto had no choice.

Sighing, I stepped forward to meet him in the middle. I could sense his impatience. He wanted this to end. "Read his intentions!" roared Antoni from the sidelines. I had done that already. I knew what would happen next.

Sure enough, Roberto charged. He faked high, went low, but I was ready. I dropped even lower, and my shoulder found his midsection with a crunching blow. I dug my bare feet into the dirt and elevated hard. He flew over my head and landed in the dirt behind me, the wind whooshing from his lungs. I was on him in a flash, taking him in a chokehold that lasted hardly twenty seconds before he tapped out.

Only then could we relax.

"Sloppy, but sufficient," Antoni growled. That was as close to a compliment as I ever received from him. He stalked off without another word.

Finally, we were finished.

I helped Roberto from the dirt. He offered me a quiet thanks. Then I hurried away before my father could corner me. I did not care to hear his thoughts on this afternoon's training, or whatever else he wanted to criticize me for.

I rounded the corner into the rear courtyard. It was mercifully empty. Slipping out of my dirt- and blood-stained trunks, I slid into the pool. I winced, then sighed as the cold water enveloped me. Then, taking a deep breath, I submerged myself completely.

It was silent underneath the surface. For a few blissful seconds, I was cool, quiet, alone. In a life full of endless training for an uncertain future, that was a gift sent from heaven.

But my lungs were begging me to resurface. I knew that there were more lessons awaiting me, more work to be done. If I was going to be don one day, I had to be ready. Even though I was young, scarcely thirteen, I could not slack off for even a day. "If you stop, you die"—Antoni's favorite expression.

So, with a sad exhale of bubbles, I pushed up from the bottom of the pool and speared back into the warm air of the twilight.

There were fresh towels stacked by the cabana. I took a quick look around and didn't see anyone. So, shrugging, I climbed nude up the stairs of the pool and onto the deck.

I was halfway across the tile when I heard a shocked giggle. Immediately, instinctively, I dropped into a fighting stance. Right foot back and offset for balance, fists up, head on a swivel as I scanned the surroundings. This wing of the house was typically unoccupied if my training or my brothers' was not underway. The awnings cast shadows around the perimeter, but my eyesight was perfect. I could see through the darkness.

I looked, looked, looked—there.

A young girl stood shyly in one corner. She was covering her mouth up as she giggled again. Her hair was dark like the wine my father drank at dinners, but her skin was so pale as to be almost translucent. Her eyes, too, shimmered in the light of the setting sun that reflected off the surface of the pool. So green. Like a meadow. But with flecks of coffee-colored amber mixed in.

"Who are you?" I called out. "Is this a test?" It wouldn't be the first time that Antoni had sent someone unassuming to probe my awareness and ability to respond to a threat at a moment's notice.

The girl just giggled. I saw now that she was a little older than I had thought at first. Right around my age, if I had to guess. Her breasts were just budding beneath her white T-shirt, and I could see the beginnings of a womanly curve to the thighs exposed beneath the hem of her jean shorts.

I glanced down at myself, realized she was seeing me naked, and—to my surprise—I blushed. I took the last few steps to the towel rack hurriedly to grab one and wrap it around my waist. I was still dripping water from the pool, down the bridge of my nose and puddling at my feet.

The girl kept staring.

"What do you want?" I said. It was silent back here, and with the walls of the castle surrounding us on three sides, my voice echoed louder than I had intended. I winced, lowered my voice, and said again, "What do you want?"

Again, she said nothing, just stared at me with a soft smile playing on the corners of her lips.

I crossed the distance between us warily, one step at a time, like I was trying to sneak up on a wild deer. She stayed still for now, but she looked like she might flee at any moment, so I moved carefully. I stopped a dozen steps away.

"What do you want?" I said for the third time.

"Nothing," she answered. I saw her eyes trace down my body, from my tousled black hair to the v-line where my abs disappeared beneath the

towel. I was well-muscled for thirteen, courtesy of the extensive training my father and Antoni put me through.

"Then who are you?"

In response, she pointed to the pool shed at the far end of the courtyard. The door was slightly ajar, and when I held my breath and listened close, I could hear the clink of tools on machinery and the muffled cursing of a man at work.

"My father is fixing the pool," she explained. "I had to come with him today. Since it's not a school day. What school do you go to?"

I blinked. It was a strange question. "I go to school here."

"Here?" Her nose wrinkled. "What does that mean?"

I pointed to the castle behind me. "Here. At home."

"You go to school the same place you live? That's weird."

"No, it's not. I have to learn special things. So I can be—" I was going to say, "so I can be don one day," *but I stopped myself short, remembering my father's lessons. I didn't know who I was talking to, so it was best not to blab needlessly. But for some reason, I wanted to impress this girl.*

She was beautiful. So ... untarnished. In comparison to the scars and bruises crisscrossing my young body, she looked like she hadn't been touched by a single soul since the day she was born.

"What kind of things do you learn?"

"Fighting. Tactics. Business. Like, numbers and accounting and stuff."

She wrinkled her brow like she pitied me. "What about like, art?"

I scoffed. "What use is art?"

"I like art." She shrugged. "It's fun."

"I don't have time for fun."

"That's sad."

I didn't know what to say to that. It hadn't ever occurred to me before to have an opinion about what I was learning or why. It was just the way things were. The way things had to be. Why question it? That would be like questioning gravity or the pattern of the sun rising and setting. Didn't do anybody any good, because it couldn't possibly be changed.

We both turned our heads at the same time when we heard the door to the pool shed thump closed. A man emerged. He was in his mid-forties, medium height, a bit portly around the middle and starting to go bald in the center of his scalp. He had a bag of tools in one hand and was wiping at his face with a filthy, oil-stained rag in the other. The rag kept him from seeing us until he was almost all of the way around the pool, headed in our direction.

When he looked up and saw his daughter talking to me, he blanched. "Audrey!" he called at once. His eyes shifted to me. "Please forgive me, sir, I didn't intend to disrupt your evening. Audrey, come here!" He sounded panicked, like all of the other servants and workmen who encountered any member of my family around the grounds. They didn't like to talk to us anymore than they had to.

Audrey lingered in front of me for a moment. Our eyes were riveted on each other's. Something passed between us, like an electric current running along a wire. I would have recoiled, were it not for the training that kept me rooted in place resolutely. "Stand your ground. Show no fear." One of Antoni's lessons.

Then her father said her name again. She swished her long, dark hair over her shoulder, turned, and followed him away. She didn't look back for as long as I could see her, though part of me hoped she would, if only so I could see her eyes again.

The two of them rounded a corner and were gone. The courtyard was silent once again. The pool water still puddled at my feet, growing colder by the second.

I said her name out loud. "Audrey." I liked how it sounded coming from my lips. "Audrey," I said again. "Her name is Audrey."

I claw my way back to the present. Glancing around, I'm suddenly unsure of how much time has passed since I started indulging myself with memories that would be better off forgotten. No one has moved or spoken since Mateo. But no one seems to have noticed me disappearing into my own head, either. That is for the best. If any of my brothers knew the kinds of things that occupy me in the middle of sleepless nights, they would not even know where to begin.

"So," I say, clearing my throat. "The girl."

"What about her?" Leo answers lazily.

"We need to plan our next steps carefully."

"Just poke her with something sharp until she squeals," Dante suggests, stabbing his knife in the air a few times.

I wince. "Do you want to start a war?"

"What I *want* to do, *fratello*, is castrate a few Russians. What I'll settle for is making their princess bleed." He shrugs. "Or maybe just fuck her until I've had my fill."

"No," I answer swiftly and firmly. "What I said stands. We don't touch her. Especially not you."

"Afraid she'll fall for me?" Dante taunts me. He grinds his hips and thrusts into the air like he's making love to the fireplace. Laughing, he slumps back down and waves a hand carelessly in the air. "That's more Leo's style, not mine."

"True enough," Leo answers with a wry grin. "Perhaps that's the way then? I'll just bed her until she sings like a bird."

"No," I say again. I can feel myself losing my grip on the conversation. Getting my brothers in line is like herding cats. It always has been that way, and nothing has changed now that I am the acting don. They are willful, impetuous, impossible to rein in. Even now, I can see Leo's expression turning wistful as he no doubt pictures stripping Milaya bare and taking her into his toy room like she is just another of his whores.

"It could be the simplest solution," Leo argues suddenly. "If she is putty in my hands, then we can mold her into anything we like. An ally, even."

"That's not—"

"An ally is a good thing, yes," interrupts Mateo. "But I hardly think your cock is going to brainwash her into cooperating with her family's enemies. We have to persuade her to join us voluntarily."

Dante rolls his eyes. "Why do you always prefer a mind fuck over the real thing, you nerdy bastard?"

"There is more to life than the pleasures of the skin, brother."

"Spoken like someone who's never been laid."

Leo chokes out a harsh laugh as Mateo and Dante continue to bicker. I tune them all out.

It is clear that each of us is playing exactly to character. Leo wants to seduce her into cooperating, Dante wants to threaten her into it, Mateo wants to convince her, and I want to leave her out of it entirely. If I had my way, she'd stay chained in the basement and serve as bait, a bargaining chip, nothing more than that. No need to involve her at all. That would be best for everyone, I think. Certainly it would be best for me. I can hardly stomach the thought of looking her in the face again. I want to do it as little as possible.

So, if I were truly don, it would be simple: issue the order and watch it become reality. But the fact is that I am not the dictatorial mafioso leader my father was. My brothers will not be cast to the wayside so easily. Leo could be tempted into other distractions; Dante could be set loose on a minor enemy while I figure out what to do with the Volkov situation. But Mateo is stubborn.

I wish Sergio were here. He was truly the best of each of us. My fist tightens on the arm of the chair in which I'm seated. Again, I picture him jumping out of the car—the bullets splicing through the air—the burst of red blood. My skin grows clammy, my gaze distant.

This was Father's fault. And it was my fault for not properly dissuading him.

I as good as killed them both.

"Fuck," I growl under my breath. No one notices me, too lost in their own arguing. The only thing to do is put one foot in front of the next. *If you stop, you die.* Those words are ingrained into me like they were carved on the walls of my heart. I cannot stop to mourn or wish for what might have been. All we have is the here and now. All we can do is the next best thing.

But what is that thing?

If we bring the Volkov girl into our world the way Mateo and Leo want to do, I know with bone-deep certainty that she will ruin us all. Something about her is poison to men like us. I can sense it, even from here, floors above where she shivers in the dungeon.

And yet, I cannot bear to just dispose of her like Dante suggested. She might be poison, but like any good drug, she makes overdosing on her seem like it's worth it.

Once again, I am caught in the middle. I feel helpless and dim-witted. This is all wrong in so many ways. We have to figure out what to do, find a common ground to agree on. Otherwise, we'll tear each other to pieces.

In fact, we've already started to do just that.

11

MILAYA

When I was young, no older than eight or nine, my father locked me in a closet with a set of lockpicking tools and told me to figure it out myself. He was there to greet me when I emerged, bawling. I was mad at him, but he swept me up in his tightest embrace and told me that he was sorry, this was just how he had to do it. He knew that I would never forget the lesson. Like being thrown in the deep end of the swimming pool, some experiences have to be taught in the harshest way possible so they sear themselves into your brain.

He never did anything like that again though. I think Mom screamed herself blue in the face. *How could you do that to our daughter? After everything she went through?* The lessons were cut off abruptly. Dad resolved that I would be kept out of his life, as best as the two of them could manage. So off I went to boarding school.

I only ever heard little snippets of Dad's business. Same with the things that happened just after I was born. I had to piece the story together from tiny overheard scraps of conversation. Something about a cartel, a kidnapping, Irish something. It sounded almost made-up. If I hadn't seen some of the things I'd seen in my family's home with my own two eyes, I might not've believed it.

But there were things I saw that told me all of it was true. My father was exactly what people whispered he was. And when the housekeeping staff bowed their heads deferentially or scurried out of any room into which he walked, I knew with certainty that his reputation was deserved.

He always loved me, though. He loved me so much that it was tangible. When I let myself out of the closet with the lock picks and he was there waiting for me, I could swear I remember glimpsing a tear in his eye. Just for a moment before he hugged me, and when he set me back down, he was just the same old Dad. Stern but loving, tough but fair. I didn't want to hug him because I was so mad, but he wasn't the kind of man you could say no to. He knew how to push my buttons to get what he wanted from me.

If I could see him now, I would hug him and never let go. That's one of the things you learn as you get older, I think—that your parents are people too and you have to hold onto them for as long as you can. You learn to understand them, to see why they did the things they did to you and for you. Only recently have I begun to appreciate my parents as mentors and role models, rather than just dispensers of cash and discipline.

I can't hug my dad though. He's far away, blissfully oblivious at home, and I am locked in the dungeon of some very bad men who want to spill the Volkov blood that's running through my veins. So I just offer up a silent, "Thanks, Dad," as I apply just one more ounce of pressure to the bobby pin and the shackles pop loose.

I rub my wrists and ankles to coax some blood flow into my limbs. But I have to move quickly. There's no telling how much time I have before one of the brothers returns. The thought of it makes me shiver.

It's funny—when I was on the table, I felt exposed and threatened, especially when Dante ran his knife down my midsection. But I felt safe in the strangest way, too. Like I was a prized painting hung up on a wall, and none of them would dare to touch me in any way that could hurt.

But I know that if I see them now, it won't be like that. I'll be just a helpless girl in an unfamiliar place. And they'll be men—powerful, strong, violent men—who are free to do anything they please to me.

I have no choice. It is either face them out in the open or die as their prisoner. I can only cross my fingers and hope I don't cross paths with another Bianci brother for the rest of my life.

The locks on the door are easier than the cuffs. Leo was careless when he shut me in here. He didn't realize that the deadbolt didn't slide fully into place. So, after I make short work of the bottom lock, I have only to wiggle the deadbolt out just the tiniest bit in order to make my way out.

Sizing it up, I take a deep breath, step back, and then ram into it with my shoulder as hard as I can. "Shit!" I yelp when I hit it. The door is solid, thick steel. I am already bruising from the contact. I hope the noise wasn't too loud, but I can still hear the echoes of metal on stone reverberating throughout the dungeon beyond. With any luck, the brothers are all far away, and there is no one else in this section of wherever it is that I'm being held.

I take a deep breath once more, back up, and ram it a second time. Again, it aches, rattling my entire skeleton. The muscles of my shoulder are begging for mercy. I don't have time for that though. An idea occurs to me—I reach over and grab the blanket I'd discarded and wrap it around my upper body as a buffer against the pain of charging forward.

It takes five more charges before the deadbolt finally shimmies all the way out of place. The door swings open, creaking loudly before I can grab it to stop it from making any more noise. I wait a moment inside the cell for the echoes to fade away.

Then I run.

There are too many doors to choose from. The first few I try are all locked. "Shit, shit, shit!" I whimper under my breath. One of these has to be open and lead outdoors. If I can just get to the street, I'll flag down a passing car, borrow a cell phone, and tell my father where I am. He'll have men nearby ready to pick me up. Maybe he's even already missed a check-in from Anton and Matvei and he's got people out looking for me. It's entirely possible. For the first time in my life, I pray that my dad is more overbearing than normal.

But as I go down the row of doors, my hope begins to dwindle. Everything is locked. I'm eyeing the spiral staircase at one end of the room, the one that the men always emerged from. I have a creeping feeling that that way leads deeper into the place, which is the last direction I want to go. I want OUT, not IN.

And yet it seems I have no other option. The last door I have yet to try doesn't budge even a bit. All the ways are locked ... except the one that leads me right into the arms of the men who took me.

So be it.

I curse once more under my breath and pull the blanket tighter around myself. There is a long sword-looking thing hanging from a hook on the wall. I grab it and give it a few practice swings. It's heavy, unwieldy, and I have no earthly clue how to use it. But it's better than going in naked and unarmed.

I make my way towards the bottom of the staircase. Each step adds another tremor to the pool of nausea in my stomach. I feel like I'm stepping up to the mouth of a volcano and swan-diving in voluntarily. Hopefully, I'll find another exit on a different floor. But as I reach the stairs and start climbing tentatively, one bare foot at a time, I have a sinking feeling that that will not be the case.

The stairway is long and winding. After so long spent in captivity, my thighs are weak and sore, and I'm quickly out of breath. But I keep moving. I have to. I can't stop now. I can't give up. My dad wouldn't want that. And I made a promise to myself, didn't I? I swore I would not die in here.

"Climb, you silly bitch," I mutter to myself. Despite the doom and gloom of the whole situation, it makes me laugh, if only a little. So I keep climbing, sucking wind, hefting the stupid sword and keeping the blanket pulled tight around me, even though the chill seems to lessen just a touch as I get higher and higher.

I look up an eternity later. It seems like the end might be in sight. A few dozen turns later, the staircase concludes in a small concrete landing. There is a rough doorway cut into the rock walls. Something is hanging just in front of it, on the other side. I can see a tiny sliver of warm, flickering light between the thing and the floor. It's too dark to say for certain, but it looks to me like a tapestry of some sort, judging by the tassels that tickle the smooth stone floor and the way it seems to ripple a little bit with the air circulating in the space beyond.

I creep closer and reach out a tentative hand to touch it. Yes, some kind of hanging or tapestry. It's soft to the touch. I step up to it and lean my ear forward. I think I can just barely make out voices. Deep, rumbling voices.

It's the brothers.

I immediately hold my breath and try not to make a sound. Before I just barge into this room and reveal myself, I need to get some idea of the lay of the land that awaits me on the other side of the tapestry. I grab the sword in two hands, being careful not to cut myself on its edge, and set it down on the ground without letting it make any noise. Then I lower myself down after it. Pressing my belly to the cold floor, I scoot closer to the tapestry.

There's maybe a half inch or an inch of space between the tapestry and the floor. It's just barely enough for me to squint between the tassels and get the gist of the room layout.

It looks like a massive main room, a den of some sort. The ceilings stretch way above into the distance. The flickering light I noticed was from a fire in a huge central fireplace. There are armchairs circling around it. Even though they're facing away from me, if I stay as quiet as possible, the voices of the Bianci brothers echo enough for me to just barely make out what they're saying, interspersed with the crackling of the logs in the fire.

"... more to life than pleasures of the skin, brother."

"Spoken like someone who's never been laid." That's Dante, I think, judging by the harsh cackle.

"I've never stuck my dick in something I had to pay for, unlike you, oh brother of mine."

"You're missing out. Nothing like store-bought pussy."

"Ah, but you're more a bottom-shelf kind of guy, aren't you?" Leo chimes in. I recognize his smooth voice, like glacial melt running past rocks in a stream.

"The only thing I'd stick up the stuck-up queens you prefer is a fist," Dante snaps back. They all chuckle, and I can't help but do the same. He's obviously insane, but once you get past that, Dante is—well, still insane, actually. But in a funny way. He seems like he has a death wish. You can see it in his face, hear it in his words, sense it in the way he walks and carries himself. He is like a train wreck, one I can't help but watch.

Leo, on the other hand, is the exact opposite. He is so put-together, elegant in the strangest way.

The other two are harder to puzzle out. The fourth one, whose name I don't know, seems studious and brooding. He was the one who brought me the blanket, I think, though I was still a little loopy from the drugs when he did.

And then Vito. He seems conflicted. There's a lot of darkness raging in him. Even when I was drugged up and chained to a table in a castle dungeon, I could see that.

He's stayed quiet so far. But, as I watch under the hem of the tapestry, he snarls, "Enough."

They all stop at once.

He's got an undeniable power in his voice. The kind of tone that says he was born to be a leader. It's dark and irresistible. Even here, where I'm lying huddled in the shadows fifty yards away from them, I feel his "Enough" like a physical touch, almost like the sharp crack of a bullwhip on my bare skin.

"Well then," Dante scowls, "what are we gonna do with her, *don?*" He says the last word with a lash of cruel sarcasm.

I know they're talking about me. I try to tell myself to stay calm. This is just information gathering. It's a good thing that I'm here. If I know what they are planning, I can counter accordingly. That being said, I'd prefer to be a thousand miles away before they get their chance to execute their plan. I just need them to wrap this conversation up quickly before someone tries to go up or down these stairs. I spy a large patio door about halfway down the right-hand wall. Through the glass panes set in the wood paneling, I can see the moon outside turning a palm tree into a stark silhouette. So that way is out. I can run the distance in twenty seconds or so, I think. For now, I'm just going to wait. They'll disperse soon enough, and then I'll have my chance.

"We leave her down there," Vito says. "Keep her fed and locked up, out of harm's way. We can negotiate with her father directly. If he gives up all the men who were at that warehouse, we'll release her unharmed."

"Fuck that!" Dante snarls. He has stood up suddenly, exploding from his seat with enough force to send it toppling over backwards. I wince as it clatters to the flagstones. His fist is balled and he is trembling with anger. "After what those motherfuckers did to our family? We should skin her alive and send the bastard her head in the fucking mail!"

"Sit down," Vito grits.

"Come here and make me, brother."

"Mateo, put his ass in the fucking chair."

Mateo. That's the fourth one. Vito, Leo, Mateo, Dante. The Bianci brothers. I shiver. It feels like a final puzzle piece clicking into place. For some reason, I feel like I know them intimately now. Like we're connected in a strange way.

"Let him speak his mind, Vito."

"His mind is filled with nothing but violence. That won't get us anywhere."

"Please," Dante drawls sarcastically, "continue talking about me like I'm not here."

"Act like an adult and you'll get treated like one," Vito responds.

"Why don't you *act* like you didn't just say that, and I'll refrain from slicing a second smile into your throat?"

Now, Vito takes to his feet. The two of them move towards each other and bump chests in front of the fire. They look like two brawling grizzly bears, so big and burly. "Get that pretty little knife out and do it then, you coward. You don't have the balls."

"You're the one who will be lacking balls soon enough."

"Both of you, sit the fuck down!" bellows Mateo. He has stood up and joined them. Putting one huge paw on each of their chests, he pushes Dante and Vito apart. "This is not the time to be bickering like kids on the playground. If you can't even have a civil goddamn conversation like men, like *brothers*, then maybe we deserve everything that has happened to us."

No one says anything to that. I can hear Vito and Mateo breathing heavily like boxers in the ring. Gradually, reluctantly, they step back from each other. Mateo helps Dante pick his armchair back up as Vito settles back into his.

My head is whirling. The four of them presented such a united front in uniform at the hotel room and during their turns watching over me in the dungeon. But now, I'm seeing that front splinter into pieces. They don't even know what they want to do with me. Vito wants to spare me, to use me as a hostage. Dante wants to make me suffer to pay for something, whatever it is that my father did to them. Leo and Mateo haven't spoken up since I started listening, so I don't know what they want. All I know is that my life just might hang in the balance.

My arm is falling asleep, so I shift position. As I do, I accidentally nudge the sword where I had set it down.

To my horror, it promptly falls over the edge of the landing.

I feel like time condenses into honey, into molasses, like a thick, viscous substance that slows the passing of seconds to a crawl. I see the sword skittering across the concrete, the metal clanging. The tip of it moves over the darkness below. It keeps going, more and more of the blade sliding from the safety of the stone to the emptiness beyond the landing. I reach out a hand, trying to stop it, but it's too little, too late. I can't stop it now. I can only watch as the handle follows the blade and the whole thing tips.

Going, going, gone.

I close my eyes and wait for the sound. There's an excruciating one or two seconds where the sword must still be falling through the air.

Then it hits the first step and I hear, *CLAAAANG!*

Again and again, the noise rings out into the stairwell as the sword bounces its way down.

CLAANG!

CLAANG!

It falls for a good while before it finally finds a resting place.

I could run back to my cell and try to hide, but even if I did, there is no way to lock the door behind me. The brothers would know right away that I'd gotten out.

What I should do is get up and try to make a break for the patio door that leads outside. I'm screaming at myself to get up and go. But it feels like my body has stopped listening to my brain. I'm frozen, unable to move even a muscle. All I can do is stare at the ledge where the sword fell over and wonder, *Why?*

Why me? Why this? Why now?

What did I do wrong?

Or is it not my fault at all? Am I just paying for the sins of my father?

The shadows don't contain any answers.

And when the tapestry is swept aside and I look up to see the four faces of my captors, staring down at me sprawled pathetically on the landing of the stairway, I don't see any answers there, either.

I hear only Dante's voice. "Tsk-tsk, Princess Volkov. You've been very naughty indeed."

12

MILAYA

I haven't had food or water in three days. They took the blanket away, too, and the thin, lumpy mattress, so I have nothing in my cell but a bucket and the chains fastened to my wrists and ankles. I sleep on bare rock. All I can use to mark the passage of time is the tiny beam of light filtering through the hole cut in the upper portion of the wall.

I am being punished for sneaking out of my cell and for spying on their meeting. They wanted me to tell them what I heard, but I couldn't even find the words to speak. I feel shell-shocked, mute, like the victim of a car crash who is having trouble remembering how to make her lips work. They gave up without trying too hard. It didn't particularly matter what I heard. It's not like I will ever have the chance to do anything with the information.

The thirst came first. Then the gnawing hunger in the pit of my belly. The hallucinations arrived not long after that.

I imagine I see my old family dog, Charlie—who's been dead for five years—licking at something in the corner of the cell. When I reach out to pet him, he turns into a snarling, black-faced, red-eyed rat and nips at my hand before scurrying up and out of the light hole.

Other things come and go, mostly insubstantial and inconsequential. I forget them as soon as they're gone. My brain is having trouble holding onto thoughts and memories. Thoughts happen and then slip away like sand through my fingers.

Mostly, I just sit slumped against the wall, curled into a little ball and shivering. Occasionally, though not very often, I manage to sleep.

When I do sleep, I dream.

The dream starts the same way every time.

I am standing in a huge bedroom. There is a massive four-poster bed made out of rich mahogany, with carved lions and eagles racing each other up and down the posts. I am wearing a lavender silk bathrobe, loosely knotted in the front. The air in the bedroom is cool, though not uncomfortably so.

Behind me, I hear a door swing open silently and feel the rush of warm air that comes from it. Footsteps move towards me, several of them in unison. I don't turn around. I keep my eyes facing directly forward—until the four Bianci brothers slide into view in front of me, shoulder to shoulder. If I wanted to, I could reach out and touch them. They are all shirtless and barefoot, wearing only suit pants.

In my dream, I am not afraid, although objectively, I should be. Somehow, the dream Milaya knows that they aren't going to hurt me. Waking Milaya would beg to differ. But when I am asleep, the thought doesn't even cross my mind.

Still, at the point in the dream when Leo and Mateo each step forward to untie my bathrobe and slip it from my shoulders, leaving me standing naked between them, I always force myself to wake up.

At least, that's what I did the first two nights I dreamt.

But on the night of the third day, I find I have suddenly lost the power to wake myself. I'm caught in the throes of the dream, and I know right away that this time around, I will have to see it through to the end.

It starts as it always does. The room, the robe, the door opening, the feeling of heat licking the back of my neck, the brothers assembling before me. Leo and Mateo disrobe me. Dante and Vito stand in place, their gazes both inscrutable.

"Are you sure?" they ask me as one. Their baritones make my skin prickle up in goose bumps. The words are like a physical caress, trailing down the nape of my neck and between my thighs.

I want to scream, *No! Stop! Leave me alone!*

But, caught in the fabric of the dream, all I do is nod.

They step forward. Now, all four brothers are pressing against me in a tight ring. It's a wall of muscled, scarred flesh. I raise my hands and lay one each on the bare chests of Leo and Mateo where they stand to my left and to my right. I can feel their hearts beating in my fingertips.

"Are you sure?" Vito and Dante ask me in unison one more time.

Again, I nod.

Then it begins.

They descend on me. Mateo's teeth find and nip at my earlobe at the same time that Leo immediately winds his fingers through the roots of my hair to pull my head back and run a teasing tongue down the curve of my neck. Dante and Vito both fall to my knees, each of them suckling at one painfully hard, peaked nipple. It is so tender and so intense at the same time. I press my thighs together, trying to prevent what I know will happen next—the gushing of heat from my core.

As if he can tell that I am trying to slow this down, Vito kisses from my nipple down past my belly button. Gently but firmly, he pries my thighs apart. I know he won't relent, so I have no choice but to let him. When his tongue then finds my center, lapping with just the tip, I groan out loud and let my head fall back further. My gaze is pointed straight up, towards a ceiling that seems like it is farther away than any night sky has ever been.

Vito's tongue twists in a way that forces my attention back down to earth. I am opening up for him, blooming like a flower. Then, all at once as if by some unspoken command, the four brothers pick me up and move me to the bed.

They set upon me like starving lions to fresh prey. Mateo kisses me on the lips, his tongue delving past my moans to flicker against mine. Leo moves to the nipple that Vito left behind, while Dante kneads my breast and squeezes my hip hard, so I can feel through his hand the tremors that are coursing up and down his body. He wants me so badly that he can't bear it, can't sit still with it, can't wait much longer before he explodes.

Between my spread thighs, Vito licks at my clit. And, as I groan into Mateo's kiss, Vito adds a finger to probe at my opening, pushing into me millimeter by millimeter, letting me sigh and part for him as he goes. Already there is the telltale pressure of an orgasm building in my core, although it's not there yet.

Soon, though, I will tumble over that edge. I may never come back from it.

Leo lets his fingers trace from my shoulder, down the length of my arm, to force my fingers to splay open. He guides my open hand to the erection pressing behind his zipper. "Do you want this, darling?" he murmurs.

I say the only thing I know how to say anymore: "Yes."

He nods and frees his length from his zipper. I wrap my hand around the base of him. His manhood is slender and slightly curved, with a drop of precum glistening at the head. I stroke slowly with my hand.

To my other side, Mateo is doing the same. I wrap my hand around his cock too. His is thicker than Leo's and ramrod straight. At the nod of my head, he slides forward to bring his tip to my lips. I open my mouth and greedily take him in. He barely fits, but I suddenly have an insane craving to swallow as much of him as I can. I want all of him. I want to hear him moan as I work my tongue around his girth.

I want to know that I have all the power here.

And he gives me that in spades. As does Leo. At the touch of my fingers and my lips, both of them are vacant-eyed and sputtering. They want me as badly as I want them.

This was inevitable from the beginning, wasn't it? We were always charted on a crash course to this exact moment, of me sucking on Mateo's manhood and stroking Leo's while Vito and Dante pay homage to the rest of my sweaty, needy body.

Fate brought us here.

And it feels like heaven.

But when I feel a sudden coldness and absence, I glance down to see that Vito and Dante have stepped away from me. I let Mateo's member fall from my mouth so I can watch the two of them unzip and unbuckle their pants, then step out of them. Their cocks spring free of the fabric.

Vito is shorn, but Dante has a short crop of dark, curly pubic hair. Vito's is the biggest dick of them all. I eye it warily, wondering how on earth I could ever possibly take that into me. But when I shift my gaze to his eyes, I see the pained tenderness there.

Suddenly, I want to take that pain away from him. I know how.

"I want you," I whisper. To both of them. To all of them.

Vito moves first to position himself at my entrance. I spread my knees apart even wider for him. He extends a gentle finger to stroke at my folds, prompting me a little wider, a little wetter. I need him so badly.

I'm aching without him, my whole body clenched up like a fist that cannot relax until I feel all of him fill all of me.

"Vito, please," I whimper.

He touches the head of his manhood against my opening. Mateo and Leo have moved back for this moment, so it is just Vito I focus my attention on as he is the first to slide his hard cock into my wet, ravenous pussy.

The slow seconds that trickle past as he pushes into me are the sweetest agony. I gasp, writhe, squeeze the silken sheets in my fists.

When our hips finally meet flush and there is no more room to go, only then can I let loose the wracking, soul-deep cry I've been holding back from the very beginning.

It is utter chaos from there. The chains have been broken loose on the rampant desire that I've felt for them and they've felt for me since the beginning. All the torture, the mind games, the cruelty—all of it was just foreplay to this moment, to delay it so that it was that much better in the end.

And God, it is so fucking good. It feels like I'm splitting open from the inside out. I can't moan loud enough or grab the sheets hard enough or lock my heels behind Vito's now-pumping hips tight enough to express how good it all feels, how badly I wanted this, how much I needed this.

"Fuck me!" I cry out into the air of the castle.

I come, hard, before Vito is scarcely a dozen strokes in. But we are far from finished.

Mateo moves back to my mouth, Leo places himself back in my hand, Vito pulls away to let Dante slide his own wickedly curved cock into me, and then there is so much happening on all sides that I can hardly keep track of it.

My lips are stretched to accommodate Mateo's thrusting thickness, and in my hand, I can sense that Leo is eager for his own turn. I switch back and forth between them as, below my waist, Vito and Dante take turns fucking me while the other rubs a frenetic circle with his thumb across my clit.

Then they all shift, and now it is Vito I am blowing and Mateo I am jerking off and Leo who has buried himself in me to the hilt. I didn't know it was even possible, but somehow I am even wetter, as the curve in his cock finds places in me that have never been reached before.

I come again in an instant when Dante's spit-slicked, teasing thumb finds my other hole. I have to fight the urge to recoil. He urges me, "Relax, princess, relax," and slowly I find myself obeying his instructions, relaxing enough for him to slip a finger inside me from behind while Leo continues to fuck and fuck and fuck me.

When I have opened up enough for him, Dante replaces his finger with his cock. Now, I am truly as full as it is possible to be. As if on cue, I can feel all the brothers' groans growing louder, each of them building to their own respective peaks. I'm urging them on with whimpers and moans.

I want to take all their pain from them, to be their core, at the same time that they are worshipping me. I am their queen and their rock, the center of their universe, the only thing binding them all together and keeping this entire castle from crumbling to pieces.

A bell rings in the distance, like someone knows that it is time for the crescendo. Vito erupts into my mouth with hot, sticky, salty cum. I swallow it hungrily as it arrives in spurts. In the same breath, Mateo unleashes ropes of his own seed in my hand. I keep stroking until he is emptied of every drop. Dante and Leo come as one. They fill me in front and back with all they have to offer.

I am full of the Biancis, and they are full of me. We collapse into a sweaty, flesh-on-flesh pile, all panting and groaning with the aftershocks of God-knows-how-many orgasms that burned through each of us like shooting stars.

And as soon as I fall asleep in the dream ...

That's when the real Milaya wakes up.

13

MILAYA

I'm breathing hard and sweating like a pig when I awaken. Cold sweat like glacier water trickles down my forehead. My hair is hanging in damp, messy ringlets. I don't even want to know what I look like. Actually, I know exactly what I look like: a prisoner being kept in a barren dungeon cell.

My body is still buzzing as though everything that happened in the dream is real. For a brief moment, half of my brain hasn't even realized yet that it was in fact a dream. I can still feel the sticky heat of Vito's seed in my mouth, the thighs-spread fullness that each of the brothers gave to me.

Above all, I feel the sense of power. I feel the desire that radiated from them like nuclear reactors. They wanted me so badly that they couldn't stand to even blink one more time without laying their hands on me.

I feel intoxicated by the whole thing. Like I, too, am glowing radioactively.

I shudder.

"No," I say out loud into the cell. When my voice reverberates back to me, it sounds tinny and pathetic. I say it again, louder and more seriously. "No. No. No!" I hope they're watching on the cameras they installed in here after my failed escape. I hope they see me denying them and that they know deep down in their bones exactly what I'm screaming about.

That will never come to pass. I need to start seeing these men for what they are: my enemies. They snatched me up from my happy life and chained me to a table, for fuck's sake. How much do perfect bone structure and brawny forearms really matter in the face of a hideous crime like that?

To my unconscious brain, it apparently matters a lot. But fuck my unconscious brain, because if it thinks I'm ever going to let the Four Horsemen of the Acockalypse go down on me like that, then it's got another thing coming.

I close my eyes and curl up in a corner of the cell. I feel so thin and stretched out. Three days without food or water have sapped me down to the core, and yet somehow I'm still finding the energy to have hot wet dreams about my captors. I can feel that the insides of my thighs are drenched. Ugh. It just seems like a waste of moisture.

It is nighttime now. I can tell by the tiny sliver of moonbeam that is peeking through the inches-wide hole in the upper corner of my high-ceilinged cell.

I'm wide awake now, but still so shaken by both my dream and my physical suffering that my mind is pinwheeling through memories, some of them real and some of them made up.

I remember losing my virginity. A high school boyfriend back home, Robbie Holmes. He was cute, nice. A little nerdy type. Had floppy hair with a pleasant smile. We snuck into his parents' friends' house while they were on vacation, laid out a towel on their guest bed, and got carefully into the whole thing. He told me he loved me after it was over, which was nice, even if it wasn't necessarily needed. I told him I loved him too, which felt like the right thing to do, even if it wasn't necessarily true. The sex itself is weirdly absent from my recollection. I only remember being a little sore and a little bored but mostly just relieved that the whole thing was over and I could go about the rest of my life without that monkey hanging on my back.

I remember further back, to my first kiss. Timothy Pearson, seventh grade, at the county fair behind the Ferris wheel. The way I'm remembering these things makes me laugh. It's like a game of Clue. *Colonel Mustard, with the wrench, in the drawing room.* But that's how it's coming back to me. I can still close my eyes and smell the scent of fried Oreos and funnel cakes and, vaguely mixed into the background, horse shit and cigarettes. But it's a good memory, for the most part. We were playing truth or dare with our friends and they knew he liked me, so they dared us to go behind the Ferris wheel and make out. We did, hesitantly at first and then sloppily, and then we abruptly parted like we got zapped by electricity. He looked at me and I looked at him and I said, "Guess we should go back now?" Which, in retrospect, was probably a devastating blow for a thirteen-year-old boy who'd been holding out hope of feeling my tits up.

That, too, makes me laugh. I guess it's good that I have these memories to laugh at.

Because the world I'm in now is utterly devoid of laughter.

Those little moments frozen in time like insects trapped in amber—they seem so sweet and innocent and weirdly perfect in their own way. But they don't feel real.

They don't feel real the way the stones under my body feel real—cold and hard and painful. They don't feel real the way the hands of the brothers on my wrists and ankles felt real when they picked me up from the top of the staircase landing three days ago and carried me back down, kicking and screaming, to this cell. They don't feel real the way Vito's eyes felt real when he looked at me and said, "I didn't want to have to do this, Volkov," before slamming the door shut and locking it securely into place. Those things felt so real that I'm cowering from them, hiding away by drifting through my past and trying desperately to ignore how hungry, how thirsty, how tired, how agonized I am.

I miss my father. God, I miss him so much. I never realized how much I relied on him. His strength, his certainty, his convictions. I know I have those things in me, but as I waste away in this cell, I feel like a battery that's gone too long without a charge. If I could just see him again, get wrapped up in a hug from him or my mother or both of them, then I would feel again like I could survive this ordeal. Even if Dad just hugged me and returned me to this cell, that would be enough.

As it is, though, I am alone. No one knows I am here. No one is coming for me.

I have no one but myself to rely upon.

I think I fall asleep for a while, but maybe I'm just pretending. There's not much difference at this point. Day is blending into night and reality is blending into fantasy. It's all a confusing mishmash of past and present and future, as well as things that have never happened and never, ever will happen.

I dream a second time of the brothers devouring me with their hands and mouths and cocks, and when I wake up, my thighs are slick once again.

It is still nighttime. Or maybe it is nighttime of the next day. Who's to say, really? Not me. I'm losing it. Like a boat with only a frayed knot keeping me tethered to the dock. I don't have long left before I slip away and never come back.

I hear a creak outside my cell. Or maybe I just think I do. Either way, it's enough to send me hurtling back into the arms of yet another memory.

I'm thirteen years old. It's late at night. I've just gotten my period for the first time. Part of me wants to cry, but part of me is proud. Mom coached me on this, told me it was coming, and we got ready for it together. But it's happened now, and despite all the pep talks, I'm a little scared. I just want her to tell me it's okay. Just those two little words, "It's okay," and I'll be able to take care of all the things that need to be taken care of and go back to sleep. But I need those words.

So I've gotten up from my bedroom and slipped out. Our home is dark, cool in the late autumn, and silent.

Until I hear it.

A whimper.

It is a man's whimper, ragged and deep. Someone is in pain. My mind flashes immediately to my dad being hurt, but then I hear the whimper again, and I know it's not him. He would never plead like that.

"Please, God ..." the stranger's voice says before trailing off again into wordless agony.

My heart leaps into my throat. I've known for a long time that my dad isn't like other dads. He does ... things *... that other dads don't do, won't do, couldn't do. He's quiet about it, but I know that he and Mom argue a lot about what I should or shouldn't know. I try to keep quiet and listen during those arguments. I learn more by doing that than I would ever learn from what they actually compromise on telling me.*

Dad wants me to know things. He says living with your head in the sand just makes you an easy target for people who are more aware. But Mom says I'm too young. She says I'm just a little girl. She's just as hardheaded as Dad, in her own way. So I decide to keep doing what I've been doing—stay quiet and listen. The whimpers are fainter now, though. I need to get closer.

I keep my breath hushed as much as I can and pad up the stairs, turn the corner, and head down the hall in my bare feet. Pictures of the three of us line the wall. The Volkovs—picture perfect, pretty, happy together. Me playing softball and violin, Dad accepting some civic award, Mom in her chef's whites at the opening of her restaurant. As I glide down the hall towards the source of the whimpering, my eyes trail along the shadowy picture frames. It's like watching me grow up again, from baby pictures of a plump bread-loaf-sized Milaya, to a toddler chasing after bubbles in the garden, to a lanky young girl with green eyes that seem too old for her somehow.

I see that one of the doors about halfway down the hall is cracked open. It's a door that Daddy keeps locked most of the time. He says I'm not allowed to go in there. It's for work, and there are some things he keeps inside that only he's permitted to see. I snuck in once when he had to leave the house in a hurry and left the door unlocked behind him, but there was nothing interesting inside. Just a couple of filing cabinets, a small desk, and some file folders. I peeked through them, didn't see anything I cared about, and left quickly. It wasn't anything worth getting in trouble over. The only memorable part of the whole room was the lattice of steel pipes crisscrossing the ceiling. That seemed out of place, but I couldn't puzzle it out, so I just forgot about the whole thing.

Dad must be in there now, though, along with whoever is doing the whimpering. And, as I get closer, I hear a meaty thwack and freeze in place.

It sounds like somebody getting hit.

The whimpers spill over again. Pained grunts come one after the other as the sound of fist on flesh continues. I've only ever seen one fight in person, between my classmates Mitchell Cook and Trevor Hawkins after Trevor poured milk on Mitchell's head during lunchtime at school. Mitchell punched Trevor in the face and broke his nose. There was a lot of blood.

The sound I hear now is like that, but way worse. When I sniff, I can smell the tang of blood again, just like I did that day on the playground.

I peek around the corner and see something that makes me stiffen up like a board.

There's a chain fastened to the steel pipes in the ceiling of Dad's office. Hanging from the chain by his wrists is a man. He has dark, oily hair and a strong, proud nose. The rest of his face, though, is an ugly mess of blood, cuts, and bruises. He's shirtless and I can see that the rest of his body is also bruised really badly. There's another man I recognize—one of Dad's employees, a guy he told me to call "Uncle Alexei"—with his shirtsleeves rolled up to his elbows. His hands are slick with blood. As I watch, he winds up and slugs the upside-down man in the gut with a compact fist.

The chained man cries out. "Please, God, stop," he begs in a foreign accent. "Per l'amor di Dio!" He's speaking Italian. I recognize it from one time when I overheard Mom speaking Italian to some distant cousin or something like that.

Dad has always said that he doesn't trust Italians. So why is there one hanging from his wrists in his office? And why is Uncle Alexei hurting him so much?

My eyes swivel to the far corner and I see my father standing there. He's still wearing the suit he left the house in this morning, the dark navy one that I think looks best on him, with a clean white pocket square. His arms are folded across his chest and there's that look in his eyes, the one I know means "Stay away."

Why isn't he doing anything to stop Uncle Alexei? Why is he letting this happen?

Uncle Alexei punches the man once, twice, three times, and then I decide I've had enough. This must all just be a bad dream. I'm going to go back to bed now and try to forget this ever happened.

As I turn to leave, I hear my father's voice ring out softly into the dark quiet of our house. "Have you had enough, Marco?" he asks. "Or will we need to continue?"

I plug my ears and run away before I can hear the man's answer.

14

MATEO

I open my eyes. Another day in hell begins.

It has been scarcely a week since we lost Sergio and Father to the warehouse debacle. Yet the days and nights creep past like panthers in the underbrush, slow and fast all at once. There is not enough time to do all the things that must be done to ensure that the Bianci family retains its spot—both literal and metaphorical—atop the hills of Los Angeles.

And yet, there is too much time—too much time to think. Too much time to ponder. Too much time to consider, *What if?*

Such questions will not resurrect my dead father and brother. Nor will they help devise a plan to snatch back what we have lost to the Russians. Eye for an eye, blood for blood—these things are soaked into the DNA of our family, programmed into us like computer code. However, if I cannot even find my enemies, how am I supposed to take from them what they owe me? The Russians remain stubbornly elusive, like smoke in the wind.

Finding the Volkov girl was an unbelievable stroke of luck. A whispered rumor from a source who refused to step into the light. I still don't quite understand how it bore out to be true, but it did. She is who we thought she was, and now she is ours to do with as we please. A gift I never expected. A blessing we surely did not deserve.

When I sit to drink wine and ponder, as I am doing now, what I come back to again and again is that we brought this apocalypse down upon ourselves. Each of us saw the signs of madness brewing in Father. But we did nothing to combat it. We let him spit and swear and work himself up into a rage night after night. In the end, we let it kill him. We let it take our baby brother to the grave too.

"We earned what we have been given," I murmur to myself.

The study in the west wing is quiet. This is my area, my thinking place, the only little corner of the Bianci Castle that none dare disturb, not even my brothers. It is filled with rows and rows of books reaching up to the high ceiling, save for one wall that is a cacophony of computer screens and complicated technology.

It is an underappreciated room. Dante thinks that our wars are waged on the streets, with guns and knives and spilled blood. Leo thinks they are waged in the bedroom, with seduction and betrayal. Vito thinks they are won in the boardroom, negotiated between enemies like we are diplomats or lawyers.

Only I know the truth: war is a state of mind.

To win it is to occupy your enemy's head and know what he will do before even *he* knows it. Information is not merely an advantage to be weaponized—it is the only weapon that exists at all. Our wars are won before a single Bianci soldier takes up arms.

My thoughts slink downstairs, to be with the Volkov girl in the dungeon. She knows what I mean when I talk about wars of the mind, about knowledge as a sword. It took only a glimpse into her hazel eyes to see the intelligence that glimmers there. Who sneaks out of a cell and eavesdrops on her captors instead of running for the hills? The answer: someone who wants to know how to strike back. Someone who wants not just freedom, but revenge.

We need to tread carefully with her. There is no telling how much she heard, what conclusions she has drawn from the snatches of conversation she witnessed.

But my initial hunch still stands, I think, though my siblings refuse to see it through my eyes. If she can be persuaded to cooperate, then she will become an invaluable asset. However, with how Dante and Vito are proceeding—trying to frighten her or bludgeon her into submission—I think it is more likely that she will end up hurting us when all this is said and done.

I tighten my fist on the arm of my chair. If my brothers don't listen to me, we might all end up going the way of our father. The Russians are ruthless. My research into their operations has shined a light onto an organization that moves silently and efficiently. They are as loyal as they are vicious.

And now they are coming for us.

Truth be told, this has been in the cards for a long time now. Ten years have passed since they first struck. This didn't start last week—it started long before Father lost his way.

In fact, the event that ignited our hatred for the Russians may have been what broke his mind in the first place.

TEN YEARS AGO

I was waiting outside on the street corner. A luxury apartment building rose into the night behind me. "I am here," I said into my cell phone.

An intermittent drizzle had begun to come down from the heavens, masking the earliest dawn light, so I turned up my collar against the rain and shoved my free hand into my pocket. A black car purred around the corner and came to a stop in front of me. The back door swung open to reveal Dante's grinning face. He had only one piercing back then, the ring above his eyebrow, and his neck was still bare, though he'd been making noise about getting it tattooed, if only to thumb his nose at Father.

"How was she?" he cackled at me, waggling his tongue suggestively.

"A gentleman never tells," I answered soberly as I clambered into the back seat. My serious face lasted all of five seconds before I broke into a smile. Within the car, my brothers all started laughing along with me. Vito was behind the wheel, Leo sat in the front passenger seat, and Sergio, Dante, and I were all crammed into the back.

It had been a raucous night. An auction in Beverly Hills had turned into drinks at Vertex, a nightclub downtown in which Father owned an interest. That, in turn, had led to an after-party of sorts at the VIP room of the city's premier strip club. At the end of it all, my brothers and I each took home a girl or two to satisfy the carnal cravings that our partying had stirred up. Now, with the dawn approaching, it was time to go home. Thus, "the wagon"—our joking name for this nightly round-up ride—arriving to pick me up.

Leo looked drowsy, slumped in his seat. He had taken a pair of dancing girls back to a suite at the Four Seasons. They must have drained him thoroughly.

"Good night, Leo?" I asked, leaning forward to clap him on the shoulder.

He merely grunted in response.

Seated to my left, Dante was a ball of energy. He had purchased a new knife recently and seemed to think that we would all be impressed by his twirling it around in his hands like a snake charmer. "So tell us how you fared," he drawled. "I bet that blonde was a shot of life."

"More plastic in her than the Pacific Ocean," I retorted. "Though still less dangerous than the coven of witches you went cavorting off with."

He grinned. He'd found himself a strange trio of gothic girls, all pale skin and dark hair with far too much makeup on. There was no telling what kind of strange and fucked-up shit they had gotten into. Even at his young age—scarcely nineteen years old—he had peculiar tastes. "Oh, I had myself a fun night, don't you worry."

On the far side of the vehicle, both Sergio and Vito were quiet and brooding. I had often thought that they both had too much of Father in them. Too prone to inner darkness. Even after a night of drinking and sex and fun, a night of being kings of the city, they each looked like someone had just run over the family dog. I decided to leave them alone.

It was a long ride from downtown back up to the Castle. I watched the city pass us by as we wound up the hills. Lights glimmered in the darkness like gems studded into a sheet of velvet.

By the time we pulled into the drive, I was nearly asleep.

Something caught my eye as we parked. It was a dark bundle of sorts, slumped at the corner of the stone steps that led up to the grand front entrance, lying just out of the light.

"Stop," I ordered Vito. He braked the car at once. All of us reached for our weapons instinctively.

"What is it?" he asked me. But I was already out of the car and racing towards the bundle with my gun drawn.

I knew before I had even gotten halfway there that it was a dead body.

The only question that remained was, Whose was it?

I held a breath to fight back the stench of decay and rot that emanated in waves from the corpse. It had been dead for a few days at least. Reaching forward, I grabbed the shoulder and rolled it over.

"Fuck!" I growled, leaping back.

The dead, broken face of my uncle Marco stared back at me.

My brothers came to stand by my shoulders. Each of them had the same reaction. They saw who it was, grimaced, and spat on the ground behind us.

"Who did this?" Leo asked in a quiet voice. No one answered. We Biancis had many enemies, though few of them were bold enough to strike so close to the heart of our family. There would be hell to pay for this. In the coming days and weeks, many people were going to die.

"We'll figure that out later," Sergio said. "For now, we need to move the body before Father sees. This is no way for any man to find his brother."

"Sergio is right," Vito announced. "Grab blankets from the trunk. We will take him to the basement. Quickly, before Father returns home."

"Too late," Dante announced grimly. We all turned to follow his voice and saw him looking down the drive.

A pair of headlights had appeared beyond the gates. As we watched, the gates swung open to admit Father's vehicle. I sighed and rubbed the bridge of my nose as his car wound through the craggy old trees and came to a halt just behind the sedan we'd arrived in. The uniformed driver popped out and hurried around to open Father's door.

Our father emerged from the back seat. He looked like what he was—Giovanni Bianci, don of the most powerful Mafia in the western United States. Tall, proud, elegant. Not yet graying, not yet crippled. That would come later.

He strode towards us, calling over as he went, "Why are my drunken fool sons standing at the foot of the stairs with their cocks in their hands?" He had what passed for a smile on his face—until he shouldered past us and saw the body sprawled on the gravel.

The blood drained from his skin. "Marco," he whispered. He fell to his knees and grabbed his dead brother's hand. "Marco, oh, for fuck's sake."

I'd never seen that kind of emotion from him. My father had cut a fearsome figure for as long as I could remember. He was a god of war, a grim reaper.

Stoic to the core.

But not now. The death of his brother had undone him. And there was nothing for any of us to do but stand there and watch as our father cried out to the heavens and offered to trade his brother's life for his own.

No god answered his prayer.

I check the security cameras. The coast is clear. It's time.

I have to make my move now, before my brothers do anything stupid. Once upon a time, we were thick as thieves. We were an indivisible unit. Now, though, I fear that we are fragmented beyond repair. But that is an issue for another day.

Tonight, I need to talk to Milaya.

Standing from my seat in the study, I exit the room and lock it behind me before proceeding to the spiral staircase at the rear of the great room. My brothers are each squirreled away in their own sections of the castle. Still, I am careful not to make too much noise lest I draw unwanted attention.

I sweep aside the tapestry and go down the stairs. My footsteps echo in the drafty space. I still get the shivers every time I descend into the dungeon. Too many bad things have happened down here not to feel the presence of the lost souls whose lives ended on these stones.

The stairs deposit me into the torture chamber. It looks as it always does—jagged, poorly lit, with leather and metal tools strewn about the floor space. Milaya's cell is the one four doors down on the right. I pluck the key from my pocket, walk down, and unlock it.

She is shivering inside, curled up in one corner like a stray cat. I stand still for a moment and watch her. But I don't have much time to waste.

"Get up."

She rolls over and blinks at me. I wonder briefly if we have pushed her too far. Three days of no food and no water might have been excessive. It was Dante's idea, of course, but Vito and Leo eventually acquiesced. I was the only one to argue against it. Little good it did me—or her, for that matter. She looks wan and weak. I hope the protein bar and bottle of water I brought for her are enough to screw the head back on her shoulders. I need her to be present and alert for what comes next.

Seeing that she won't get up on her own—or can't—I enter and crouch down. A thought crosses my mind—is she playing me? Does she have a weapon of some kind? We searched her before putting her back in the cell, of course, but who knows what sliver of rock she may have pried up from the floor to stab me with. She keeps staring into my eyes though, and I realize that mentally, she is far away from here. She is not a threat right now.

I lower myself to a seat on the floor next to her before offering the blanket that we took from her at the beginning of her punishment. I tell myself to avert my gaze, but it's drawn to her body like a magnet. Her bare hips are curvy and feminine, rising to that petite waist, to breasts pale and unblemished. They each peak in a ghostly nipple, so faint it is almost invisible.

Finally, my eyes settle on her face. Despite the fog of hunger and thirst clouding her, I still see what I saw that first night in the hotel room—the flicker of undeniable intelligence. I feel my cock stir. It takes every ounce of willpower to coax myself back on track, instead of just pinning her against the wall and fucking the daylights out of her.

Dante thinks that I don't have the same hunger he does. But what he doesn't see is that I merely do a better job of hiding it. I tame it and make it work for me instead of the other way around.

Still, there is no denying that it wants this girl. *I* want this girl.

“Eat,” I order softly once the blanket is wrapped around her. She takes the offered protein bar with trembling fingers. When she tries to tear the wrapper open, though, she can’t even get it started. My frown deepens. I pray again silently that we are making the right choices with her. She is far too valuable to lose so carelessly. We almost lost her once through sheer negligence. Losing her to needless cruelty would be a tragic mistake.

“Here.” I trade her the bottle of water for the bar she cannot open. I make sure to unseal the cap before handing it to her. She takes a greedy suckle of it at once.

I snatch it away. “Slower,” I command. “You’ll vomit.”

She fixes me with a wary gaze, but nods slowly. I hold the bottle up to her lips and force her to take small sips.

I can see the color coming back into her face almost instantly. Tearing away the wrapper and plucking off a bite of the protein bar between my fingers, I offer it to her. Not to her hands, though, but up to her mouth. My thumb grazes her soft lip. Again, my manhood strains at the zipper of my pants. It wants out. I’m nearly overwhelmed by the sudden and vicious pang of craving.

Easy, Mateo, I tell myself. *Remember what you came for. Remember what you have lost already to rash decisions.*

That calms me. Enough so that I let her tongue flick out and take the crumb from my fingers and don’t feel quite the same level of urgency to rip the blanket away and press my mouth to her breasts, just so I can hear her moan.

We sit there for a few long, silent minutes. Just me and the daughter of my sworn enemy. I feed her water and food and say nothing. It is one of the most painful experiences of my life.

She is reviving before my eyes, though. Soon, she speaks. “Is this the part where you kill me?”

"No," I answer at once. "Not yet."

"Will you eventually?"

"Maybe. I am not certain yet." I see no reason to lie to her. There is every chance that this will end with her blood being spilled. I hope to avoid the needless sacrifice of life, certainly. But in all the scenarios I've played out in my head and in my notes, quite a few end with the light fading from Milaya Volkov's eyes.

She nods as she digests that information. She doesn't look afraid, though. I can't help but admire that. Here she is, in the belly of the beast, and she doesn't quiver or scream. She's strong, this girl. And cunning. That much is obvious. I need to stay wary.

"Have you had enough to drink?"

"For now. I think."

"Then come. I have something to show you."

I stand in one swift motion, then turn to help her to her feet. She struggles up, like a fawn just learning how to walk. She is putting on a brave front, but as she moves to follow me out of the cell, I can see that this captivity is taking a serious toll on her. She looks thin and worn.

"This way."

I take her down a hallway, deeper into the recesses of the dungeon level. Left, left, right, down the short stairs, left. We reach my destination. I turn to face her before I unlock the door. Her face catches the lamplight. She looks—I suppose beautiful is the only word for it, though it feels inadequate. The skin of her face and shoulders looks sculpted from marble and she is scantily clad, yes, but her beauty runs deeper. It is in the jut of her jaw, the fire in her eyes, in the way I feel like she is looking through me. I have all the power here, and yet something tells me not to underestimate her.

"I am about to show you something that is ... difficult. You will not like it. I want you to understand a few things before I open the door, though. What I am showing you is not a threat—unless you choose to interpret it that way. I won't deny that we are capable of doing very painful things. But I don't want to have to do that. I want you to choose to help us of your own accord."

"Fat fucking chance."

I laugh bitterly. "I understand why you would say that. Still, I have to try. You can cooperate with us, or I will have to resort to—shall we call it other methods?"

"Cooperate with you *how*?" she snaps. "None of you will even tell me what you want. Is it my dad?"

I nod gravely. "It has to do with your father, yes." I clear my throat. "But you must understand that before we can even present our requests, we need to feel that we can trust you."

"I wouldn't, if I were you."

I can't help but smile again. So much fire in this girl. "I thought you might say something like that. Let me show you what is behind the door."

I unlock the door and pull it open slowly. I know what is inside, so my eyes stay rooted on her face.

Seconds pass. I hear the bell chime from far above us. The hour is late.

Frustratingly, she doesn't give me as much of a reaction as I wanted. She blinks, shudders imperceptibly, then tightens the blanket around her shoulders. The only giveaway is how her eyes seem to retreat within her just a bit farther.

"You killed them." She says it flatly, like it's as much of a statement of fact as it is an accusation.

I turn my eyes to the cell. Four bodies are laid out on the floor, hands and ankles bound. They are young men, college-aged. One redheaded, one blond, two with darker brown hair. Each man is wearing what he was wearing the night we barged into the hotel room, and they all bear identical tattoos on their chests—the Greek letters chi and omega.

"They confessed they tried to rape you," I say.

"So?"

"So did you not wish them dead?"

She doesn't say anything for a while. "Maybe I did in the moment. I don't know. Not like this." She looks to them, then back up at me. "Did you torture them?"

"No. We asked them questions. When it was time, their end came quickly."

"All right."

I see suddenly that she's shivering. I frown. "Are you okay?"

"I'm going to sit down," she says in a very careful, clipped voice. "I think I might fall over if I don't."

She promptly collapses.

She would've cracked her head against the corridor wall if I hadn't stepped forward to grab her and ease her transition to the ground. I prop her up into a seating position against the wall.

When I am satisfied that she is in control of her body again, I settle into a position next to her, just as we were in her cell a few minutes ago.

I see a tear trickling down her face. "Why are you crying?"

"They're dead, in case you didn't notice."

"But they were bad to you."

"It's ... it's not that simple."

"No," I muse, more to myself than to her. "Perhaps not." I'm watching her carefully the whole time. Is she playing me? Or is she approaching the state I want her to be in—cooperative, suggestible? It is a delicate operation. One wrong move could send the whole affair careening in the worst possible direction. I need her submissive and compliant, but alert and aware. Right now, we stand on the precipice, the knife's edge, close to falling in either direction.

She has her eyes closed and her head tilted back to rest against the stone wall. We sit in silence for a few slow heartbeats. "Can you tell me now what you want from me?"

I almost tell her. In that moment, I almost open my mouth and lay out the whole plan for her, start to finish. In the length of one brief, idiotic impulse, I almost ruin everything.

I catch myself just before the words slip from my mouth.

"Not yet," I answer in a strained voice. I wonder if she notices my internal struggle.

How is she doing this to me? What is she coaxing out of me? She is a helpless captive. I have dealt with hundreds like her in my time.

But this one is different.

Perhaps it is because the look in her eyes demands I treat her as my equal. It is the same look that Dante wants to break, that Leo wants to dominate, that Vito wants to imprison. I, on the other hand, want to engage it. To set it free under the Bianci banner.

She is not yet ready for that, though. If I tell her the truth—*we want you to betray your father and help deliver him to us unawares so we can make him pay for what he did to our family*—she will never willingly participate. We have to stick to the plan—mold her mind according to our needs. This—the reveal of the dead frat boys—is merely the next step.

I reach into my pocket, retrieve my cell phone, and prepare the second.

The video feed I pull up is in crystal-clear high definition. "Look," I tell Milaya, holding the screen towards her. She opens her eyes reluctantly, as if it pains her, and focuses on the phone with a frown.

I don't have to look. Like the bodies in the cell, I know what it shows.

An apartment. One that Milaya is very familiar with. Secondhand leather couch, the countertop of a kitchen island. The room is empty. I swipe over to reveal the second feed.

This one is a bedroom. Queen bed jammed into one corner, rickety nightstand covered with makeup. A girl is sleeping on top of the comforter, curled up into a little ball. She is petite, feisty, with long blonde hair. Milaya knows her well.

"Anastasia!" she gasps. She looks at me. I blink, betraying nothing.

"There is blood on your hands already," I tell her. I point towards the cell across from us where the frat boys lie cooling. "Thus far, only your enemies have been harmed. Innocent or not, it doesn't matter. But next, it will be people you care about. Your friends are waiting to meet the same end, whether or not they know it."

The lone tear carving its way down her dirt-stained cheek becomes a flood of them. She doesn't redden or sob, just cries silently like that as I watch her. If she is manipulating me, she is a master of her craft.

I think not. I hope not. I want to believe that this is Milaya Volkov nearing her breaking point, the point that will turn this whole war around for my family.

But I can't be sure just yet.

"Please," she begs, "just tell me what you want me to do. I'll do it, I'll do anything. Just don't hurt her."

Amazing, I think to myself. What kind of daughter has Luka Volkov raised? Perhaps he is not the ruthless killer that his reputation suggests. If this is his child—overflowing with compassion even for men who tried to rape her, for a friend who betrayed her—then perhaps I have overestimated my enemy. She is wracked with grief for the worst kind of man alive, the pig who takes what he has neither earned nor been given. She wants to protect a companion who stabbed her in the back. I can't pretend to understand either impulse. But it amazes me nonetheless.

Is this the moment? Have we reached her breaking point far sooner than I anticipated? I see the liquid fear in her eyes and wonder if it is time to tell her she must now turn on her father. If I reveal what he has done, the full extent of his sins, then she will be putty in my hands, won't she?

I don't know. Fuck, I don't know. I despise those words more than any others on this planet. I have to make a choice, right now. Tell her or don't? Return her to her cell or make her my ally?

I make a choice.

But when I open my mouth to deliver it, the door at the end of the hallway clangs open. Vito comes storming in.

His nostrils flare and his brows form an angry V. "Get up," he seethes. Milaya starts to struggle to her feet, but he holds up a hand. "Not you. Him."

Goddammit. I sigh and rise gracefully to face him. Though I am younger, I am three inches taller, meaning I can look down into his eyes. He hates that, I know, the vain prick.

"You were not invited to this little powwow, *fratello,*" I say. I let a faint edge of mockery creep into my voice. He hates that too.

"You should not be here, Mateo."

"I wasn't aware that my movements were restricted now."

"You know better."

"Do I?"

"We do not make decisions on our own."

"Once upon a time, perhaps not. Things are different now."

He growls. I know he wants to hit me. It is written on his face, in the clench of his fists at his side, the set of his jaw. A younger Vito would not have thought twice about striking me. He is different now than he once was. Our father's death has aged him decades in a mere few days.

"Put her back," he hisses. "Then meet me in the great room. So we can have a 'powwow' of our own."

He stalks away before I can answer. The door slams shut behind him forcefully.

I turn to face Milaya, who is still seated on the floor. "Come," I tell her. "Time for you to go home."

I make her walk in front of me as we wind back to her cell. She steps inside willingly, keeping the blanket tight around her shoulders to hide her nakedness.

She pivots in place before the door shuts and looks at me. "You don't have to do this," she says in a soft voice.

"Do what?"

"Any of it."

"This choice was made a long time ago, Milaya."

Then I shut the door in her face. I try to forget her words as I go upstairs to argue more with Vito.

But I can't.

15

MILAYA

"Get up."

"No thanks."

"It wasn't a question."

I crack open an eye. Leo is leaning against the doorjamb. He is wearing a long-sleeved white linen shirt with the sleeves rolled up to his elbows, exposing strong forearms and a smattering of dark hair. The top three buttons are undone too, so I can see the outline of his chest muscles. His head is cocked at a listless angle, almost like he's bored with having to come fetch me for whatever nightmare the brothers have planned next.

"Are you going to make me throw you over my shoulder like a sack of potatoes?" he drawls.

I can't help but notice that he has such a pretty mouth. Sinfully twisted, with a smile that oscillates between wry and cruel. It must drive women crazy. Even here and now, when he's my warden and torturer, I want him to smile at me. I want him to want me.

What a wild thought. Maybe I really am becoming unhinged.

"I'd prefer if you didn't."

"Then get up."

"Why?"

"You're being invited to dinner."

I laugh and curl back up in the folds of the blanket. "Now I know you're just screwing with me. Why bother?"

He clicks his tongue in irritation. "I'm not going to eat cold food because you decided to pitch a little fit. Get up and come with me. Or would you rather stay in a musty cell for the rest of your life?"

I eye him warily. There's a catch coming somewhere soon. I have been in this place long enough to know that the other shoe is always about to drop. But he's tapping his toe impatiently against the steel door and checking his watch like he has somewhere important to be.

I weigh my options. I can continue refusing to cooperate, and likely suffer as a result. Or I can just go along with him and hold out hope that maybe there really is dinner at the end of the rainbow.

What choice do I have?

"Fine," I say, rising. I tug the blanket firmly around me and shoot him a glare. "But it better be steak. I've been craving steak."

Leo laughs sardonically. "You have very little influence in the matter, darling." He turns and leaves. I follow him, watching the muscles of his shoulders ripple beneath the thin fabric of his shirt as we go.

The stairs are every bit as long as I remember them being. My thighs are burning by the time we get halfway up.

"Wait," I plead, panting. "I need a second."

He glances back at me over his shoulder. His lips stray towards condescending. "Not such an athlete, are we?"

"You've been feeding me gruel or nothing at all for nearly a week now. I wouldn't say I'm exactly in peak condition."

He's on me in a flash, before I even realize what's happening. One hand grips my throat as he turns my head from side to side, examining me like a prize horse at auction. The other hand snakes between the folds of the blanket and cups me between my legs.

I gasp out loud. His fingers are cool but not uncomfortably so. He doesn't slide his finger into me the way the monster of desire in my core suddenly wants him to do. Instead, he just keeps his right hand on my jaw and his left palm pressed flush against my center.

His face fills my field of vision. Up close, he is just as beautiful as he is from farther away. Flashing blue eyes, cruelly sharp chin, the proud Bianci nose that all his brothers share.

And those lips. Luscious, almost feminine were it not for the coarse, haughty, disdainful way they let words slip between them.

"I'd say you are in perfectly fine condition, darling," he hisses in a voice that makes the hair on the back of my neck stand on end. "Good enough to eat, you might say."

"Stop ..." It is halfway between a word and a whimpering exhale.

"Oh no," he murmurs, "I don't think you truly want that, do you?" His palm between my slick thighs shimmies from side to side, just slightly but enough to make me squirm in his grasp.

I babble nonsense. It's just air coming from my mouth, not real words. My brain is screaming at me to yell at him, hit him, curse at him. *Get away from me!*

But that would be a lie. I don't want his hand to disappear. I want more of it. I want those lips where his hands are. I want him to choke the air from my throat while we find out just how deep those fingers can go, how wide I can spread for him.

There's no maybe about it anymore—I'm truly falling to pieces.

"I don't think you want that at all. I think you are dripping wet for me, darling. I can feel it. Oh yes, dripping wet indeed. But," he says, looking fake-thoughtful for a moment, "just say the word and I'll let you run along." His eyes sparkle. "If you want, that is."

My mouth parts. I don't know what to say. I'm on fire, burning up from the inside out. My lower belly is knotted up so tight that I'm afraid it'll snap my spine in half. His touch, his scent, his lips, his words—they're all washing over me like an ocean of fire.

"Let me go," I whisper finally in a hoarse voice. It's pathetic, but it's the best I can manage.

Leo holds onto me for one moment longer. Then his face splits into that cruel smile and he releases me. His hand retreats from between my legs. I feel cold and incomplete in its absence, like someone just ripped out a crucial part of me.

He whirls away without another word and continues up the stairs. "Hurry up," he commands as he vanishes around the bend above me. "We don't have all night."

I try to examine my surroundings as we push the tapestry aside and move through the interior of the mansion, but Leo is walking fast and I'm having a hard time keeping up. Each of his strides is long and athletic. Meanwhile, I've spent a week or so chained in a damp dungeon with little to drink and less to eat, so I'm not exactly ready for the Boston Marathon.

What I do manage to observe is breathtaking. The room beyond the tapestry that hides the spiral staircase is even bigger than I realized on the night I tried to escape. The ceilings are impossibly high. I could swear that I see a bat or two flitting around in the upper reaches. Up here is made of stone, too, though the floors are marble and covered with exotic-looking rugs. The fireplace in the center is massive and surrounded by comfortable-looking plush armchairs. I see mahogany tables displaying jewelry and chandeliers dripping with thousands of crystals that refract the firelight. Hanging on the walls everywhere I look are oil portraits of proud men and women. They all have the same hard set to their jaw and the same aquiline nose that tells me I'm looking at generations of Biancis.

But I don't have time to stop and gawk at the family lineage. Leo is walking down a long corridor that extends away from the left-hand side of the great room. I follow him in a hurry, keeping the blanket clutched close. I have the sudden burning realization of feeling so naked. In the cell, it almost became an afterthought. Up here, though, I feel wildly out of place. This isn't just a home. This is a mansion, a historical landmark. The walls themselves feel old and important, like they're looking down at me in stern disapproval.

I shrink into myself and walk faster.

There's no sign of the other brothers or of anyone else as we move down a dark hallway and emerge into another small, circular common room area. Five hallways branch off it, radiating out like spokes on a wheel. He selects the farthest to the left without breaking stride.

A few steps down it, we stop outside of a huge wooden door that reaches all the way up to the double-height ceiling. Leo turns the handle and ushers me inside.

As soon as he does, my jaw drops.

This is it. The bedroom from my dream.

I step into the room and marvel at details that I know I have seen before. The four-poster bed sits against one wall. It is carved with lions and eagles in pursuit of one another. I step close and run my fingers up and down the fine woodwork.

Turning, I look to the far wall. The double doors to the bathroom are propped open, revealing an expanse of white- and gray-swirled marble. It gleams like it's glowing.

I keep turning in place, surveying my surroundings. The walls of the bedroom are a deep sea green, flecked subtly with gold. I circle slowly around the room. I have an insatiable need to touch everything. My fingers ghost across the rich wooden credenza, the dresser, the nightstand, the gilded frame of a stormy scene depicted in dark, slashing oils.

I almost want to cry.

It's too much. Like drinking from a firehose after nearly dying of thirst in the desert. The sensory overload is short-circuiting my brain. I turn to look at Leo, tears in my eyes.

"Why did you bring me here?" I ask in a voice that I'm trying and failing to keep from quivering like a little girl on the verge of a meltdown.

He looks at me oddly. "This is where you're going to stay now."

"Here?"

"Yes," he says, almost with irritation. "Here."

I want to ask why, but I'm afraid to know the answer.

Just let yourself have this moment, I beg silently. I've been through so much. Even if this is merely foreplay to another horrible twist of events, just enjoy it while it lasts. After all, I might not ever get something like this again. Life is turning out to be far bleaker than I ever imagined it could possibly be. If I can have just sixty seconds of perfect, then I owe it to myself to take it.

So I do exactly that. I sigh and savor the scent of a cedarwood candle burning on the nightstand. I look at my feet and see the teasing play of evening sun streaming through the gauzy curtains and lighting up my skin. I let my fingertips rest on the down comforter. It feels like a cloud.

"Anyways," Leo says after a moment. He doesn't sound quite so irritated now. He must be pitying me. I'm sure I look like something worth pitying, though I didn't think any of the Bianci brothers were capable of that emotion. "Dinner is in ninety minutes. You'll need to shower and dress before then. As delicious of a morsel as you may be, time in those dungeon cells doesn't do anyone's beauty any good. I am here to supervise."

"To supervise what?"

He waves a hand towards the bathroom. "The process."

"You want to watch me shower?" I ask in disbelief.

"Want has little to do with it, darling," he says drily. I'm not sure he's fully telling me the truth. His eyes rake up and down me. "Though I won't stop myself from enjoying it if the mood should strike. I am merely acting on my brother's orders."

"Vito told you to watch me shower?" I've seen enough of the brothers' dynamic to know which one fancies himself the leader. Still, something about Vito doesn't quite add up for me yet.

Leo rolls his eyes. "Dante said you were an inquisitive one. I see now that he was spot on."

I still can't quite wrap my head around this. I know that's stupid. They stripped me naked and cuffed me to a metal table. After that, why does watching me shower seem like something even more invasive?

I don't know why I feel that way, but I do. Maybe it's because I always loved showers. I used to take long ones, back in my pre-dungeon life. Long, luxurious, self-indulgent showers. I'd sit, stand, lie down, sing, dance, wash my hair and scrub my skin a dozen times. I loved feeling warm, enveloped in steam, and then the coolness of the outside air like a fresh breeze taking you over once the water was shut off.

Now, thinking of that cozy interplay of hot and cold air just reminds me of my dream, the one that takes place in this very room. Of the silk bathrobe slipping from my shoulders. Of the four brothers consuming me, devouring me, claiming ...

"Fine," I snap. "What the hell do I care anymore?"

Leo raises an eyebrow but says nothing. We have a brief staring contest before I scowl again, shrug, and toss the blanket to the side as I stride away from him towards the bathroom. I can feel his eyes on me while I walk. They're searing into me, like he's memorizing every curve of my body.

I try to ignore him as I move from the carpeted bedroom onto the cold marble of the bathroom floor. The shower comes to life in a smooth stream of water that steams almost instantly. I stick my hand under the flow and gasp out loud.

It's incredible, but just like my first steps into the room, it's too much. I have to close my eyes and breathe. Otherwise, I'm going to black out. Finally, I get control of myself again.

I wonder idly if they're going to kill me here in the bathroom. For easy cleanup, or something like that. But as I step under the showerhead, I see that Leo hasn't moved. He's still standing against the wall just inside the door, eyeing me carefully.

There are bottles of shampoo, conditioner, and face wash waiting for me. I try not to focus on the fact that they're all my preferred brands. The implications of that—that someone was watching my apartment or has been there since my capture—are too much. For right now, I just want to enjoy the shower. The horrors of my future can wait until the hot water runs out at the very least.

But it's hard to relax. Every time I try to lose myself in the blissful heat of the shower, I feel Leo staring at me and I can't help but look to see if that's still the case. It always is. He doesn't move for the entire twenty or thirty or forty or however many minutes. I try not to care. *Let him wait,* I tell myself. *Take your moments of perfect while you still can.*

Finally, though, I'm pruning up and damn near sweating from how hot I have the water cranked. I kill the flow reluctantly and look at my feet to watch the suds swirl away down the drain. I want it back at once.

I have a memory—not even a fully-formed one, just a kind of brief flash, verging on deja vu—of my mother setting me on the edge of the bathtub after a shower to comb out the tangles in my hair. I feel the ghost of her fingers and the burls of the brush. "So tender-headed," she told me. She wasn't wrong. I always had to yell at her to be more gentle. She'd tell me to toughen up, but she also softened her touch at once. Her bark was always worse than her bite, my mom's. Though I would hate to see how hard she would bite if she could get near the men who have stolen me away.

I wonder again what my parents are doing right now. Surely by this point, they're aware that something has happened. I've missed a week of classes. Anton and Matvei haven't reported back to whichever chief goon is in charge of my security detail ...

But do they have any leads? Are they anywhere close to figuring out where I've gone? I suppose it doesn't matter. I gave up hope of being rescued a long time ago. I have only myself to rely on.

"Here." I look up in shock, lost in thought, to see Leo standing in front of me with a towel in his grasp.

It takes me a second to find my voice. "Thanks," I murmur. I feel shame blush in my cheeks suddenly and I look back down at my feet.

Just a few minutes ago, when I was a dirty little dungeon rat, I didn't care about being naked in front of this dark, sexy, mysterious man. Hell, I even ditched that nasty blanket on the ground and strolled butt-naked into the bathroom for all the world to see. But now that I'm clean from the shower, I feel *especially* naked.

Leo's eyes don't help. They aren't even slightly interested in protecting my modesty. Instead, they roam up and down my body, drinking me in like a fine wine. I don't know what it is about his face that says he's savoring me, but I know for a fact that he is. He doesn't miss a single detail. Not the birthmark on the left side of my rib cage or the scar on my knee from falling down a steep sidewalk when I was eleven. Not my too-small B-cup breasts or the freckle in the dead center of my bottom lip.

He sees *all* of me.

I reach out to take the towel to wrap myself up so I can feel like there is at least something these men haven't yet stolen from me. But before I can get it, he jerks his hand back, leaving me grasping at air.

"What are you, six years old?" I snap. "Give me the towel."

"No, darling," he demurs. "I changed my mind. Come here." He lets the towel unfold and hang in the air to his side like a bullfighter's cape.

"Not a chance." I cross my arms over my chest and fix him with an icy glare.

He just smiles. "Normally, I would tell you that it is unwise to refuse a man like me. Under the circumstances, I think I'll give you the benefit of the doubt and tell you once more: come here." He flicks his wrist so the towel flops in place, then looks at me again.

"Or what?"

"Or else, darling, I'm afraid that I will have to finish what I started on the staircase."

That sends a cold chill running through me. What he started on the staircase was his hand between my legs, stirring to life something that I didn't even know lived inside me. How can I possibly want this man in a physical, sexual sense? He is my captor, my warden, my enemy. He wants to hurt me. I heard the brothers talking between themselves. I know that they don't have good things planned. But I also know that they aren't in alignment on what exactly to do with me.

It's becoming clearer and clearer though: Leo wants to swallow me whole.

Like a marionette on strings being controlled by someone far above me, I find myself taking a step towards him. The droplets of quickly cooling water slide down my hips and from my wet hair, splattering quietly against the marble floor. I'm not in control of my own actions anymore. That *thing* inside me—the same thing telling me to enjoy perfection while I can get it—is telling me to go to Leo, to do what he says.

I shiver. As I do, he closes the remaining distance between us and wraps the huge, fluffy towel around my body. There's an almost loving tenderness to his touch. It contrasts with the dangerous gleam in his blue eyes.

"There, there," he mumbles softly. He's close enough that his lips graze my earlobe. "That wasn't so hard now, was it?"

I say nothing. I can't. I don't trust my voice not to tremble.

Keeping his hands on my shoulders, he steers me out of the bathroom towards the bedroom. I see that he's opened the huge armoire that sits in one corner. In it is a single garment—a golden dress. It catches the light of the chandelier overheard and the light of the setting sun and scatters both sources in a million different directions. Placed just in front of the armoire is a pair of impossibly high black stiletto pumps.

"This is what you'll be wearing this evening," he informs me quietly. He points to the vanity in the opposite corner. "There is makeup and whatever else you need over there. Dinner is in half an hour. Do not be late."

For the third time this evening, he turns and slips away before I can figure out what to say. I'm left in this empty room, still wet, still feeling the buzz where his lips brushed against my ear, where his palm cupped my center, where his eyes bored into my soul.

I don't even have the chance to ask why there isn't a scrap of underwear to be found.

But, as soon as he's gone, I realize it doesn't matter. I'm not going to stick around to find out.

There is a huge window next to the vanity that stretches nearly from the floor to the ceiling. I reach over and test the weight of the little stool set in front of the makeup mirror. This ought to do nicely.

Picking it up, I take a deep breath and steel myself. I'm only going to get one chance at this.

With all the force my aching body can muster, I hurl the stool at the window.

It merely bounces back.

I shriek and leap out of the way, narrowly avoiding being decapitated by my own idiotic mistake. It takes a long time to get my heartbeat back to something resembling normal.

Of course these psychopaths would have bulletproof glass. There isn't even a scratch on the pane. My dad showed me once on his car how bulletproof glass could repel slugs fired from close range. I didn't have the boldness back then to ask why a man like him needed such a thing. We both knew that I wouldn't like the answer.

I lie on the floor for a while looking up at the ceiling above me. The rug beneath me is soft and warm. I wouldn't think that would be the case, but even after days of captivity, it feels good to do nothing for a moment. The other shoe will drop soon, after all. Might as well soak up the last few moments of peace.

The clock on the wall chimes out the half hour. I need to hurry up and get ready before I am late. I shudder to think what they will do to me if I don't show up when Leo told me to. My escape will have to wait until after dinner.

Besides, maybe dining with the Bianci brothers will give me some clue I need to get away from here. At the very least, I'll get to see more of this castle. Leo was careful to lock the door behind him, so it's not like I can just sneak out that way anyhow.

The only way out is through.

I don't know where that phrase came from, but it pops into my head suddenly and loudly. *The only way out is through.* Through the castle. Through the brothers.

I shudder again and hurry over to put on some quick makeup and pull the dress over my head.

I am tottering like a newborn deer when I head towards the door of the bedroom right as the clock tolls out the top of the hour. I was never great at walking in heels under the best of circumstances. Fear, malnourishment, and nights spent sleeping on hard rock haven't done me any favors in that department.

I pause a few steps shy of the door when I remember that Leo locked me in. How am I going to get out of here? I turn halfway around to see if there's a bell I'm supposed to ring or something.

But my dilemma is answered immediately. The door sweeps open, revealing Vito.

He is wearing a midnight-black tuxedo. He looks like an honest-to-God model. Those high cheekbones, the dark windswept hair, the piercing eyes and pout. He fills it out better than the pale, scrawny boys they put on high-fashion runways, though. His shoulders are massively broad, his biceps thick.

"Good even—" he's in the midst of saying as he steps through the door. When I turn all the way around, the words die on his lips.

Something inscrutable passes over his face, like a rain cloud moving over the sun. I don't know him well enough to be able to say for sure, but on anyone else, I would say that it looked like the grief of seeing the ghost of a loved one. Since that doesn't make even a lick of sense, I'm left grasping at straws. Maybe it's just the shock of seeing his prisoner tarted up in a gold dress like an expensive hooker. Who's to say? I don't know this monster, and I don't want to. Psychoanalyzing my captors isn't high on my to-do list. At the moment, it mostly consists of one, get the hell away from here and two, see number one.

Vito is frozen stiff for just a second, maybe two. But it is long enough to leave an indelible mark in my head. I see his expression and I know at once: this is a haunted man. He is irretrievably broken in some deep, essential way. I feel like a crackpot for even thinking those words, but they're so powerfully true that I know I'm right. This man has suffered. Immensely. How, when, why, I don't know. I just know it's true.

The look on his face is gone as quickly as it came. The cloud passes and his careful mask of self-control settles right back into place.

He clears his throat. "Good evening," he repeats. "It is time for dinner. Come with me."

He offers me his elbow, which I take, not ungratefully. It makes walking through the doors out into the hallway much easier. He is so solid, so muscular, that I feel like I'm floating. He's careful to walk at my pace too, unlike Leo, who could barely be bothered to check over his shoulder and make sure that I hadn't cracked my head open on the flagstone floor.

We pass through the common area where the five hallways join up. It occurs to me that there is one hallway for each of the brothers, but with one leftover. I wonder what the significance of that is. We don't linger long enough for me to figure it out.

Vito guides me into the main hallway and back towards the great room with the fireplace. As we round the corner and emerge out under the high arched ceilings, I see that there is a large banquet table that has been arranged.

Strange—I haven't seen a single household staff member since I arrived here. But there must be some somewhere, or else the place wouldn't be so clean. I picture these four animals mopping the floors and start laughing silently. Then I picture Vito in a frilly French maid's outfit with a feather duster and fishnet tights and snort out loud.

"Is something funny?" he asks soberly.

"No, I just, uh—it'd be too hard to explain."

"I didn't think you'd be in much of a laughing mood, given your ... circumstances."

I sigh. The laughter fades away, though I file away the image to chuckle at again later. If there is a later, that is.

"I'm ... I'm not, I guess. I don't know. Nothing feels real anymore."

"I don't feel real to you, Milaya Volkov?"

"You do, you just—shit. I mean, shoot. I don't know." I pause. "Why do you say it like that?"

"Say what?"

"My name."

"Is that not what you are called?"

I wrinkle my eyebrows. "It is. It just sounds like you're saying it on purpose. Like, forcing it."

"I don't want to forget who you are."

I think about that. On the face of it, it sounds stupid. That's what names are for, right? Remembering who people are?

But I know that that's not what Vito meant by his phrasing. There's a deeper meaning lingering below the surface. Like he wants to remind himself of *what* I am. Where I come from or something.

The question remains: why? What do I mean to him?

"There she is!" crows Dante, interrupting my thoughts.

He's seated at one end of the long, white-cloth-covered table. He, too, is wearing a tuxedo, though he's opted to leave the bowtie hanging untied around his neck, unlike Vito, whose tie is knotted perfectly.

"The guest of honor. Or is she the main course?"

He laughs when he sees me blanch. They're not that sick ... are they? To go through everything they've put me through, only to be *eaten*—it seems wrong. Not to mention a serious violation of the "don't play with your food" edict. Still, I've looked right into Dante's eyes and seen the craziness there. At this point, I wouldn't put anything past him.

"My brother is kidding," clarifies Mateo, who is seated across from Dante and scowling at him. "He has a twisted sense of humor sometimes."

"Am I, though?" Dante muses.

I see Leo in another chair. His tuxedo is a bold navy that brings out his eyes. No tie at all for him, and like before, the top few buttons of his shirt are undone. If I had to guess, I'd say he thinks it makes him look sexy and dangerous. He's not wrong.

Vito walks me around to the seat at the head of the table. He pulls it out for me and helps me into it—the picture of a gentleman, if we only forget about the fact that I'm not here by choice and they drugged me and killed those frat boys and blackmailed my friend into giving me up and—

Oof, I'm getting lightheaded. I take a breath and close my eyes for a second.

When I reopen them, I promise myself to do just one thing at a time for the rest of this meal. One bite. One drink. One question. One answer. It's the only way I'm going to get through the whole ordeal.

A quote pops in my head, originally about writing a book, but equally applicable to the nightmare I'm living through right now: "It's like driving a car at night. You can see only as far as your headlights, but you can make the whole trip that way."

One thing at a time.

I can do this.

16

MILAYA

I'm seated at the head of the table. Vito and Mateo are to my right, Dante and Leo to my left. Our voices echo in the huge room. There's a slight chill in the air, though the fire in the hearth helps take the edge off it. All in all, I feel like I've been transported back two or three hundred years in time. I'm eating dinner in a godforsaken castle, for crying out loud, surrounded by four men who carry themselves like princes. Their ancestors are looking down on me from their portraits on the wall. The whole thing is too surreal.

"Am I supposed to say thank you now?" I ask sarcastically. "That's what this is, right? A little good cop/bad cop routine? First, you drug me and threaten me and imprison me, then when you let me upstairs and treat me like an actual human being, I'm supposed to fall over myself trying to please you?"

"This is dinner," Vito growls. "Nothing more."

I resist the urge to roll my eyes. I'm sure he's being purposefully dense, but it annoys me anyway. At least have the balls to say to my face what is actually happening.

Part of me almost preferred being a prisoner. Things were clear back then when I was in the cell. They were my enemies; I was their captive.

Now, it's all muddled. Dante is refilling my wineglass aggressively, servers keep materializing from the shadows with endless courses of food, and the brothers are all looking at me with gazes that fall somewhere between curious and predatory. I just try to focus on my food. One bite at a time.

The only way out is through.

Leo said I didn't have a choice in the meal, but my request for steak was apparently fulfilled, because the main course is a thick, juicy slab of expensive filet mignon, smeared with chives butter and crispy fingerling potatoes on the side. The smell is heavenly. I can see the lines of delicious fat marbled in the cut.

I practically blink and it's gone.

Mateo chuckles. "Would you like more?" he asks.

I nod and wash down the food with a huge gulp of wine as he snaps his fingers and sends one of the waitstaff scurrying off to the hidden kitchen to fetch me another plate.

I follow my first glass of wine with a second quickly on its heels. I don't even care about controlling my alcohol intake. How could I possibly wind up in *more* trouble than I'm currently in? These men have taken everything from me. Worrying about letting my guard down is stupid when there is so little of myself left to guard. So I drink. At the very least, it keeps the bad thoughts away.

Dinner is mostly silent for a while. Only the crackle of logs in the fire and the clink of cutlery. Leo, Dante, and Vito keep their eyes rooted on their plates. Only Mateo looks at me after I've finished off a second steak. He smiles again, though it's tinged with sadness. I like him the best of all of his brothers—though "like" is relative, considering that they're all murderous abductors and sadists.

Something about him is different, approachable. Even when he was showing me the bodies of the Frat Stars—something I've steadfastly refused to think about since the second the door closed on those poor boys—he did it in a way that said he didn't want to be doing this. That he wouldn't be doing it if he didn't have to, for whatever mysterious reason they still refuse to reveal.

"Do you know who we are?" Mateo asks me suddenly.

I pause. The way he posed the question feels like a test of sorts. I don't know why it would matter, but I sense that it somehow does.

I look from brother to brother, starting at my left and going in clockwise fashion—Leo, Dante, Vito, Mateo. I must be a little drunker than I thought, though, because before I know it, I'm pointing my finger at each in turn and saying, "Oh, I know you all right. That's the Playboy, he's the Nutcase, there's the Big Bad Wolf, and you're the Nerd."

Dante snorts and coughs up flecks of wine on the table. I see Vito suppress a grin as his hand tightens on the silver fork he is holding. Even Leo cracks a smile. Mateo just sighs.

"More fight in her than we anticipated," Dante chuckles after his coughing fit subsides. "You might be a little bit of a nutcase yourself, Milaya."

I smile despite myself. "Maybe I am."

No one says anything for a minute or two. For a second there, when everyone was laughing, it felt like a moment of genuine—well, genuine *something*. Connection? Friendship? Something like that. That's how it felt, at least, as bizarre as that seems.

But the feeling slips away into the silence. The chill in the air deepens as the smiles fall off each of our faces.

Eventually, Mateo looks to me again. "I mean, do you know who we *really* are?" he asks.

I hesitate, then shake my head and tell him the truth. "I don't know much. Your names. That's about it."

"You've heard of us before?"

"No."

"Our family?"

"No."

He strokes his chin. "Interesting. I would've thought that your father would tell you something about the Biancis."

"He would have if it was just him, probably. But my mom didn't like him to talk about anything that might upset or endanger me."

Leo laughs. "Fat lot of a good that did you."

I nod. "Sure doesn't feel like it."

"Our family is old," Mateo says with the air of a historian launching into an origin story. "We go back nearly seven generations."

"Here comes the boring part," Dante drawls. He refills his wineglass and offers me the bottle to refill mine as well. I bite my lip to keep from laughing as Mateo fixes his wild younger brother with a glare.

"As I was saying," he continues, "the family business has taken different forms over the years, but it has always been just that—a family business." He points at the building around us. "This is the Bianci Castle. My grandfather's grandfather built it nearly two hundred years ago. Since the walls went up, this has been the beating heart of the Biancis. We live here. We work here."

"You drug and murder people here?" I cut in.

Mateo tilts his head and gazes at me soberly. "When our duties call for it, we do what must be done."

"That's some cryptic bullshit," I argue. "You're criminals. Don't act like you're some holier-than-thou guardians of the city."

"We do what must be done," he repeats.

"She's right, you know," Dante interjects. "This city is our cash cow, not our fucking ward or whatever. We don't do this shit for our health."

"We keep the peace," Vito says in a quiet, steely voice.

"We *did,*" replies Dante without missing a beat. "And look where that got us."

"Shut up," Mateo snarls. "This is neither the time nor the place."

"What is the time and place then, *fratello?* Eh? How long are we supposed to play mind games with this fucking Russian whore? Eh?!"

He pounds the table with a fist. I jump at the sudden noise. There's a tinny little voice in my head that wants to be offended at what he called me. A fucking Russian whore? He's not exactly mincing his words here. It's clear that, out of all the brothers, Dante is the most violent one and the one least inclined to keep me alive and breathing. For whatever reason—whatever is the cause of the pain that lives behind his eyes like a wild beast—he sees me as the cause. He also sees my death as the solution.

Vito stands up, his chair screeching out behind him. "You are out of line," he says to Dante. When Dante starts to respond, Vito jabs his fork through the air. "No. No more. Not in front of the girl."

"Let him talk!" I blurt.

I want to hear what Dante really thinks. He might hate me and want me dead, but he's the only one who is willing to speak the truth around here. Vito and Mateo think that they can just crack my mind wide open and rewire me, and Leo doesn't seem to give a damn one way or the other. Yeah, Dante wants to kill me. He's honest about it though. For some reason, that honesty seems terribly important to me.

Vito settles back into his chair. He looks so impossibly weary all of the sudden. He can't be more than thirty-five at the most, and yet the exhaustion in his eyes is decades greater than that. I can see how tired he is in the slope of his shoulders, the grimace he wears at all times. Part of me wants to comfort him, inexplicably. To lay his head in my lap and tell him to sleep, that everything will be okay.

Then I remember who and what he is, and that feeling disappears at once.

"Fine," he grits out. "The floor is yours. I don't give a fuck anymore."

Dante offers Vito a mocking half-bow. Then he turns to fix me with his cold, hard stare. "Our family has had a hand in just about every crime that's been perpetrated in this city for the last hundred-plus years. Either we did it or we gave permission to someone else to do it. If some granny got mugged on a street corner, the mugger only did it with our okay, or else he got what was coming to him. We ran shit, we took our cut, we hid the bodies when they needed hiding. And it made us richer than God. That's our story, little Russian. Nothing more to it than that. No matter what my esteemed brothers like to think."

"Okay," I whisper. I don't know what else to say, although "okay" is a pretty stupid answer by anyone's standards. I mean, am I supposed to say they're forgiven? That they're bad men? Dante doesn't seem to give a rat's ass about absolution or condemnation, even if I was in a position to give him one or the other. He just seems *angry*. Burning up with such an intense rage that—even now, in the midst of a peaceful, ostensibly classy dinner in his own family castle—it threatens to overwhelm him and anyone in his vicinity.

I clear my throat and, in a quiet, hoarse whisper, ask Dante—the only one willing to tell me the truth to my face—the million-dollar question: "What do you want with me, then?"

His face hardens. The fire crackles. Leo takes a sip of his wine and looks up to the rafters, unsmiling. Vito scowls into the distance, and

Mateo is clearly lost in thought. It is a pure, powerful moment between just me and Dante, like we're the only ones in the room.

"Your father took something very precious from us," Dante says in a lethally soft voice. "So we took something very precious from him in return. And we're going to use you in whatever way we need to in order to make things right."

I swallow. I can feel a bead of sweat sliding down the nape of my neck despite the chill in the air. "So this is about revenge."

"This is about justice," Dante corrects. "So let me make one thing clear, princess: if I get the chance to hang you upside down, cut your throat, and drain you of every drop of blood you have, then I will do it without hesitation. That is *my* form of justice." His eyes flash as if he's picturing doing exactly that. Then the anger recedes slightly. He folds his hands in his lap and leans back. "Luckily for your beating heart, my brothers don't agree."

"What do they think?" I ask.

He waves a hand dismissively. "You'll have to ask them. Know this though: you will stay here until all this is over."

"I'm your little crown jewel prisoner then?"

"Don't flatter yourself. You're a pawn in this game," he answers at once. "It's up to your dear old dad to make the next move." He rises, throws his napkin over his plate, and walks away without another word, leaving the four of us sitting in stunned silence.

It's going to take me a long time to digest everything I've heard tonight. That much is certain. My dad, Dante, the Bianci family legacy—the puzzle pieces are slowly revealing themselves to me. I guess that's better than being kept in the darkness, but I can't deny that the picture being formed scares the daylights out of me.

This is so much bigger than just one college girl. This is a massive, powerful crime family going to war against my own father. And I'm caught in the crossfire.

I wasn't lying when I told Mateo that my mother tried to protect me from my father's underworld. She said it was safer for me not to know things. Dad loved her too much to argue. Whether that was for better or worse, I can't say for sure. All I know is that I spent my whole life knowing that my father was somehow at the head of a huge, shadowy organization that did things that weren't always good. I was content not knowing.

That feels so stupid now.

I'm astonished that I'm feeling something I haven't felt once in my entire two-plus decades on this earth: the first curdle of anger at my dad. Not normal daddy-daughter anger over stupid things like what I'm allowed to wear or can I be excused from the dinner table, but real, true anger.

How could he leave me so vulnerable? I'm clueless and defenseless, like a little baby thrown into the heart of the jungle. He just wanted what was best for me. But he was so wrong.

I'm lost in thought when Vito suddenly stands and paces away without saying a word to us. We all watch him go.

When he is gone, Mateo turns to me.

"I am sorry for my brothers' behavior tonight," he says.

I don't know what to say to that. Maybe he ought to apologize for keeping me in a cell, for starving me, etc., but I don't think I'll ever be hearing that particular mea culpa, not even from Mateo.

"It's okay," is what I eventually settle on.

"We are still ... learning," he says.

I ask, "Learning what?"

"How to cope."

"To cope with …?"

But he just shakes his head. "Now is not the time."

I sigh. I know he won't give me anything more than that. For as different as these men are from each other, they have at least one thing in common: they're all stubborn as mules.

Mateo stands to his full height and offers a little bow in my direction. "It was a pleasure dining with you this evening, Miss Volkov. Leo," he adds, "explain to Miss Volkov her new living arrangements." Then he follows in Vito's footsteps and is gone.

The great room is quiet once more. I feel Leo's eyes burning a hole into me. It is just the two of us now, and suddenly, I feel ridiculously nervous. Not nervous the way I feel nervous in Dante's presence, which almost has an adrenaline edge to it, like I'm putting my life on the line every time I so much as look at the man. With Leo, I feel nervous like I'm walking down a dark trail in the woods at night, and a snake might leap out from the underbrush at any moment. It doesn't help how good-looking he is. I think back to his hand between my legs on the stairwell, and that face pressed up close to mine …

"Where are your thoughts, princess?" he asks wryly. His long fingers are toying with the stem of his crystal wineglass, twisting it back and forth in the firelight.

"Er … nowhere," I say stupidly. "Here."

"Ah," he says, nothing more. It's a kind of sarcastic, almost-condescending answer. I feel my cheeks burning. That subtle sneer is teasing at the corner of his lips like it always does when he looks at me. My thighs clench together involuntarily under the hem of this ridiculous golden cocktail dress that he insisted I wear.

"Ah?"

"Here is good."

"Uh ... right." I gnaw at my lower lip, glance at my plate, then force myself to wrench my gaze back up to meet his again.

I can't show weakness. That was the first lesson my dad taught me when he took me camping in the Adirondacks the summer after fifth grade. *"If you run into a wild animal and you show fear, they'll know it,"* he said. *"They can smell the fear on you. That's the only time you're in danger."*

Welp, so much for that.

I'm exuding fear like it's the hottest new perfume. Try as I might, I can't wrestle it back down. The truth is that I'm very afraid, and Leo has given me no reason not to be. He will pounce at any moment. He's come close already, but I was lucky enough before to get away with just a little nibble. I'm terrified that if he strikes again, I won't be quite so fortunate this time around.

"What are my new, um, living arrangements?" I ask. I'm desperate to give voice to the dynamic between us. Maybe, if we're exchanging words, I'll have a chance of redirecting the conversation somewhere that feels less sinister, less threatening to my physical well-being. Not to mention less arousing to the sick, twisted urge in me that wants Leo to come take what he so clearly wants.

He looks at me levelly for a while before answering. "You'll be staying up here with us from now on. The room I showed you to earlier is yours now. You will have clothes, towels, food, all that. If you are well-behaved, you will keep it. If you try to run, you will be returned to the cell downstairs." He says all that lazily, like he doesn't give a damn about the outcome. He's so coolly detached from everything. The anger that is raging inside Dante and Vito hasn't even touched Leo. It's strange to see men who are so similar and yet so different at the same time.

"Okay," I say. "I won't run."

He laughs. "Do what you want, princess. I am merely telling you the consequences of your choices."

I shudder. Something about the way he says the word "consequences" sends a shiver down my spine. Like this is all merely a game, and something as arbitrary as the roll of a dice could decide what happens to me next.

I shuffle uncomfortably in my seat. This dress is too short, too revealing. I can feel the cool castle air drifting between my thighs.

"Would you like a tour?" Leo asks me a moment later.

I'm holding my hands together to keep them from trembling noticeably. "Oh. Uh, sure. A tour sounds, um ... nice."

"Then come. Let us tour." He pushes away from the table and strides away, just as fast as he did before. I follow him, leaving the now-empty dinner table in our wake.

Leo isn't much of a tour guide. For the last half hour, as we've wound down countless labyrinthine hallways, he has said little aside from "This way" or "Here." I can't exactly ditch him though, because there's not a snowball's chance in hell that I'll be able to find my way back. This castle is a maze of winding, twisting corridors that branch and coalesce in seemingly random patterns. It's a treasure trove of musty tapestries, ornate jewelry, and—glaring down at me from every single wall—portrait after portrait of Bianci ancestors. The whole thing is downright spooky. I keep expecting to see the eyes moving in one of the oil paintings, like an episode of Scooby Doo.

"Wait!" I call ahead as Leo rounds a corner thirty yards ahead of me. His footsteps are fading away, so I put a little pep in my step and hustle after him. My stilettos clack against the flagstones. I miss Vito's strong arm supporting me.

After a full dinner, I'm stronger than I was earlier today, but all the wine I drank is making my head feel stuffed full of cotton. All I can think is, *"Don't get lost."*

So, needless to say, I have a full head of steam when I chase Leo around the corner, and—*whoompf*—collide full-on with his chest.

Just like his brothers, he is built solidly, even though he doesn't look like it. As slender as he appears in his navy tuxedo, he is all muscle. I would have bounced off like I'd run into Superman himself, were it not for his hands reaching out to snare my elbow and keep me from tumbling ass over elbows.

I stabilize myself and blink a few times to orient the dizziness in my head.

But Leo doesn't let go of me. His blue eyes are unyielding as they stare straight into mine.

"Th—thanks," I stammer awkwardly. I curse at myself in my head for sounding like such a bumbling idiot. I have that dumb, lovestruck, girly *can't-talk*-itis, as Anastasia used to call it.

"It is my pleasure, darling," he murmurs. As with a lot of the things he says, there's an undertone to the word "pleasure." It's kind of menacing and kind of seductive, and the wine surging through my system is not helpful in any way as I try to figure out which of those two things is worse.

"Menacing" would be bad, obviously, because I'm hopelessly lost deep in the guts of enemy territory. Leo could slice my throat open right here and no one would ever find my body.

But I think that "seductive" is the more frightening of the two, for several reasons—not the least of which is because part of me wants that very, very badly.

It's his smell. His eyes. His hands. His cruel, uncaring sneer. It's all of that and none of it at once. I can't deny that my body craves his touch.

I want to make him smile at me. I have since the moment I first laid eyes on him.

"I'm not your darling," I protest, but it's weak and ineffectual. He knows it; I know it; hell, even the freaking portrait of Great-Granddaddy Billy-Bob Bianci hanging on the wall to my left knows it. So Leo doesn't have to say anything in response. He just smiles.

"I'd like to show you something," he says.

I swallow hard. My heart is pounding so freaking loudly; I can't hear anything else over the *ba-boom, ba-boom* in my eardrums. "What is it?"

"You'll see."

I shake my head timidly. Why am I being such a little weakling right now? I've stood up to these brothers before. But for some reason, I feel very small and pathetic in this yawning corridor. My dad would be ashamed of me. He raised me to be tough and independent. This is ... not that.

"That didn't work out for me so well last time."

Leo grins savagely. "Perhaps you will enjoy this more than my brother's gift to you."

"Okay." What else can I say? I'm out of options. And, again—I want this. Whatever it is, I want it.

Leo takes my hand in his. It's oddly affectionate, especially coming from a man like him who seems so aloof and distant. Together, we walk down the hallway silently. There's a small wooden door, reinforced with steel, that's set into the wall down on the right-hand side. Leo lays his other palm flat on the emblem that's set into the heart of the door. It must be some kind of biometric security device, because I hear a few electronic beeps, then the mechanical whirr of a deadbolt retreating.

The door swings inward on silent hinges. Darkness beckons from within.

I look to Leo. He's waiting patiently for me.

"After you, darling," he says so quietly that I can barely hear him.

I gulp and walk inside.

It's pitch-black. I can't see anything, not even my own hand in front of my face. I hear Leo follow after me and shut the door behind him. I'm having a hard time breathing, like there's not enough oxygen in here. The sound of the automated lock sliding back into place does nothing to reassure me.

"Leo?" I ask.

He doesn't answer.

The only way out is through. I breathe and try to quell my tremors. I can sense Leo move off to my left, followed by another soft clicking noise.

Suddenly, I'm aware that there are lights slowly coming to life. They're set in the walls like sconces, and every one of them is tinged a dark reddish-gold. They don't brighten very much, but it's enough to cast everything in an eerie glow.

What they reveal makes my jaw drop.

It's a full-on sex dungeon.

There are whips and studded paddles hanging neatly on a rack along one wall. The far corner houses a huge pair of wooden masts fashioned in the shape of an X, with cuffs on each end. I see what looks like a sawhorse, only the top portion is covered in thick leather the same color as the lighting. All manner of dangerous-looking devices are arranged around the room, and everything is bathed in that deep red-gold color. It doesn't seem real. It's too vivid and too vague at the same time. My brain can't make sense of it.

I turn to face Leo. His eyes look somehow even bluer against the contrasting color of the light. It casts his pale skin in a fiery pallor. He looks imperial, like he got taller and broader and more intimidating since we first entered the room thirty seconds ago.

"What is this place?" I ask him.

He blinks once, slowly.

Then he asks me a question that forever changes the course of my life.

"Would you like to find out?"

17

LEO

I am on the verge of losing control. I cannot allow that to happen.

But I am so close.

This girl is a delicate flower waiting to be plucked. What she doesn't yet realize is that plucking a flower kills it.

I will relish the process.

Milaya, though ... she will suffer immensely.

What she also doesn't understand is that it will hurt me too, in its own roundabout way. Yes, I intend to savor the lashings she is about to receive. Yes, I have dreamed of this moment since we first brought her into our home.

But part of me is beginning to feel things for her that I have never felt for another woman, not as long as I have lived.

How many have there been? Hundreds? Thousands? And yet not one of those nameless, faceless whores has stood in this room and looked at me with the same mixture of fear, trust, and unbridled arousal that is burning in Milaya Volkov's face right now. She is as fragile as a china doll, as strong as a willow, an impossible combination that is doing to me what no one else has ever done: pushing me to the edge.

I pride myself on control. On living my life far removed from the petty ebbs and flows of this misbegotten little world. Nothing can affect me, nothing can disturb my peace.

Until now.

She has come in like a bull in a china shop and trampled my resolve into dust. My face does not betray it, but inside, I am desperate to touch her, to hear her cry out and moan. I want to do that to her so badly that I fear it might kill me if I go another second without it.

This is all so fucking wrong.

There are rules that govern this room. Inside these walls, my word is law. I am king, I am God, I am undeniable. Any woman lucky enough to join me in here must accept that as unquestionable truth. Not even she is exempt.

But as I open my mouth to explain that to her, I falter for the briefest of moments.

I take that second to look at her. So much blood has been spilled to bring her and me here together in this moment. The blood of my father and my youngest brother stains a godforsaken concrete wasteland. Even now, Russian boots stomp over their remains.

I am not prone to overwhelming emotions the way Dante and Vito are, but even I cannot deny that I have felt grief knocking at the door of my heart, demanding to be let in. I will not answer, of course, but the beast is insistent.

The only salve is standing in front of me. She is flawless porcelain. She wants badly to be conquered. I have seen the look in too many women's eyes to mistake it for anything else.

So why can't I bring myself to do it? I have done it before. *Just do it again, you fucking coward. Give her what she wants. Break her, hurt her, make her beg for mercy.*

No.

That is all I hear, like my own voice shouting to me from the bottom of a well. It feels painfully wrong to reach for the cuffs and whip hanging just a few yards away. If I take down my tools, then we will have begun a ritual, and there can be no turning back from that point. I will be required to mark her skin. I will be required to demand her obedience. I want that in so many ways—except for in the most crucial way of all.

What is she doing to me?

My invitation to Milaya still hangs in the air between us: *would you like to find out?* It has been just a second or two since I spoke it, and yet I feel like I have lived for an eternity in that time. My cock is a steel rod in my tuxedo pants. It is requiring the full extent of my willpower to keep my hands clasped behind my back patiently.

Say no, I beg silently. *Tell me you want to go, and I will set you free.*

She has all the power now. If she denies me, then I will open the door and be grateful that she has chosen not to indulge my wickedest impulses.

But if she says yes, I will do what I have to do. I have no other choice.

I try to tell her all that with my eyes. The truth is that I cannot decide for her. She is the one at the crossroads. All I can do is tell her which road leads in which direction. She must walk the path herself.

Say no, I urge in my head. *Say no and run, before I do these things to you.*

But I know before she answers what she has selected.

Milaya's gaze falls to her feet. Her voice is trembling as she asks, "What if I say yes?"

I sigh. It feels like a sigh that originates in my soul and passes through every cell of me before escaping through my lips into the cool air of my workshop.

"If you say yes, then we can begin."

She glances around nervously, gnawing at her lip. Such an innocent affectation of hers. I do not think she even realizes that she is doing it. Her eyes take in the breadth of the room and the depth of the things it contains before settling back on me.

"Okay," she answers finally. "Yes."

"Are you sure?" I ask her. It is a question I have never asked anyone else. I do not like to repeat myself. But for her sake, I will.

"I think so," she answers. Fear and desire are fighting a war in her. The desire wins.

"Then listen to me very, very carefully. There are only two words you are allowed to say from here on out: 'yes, sir.' Is that clear?"

She nods.

"Out loud."

"Yes, sir."

"Good. There is a single exception to that rule. If at any time you wish to leave, you say your father's name. And then you run. Is that clear?"

"Yes, sir."

I take down my riding crop from where it hangs on the wall. Turning back to her, I rest it gently on her shoulder. "Kneel."

She starts to do as I told her, but I place the end of the crop under her chin. "Ah, ah, ah," I tut, shaking my head sadly. "You did not answer. That is one."

"One what?"

"You will find out soon enough. And now it is two, because you broke the first rule. Kneel."

She bites her lip as she whispers, "Yes, sir." Then she sinks to the floor.

I let her sit there for a moment as I circle behind her. There is a chest of drawers on the far side of the room, filled with paraphernalia. I retrieve a knife from there and go back to stand behind her.

"Eyes forward," I command when I can feel her desperate to look at me.

She stiffens.

"And what do we say when I give you a command?"

"Yes, sir."

I reach down with the knife and set its edge against the left shoulder strap of her golden dress. It's a ridiculous outfit. Dante chose it. I'm sure he intended to humiliate her, because it looks like the kind of thing a cheap hooker would wear.

But on her, it looks like anything but trash. She makes even this gold horror show appear elegant and feminine.

That scares me.

It scares me because she has a power over me I don't understand. And I've seen enough of the shellshocked look in my brothers' faces to know that she is doing things to them, too. At a moment when we need to be more united than ever, this girl has come plowing into our midst like a wrecking ball. She shouldn't be here—in this room, in this castle, in this family. And yet she's here, and not a single one of us is willing to let her go. Me least of all.

I can't delay much longer, no matter how badly I would prefer to lay her to rest and kiss her body. I want to take her back to the shower, but this time I want to help rinse her hair, to mop the blood and sweat and dirt from her skin. I barely resisted the impulse before dinner. I am running dangerously close to falling prey to it now.

So I force myself to finish what I've started. It is the only way.

I saw one strap of her dress off, then the other. The top falls down. From behind, I can't see her breasts, only the rise and fall of her spine and the thin winding path of a single blue vein tracing its way along the curve of her neck. It is perfection incarnate. Somehow more sexual than anything I've ever seen before.

"Stand," I order her.

"Yes, sir." She rises gracefully to her feet.

"Don't look back. Eyes forward."

I stay behind her and cut off the rest of her dress. She isn't wearing any underwear, because we didn't provide her any, of course. But rather than being turned on by the sight of her bare ass, I feel almost ashamed. I know she is choosing to be here. I know she wants this.

It just feels sinful.

I can't resist though. My cock is yearning for more. My hands are damn near shaking. I'm falling to bits and we've barely even begun.

This will need to end quickly.

"Come with me."

I turn and walk over to the pommel horse. It is a low contraption, about waist-high, standing on four legs with a broad leather-bound spine. I point at one end and tell her, "Stand there."

"Yes, sir." She has her hips pressed flush against one end of the device and facing the other end. I stoop down and tie her thighs and ankles to the legs of the pommel horse. Now, her lower body is locked in place.

Rising up behind her, I press one hand between her shoulder blades. "Bend."

"Yes, sir," she rasps.

I guide her down so that she is bent over the leather spine. Her hands are folded beneath her forehead. I stand still for a few seconds and watch the rise of her back as she inhales and exhales. Then I order myself to keep going.

Striding to the other end, I find the leather ties there and secure her hands to the other set of legs. She is fully captive now, straddling the structure and completely exposed.

I feel like my skin is crawling with ants as I return to the first side of the pommel horse. Normally, I am the picture of calm in these sessions. I live for the moment that is about to come—the first strike, the first reddening of the skin, the first cry out into the silence. But tonight, I am restless and uncomfortable. It takes everything I have not to lean forward and kiss that gorgeous ridge of her hip bone.

"Are you ready?" I ask her.

To her credit, she only hesitates for a moment before she says, "Yes, sir."

Then I swing the riding crop.

She can't help but cry out. I don't blame her. The first strike is hard for anyone, especially someone who has never been here before. But as the flush of her skin deepens and spread where the riding crop landed on her right ass cheek, I almost erupt in my fucking pants. It's too much, too soon, too wrong, too right. I shouldn't be here, but I can't imagine being anywhere else.

Fuck, fuck, fuck.

To quiet my thoughts, I boom, "Again!" I don't hesitate before I bring the crop down a second time.

Milaya cries out once more, a wordless whimper that sets my blood on fire.

I don't know how many times we repeat that cycle before I know that I can't resist my urges anymore.

I have to touch her.

I drop the riding crop and fall at once to my knees behind her. Her bare pink pussy is wet and glistening. I can still see the bright red welts blossoming on her ass. Without thinking, I plunge my face into her and lap up her juices. My tongue finds her button and whirls as fast as I can muster. When it does, the tenor of her moans changes. It goes from red-hot whimpers of pain she tries desperately to resist, into the half-choked, half-gasped panting of unbearable pleasure.

Before I know it, she's crying out, "Yes, sir!" as she comes on my mouth. She spasms hard, but the ties are secure and I bound them tightly. I just keep whirring my tongue over her and kissing her center until the aftershocks of her orgasm finally fade.

When it is done, I fall back onto my haunches. Her pussy is still there for the taking if I want it. I could unzip my pants and bury myself in her right here, right now.

But this has gone too far already.

I need to retreat into myself before she makes me do something I'll regret. I've already come too far out of my shell, beyond my boundaries. I have broken every rule I've ever had for myself. Because of her. My enemy's daughter. I shouldn't give a shit whether she lives or dies. But the longer I stay here bathing in her blissful moans, the more I find that I *do* care.

I am no longer in charge here.

I untie her as fast as I can. When she is free, I don't turn around.

"Run," I say, still facing the wall. I can't bear the thought of administering aftercare, of even a single ounce of tenderness passing between us. I need her gone—before she breaks me.

I can hear her hesitation. She wants to know what happened. Why the sudden change? She could see before that I wanted her like she wanted me.

What she didn't see was that I shouldn't have ever allowed myself to want such a thing. I've gone too far. We have gone too far. This needs to end—now.

"Run," I repeat. "Run and don't come back."

Then she is gone.

18

VITO

THE NEXT NIGHT

I spent years dreaming about tonight. All through the training of my youth, I endured just so I could get to this moment. It was my birthright, my destiny, my inevitable destination.

Yet here I am, and all I can think about is when it will be over.

The lieutenants—the newly promoted ones, filling the shoes of those lost in the massacre at the Russians' warehouse—are gathered in the meeting chambers, as are my brothers. The ceremonial knife sits on a velvet-covered pedestal in the middle of the circle. It's waiting for me to do what generations of Bianci dons before me have done: slice open my palm and declare my reign begun.

Fuck that. Fuck this. Fuck everything.

I was meant to be here, yes. But not like this. Never like this.

"Let's get this shit over with," I mutter to Mateo.

"That is a bad way to begin things, brother."

"Since when are you superstitious?"

He just grunts. Leave it to him to go silent at the worst possible moment. Can't get him to shut up when he's lecturing, and yet when all I want is for someone to tell me that I do not bear the responsibility for my father's and brother's deaths, he says nothing. Lie to me if you must—I don't fucking care. But for one second, just one single goddamn second, can't someone lift this weight off my shoulders?

No. They can't. It's my cross to bear. I am the don. I must drag us kicking and screaming into the future. If I don't, we'll all die. Those are the only options.

"Let us begin," I announce into the room.

Everyone falls silent at once.

Mateo looks at me. I give him a curt nod and he begins reading in Italian. I don't bother listening. I studied the text he's reading from in my younger days. My thoughts on it haven't changed since my father first threw it across my desk when I was scarcely thirteen years old. It is all bullshit mumbo-jumbo, the rantings and ravings of a long-dead Bianci don from back in the old country. Practically meaningless today. Nowhere in there is anything that will help me now. Supposedly, it contains the guiding principles of our family. The Bible of crime lords, so to speak.

But there is only one rule that matters anymore.

If you stop, you die.

Simple as that.

It is a long passage, so I have plenty of time to think while Mateo lilts nonsense in our mother tongue. I choose to daydream and reflect on better times.

My thoughts stray to Milaya. She has been upstairs for scarcely a day and a half, and it already feels as though the entire castle has become imbued with her spirit. Her smell lingers in the hallways. I found a stray hair of hers on the bearskin rugs in front of the hearth early this morning and it damn near floored me.

I cannot look at her without thinking of Audrey. And because of that, I am undone, a blubbering fucking mess, at the perfectly wrong time for that to happen. It's like she is ripping me apart at the seams, merely by having dark hair and pale skin and shining green eyes. How many thousands if not millions of women does that describe? It doesn't matter to my heart though. It sees what it sees. It wants what it wants.

And it has decided that it wants her.

I should know better. I trained to prevent exactly this. Meditation and fighting and psychological warfare—these were the things that filled my childhood days from sunup until sundown. I was taught to turn myself into an impenetrable fortress. I am failing at that simple task.

My walls were breached once already by the daughter of a mechanic. And now—magnitudes worse—they have been breached again, this time by my enemy's spawn.

I shudder.

I wish badly that Sergio were here. He always knew what to say in moments like these, or even when to say nothing at all. He would have been able to look at me and, just by placing a hand on my shoulder, ease the pain that has been wracking me since we first brought her home.

But he is dead. He cannot help me. No one can.

The ritual unfolds as it has done dozens of times before me, and as it will dozens of times after me, if the Biancis survive what is waiting for us on the horizon. Mateo finishes speaking and directs me to the middle of the circle. I repeat what he tells me to repeat, then I pick up the knife and cut my hand open and let the crimson droplets drip onto the stone pedestal. I think of Milaya the whole time. I might as well not even be here, for all the attention I'm paying to proceedings.

I am on autopilot, wondering what to do, what not to do. What is right, what is wrong. What is behind us, what is yet to come.

Another memory strikes me, apropos of nothing.

My father took me camping, years ago. It seemed like an oddly innocuous activity for a man like him. But I didn't think of that until much later. "Just you and me, my oldest," he said with a friendly clap on the back. "Father-son bonding, eh?"

We drove miles into the northern reaches of the state, chattering idly about my training and education. By the time we arrived at our campsite, it was nearing dark. We hurried to construct our tent and cook a meager dinner. He told me that we would go for a hike early the following morning, so it was an early bedtime for the two of us. I fell asleep easily.

When I woke up, he was gone.

There was a scrap of paper tucked under a log at the mouth of the tent. "Find your own way home." It was in his handwriting. He'd taken the rest of the supplies, so I had nothing but a compass and a walking stick. The tent was too much to carry; I left it behind.

It took me a day and a half to find my way out of the thick woods.

I arrived home just in time to blow out the candles on my tenth birthday cake.

That, too, makes me shudder, and I file it away with so many other similar memories. Father is dead, just like Sergio. There is no bringing him back.

"Sir?"

I look up. One of the lieutenants, Carlo, is looking at me. "Yes?" I snap, harsher than is required.

"We are awaiting further orders, sir."

I glance around. All eyes are on me. Leo looks distracted, as he has for the last day or two. I make a mental note to question him later. Maybe he is suffering from the same Volkov-induced sickness that I am.

"You men are dismissed," I say. "I need only my brothers to remain behind."

Carlo nods. He and the rest of the second-tier leadership file out, each offering me a bow and a shake of my uninjured hand as they leave.

When they are gone, I look at my brothers. "We have a mission tonight, *fratelli*," I tell them. "It is time to go hunting for Russians."

I was going to be in a lot of trouble when I got home. Father would punish me. Antoni would run me ragged. My schoolteacher, Signora Arianna, would drill me ruthlessly.

But I didn't care.

Because this was heaven.

Audrey's hair draped over my face like a curtain, shutting out the world. It was dark in here. Quiet. Still. There were no yelling taskmasters, none of Father's cruel jabs or stony silences. I could finally breathe.

I let out a sigh that came from somewhere deep within. It picked up steam, collecting things as it went, and when it finally passed my lips, it was full to the brim of the weariness and sadness I had carried with me since the day I was born. I let it all go.

I felt a million times lighter when her lips brushed mine. When her hand stroked my chin. I could sigh and mean it and actually feel—well, if not free, then something akin to it. As close to freedom as I would ever get.

The sad truth of my life was that I would never be truly free. It was my birthright to bear this burden. A hundred-plus years of family history sat squarely on my shoulders, and there wasn't a damn thing I could do to shake it. Not now. Not ever.

But with Audrey, I could snatch away a brief moment in time where I forgot that I was carrying that immense weight. That was enough. That was bliss.

"You're not going to fall asleep on me, are you?" she teased.

I reached up and ran a rough thumb gently across her lips. "Am I not sleeping already? Isn't this a dream?"

She rolled her eyes and pinched my side. "I knew Italian men were supposed to be romantic, but that's awfully cheesy, V, even for you."

She was the only one who could get away with calling me nicknames. I let her, because I loved her. I loved her in that way that only a teenager can love: with the all-consuming intensity, the unwavering belief that every other thing in the world could burn away, but if I had her, it would still be fine. I loved her like air.

It would be my undoing.

But in that moment, I didn't know it yet. All I knew was that when she kissed me, I could breathe. That was the only thing that mattered.

I heard her watch beep, signaling the top of the hour. I frowned. "I'm going to have to leave soon," I muttered.

"No!" she yelped plaintively. She grinned. God, how I loved that grin. "Don't. Stay." We were curled together, naked bodies aligned, in a dingy motel in the San Fernando Valley. Far away from prying eyes. We purchased the room with cash, arrived separately, would leave separately. But still, I couldn't stop myself from glancing at the curtain-covered windows every five minutes, or checking to make sure that the gun I'd laid down on the bedside table was loaded with the safety off. "Enemies are

everywhere," went the lessons that had been as good as carved on the inside of my skull from sheer, mind-numbing repetition. "You can never rest."

Seventeen years old and I lived like I was ten times that age. So much depended on me. If I stopped, I would die. We would all die.

Perhaps that is why it felt like such a sin to steal these silent, unmoving moments in this shithole motel. To lie there and breathe in time with Audrey was like spitting in my father's face. I relished every second of it.

I could see the early gray light of dawn peeking through the curtains. My brothers would be waking soon and the day's training would begin. I had to be on the move before then, so I could take the taxi back to the gates and find the gardener who would let me in the side entrance. If I wasn't at breakfast with my siblings, all hell would break loose. Questions would be asked, questions for which I had no good answers. It was better to avoid that storm entirely.

So I had to leave soon. But I wanted just a moment longer here. With Audrey's hair splayed across my chest, her scent in my nose, her hand idly tracing the crests and valleys in my abdomen. "Tell me a secret, V," she whispered breathily in my ear. "Something you've never told anyone before."

I laughed. "If I told you, I'd have to kill you."

"I'm serious," she snapped, swatting me on the arm. She softened. "You can trust me, V. I won't tell anyone. You're the only person who matters to me anyway."

I couldn't deny the truth of that. I was *all she had. Her father had passed away two years prior from a heart attack. She was lucky that it hadn't happened on the castle grounds, or else his body might have disappeared forever. No funeral, no trace to be found. My father didn't want any police or paramedics to set so much as a single foot on our property, no matter the reason.*

As it was, he had died peacefully in his sleep. He had been a hardworking man, a kind man, but an irredeemably sad one. He spent his whole life sweating his ass off just to scrape a meager living together for him and his daughter. And then he died. I almost pitied him. Life was cruel.

I wondered what kind of secret Audrey wanted to hear from me. My life was full of secrets, of course, but not the kind she gave a damn about. The secrets that filled my days were more about offshore bank accounts, the movement of product across state and country borders, the art of making people disappear. But that was all just business, and Audrey hated business. She liked to pretend that I wasn't: the son of the Bianci Mafia don, the heir apparent, the crown prince. That's why she called me "V," I think—so that I was just hers, so that I didn't belong to my family or my father or my responsibilities. Just a seventeen-year-old boy in a motel room, placed on this earth for the purpose of loving her.

I liked being her V.

But I knew from the tone of her voice that she wanted a real secret. She wouldn't be content with a joke or a deferral. She wanted truth. Honesty. Vulnerability. Things that were foreign and frightening to me. I could face down a man and kill him with my bare hands, but the thought of baring myself to another human being was incomprehensible. It just did not compute.

And yet, when she kissed me, when she touched me, when she looked at me —it felt possible.

I opened my mouth to answer her question, then let it fall closed again. "I —" No, not like that. Try again. Tell her a secret. *"I ..." I was floundering. Such a simple question. Just tell her a secret that I'd never told before.* Do it, you coward. Open your fucking lips.

I seized the words in my head, the ones that were desperately trying to wriggle away from me, and I let them loose before I could chicken out again. "I am a bad, broken person. I want to kill my father. I want to burn down my home. I want to run away with you and leave all of this behind."

When I was finished blurting all of that, I fell silent. My chest was heaving with effort, though I hadn't moved a muscle, and I could feel sweat dripping down my brow.

Saying those things was a violation of everything I had ever been taught. It wasn't just spitting in Father's face to say I wanted to leave—it was stabbing him in the heart and watching him bleed out at my feet.

But God, it felt good. I knew I had spoken honestly because of how good and cleansing it felt. I hated my training. I hated the future that had been laid out for me. I just didn't know it until now. There had never been an alternative. Until Audrey.

She looked me in the face. Those hazel eyes glistened in the dim lamplight. "You are not a bad person, V. You aren't broken. Not unless you choose to be."

I wanted so badly to believe her. That urge rose up in me until it choked me out and brought tears to my eyes. For the briefest of moments, I think I actually did. Everything felt possible. There was another future I could reach out and grab. A future with her. A future far from here, free from blood and anger and cruelty and revenge and all the other dark things that clouded my day-to-day. I could have it.

Reach out and take it. Do it, now.

"Come here," I told her. I turned on my side to press my forehead against hers as I cupped her face in my hands. "I want to make love to you once more before I have to go."

I pulled her into a kiss and we joined our sweaty bodies together. I bathed in freedom I'd never felt before.

I should have known it was never going to last.

The man in front of me is scared for his life. As he should be. If I have my way, he will not live to see the dawn.

"You know who I am, yes?" I ask him.

"*Da*."

"Speak English, motherfucker," Dante snarls. He's standing behind the Russian, who is cuffed and kneeling. One of Dante's hands is keeping a tight grip on the dog collar that's been fastened around our enemy's throat. The other hand is fiddling with his knife. He is antsy to use it, though the blade is already stained with the blood of the other men who were drinking with our target at a grimy nightclub in Brentwood.

"Y—yes," the man says. He's a sweaty, heaving mess. He has already been worked over thoroughly enough to mark him for life. His big, hooked nose will never sit straight again, that much is guaranteed.

"Then you know what I have come for."

"No! I don't—fuck, shit, I don't know."

"Come now, Dmitri. Don't play me for a fool."

"No, no, I do not know," he whimpers. His bottom lip is trembling now. How pathetic. I want badly to slice his throat open here and now, just so I don't have to look him in the face anymore. But I need answers. I need to know where the bodies of my brother and father are. And I need to know some things about Luka Volkov.

"That is very much a shame," I say coolly. I crouch down on one knee to look the man in the eyes on his level. His stench is repulsive. He must have pissed himself. "Because if you do not know what I have come for, then you are no use to me."

"Please, please," he begs, "I have a family."

I laugh bitterly. "Do I look like the kind of man who gives a fuck?" I point at Dante. "Does *he* look like the kind of man who gives a fuck?"

Dmitri tries to look over his shoulder at Dante standing behind him, but Dante slugs him in the face with a closed fist. "Face forward," he growls like a feral beast. “Don’t look at me. I am the least of your concerns, friend.” No one has ever made the word “friend” sound more sinister.

I wonder if I have underestimated the toll that Sergio’s and Father’s deaths have taken on Dante. He was always a loose cannon, but lately, he has thrown what little caution he once had to the wind. When I told my brothers of the intel we’d received about this lieutenant, an area chief for the Volkov Bratva, and how he liked to drink and grab ass at that shit-hole club, you would’ve thought it was Christmas morning by the way Dante’s eyes lit up. And when we arrived on the scene, he was in the club almost before the car had stopped moving. That damn knife never left his hand as he killed, killed, killed, until we found the man we were looking for. It doesn’t look as though those lost souls dulled his appetite for blood in the slightest.

Now is not the time to worry about my brother. Besides, I feel much of the same rage. I just happen to burn inwards, whereas he cannot contain his anger. Two sides of the same coin, I suppose.

I grab Dmitri’s cheeks in my hands and pull my face close to his. “I want you to tell me what you know about Luka Volkov,” I say, enunciating each word crisply. “I know that you understand what I am saying. And I know that you understand what will happen if you do not answer my questions.”

“I—I can’t ...” he whispers in a high, strained voice.

I glance up at Dante and give him a short nod. Standing, I turn away and face the opposite wall.

Behind me, I hear a squelch, a crunch, a scream. I wait until the scream recedes into agonized whimpers before I turn back around and look down on the bloodied man once more.

“I did not want to do that,” I tell Dmitri sadly. “You forced my hand.”

“Please, God ...” he moans.

I laugh for the second time this evening. "There is no God here, Russian. There is only me."

I can sense Leo and Mateo looking on uncomfortably from the corners of the room. Neither of them likes to get their hands dirty in moments like this. That is fine—Dante prefers to handle the hands-on work himself anyhow.

Dmitri, Dante, and I go back and forth like this for a while. Blood is spilled, moans are ripped out of the Russian's quivering lips, but eventually he tells me part of what I want to know. As much as he can, at least. It is clear that there are some pieces of information he is simply not privy to. That is no surprise. Luka Volkov would not be much of a mob boss if he wasn't careful with who he confided in.

Still, it is enough for now. I have what I need to bring Luka to the negotiating table.

"You have done well," I tell the slumped, trembling man before me. I pat him on the head and hand him a rag. "Clean yourself up."

I rise once more and go to leave the room. I can feel the man's relief when he thinks the worst is over. Whether we kill him or let him go, at least the torture has concluded, or so he thinks.

I almost feel bad that it is a fake out.

"Oh," I say, softly but just loud enough that he can hear me. I peek over my shoulder and see Dmitri stiffen up like a board. His eyes find mine as I pivot to face him again. "I forgot to ask. Tell me, if you would be so kind, where I might find the bodies of my brother and father?"

He shakes his head. His mouth is moving, but no words come out.

"I'm afraid you'll have to speak up."

He tries again. His second attempt at speaking is hardly better than the first, but I think I hear him say, "*Ushel …*"

"What did you say?" I snap. I pounce back over to him and wrench his face up. "Repeat yourself."

"*Ushel*," he says. The lights in his eyes are fading. "*Ushel, ushel.*"

I swivel my gaze to Mateo, leaning against the far wall with his brows furrowed, deep in thought. "What does that mean?" I ask him.

"It means gone."

"Gone?" I squeeze Dmitri's face harder. His skin is cold to the touch now. He has lost so much blood. "What the fuck does that mean?"

He just shakes his head and says the Russian word again. *"Ushel ..."*

"Where are their bodies?!" I roar. I wind up and punch him in the face. "Tell me where they are!" Another strike. Flesh gives way beneath my knuckles.

I roar again and again and punch again and again.

He doesn't say another word.

That doesn't stop me from swinging as hard as I can until I feel my brothers pulling me off and I realize that Mateo is hollering in my ear as loud as he can.

"Vito! He is dead, Vito! Let him go!"

It takes all three of my brothers to haul me away from the corpse of the Russian and throw me back against the far wall. My ears are ringing and my fists are throbbing. All I can think is that I lost control. I have never done that before. The man might have still been useful.

But I killed him.

Needlessly. Carelessly. Stupidly.

What the fuck is happening inside my head? I am being crushed by the most immense, invisible weight I have ever felt. It's hard to breathe, hard to think. I need out of this room. I stumble to my feet and race out into the hall.

I make it maybe five or ten steps before I have to stop, lean up against a stone wall, and hurl my guts up. I keep puking until there is nothing left in me.

When my head finally begins to clear, I look up. Mateo is standing in the doorway of the room I just left. He is looking at me with an inscrutable expression on his face.

"I don't want to hear it," I tell him in a hoarse voice.

"I wasn't going to say anything."

"Good. Don't."

He nods slowly. "What next?"

I point into the room. I am cooling off from my violent outburst, and in the wake of it, I feel so impossibly tired. I want to sleep for days.

"Use what he told us. Set up the meeting." I wipe the last vestiges of spit from my lips. "It is time we sat down with Mr. Volkov. Face-to-face."

19

MILAYA

I haven't left my room since the encounter with Leo.

The staff bring me meals and leave them outside my door, but I'm not hungry. I can't stop thinking about what I did—and most of all, why?

I let him touch me. I let him hurt me.

And I loved it.

Am I certifiably insane?

I crossed a line in the sand that was impossible to miss. It might as well have had blinking lights and big, bold signs saying "DO NOT PASS" and freaking air traffic controllers warning me to stay away. But I charged over it anyway. Lust made me do something that can never be undone. I'm an idiot. I'm a skank. I'm a traitor—to my dad, my mom, my family, but most of all to myself.

I've relived the moment again and again in the two days since. Every time I close my eyes, I see his lips and hear his question again: *would you like to find out?*

To say I don't regret it is a lie.

To say I *do* regret it is a lie.

I've never felt that way in my life. When I was strapped down to whatever the hell that thing was called as Leo whipped me, I'd never felt so weak. And then, when he lost himself to his lust and buried his face between my legs, I'd never felt so strong. I never knew until that very moment just how badly he wanted me. He couldn't resist for even one millisecond longer. He fell to his freaking knees and licked me until I came like a shuddering train wreck.

And then he kicked me out?

None of it makes sense. If my ass wasn't still welted and sore, I might've assumed it was all just a dream. But there's no denying that I did the damn thing.

And there's no denying that I want to do it again.

What a stupid, repetitive cycle of thoughts. How many times have I been down this road since I ran back into this room? When I jumped straight into the shower, still stinging from the spanking I'd suffered at Leo's hands, I scrubbed and scrubbed my skin. I sat there under the jet until the water ran cold, and even then I didn't move. I felt so dirty, so alive, so confused.

"Stupid and repetitive" doesn't even begin to cover it.

The thought of doing that again is so overwhelming that I can't even begin to address it head-on. It sneaks up on me like a mirage in the corner of my eye. Like some other voice in my head is sneakily suggesting, "What if you went back and …?" The in-charge voice, the *real* Milaya voice, has to scream back "NO!" If I don't resist, I might do what I've been dreaming of doing: opening my bedroom door, searching for Leo, and pleading with him to tie me down once more.

The light outside is fading. Two days have passed since I last talked to another human being. I don't have a clue why the brothers are leaving me alone, but the bedroom is such a huge upgrade from the cell that I don't want to ask. I just soak in the silence and try to focus on anything other than the here and now.

I still can't get over the fact that I dreamed of this room almost exactly. The walls, the posters of the bed, the floor—I saw it all when I was hallucinating in the cell. I wondered idly for a little while if maybe they heard me babbling in my sleep or something like that and recreated it. That'd be a crazy conspiracy theory, and it's definitely not true, but I'm having a hard time shaking the eerie feeling of seeing my dream world come to life. I only know it existed already because I can see fingerprints worn into the edge of the nightstand. This room was occupied before I got here. It predates my arrival at the castle. Who exactly was in here, I don't know. But someone definitely was.

I've been pacing all day long, back and forth, practically wearing a ravine into the carpet where my footsteps have passed over a thousand times. I try to count my strides, to think of other things, but every time I close my eyes, I see Leo's face again, and his lips forming those words—"Would you like to find out?"—and I start my pacing all over again.

Finally, when my ankles are aching and my lower lip is raw from gnawing on it since I woke up, I decide to try meditating. Supposed to be the hot new thing these days. My hippie organic chemistry professor, Dr. Lovelady, was always getting on us to give it a shot. As left-brained science nerds, all her students were all doubtful about it, not to mention constitutionally inclined to be skeptical. But Dr. Lovelady showed us some research that seemed fairly convincing, and I found it to be useful for calming myself down whenever I spent too long looking at flash cards with chemical formulations on them.

This particular scenario I've found myself in isn't exactly late-night cramming for an O-chem midterm, but I could definitely use some calming down. So I settle into a cross-legged seat in the middle of the lush carpet, close my eyes, and try to breathe.

I do the humming the professor taught us. There's supposed to be something to the resonance of your vocal chords producing some kind of gamma brain wave—*or is it beta? Shit, I should know that*—that amplifies the calming effects. I just like it because it drowns out the world around me. I need that now more than ever.

I take in a deep breath and let the hums reverberate through me. I picture the cells of my body bumping back and forth into each other, like reckless dancers in the mosh pit at a concert. One by one, they collide into their neighbors and keep the wave going, until I feel as though my whole body is sizzling with life and energy and vitality.

Then I try to find my place amidst all of that. *Find your frequency. Breathe through it.* Unbidden, I see Dr. Lovelady in my mind's eye. Frizzled gray hair, thick-lensed glasses on a colorful bead chain, a Sanskrit tattoo that peeks out from the back of her neck. She has that eccentric old granola lady smile, the kind that says, "Of course everything is going to be okay! Everything is already okay." She smells like patchouli and lavender, she drinks chamomile tea all day long, and she is an absolutely ruthless grader. I love her.

I try to breathe all of her in too, to internalize it and pretend that I believe the things Dr. Lovelady says and does. If she says everything is okay, it must be true.

Right? Right.

Little by little, I start to convince myself. I find my anxiety slipping away, as if a fist knotted up inside of me is loosening its hold on my guts. I sigh, and that feels good, so I sigh again. It's like lubricant on my soul. Everything is easing up. The sharp edges of my thoughts are insulated, or maybe I'm insulated from them. It's calm. It's cool. Everything is okay.

I stay there for a long time, breathing and buzzing.

Then I open my eyes.

Dante is sitting in front of me.

"Jesus fucking Christ!" I screech. I jump up, trip, fall back down, then scramble backwards on my hands like a crab until I'm a couple yards away from him, safely out of arm's reach. "What the fuck are you—goddammit, don't scare me like that!"

He smiles. It's kind of a lopsided version of his regular smile, off-kilter somehow.

When I finally stop feeling like I'm about to have a heart attack, I realize that he is obliterated drunk. The stench of whiskey is rolling off him in waves.

"Sorry to startle you, princess," he slurs. "Looked like you were having a moment there. Didn't wanna, you know ..." He waves a hand in the air while he searches for the right word. "Interrupt."

I feel like there are ants crawling underneath my skin. So much for inner peace. "What are you *doing* here?" I finally say.

He shrugs. "Dropping in on my new roommate, yeah?" He chuckles at his own non-joke, starts to lean over, straightens himself back up. I watch as he pulls a metal flask from a back pocket and takes a swig. "Or whatever it is that you are."

"Right," I answer uneasily. "So just a social call, then."

"Whatever you want it to be, princess."

We just breathe and look at each other for a beat. I eye the flask.

"How much have you drunk tonight?" Glancing out the window, I notice that it's completely dark out now. How long was I meditating? I feel like I time traveled several hours into the future.

He shrugs again and waggles the flask in front of his face at eye level. "This much, times a few." He taps one finger against his temple. "Keeps the demons quiet, you know?"

I can't quite decipher what's happening behind his eyes. That's strange. I've only known him—"known" being an extremely loose descriptor for the relationship he and I have—for a little while, and yet it's always been obvious to me that Dante wears his heart on his sleeve. He's not like Mr. Magic 8-Ball Vito, where you have to shake him up before he tells you what he's thinking and feeling. With Dante, his eyes are a billboard, announcing to the world exactly what's happening inside his skull.

Right now though, it's unclear. The ever-present pain is still there, but it's more muted than usual. I almost want to say that he looks a little bit sad and lost. That is stranger still. When I first woke up chained to the table in the dungeon, he was obviously a man driven by a singular, deadly purpose. Now, he is ... something else. Something less certain.

"Keeps the demons quiet," I repeat. "Yeah, I know what that's like."

I sort of do and I sort of don't. I know damn well that I've had a privileged life. My mom and dad kept me safe from everything. There were no real dangers in my world—none of consequence, anyway. But there's no such thing as running away from trouble. No matter who you are or where you're from, everyone has problems. I've been a songbird trapped in a gilded cage since the day I was born. That's a demon of its own. So when I say I know what he means ... it's not entirely false.

Dante drops his flask on the carpet at his side and withdraws his switchblade from a different pocket. He starts flicking it open and shut. I feel the first cold finger of fear creep into my belly.

Has he come here to kill me?

Drunk as he is, he must see the fear in my eyes when he glances up at me, because he smiles, flicks the blade closed, and offers it to me. "Would you like to hold it?" he asks.

I hesitate. Is this a trap? I've seen enough cheesy old spy movies to know that villains love nothing more than to taunt the protagonist right before they try to end it all. Maybe he wants me to stick my hand out so he can slice my wrist open and watch me bleed out right here.

That seems like a dumb idea though. They've invested way too much time and effort into me to just kill me right here. They've done too much, said too much, showed me too much to bleed me out like a stuck pig. Besides, Dante's eyes aren't violent right now. They're glazed over, harmless.

I decide to trust him.

"Okay," I say. I hold my hand out carefully and take the knife from him. Our fingers graze just barely, but it's enough to send a shiver racing down my spine.

I look down at the weapon in my hands. It has a black leather grip, grooved where your fingertips go. It's a little heavier than I expected.

"Press the button," he tells me.

I do as he says. I have to suppress a little shriek as the blade whips out and clicks into place. The razor-sharp metal edge gleams in the light of the chandelier overhead. I turn it back and forth, then touch my finger to the point of it as gently as I can. The tiniest bead of blood emerges when I apply pressure.

I remember him running this down my torso and tapping it against each nipple while I lay helplessly chained beneath him. I remember the anger roiling in his eyes. And, most of all, I remember what he said to me.

You cost me everything, princess.

I fold the blade away and look back up at him. He has his head tilted to one side. I count six piercings—nose, eyebrow, lip, two in one ear and one in another—plus the inky swirls of tattoos rising up from beneath the collar of his plain white T-shirt. A random thing my dad said in passing years ago comes back to me out of nowhere. We were walking through Greenwich Village in the city and saw a man with dozens of facial piercings and thick tattoos all over his face. Dad saw him and muttered, "That's a man who's hiding from something." It seemed like a harsh judgment to me at the time. Maybe he just liked tats and piercings, you know? I still don't think it's true for everyone who has those things. But when I look at Dante, I can't shake the feeling that he is hiding from something very bad indeed. Pain, maybe. Or just his past, like the rest of us.

"You told me—back on that first night—you told me that I cost you everything. What does that mean?"

I try to keep my voice quiet and respectful. I don't want to send him into an angry frenzy. God only knows how short this man's fuse is. And with no one here to save me, setting him off is the last thing I'm interested in doing. But the question is burning inside of me. It feels like getting his answer will be the key to finally unraveling the last vestiges of mystery cloaking this place. Questions like who these men are, what they want—I know bits and pieces, but it all comes back to this. They blame me and my dad for something.

What happened to them? What was stolen?

Dante blinks, then looks down at his hands resting in his lap. I wonder for a moment if he's too drunk to answer. Then he starts to speak.

"Did you know I played the violin when I was younger?" he asks. "I was good. It came naturally to me. Dunno why—no one else in my family has a musical bone in their body. No one gives a shit about music either. But I did; I cared. I was good at it. Our schoolteacher had a friend who was a music teacher out near Malibu, and she used to take me there for lessons a few times a week. Never told my dad about it, or any of my brothers. Dad wouldn't have liked it. 'Waste of fucking time,' 'won't have my boys being pussies'—that's the sort of thing he would've said. And my brothers just didn't care about that kind of thing. But I was a wild kid, and the music calmed me down for whatever reason. It makes me laugh now to think about it.

Signora Arianna might've gotten her throat cut if Pops found out she was doing anything behind his back. I wonder why she took that risk. Pretty fuckin' stupid thing to roll the dice on if you ask me."

He pauses. I realize I'm holding my breath. It seems like an innocent story, albeit a super strange one. Why does it feel like it's so important to him? Why is my heart beating so fast? What does this have to do with me, with my question?

He looks up from his lap and makes eye contact with me. "But one day, Sergio found out about it, and he decided he wanted to play too. So Signora Arianna got him a violin. And he was better than me right away. God, I hated him. I hated that shit more than anything! But he was fucking beautiful when he played. A goddamn prodigy, I swear. Wildest thing. This sad-faced little kid, pale as hell, crazy purple eyes like a demon, but he could *do* the damn thing. He could play. We'd sneak out to the garden house, far away enough from the castle so that Dad couldn't hear us. We said we were going to practice, and I guess we did sometimes, but mostly I just made Sergio play. He couldn't read sheet music or anything. He just had a feel for it. I'd sit and watch him play violin in that cramped, dusty little shed, with cockroaches and rats and snakes moving around in the corners. It was the only time I ever wanted to be alive."

I notice with sudden horror that there is a tear sliding down his cheek. One sad, lone wolf tear. It hits the edge of his beard and disappears. I can't look away from him now, as if he has my head locked in position. I can hardly blink. I can hardly breathe.

"Then Dad found us one day. He beat the bejesus out of both of us. That was back when he was still fit enough to do something like that, rather than have someone else administer the beatings for him. He beat us real good. I've still got a scar somewhere from that one, I think. Afterwards, he made us throw the violins in the firepit and watch them burn. Neither of us ever played again."

Silence reigns, thick and immutable.

But I know what I'm supposed to say next, just like we're reading lines from a play.

"What happened to Sergio?" I ask softly.

Dante doesn't say anything for a long time. I realize suddenly that I'm reaching forward now with my free hand to wipe the tear away from the edge of his beard. I feel the dampness on my finger and the heat of his breath. I'm barely aware of what I'm doing. That feeling that everything is scripted, everything is predetermined—it's so powerful that I can't possibly resist. I was *meant* to be here, hearing this, touching him.

I scoot closer. We're just a few inches apart now, seated on the thick white rug in this grand bedroom. I can feel his body heat emanating from him. And that smell—so different than Leo's. Dante smells grittier, sweatier, muskier. There's a raw manliness to it, like he just killed a sabertooth tiger with a club on his way over here. He's a feral beast. The lines on his face are the same as all his brothers', but his eyes are wilder, his mouth is twitchier and more savage. None of that makes sense but it's so unbelievably true that I can't help but think it. It's just what he is. He is pure wilderness, through and through.

"What happened to Sergio?" I repeat.

I know what the answer to my question is going to be. But when Dante finally opens his mouth and says it, it hits me in the face like a slap nonetheless.

"He's dead," Dante says in a half gasp, half moan. "My father and brother are both fucking dead."

I take a deep breath.

Five or six minutes have passed since he first handed me the knife, since I first hatched the plan that's about to unfurl itself. The climactic moment has to happen now, while he's distracted and looking away, or it will never happen at all.

So I do it.

I free the knife from its clasp with the press of the button, shove Dante onto his back, leap on top of him, and bring the blade to his throat all in one motion. I don't know whether I truly caught him by surprise or if he's just too drunk to give a damn, but either way, it works.

I could kill him right now.

Do it. Do it.

The only way out is through.

He's drunk and distracted and teary-eyed and I have his weapon in my grasp, pressed against the vulnerable flesh of his exposed throat, so the only thing left to do is what I've planned on doing from the start: slice his throat open, grab the car keys I saw jangling in his pocket, and get the fuck out of this nightmare castle. All the conversation, the lulling him into a false sense of security, has led to this, my first and only real window of opportunity to escape.

But now that I'm here ...

I can't.

He must see my hesitation, because the shock that filled him at first turns into the saddest laughter I have ever heard in my life. It starts as just a small chuckle, like he can't help himself, but as I watch with the knife held in my trembling fist, his laughter grows and grows, until he's full-on belly laughing, cackling like a loon. I'm riding him like a bucking bull, one knee planted on either side of his torso. But when his head jerks with each bale of laughter, the blade draws a thin red line against his skin.

Finally, his laughter settles down, and he fixes me with an amused stare. "You planned this the whole time, eh?" he says. "Well done, princess. Well fucking done. I warned the others you had more to you than met the eye. Look how right I was. Look what it's going to cost me."

I swallow past the knot in my throat. "I have to do this."

He nods as much as he can. "Oh, I know. I'm the last person on earth who's going to blame you. You do what you have to do." His eyes flutter closed. So calm. So stoic.

Tick. Tock. The clock on the wall tolls out each passing second. I do not move.

Dante's eyes flicker open a few moments later. "Cold feet, I see."

"No."

"No? Then do the damn thing, princess."

"Stop calling me that."

"What?"

"Princess. I'm not your fucking princess."

"You are wrong there," he murmurs.

I grip the collar of his shirt in my free hand and ball it up in a fist. "What the hell does that mean?"

"You're the heir to a vast kingdom, living in a castle with four dark princes, love. If that doesn't make you a princess, what does?" He laughs, loud and carefree, as if his sworn enemy isn't holding a knife to his throat.

I marvel at that. I always said I wanted to be carefree. Is this what that looks like? To stare death in the face and laugh—not just putting on a brave front, but to truly *laugh,* like he means it—is that freedom from worry? Is that what I want? I don't know. I don't know anything anymore.

I don't know why I'm here.

I don't know why I care that his brother is dead.

I don't know why it breaks my heart to think of a little boy with honey-colored eyes watching his violin burn.

I don't know why I let my hand fall slack.

I don't know why I let go of his shirt, why I let Dante lean up on his elbows.

I don't know why I lean forward to kiss him.

And I don't know why he stops me with a finger on my lips.

"Wait," he says. He reaches over to wrap his fingers around my wrist and pull it up so he positions the knife back against his jugular. "Keep it there," he tells me softly, his eyes riveted on mine. "Make me feel like I'm alive. It's been a long time since I've felt that, princess."

Then he kisses me, and I feel like I'm diving into the heart of the jungle as his tongue slides past my lips and his smell consumes me. His hand finds the edge of the T-shirt I'm wearing, the one that appeared suddenly in a chest of drawers two mornings ago, and moves underneath it to palm my lower back. His other hand moves to the back of my head and tugs gently at the roots of my hair.

I feel what I felt with Leo, the same feeling I've been wrestling with for so many days and nights now: I want this man more than I've ever wanted anything in my life.

With Leo, I felt like he might swallow me whole at any moment.

With Dante though, I feel like I'm closing my eyes and jumping off a cliff. It's adrenaline, yes, but the kind filled with uncertainty and wind rushing past your face and the cloying, unfiltered sense that there is nothing between you and the next moment and the next.

I feel wild. I feel free.

I also feel his cock stiffening beneath me. I'm still straddling him, but as he sits up further and further—keeping the knife pressed against his neck; he truly wants it there— he shifts me back, until his thickness is rubbing against my own core heat, separated only by the thin lace of the panties I'm wearing. His hand on my back slides around front to find one breast and squeeze it. He's careful at first, but as his thumb flicks across my taut nipple and draws a low moan from me, he gets messier and hungrier and less tentative.

Devour me, is what I would tell him if my mouth wasn't caught in his, if his teeth weren't finding my lip and biting and his hands weren't lifting my shirt over my head to expose my naked torso to the moonlight streaming in through the window.

The strangest mix of emotions is rising up in me as Dante's thumb keeps flicking back and forth over my achingly hard nipples. I feel the familiar lust that I've ignored since I was first brought here. It's been a betrayal of myself since day one to admit how bad I want these brothers. They're physically gorgeous, and that's part of it of course, but it runs deeper than that too. Each of them speaks to something different in me. Now, as Dante kisses me and grinds his hips into mine, I feel a savage fury rise up from deep in my core.

I want to hurt something. I want to break something. I want to beat something into submission, to master it, to go at it like a wild beast with my teeth and fists. The heat of that foreign, brutal feeling keeps building in me, to the point where I can't ignore it anymore and I let it take me over.

I plant my free hand in Dante's chest and shove him flat on his back. He falls back with an ungainly thump and a surprised look in his face. He smiles up at me, that laughter still teasing at the corner of his lips, but I don't smile back. I feel like a warrior princess. This isn't what I shared with Leo—an exquisitely crafted dance of pleasure, pain, denial, reward. This is much more primal than that.

This is a claiming.

I move my hand down to the zipper of Dante's jeans. I yank it down and free his cock from the denim. It springs free at once with a shocking curve to it, aiming back up towards his belly button. He is hard as a rock.

But there's no time to waste. I have a desperate energy to my actions as I pull aside the fabric of my panties and position him at my entrance.

I don't move the knife from his neck. Not as I slide down his length until he fills me so completely I might explode. Not as I start to rock up and down on him. I keep the blade there so he knows that he is fucking the queen of death. I have his life in my hands. There is only this second for him to enjoy, because I could end this at any moment. He knows that; I don't have to say it. He wants to be tortured like this. He wants to be punished. He thinks he deserves it, and maybe he does. Maybe, after all of this is over, I'll slit his throat and end his pain-filled life the way that part of him desperately wants me to do.

He tries to reach a hand up and grab my bouncing hips, but I pin it to the floor with a ruthless thump. "Don't fucking touch me," I snarl. "I'm not your princess. I'm not your prisoner anymore."

He smiles, but it turns into a groan as I lean forward to press my forehead against his and writhe harder and faster on his cock. My thighs are burning but all the money in the world couldn't stop me. All the Bianci men in this house couldn't pull me off him right now. I'm riding him like my life depends on it, and like his does too—which is the truth.

"Tell me you need this," I pant in his face as he pierces me and withdraws and does it all over again. "Tell me you fucking need me."

"I need you," he answers at once in a husky voice. "I—ah fuck, princess—I need you on my cock like I need air. Fuck me, kill me, do whatever you want."

"That's right," I gasp back. My hand that's holding the knife is starting to shake as the telltale pressure of an orgasm accumulates right where the curve of Dante's manhood is finding part of me that's never been touched before. "I'm your—fuck, fuck—I'm—" I run out of air, but Dante knows what I want to say.

"You're my queen," he says. The drunken haze is gone from his eyes now, but it's been replaced by oceans of lust. He said he wanted to feel alive again, and as each thrust sends the sound of flesh meeting flesh echoing around the high ceiling, I know that's exactly what he's feeling.

I reach my free hand up to wrap around his throat and apply pressure there in addition to the knife. His face starts to turn red. Veins stand out on his forehead and at the base of his throat. And still all the while, I keep riding him. The carpet is wearing rug burns into my knees, but I don't give a shit. I've never felt so unrestrained. I'm a predator, a lioness consuming her catch. It's bloody, it's messy, it's violent, and it feels so fucking good that I am either going to come or die—there is no other alternative.

"Don't ... stop ..." he gasps past my hand choking him and the blade that is now dripping with a small trickle of his blood from where our motion has cut him open.

He knows damn well I won't stop. I'm right on the edge. He starts to grind up into me from below, and then I can't multitask anymore, so I let the knife fall onto the carpet next to Dante's head and I sit up so I can squeeze my breasts as I look up into the ceiling and cry out at the top of my lungs. It's a long, wordless cry, a moaning orgasm that starts at my toes and gathers speed as it rips through all of me and tears me up like wildfire.

Dante comes moments later, adding his rasped roar to my own noises. He fills me with one, two, three spurts of his seed, and it doesn't even occur to me what we've done. I just know that, right now, that's the only possible outcome. I let it happen because I need it to happen.

Only when I've fallen to my side, face buried in the carpet, and the aftershocks of the orgasm have finally stopped rippling through me, do I notice the sensation of his warm seed leaking out between my thighs and realize with horror what I've done.

If submitting to Leo was betrayal, this was fucking mutiny. I just had sex with the Bianci brother who most wants me dead, all while holding a goddamn knife against his throat.

What am I becoming?

I feel like I was possessed and the ghost has let me go now, leaving me terrified and trembling in its wake. I look over to see that Dante hasn't moved. His cock, still half hard, is wet with my juices. His eyes are staring straight up into the upper reaches of the ceiling.

"I shouldn't have done that," I say.

He doesn't look at me or say anything for a long time. The knife is right next to him. Even if I lunged for it, I don't think I'd get it, though I'm also not sure whether or not he'd stop me. All the rules have gone out the window now. What am I? What is he? What are we to each other? Answers that were once clear-cut are now so tangled up that I can't make head or tail of them. He's not just my enemy anymore. When I look at him, I see more than just the man who wanted to bleed me dry.

I see a little boy, face lit by the dancing shadows from a burning violin.

I see a mourning brother.

I see a savage beast suffering from an invisible wound that's awfully close to killing him.

And when I look in the mirror, what will I see? Who the fuck knows? I'm terrified of that too.

"What happens next?" I say again. He looks at me this time. I expect to be punished. After all, I lulled him into a drunken ramble, then damn near killed him with his own knife in an aborted escape attempt. He should throw me back in the cell at the very least, right? Or kill me before I get the chance to kill him again?

But he doesn't do either of those things. He clambers slowly to his feet, tucks himself away back in his jeans, then bends down and picks up the knife. To my surprise, he turns and sets it down on the vanity.

"This is yours now," he says.

Then he leaves without another word.

20

DANTE

I committed a sin.

Now, payment is due.

I walk out of the girl's room under control. But as soon as the door shuts behind me, I start to run. My feet beat into the stone floors as I race down the corridor, into the common room, then down my own hallway. I find the staircase at the far end and climb until I get to the top of my private tower.

A barren room awaits me there. I waste no time in slamming the wooden door shut behind me and throwing the deadbolt. Turning back, I drop to my knees and strip off my shirt in one motion. There is a mirror to my right. I rotate around so I can look at my back.

It's mottled with thick scars and a massive tattoo that stretches all the way from top to bottom, side to side.

The ink depicts a massive demon, wings spread, blood dripping from the claws on its hands and feet. The whole thing is rendered in vividly real black-and-white.

But the scars tell the true tale. Skin that has been torn apart and healed and torn again.

I am about to add another chapter to that story.

My rope awaits me. It is fraying and old, though clotted blood crusted along its length keeps it from crumbling completely. Fat knots are tied at regular intervals along it.

It has done this before. It knows its job.

I seize it in one hand and, with a deep breath, whip it backwards over my shoulder.

Only when the knots strike my back and I feel the first blush of sharp, cracking pain can I finally breathe again.

But I do not stop there.

I whip myself again and again until I can feel hot blood stream from the breaks in my skin. Until my breath comes in sharp, agonized spurts. Until I feel that I have paid what is owed for the promises I broke.

I go longer than I ever have before, because this was a special kind of sin. I touched what I should never have touched. Went where I shouldn't have gone.

I don't give a fuck that Vito told me to stay away from the girl. I haven't cared what he tells me to do in a long time. I am here castigating myself because I swore to myself that I wouldn't go there.

I knew from the moment we found her that this would not end well. My brothers think I am too caught up in my own madness to see that they are each victims of their insanities. But I see in them what I feel in myself: this girl is the flint that sparks the fire. None of us will survive unscathed.

I should have killed her when I had the chance. That first night, I went down to sharpen my knife and end things before they went too far. She awoke just before I was ready to kill her in her drugged stupor. That was a sign from heaven or hell—I'm still not sure which. Fate dictated that this girl would come into our home, into our hearts, and wreak havoc.

Though it is also true that she had already wreaked havoc before our eyes ever met. Her skin is flawless pearl, but it is stained with the blood of my brother and father. By mere virtue of her family name, she is responsible for their deaths. And, more to the point, she is the sacrificial lamb that must die in order to balance the scale.

Her father stole Sergio from me. So I promised that I would steal her from him.

I told Milaya that to her face. But I fear that now she knows I can't go through with it. Maybe she doesn't know the extent of my struggle. Of how many nights I sat outside her cell door when all else was dark and quiet, picturing myself throwing open the door and finishing what I started. I failed then. I failed now.

Christ, I am a pathetic wretch. I could not protect my brother and now I can't even bear to kill for him in vengeance. I deserve the pain that is lancing through my back now as I lie huddled on the cold stone floor of this empty room. The only light comes from a steel-barred window. It is a clear night and cloudless, so the moon is bright and full. I wonder if she is looking out her window and seeing it the way I am.

After several long minutes of labored breathing, I reach for the rope again. Because I feel the lust rearing its ugly head once more. I want to go back down and do again what I shouldn't have done even once. I want to fuck her again. I want to feel alive again, the way I did when she pressed the knife against my neck with murder in her eyes.

What does it mean that she couldn't kill me? I feel bound to her by that, like an invisible chain links her heart to mine. I couldn't kill her; she couldn't kill me. Does that mean something? Does anything mean anything anymore?

I don't fucking know.

To be truthful, I haven't known anything for a long time. Maybe ever.

Mateo thinks I was born unhinged. He is not entirely wrong. But he cannot possibly know how it feels to live in the grips of emotions so powerful that there is nothing to do but submit to them or be crushed, like tumbling in the throes of a wave at the beach. If I try to resist the things I feel, I would be broken by them. So I have to let them run over me. Around me. Through me. That's the only way.

Sergio was the only one who ever understood. He knew me implicitly. My twin, my other. He saw what I saw, felt what I felt. But he knew better than me how to handle it. He found a way to tame his demons, to saddle them and make them work for him instead of the other way around. I have never been so fortunate.

He knew how to put the reins in my hands though. When it truly mattered, he could speak to me in a way that cut through the chaos and helped me find my center.

But he is gone now, and so I am a victim once again.

I let the rope fall from my hand.

Whipping myself won't undo the sex. It won't bring back my dead twin. All I have is sins compounding sins. I'm the one who has to live with it. Trying to beat them back with this blood-clotted rope or with self-loathing or with alcohol is like punching waves. I will only die tired.

I struggle to my feet and pull my shirt back over my head. The drunkenness is fading from me now. I want to sleep for days, for weeks, for years. First, I must shower and rinse the smell of Milaya from my hands and face. It is haunting me already.

Before I go, I walk over to the window and peer through. It looks out into the rear courtyard. I scan the darkness. Perhaps there are answers to my torment hidden between the boughs of the trees. But the night is still and quiet.

Until I see a dark figure meandering along the edge of the pool. It stops and drops something into the water, then watches the ripples spread. I smile, a tight, thin-lipped smile of like recognizing like. The man down there is suffering the same way I am.

And I think I know the reason why.

"Leo."

My brother turns and looks at me. He is wary, surprised, fists clenched and ready to strike if I prove to be an enemy, as we were taught. When he sees it is me, he eases but scowls.

"What are you doing out here, Dante?"

"I might ask you the same question."

"I'd rather you didn't."

"I'd rather a lot of things be different than they are, *fratello.*"

He scowls again, the infamous Leo Bianci scowl that half the city's female socialites have driven themselves crazy over. "I'm not in the mood."

"Nor am I," I tell him. I hand him the flask from my back pocket. Warm whiskey swishes around inside it. He starts to shake his head, then reconsiders and takes it from me. He uncaps it, holds it up to his lips, and takes a long swallow. I watch in mild amusement as the grimace spreads across his face when it hits his tongue.

"Christ, you drink horse's piss."

"It's best not to make your vices taste too good."

He laughs bitterly at that. "I know too well what you mean."

"I thought so. Is that what has you prowling the courtyard in the night?"

Leo turns away from me a bit, as if he doesn't want me to see the emotions that are playing out behind his eyes. He is unusually vulnerable right now, for a man who has spent his whole life burying things deep below the surface. I can see clearly the pain written in his face. It is just like I thought. We are suffering from the same affliction.

"Something like that," he mutters.

I pause before I speak my mind. If I say what I want to say, I will open a Pandora's box that cannot be sealed again. But how much longer can it live in the darkness? This thing tearing up each of us will bring the walls crashing down if we don't acknowledge it. It might already be too late, in fact.

"It's her, isn't it?"

He turns back around to face me. The moon catches only half his face, so the other is shrouded in darkness. "You too, then."

"Me too," I sigh.

"Come," he tells me. "Let's walk."

We move through the courtyard into the garden that sits at the end away from the castle. There is a dirt path lined with rocks that winds through the shadowy tree trunks. It ends in a white-painted gazebo in a small glade. When we reach it, we sink to a seat on the steps.

Leo hands me the flask and I take another sip. Sins compounding sins. At this point, what is one more? The whiskey may not quiet my demons any longer, but it's better than twiddling my thumbs idly.

"I can't close my eyes without seeing her," he whispers. He keeps his gaze rooted straight ahead like he can't bear to look at me. I glance at him, though I feel the same burning shame. But he is right—it is too much. I look away too, reducing Leo to nothing more than a disembodied voice in the night.

"We should never have brought her here."

"Don't say that," he snaps.

I arch my eyebrows in surprise but say nothing.

"Don't say that," he repeats, quieter this time and less forceful, like maybe he thinks I have a point after all.

"You think it was wise then?"

"I just ... I don't know what I would be feeling if we had killed her on the spot."

I nod. That was, of course, the only alternative. One way or another, our paths were going to cross with Milaya Volkov. But for that to be the outcome—I shudder at the thought of seeing her dead and broken at my feet. That image dissipates in my head and is replaced with the one of her riding me, breasts bared to the moonlight, holding a gleaming knife to my throat and coaxing me to come so hard it felt like I was emptying my soul into the girl. A wild princess. A savage queen. Owning me, taming me, and submitting to me all at the same time. It was a fucking conundrum like no other.

"It's too late now," I offer.

"It's too late for many things."

"That too."

"So what do we do next?"

I chuckle quietly. "If I knew, do you think I'd be this drunk?"

I can hear him scowling again. He snatches the flask back from me and drinks deeply once more. He smacks his lips as he drains the last of the alcohol, then hurls the canister into the woods as far as he can. Squirrels skitter away in the underbrush, frightened by the sudden intrusion.

"You bastard. You owe me a flask."

"Put it on my tab."

We sit in silence for a while. What else is there to say? I don't know what Leo did with her and I don't honestly want to know. Mostly because I don't want to tell him what I did with her—or, more accurately, what she did with me. It feels intensely private, like that was a moment for us and us alone.

And yet, strangely enough, I don't feel a shred of jealousy. We've never shared women between us before. But for some reason, the thought of Leo fucking Milaya doesn't stir envy in my chest the way I thought it might. What she and I did on that carpet can't be replicated. It wasn't sex, or at least, it wasn't *just* sex. There was more to it—a conversation with our bodies—that could only take place between me and her.

"He will be here soon," Leo says abruptly after God-knows-how-long has passed.

"I know."

"What then?"

"Not a fucking clue."

Quiet resumes. Little woodland creatures dash through the underbrush. An owl hoots. A few bats wing around the gazebo roof overhead.

After a while, the exhaustion has claimed me completely. Rather than inebriate me, the alcohol has just dragged me down towards sleep. I stand and offer Leo a hand to help him to his feet. "Come on, brother," I tell him. "A man can only torture himself in the darkness for so long."

He eyes me for a long moment before he accepts my offer and I pull him up.

"You've been at it again."

I hesitate, then nod.

"You can't beat the devil out of yourself, Dante," he says. It almost sounds caring.

"Well, I can keep fucking trying, can't I?" I laugh, but he doesn't.

"I'm worried for you. You will go too far one day."

I turn away from him and start down the path. "That's my problem, isn't it?"

Leo lunges forward to grab my shoulder and whirl me back around to face him. "Sergio's death is not your fault, Dante. Neither is Father's."

"Fuck Father. Let the old bastard burn in hell."

"Burn? All his friends are down there. He's fucking loving the place."

We laugh together at that. It's an unexpected moment of lightness in a night that feels so dark, heavy, and cloying. It feels wrong somehow to be laughing, but I laugh anyway, and it feels good to do that. To stand with my brother in the night and feel for just the briefest of moments like I'm not as alone as I might otherwise think.

The moment passes, but its warmth lingers. Sighing, we turn as one and go back up towards the castle, though each of us is still hurtling at breakneck speed towards a grim and uncertain future.

21

MILAYA

I wake up shivering.

I don't know what time it is. It's still nighttime outside of my window, but the moonlight has disappeared completely. I feel a painful crick in my neck and realize that I must have fallen asleep curled into a little ball on the rug, right where Dante left me. I can still feel the heat he left between my thighs, though it is sticky and dried now. My hips ache and the rug burn on my knees is irritating.

I don't want to move. As uncomfortable as this position is, I feel like if I can just stay here forever then I can pretend that what just happened didn't actually happen at all. I can pretend that I didn't just hold a knife to a man's throat and then pull him inside of me.

This was so much worse, wasn't it? I didn't just submit to Dante the way I did to Leo. I took over. *I* was the one in charge. And yet instead of killing him for what he's done to me, or at the very least hurting him enough that I could make my escape from this place, I had sex with him.

Now, two of the brothers have put their hands on me. Two of them have made me moan and whimper and come like a rocket ship.

What's next?

God, I don't want to know.

It feels like I'm living in a fucked-up version of that movie *Groundhog Day*. I need to break this cycle and get my head on straight once more. If I don't ... well, best not to think of it.

I was having a dream before I woke up. Not a dream actually, but a memory.

It was my fourteenth birthday party. I had a half dozen friends over and we were doing a spa party, pretending we were middle-aged divas with cucumbers over our eyes and mocktails in our hands. I remember that I'd cajoled my dad into joining us. I delighted in applying a charcoal mud mask on my father's face, making him wear a fluffy pink bathrobe that matched the rest of ours. Even at that age, I knew he would do anything for me. Even this, as goofy as it was.

We listened to music, ate snacks, gossiped, and played silly games while Dad looked on in amusement. It was fun; it was sweet; it was one of the last truly innocent moments of my life.

I remember the moment it all ended.

It's funny that the moment sticks out in my head at all actually, because of how innocuous it was on the surface of it. Mom had gone into the kitchen to make another tray of virgin daiquiris for us. There was a knock at the glass double doors that separated the house from the courtyard where we were all seated.

Dad frowned as Uncle Alexei entered. He was wearing a suit and he looked stiff and formal, just like he always did. He strode to my dad's side and bent over to whisper something in his ear.

Dad's frown deepened. He stood up at once and wiped the mask off his face with a nearby towel, tossing the cucumbers onto the ground as he did. Then he swept away without another word. Uncle Alexei glanced back over his shoulder before they disappeared, but Dad didn't. Dad didn't look back at all.

I stared for a long while at the mud-splattered cucumbers he left behind. My friends had barely noticed my father's departure, but it felt to me like an essential part of me had vanished. There was something so sad and forlorn about two slices of cucumber lying on the whitewashed patio, with little flecks of black mud drying on the edges.

I knew where he'd gone, or rather, what kind of thing he had gone to do. I was old enough by then to put the pieces together and understand that my father was not a good man. He was my daddy and I was his little girl, so of course I loved him. But how many times can a girl hear her father whisper ominous threats into a phone late at night before she realizes that he hurts people? How many times did I have to see Uncle Alexei or some other suited goon whisper in his ear and notice how my father's face hardened into steel? His eyes would slit, his fists would clench, and it was like he became a different man altogether. He wasn't Daddy anymore—he was Luka Volkov. I stared at the cucumber slices wilting in the sunlight, and that was the moment that I truly understood exactly what everything meant. Who he was. Who I was.

I force myself to sit up. Like I suspected, motion shatters the illusion that my encounter with Dante never happened. But I suppose I don't have much capacity for self-delusion left in me anymore anyway. I've spent twenty-two years trying to hide from my father's crimes, to pretend they don't exist. But it feels like they're finally catching up to me.

I can't keep pretending.

I try to go back to sleep, but I fail miserably. I don't know whether it is my body or my soul that needs the rest more. So much has changed since I was first brought here, and yet the basic circumstances are still the same. I'm still a prisoner. I'm still a pawn. I'm still the enemy.

But nothing is ever that simple. Especially not with the men holding me captive. It seems like, the more I learn about them, the less I know. A dead brother, a dead father? How the hell am I supposed to process *that* twin bombshell that Dante dropped on me?

The fact is that it just doesn't compute. I don't know how to make sense of it, so I choose to ignore it. Dad always told me that sticking your head in the sand just meant someone was going to come along and screw you in the ass—not an expression that Mom approved of by any stretch of the imagination, though it definitely had its own kind of folksy wisdom. But I don't see an alternative. Seeing these men as living, breathing, loving humans would break everything that's holding me together. I can't take that risk.

So I just get up and go wander. I leave my room to pad barefoot down the halls. For the first time, I force myself to stare back at the portraits glaring down at me from the walls. I feel an inexplicable calmness that has eluded me since my arrival. I'm not scared by these ancient Biancis anymore. If anything, I'm annoyed by them, like back home in New York when some creep wouldn't stop staring at me on the subway. The prevailing wisdom in those days was always to just ignore, to not engage—Lord knows the headlines are always filled with the stories of what happened to unlucky women who pissed off the wrong leering creep. But I always said to hell with that. I'm no one's eye candy.

"Fuck you," I whisper to one particularly nasty-looking portrait. It's an old man with a huge wart on his iconic Bianci schnoz and beady little eyes. "You're ugly anyway."

"That's no way to speak to an ancestor of mine," comes an amused voice.

I damn near jump out of my skin at the sound of it. Whirling around, I see Mateo leaning against the wall a dozen yards away from me. He's got a bottle of wine in his hands, but his eyes are raking up and down me. I might just be projecting my own emotions onto him, but it seems an awful lot like he's got a war going on inside his head, like he wants so badly to look at me but also feels like that's the last thing he should be doing.

I know the feeling.

"What is it with you guys and sneaking up on me like that?" I demand.

He shrugs. "We learned a long time ago that grand entrances are for men with a death wish."

I roll my eyes. "I'm not even going to bother trying to figure out what the hell that means." My gaze falls to the wine bottle he's holding. "Celebrating something?"

"Not exactly."

"Drinking to forget, then."

"That's a little closer to the mark, I'd say."

I swallow past the sudden and unexpected lump in my throat. "Something bad."

He nods slowly, his eyes never leaving mine.

"Which thing?"

He tilts his head to the side and fixes me with an understanding look. "Judging by your questions, I'd say you know that already, Milaya."

I hesitate. I could lie and deny that Dante told me anything about their father and Sergio. But Mateo has me skewered as it is. He knows I know. So I just whisper, "Yeah." It's stupid to let a sympathetic note creep into my voice. Why do I care? The less of these Biancis, the better—right?

Shoot, I don't even know anymore.

“I suspect I’m not the only one who needs a drink now, am I?” Mateo asks me softly.

I consider what he’s asking for a second—the question beneath the question. He’s standing a dozen yards away from me, but I can already feel that familiar, dreaded pull in my gut, like a hook embedded in me drawing me towards him inexorably. Reeling me in towards ... something. Something regrettable. Something I should fight.

In the end, though, all I can say is what that dreaded pulling feeling wants me to say. “I could use a drink, maybe.”

Mateo gestures behind me. “Perhaps we can go sit outside and share a drink together then. After you, Milaya.”

The late night air is hazy and thick. Fireflies drift past my head as we sit on the steps of a gazebo nestled on the back lawn.

“It’s beautiful out here,” I murmur.

“I suppose it is,” Mateo replies with the voice of someone who has never stopped to consider that question before.

“Do you spend a lot of time out here?”

“No. Never.”

“Why not? Might not have such a sourpuss face all the time if you did.”

Mateo laughs. It’s a strange sound coming from such a massive, brooding man like him, but not an unwelcome one. I feel a weird blush of pride at that for some reason I don’t want to examine any closer. “I might not,” he agrees. “But my work demands most of my time.”

"Wouldn't kill you to take a break and go smell the roses every once in a while, you know."

"It wouldn't kill me *immediately,*" he corrects. "But it would kill other men. And it would eventually kill me, too."

I fix him with a glare. "God, you boys are all the same. Buzzkill Biancis. Bunch of nihilists in ten-thousand-dollar suits."

He laughs again, louder this time. "Ah shit!" he curses. He'd forgotten a bottle opener, so he'd been fiddling with the cork with a pocketknife, trying to coax it out. But his laughter made him inadvertently push the cork deeper into the bottle. Shrugging, he pokes it all the way through so it floats in the red wine and raises an eyebrow at me.

I shrug back. "No glasses, no bottle opener. Brings me back to high school."

"To younger and more vulnerable days, then," Mateo says, raising the bottle up in a mock toast before knocking back a glug and handing it over to me.

"You always have to make things serious," I sigh. I tilt the bottle to my lips and take a long sip of my own.

"Life is serious."

"It doesn't have to be."

"It is what it is, Milaya. We don't choose it."

I wrinkle my eyebrows. "All those books you read ... don't any of them have happy endings?"

He grins sort of sadly. That also looks weird on him, but he's more handsome when he smiles than when he's wearing his ever-present grimace. "Not the kind of books I read, no."

"Maybe you should get some new books then."

"Maybe," he agrees, looking longingly into the distance. "Maybe."

An uncomfortable silence follows. I take another sip of the wine and realize we've passed it back and forth so many times that it's just about empty now. I close my eyes and feel the warm rush of tipsiness. When I open them again, Mateo is looking at me strangely.

"What?" I ask.

He opens his mouth to speak then reconsiders. "Perhaps not."

"What is it?" I repeat. I push his knee and am surprised when he flinches like I shocked him. "Tell me."

He twiddles his thumbs in his lap, diverting his gaze to look anywhere but at me.

"Are you really gonna clam up all of a sudden? This is the most words you've said to me in, like, however long I've been here, and—"

"Eleven days, three hours, and thirty-seven minutes," he says quietly, as much to himself as to me.

I blink. "Is there a countdown clock I'm not aware of or something?" I demand sarcastically.

But he doesn't laugh this time. "There's a countdown clock for all of us," he whispers.

"What the hell does that mean?"

He looks up at me. "It means that I don't think any of us are going to make it out of this one alive, Milaya."

It feels like someone sucked the air out of the night. The owls winging past overhead settle down; the wind shushing through the trees stills. All there is in the world is Mateo's murky green eyes and thick, furrowed brows. I feel myself moving closer to him on the steps. Before I even realize what's happening, I'm resting my head on his shoulder and cradling his hand between mine. He flinches again, but I don't let go.

I don't know what crazy impulse is driving my decision-making. It would be easy to blame it on the wine, but at most, all the alcohol has done is loosen my hold on the urges that have been brewing in me for eleven days, three hours, and thirty-seven minutes now. It's a knotted tangle of twin dueling urges, but I think I'm finally beginning to make sense of them, sort of. There's the obvious parts—the burning physical attraction for each of the brothers pitted against my hatred for what they've done to me. Then there's the underlying part that's harder to suss out: how much I want them to suffer for their sins, compared to how much I want to take away the pain that's eating each of them alive. That last part is what makes me touch Mateo and hold his hand in mine, even when it's so clear that he is fighting his desire to let me do that.

When I touch him, I feel like I'm siphoning away some of the sadness. I feel like he's finally drawing the kind of deep breath he's waited years to take—maybe even his whole life. I feel like I'm doing something that only I can do. I don't know how or why—I just know that it feels like what I was meant to do. What I was brought here for.

"We shouldn't," he whispers. "*I* shouldn't."

"I don't think there are rules anymore," I reply just as softly.

"No," he agrees finally. "No, I don't think there are, either."

We sit like that for a little while. Maybe minutes, maybe an hour; I'm not sure. Neither of us says anything, and yet it seems so obvious to me that this is the most essential act of healing that I've ever been a part of. Dante needed to be brought to the very edge of life and death before he could draw in that deep breath. Leo needed to be brought face-to-face with the river of desire coursing through him.

Mateo, it turns out, needed to be forced to sit in a garden and breathe. To get out of his head and into the world around him. My cheek on his shoulder, my fingers woven through his—that's what tethering him to the here and now. That's what's important.

Eventually, the moment passes, though neither of us acknowledges it. I sit up and eye the empty bottle at our feet. "I want some more wine," I say suddenly.

Like earlier in the hallway, when he asked if I wanted to join him for a drink, there's a separate question underlying what I just said. I know by the flash of recognition in his eye that Mateo heard it too. So when he stands up and offers his hand to help me to my feet and I feel the first surge of heat between my legs, it's clear to both of us what will happen next.

He doesn't look at me as he leads me back up the path to the house. He doesn't look at me as we step back into the cool interior of the castle, down a long hallway, to a winding staircase I've never seen before. He doesn't look at me as he unlocks a thick, steel-reinforced door to reveal a sprawling wine cellar, then ushers me inward and steps behind me as I gaze up at a huge rack of hundreds of dusty bottles that are no doubt worth half the GDP of Jamaica.

And because he doesn't look at me, I am not ready when I feel his lips press against the base of my throat and his arm wraps around my waist from behind. The heat of his kiss is a delicious contrast against the cool, musty air of the wine cellar.

"Mateo ..." I gasp.

"Shh," he tells me. "Don't say a word. You'll break the spell."

He's right. There's a fragile tension in the air that might shatter irretrievably if I say anything. But it takes all my willpower not to moan into the rafters when his fingers find the button of my jean shorts and pop it open before sliding past my sheer panties and spreading me wide open. I rest a hand on the shelf in front of me and let my head sag forward. Mateo kisses down my spine. He tugs my jeans down to my ankles and I gasp again as the cold rushes between my thighs.

He doesn't make me wait long before he frees himself and thrusts into me. It's a good thing I am already soaking wet, because he is girthy and rock-hard. He goes slow at first, but when I reach back to grab his hip and pull him slamming harder into me, he picks up the tempo, faster and faster, until the vibrations running through me cause the bottles to rattle on the shelf to which I'm clinging for leverage. He clamps down on my shoulder with his teeth and presses his torso against my back as he thrusts, grunting with each effort.

I'm full to bursting with him. The smell of my sweat, his spicy cologne, and the acrid musk of the wine cellar all combine in my nose like an aphrodisiac, so that when his hand swipes down to find my clit and rub urgently on it, it doesn't take long before I come explosively. I tighten my grip on the shelf as the orgasm rockets through me, every muscle fiber squeezing hard while the waves pass again and again.

Mateo isn't finished though. So as soon as I regain my bearings, I turn around and fall to my knees. The stone is rough on my bare skin, but I don't care. I want to look at him as he comes, to feel him. "What are you—" he starts to say. It turns into a strangled groan as I open my mouth and take his length as far past my lips as I can. He can't help but buck his hips into me. I encourage it with my hands on his firm, muscular ass. I taste him—the tang of his skin and his salty precum, yes, but also the *him* part of him—the melancholy, the burden, the licorice-tinged sadness—and I try to draw it into me and memorize it so that he doesn't have to carry it all alone anymore.

He lasts perhaps a minute, maybe less, before he groans once more and unleashes himself in my mouth. I bob my head again and again until there's nothing left. When I'm finished, I let his manhood fall from my lips and I plop backwards to lean up against the shelf.

Mateo drops to his hands and knees, panting. He stays that way for a long time as he catches his breath. Eventually, he sighs, rolls over, and sits next to me.

It's just like a week ago down in the dungeon, when he sat next to me in the hallway outside of the room where the dead bodies of the Frat Stars were stashed. Back then, I thought he was a monster, but as we sat next to each other, I saw the first glimmer of humanity in him. It scared me then.

What I'm seeing in Mateo now doesn't scare me quite the same way. In fact, it damn near breaks my heart. I tried to take it from him, as best I could. I wonder if I was successful. I wonder if it is even possible to put that exchange into words, or if it was just something that had to be acted out with our bodies like we just did.

But there's something else weighing on me more than that. Now feels like the right moment to ask.

"Dante told me about your brother and father," I say quietly. I'm looking at him, but his head is hanging and he isn't returning my gaze.

He just grunts wordlessly.

"My dad killed them, didn't he?"

There's a long, pregnant pause. It looks like it takes the last dregs of his effort for Mateo to raise his head and look at me. An exhaustion floats in his eyes that wasn't there before. I wait on pins and needles for him to speak.

"Your father killed my father," he says without emotion. "And also my brother. And my uncle. For ten years, he has hunted us like dogs. We took you because, frankly, we had no other choice."

His words hit me like a slap in the face.

On some level, I've known these truths for a while now. I was just too afraid to bring them into the light, to say them out loud. But something about the way Mateo says things—so matter-of-factly, so precisely, so irrevocably—is what I needed to hear. I can't keep running from the final truth: my dad is not who I want him to be.

He loves me. He raised me as best as he knew how to do, and he mostly did a good job.

But he has blood on his hands. It may not be innocent blood, but it's blood all the same. And that's a sin that must be atoned for.

22

VITO

I need to get out of this fucking castle.

Every glimpse I see of Milaya, every time I notice her lingering smell in a room she has just vacated, I blanch and feel sick to my stomach.

Fortunately, business calls me down into the city. The men need to see my presence and be reassured that they are in good hands. Our organization is sprawling, and the time is right to do a review of the troops.

But it is a delicate balancing act, because I am trying to quell their fears at the same time that I must exhort them to batten down the hatches and prepare for what comes next. We are nearing a critical point: Luka Volkov will be here soon. There is no telling what will happen after that.

The plan had come together with ease, as if it had been in the cards for us all along. Bring Luka here. Anticipate the various tricks he would stash up his sleeve and neutralize them. And then do what I intended to do from the moment his men took the lives of my father, my uncle, my brother—cut off the head of the snake and watch its body squirm.

But that will come later. Right now, it is a fine spring day. For a change, I take the time to relish it. The air is warm and lucid as it moves through the palm fronds overhead. Now that I am free of the castle walls, I feel oddly tranquil—so long as I ignore the pang of anxiety that comes from being distanced from Milaya.

I chose to drive myself, though of course there are soldiers driving ahead and behind me. The wheel of my car, an expensive convertible, thrums in my hands like a purring beast. It feels alive and connected to me just as I am connected to it. When I want to turn, to change lanes, to accelerate, it springs into action practically the instant the impulse occurs to me, like it is acting of its own accord. It is an unexpected blessing to lose myself in the simple act of driving fast. With the wind roaring in my ears, I cannot think. With the road passing beneath my feet, I cannot worry. With the sun shining down upon my head, I cannot brood.

For a moment, things are okay.

But all good things must come to an end, and eventually, as I reenter the city and slow to a halt in front of my first stop, I feel the familiar shroud of dark concern ensconce me once again. My brow furrows into its usual resting place and my fist clenches.

I step out of the car, leaving it still running. One of the soldiers assigned to my security detail will watch over it while I am inside the store. This will be a quick errand anyway.

The doorbell jingles as I walk in. It is a small mini-mart, tucked out of the way in Inglewood, far from prying eyes. The windows are dusty, cluttered with flyers, and the racks arranged in the store are filled with stale chips and a blinding assortment of candy. The man behind the bulletproof glass, a portly Hispanic male in a stained wifebeater shirt, does a double take when he sees me enter.

"Mr. Bianci!" he crows. He scrambles to his feet, knocking over his rickety stool in the process, then unlocks the door to the cashier's area and comes waddling around as fast as he can. There is a barefooted little boy playing with an action figure in the beer aisle. The man hisses at him as he passes, "Get out!", and the boy immediately turns tail and races into the back corner.

"Mr. Bianci," the man says again when he faces me.

He's got his head bowed a little bit like he's afraid to look me in the eye. I notice with distaste that he has crumbs nestled between his chins and his fingers are slick with Cheeto dust. "Jorge," I reply calmly.

"To what do we owe the, eh, the pleasure?" he asks nervously. His hands are clasped in front of his waist, but I can see that they are trembling.

"My men tell me that you are short this month," I say simply.

He blanches. "It's a, you know, it's a crazy time of year, yes? No—not, um—not much business, *sí*."

I step close to the man, though the smell of body odor hits my nose like an unwelcome heat wave, and drop my voice low. "Do you think that my father took the rules with him when he died?"

"Oh no, sir, I just saying that—"

"No. I am the don, Jorge. And I have come to collect what I am owed. I do not like these trips. I do not intend to linger here."

He nods, too scared for words now. His eyes keep flitting over my shoulder to look through the door. No doubt he can see my men waiting outside. He is too dumb to realize that I am the one he most needs to fear.

"I get it for you now, *sí?* Wait right there, sir." Turning, he hustles back behind the counter, presses a button to open the drawer, and empties it of cash. He snaps a grimy rubber band around the stack before coming back and pressing the bills into my waiting hand.

"That is better," I tell him. "Do not be late again."

"Of course not, sir."

I start to turn to leave, but as I do, I see the little boy peering through the crack of the door that leads to the employees-only area in the back. He looks just like Jorge, I see. Perhaps a nephew or a son.

A thought occurs to me, apropos of nothing: I have become just like my father. How many times did I accompany him on errands like this? *"Watch me and learn, Vito,"* he would say before we entered. *"A don must make the right impression."* And then he would storm inside and leave quivering fools in his wake, their money fattening his pocket or their sworn loyalty bolstering his empire.

Here I am, finding myself playing that same part without even consciously trying. I catch sight of my reflection in the theft prevention mirror that hangs over the cash register. It is not Vito Bianci looking back—it is Giovanni I see in my face. The angry V of my eyebrows, the storm swirling in my eyes ... it is him. *I* am him.

I sigh and rub a thumb across my temple. Whether I am in the castle or out in the city, it seems that I cannot escape my ghosts. I thought I saw Milaya in every woman on the drive over, and now that I am here, I am seeing my father in dirty mirror reflections. No doubt Sergio is lingering just out of the corner of my eye. I shudder.

Turning back, I pull a few hundred-dollar bills from the money that Jorge just surrendered to me. I slap them down onto the counter. Jorge looks up at me fearfully.

"Buy the kid some shoes," I tell him wearily. "He'll get ringworm if he keeps running around this filthy store barefoot."

Then I leave before I get any other stupid ideas.

I keep my thoughts to myself for the rest of the day. Stop after stop, I am greeted like a king. My father would have rejoiced in the adulation, the fear he inspired.

It just makes me feel sick.

But it cannot be helped. If I am to keep this kingdom together, I must show my face around our territory and remind people why they choose to follow me. Whether out of self-preservation or mere financial self-interest, I make sure to push the buttons that need pushing, pay the homage that needs paying, solidify the bonds that hold the whole thing in place. Various underlings, minor crime lords, and gang leaders greet me, toast me, and request my help with this or that as I sweep through the city. I dole out favors and call them in. I make calls and take them.

In short, I do what I was born to do.

And through it all, I keep my eyes rooted firmly forward, so I don't catch another unwanted reflection of myself and the demons that live inside of me.

"What's next?" I ask Umberto. He is a young sergeant and the organizer of today's little excursion.

"Only one more stop, sir," he answers promptly. "A stash house in Koreatown." He's sharp-eyed and competent, which I am appreciating more than usual right now. I left home buzzing with energy. But now, I just feel deflated, so it is nice to have someone else I can rely on to handle things on my behalf.

"Let's go then," I say. For the umpteenth time that day, my team piles into their cars and we depart. I follow Umberto's lead through the city.

A few minutes into the drive, I notice that there is a motorcyclist who has been following us turn after turn. In my rear-view mirror, I can make out that it is a younger-looking man, perhaps in his twenties or thirties. He has dark, tousled hair, but the bandana tied around his nose and mouth keeps me from seeing much beyond the pale expanse of his forehead. I frown and open the walkie-talkie function on my cell phone.

"Umberto."

"Yes, sir?" comes the immediate reply.

"I don't like the look of this kid on the bike. Lose him."

"Yes, sir."

The SUV in front of me immediately veers off onto the shoulder of the highway and accelerates past the standstill traffic. I follow suit, as does my trail car.

But the biker stays with us.

We make a quick exit onto a back road, some arbitrary turns here and there as we lose ourselves in a sleepy commercial stretch of warehouses, shops, small factories. It appears that the motorcycle is gone. But I want to be sure we have ditched him before I lead him to the door of a valuable Bianci property. I remember a hidden alley not far from here. That'll do.

"Split up," I bark into the walkie-talkie. "Reconvene in Koreatown."

The three vehicles immediately diverge. I head west, smoothly accelerating and cornering at high speed. The car I'm driving is built for performance like this, so it responds instantaneously. One more left turn and then I see my destination in sight. A quick glance in my mirror shows no sign of the motorcyclist. Good.

Pulling up, I whip the wheel to the right and hide my car in the small open-ended alley I remember from some random errand years back. I kill the ignition and wait. My right hand finds the gun in the glove compartment. I grip it tightly, savoring the reassuring weight. It would be insane for the Russians to strike now, with their leader due to arrive soon for negotiations. But perhaps they want to take me hostage for leverage. I start to wonder whether splitting up was a tactical error. It's just one biker, though. How much harm could a lone wolf do?

For a few long minutes, the adrenaline surges through my veins. I am ready for a fight. If this is the end, then I am prepared to go down guns blazing.

But nothing happens.

Once I'm satisfied that enough time has passed, I ease my death grip on the gun and start up the engine again. Business calls. I want to finish this final errand so I can return home and have a fucking drink.

I'm too keyed up. This will all turn out to be much ado about nothing, I'm sure. The kid on the bike was probably just admiring my vehicle. It was the sight of my father's ghost in my own reflection that has me so wired. A stiff drink will do me a lot of good, no doubt.

Releasing the brake, I ease the car forward to the other end of the alley. I'm about a yard away from reemerging and joining the early evening traffic once more when I hear the cough of a motorcycle engine.

The biker pulls across the mouth of the alley.

My first thought, sharp and clear in my mind's eye, is that I deserve to die for my idiocy. I abandoned my guards and pulled my vehicle into an alley? What kind of fucking moron does that?

I wait for the biker to pull out his gun and light me up where I sit strapped into the driver's seat of the car.

But he doesn't do that.

He just sits on his bike, idling there on the sidewalk, staring at me. The bandana across the lower half of his face hides his expression, but I could almost swear he is grinning.

Then he kicks the bike into gear again, merges back into traffic, and disappears.

It takes me a long time to catch my breath. Not because I could have been killed. Not because I made a series of stupid decisions, the kind of decisions that make me question everything I've been doing since Father died.

But because I swore I recognized those eyes.

I've only ever met one person with eyes that violet.

And that man is dead.

Right?

By the time I meet up again with my security detail on the southern rim of Koreatown, I'm doubting my own observations. There's no way that that was Sergio on the motorcycle. The sun was playing tricks on me, surely. Or perhaps it was just my own heart that caused me to see what I wanted to see.

I can't deny that I want badly for Sergio to still be alive. But if he were alive, he wouldn't be haunting me on a motorcycle like a fucking ghoul. He would have returned home to where he belongs.

Maybe I really do need that drink.

"You okay, boss?" Umberto asks cautiously as I step out of my vehicle. "You look a little wan."

I open my mouth to reprimand him for daring to ask such an invasive question, then think better of it. He is a good man. No need to put him on his heels right now.

"It has been a long day," I reply by way of explanation. "You didn't find the biker?"

"No, sir," he says. "We have teams of men out looking, but with the lead he has on us, it's unlikely we'll catch up to him."

I figured as much, but I still had to try. So be it. Best to pretend none of that happened anyway. "What time is it?"

"Almost five forty-five, sir." He glances up at me. "Do you want me to cancel your final appointment?"

"No." I shake my head.

The last thing we need is a display of weakness. Today was supposed to be about rallying the troops and solidifying my leadership. If I let one measly fucking punk rattle my cage so thoroughly, what kind of example will that be setting for the men who rely upon me?

"Let's just go," I growl to Umberto. "I'm sick of this goddamn city." That at least is not a lie.

I follow him down an alley to an unassuming storefront. Umberto opens the door for me and I step through.

It takes a moment for my eyes to adjust from the sunny afternoon to the dark, dank interior. When I do, I see that the storefront is just that —a front. Inside is not a simple dry cleaners as the sign proclaims. Instead, it is a sprawling cavern of guns, packaged drugs, and banks of computers performing all manner of illicit transactions on behalf of the Bianci Family Mafia. This is our core facility, the lifeblood of the organization. Tens of thousands of dollars flow through our fingertips every second on their way from here to everywhere and from everywhere to here.

A familiar voice calls out my name through the cacophony. "Vito, sir!"

I turn to see a gray-whiskered face smiling in my direction. "Roberto," I call back, breaking out into a grin of my own. "It is good to see you, old friend. How are Helena and the children?"

"A pain in my ass, of course." He laughs easily and freely as he walks up and shakes my hand. "But the best kind of pain. When are you settling down with a pain of your own?"

I laugh, though it feels forced. "Never, if I can help it. You are a better man than I am in that sense."

"In many senses." He winks. Only Roberto could get away with a joke like that. Any other man would lose a finger for it.

I shake my head tiredly and shoot back, "Actually, I was just thinking that you look like shit."

Roberto laughs. "I would argue that you are to blame for that, sir. You weren't exactly kind to my face back in our sparring days. I'm paying for it now, I suppose."

"I seem to remember you getting in a fair few hits of your own. Picking on a twelve-year-old boy, how could you?"

"Who, me? I wouldn't dare hit the son of the don." He blinks, realizes what he said by mentioning my father, and immediately sweeps the hat off his head and bows towards me. I can see he is going bald on top.

My, how quickly the years have passed. Once upon a time, Roberto was my sparring partner, a tough, burly man of thirty. Now, he is past fifty, if I recall correctly, and looking at least a decade older than that. But he has been loyal to the Biancis since before I was born.

"My condolences on the loss of your father and brother," Roberto murmurs with his face aimed at the ground. "I was devastated to hear of it."

"Stand up, Roberto," I reply quietly. "Thank you for your kind words. But it won't bring them back. I am the don now."

"Yes, sir," he says, straightening. "That you are. You've been ready for this for a long time."

I nod. As unexpectedly nice as it is to hear a simple and honest vote of confidence in my newfound leadership, it would be unbecoming to thank him or embrace him, especially with my security detail at my back and family employees bustling around within earshot. So I simply stay quiet and try to say with my eyes what I cannot say with my words.

A heady silence passes before Roberto coughs to clear his throat. "Come, sir, let me give you the tour of the facility to update you on the latest." He turns and gestures for me to follow.

My mind is elsewhere as he fills me in on shipments coming and going, where our capital is being deployed, what new distribution channels have been added or modified for our products. I appreciate his competence. On any other occasion, I would be keenly interested in the minutiae of the Bianci businesses.

But I cannot shake thoughts of the violet-eyed motorcyclist. Was I seeing things or not? I try to convince myself that I was, that it was all a mirage, but my attempts feel feeble. I saw what I saw. I've never doubted myself before and I don't plan to start now. The only question is—what does that *mean?* Was it really Sergio? It couldn't possibly be.

And yet I feel deep in my heart of hearts that it was.

The rest of the tour passes without incident. I make sure that I am seen by every last man and woman working in the facility. My father's voice echoes in my head—more of his endless stream of dictums and principles. *"A king is not an abstract, invisible concept. A king is a man with the power to end lives. Never let the people forget that, son. Make sure they remember what you are capable of doing if they forget you."* That—more than collecting money, more than checking in on business, more than surveying our landscape—is what today is about.

Fear.

I think of the little boy in the mini-mart—shoeless and terrified when he looked at me. I think of how sick I felt in that moment.

And, as it has done all day long, the memory makes me shudder.

I bid Roberto goodbye and return home to the castle as fast as I can.

The first sip of whiskey hitting my tongue is heaven-sent. The second and third are just as good. I can feel the alcohol seeping into my bloodstream and taking the edge off. I loosen my tie and collapse into an armchair in my study.

"Is there anything else I can do for you, sir?" Umberto asks. He's standing ramrod straight at the door, hands folded behind his back, looking at me with a respectful mix of confidence and discretion.

"No," I say exhaustedly as I slump down, resting the glass tumbler on my chest. "I don't want to be bothered for the rest of the night."

"Yes, sir." He bows and leaves, shutting the door behind him.

When he's gone, I let out the sigh I've been holding back all day long. I feel restless and tired all at the same time. It is an unwelcome combination.

So many things are hanging in the balance right now. Luka, his daughter, my father, my brother, the Russians, the castle—the whole fucking world is waiting on me to make my next move. I have to choose carefully.

I have trained for this my whole life. So why do I feel so lost and helpless? Surely I don't need my father's guidance, do I? No, certainly not. In so many ways, I am glad he is dead. He was a monster. I am old enough and man enough now to admit that to myself. I say it out loud to try it on for size. "He was a monster." It feels good to say, so I keep going, talking out loud to nobody at all. "He was a terrorizer. A predator. He preyed on people too weak to fight back. He drained Mother of her life force. He put nightmares in my head just because he could. Fuck him."

That last part feels best of all. I say it again. "Fuck him. Fuck my father. May he rot in hell."

The fiery bloom of anger in my chest makes me sit up straight. I don't know why now is the time I feel it. Perhaps I am transitioning between stages of grieving or some other such psychological bullshit. Have I really waited thirty-two years to finally give voice to the things I've known practically since the day I was born?

Maybe I just never thought to question it before. My father was never good or bad in my eyes—he was just my father. But now that I am walking in his shoes, commanding his empire, I feel like I am at long last in a position to see him for what he was.

And I am in a position to remember the night I first saw that truth clearly.

The night I killed Audrey.

23

VITO

It takes everything I have in me not to scream like a pig at the slaughter when I am awoken from my dream by a hand on my shoulder.

I was dreaming of—*NO. Forget it now, Vito,* I curse inwardly. I feel wetness at the cuff of my pants and look down to realize that I fell asleep with my whiskey glass in my hand. It fell and shattered on the floor beneath me. The shards crunch under my heel as I look up to see Umberto standing nervously. He has a stricken look on his face and is ashen pale.

“I thought I told you I didn’t want to be disturbed for the rest of the evening,” I growl.

He nods but stays rooted in place. “Sir, I wouldn’t have woken you if it wasn’t an emergency.”

“What’s the fucking emergency?”

“The stash house has been hit.”

Blood paints the sidewalk, mingled with cracked bricks and shattered windowpanes. Like a war zone in the aftermath of a gunfight, it is eerily empty and quiet. Not a soul moves, other than smoke caught in the wind.

I hold my breath as I step over a dead body and duck underneath the crumbling awning. The smell of burnt hair and coppery blood intensifies the deeper into the place I go.

I was just a few hours shy of being caught up in this. It could have been my body here along with the others littering the concrete floor. But the thought brings me no relief. I am the don—that means these people are my people. These deaths are my deaths. This attack on my property and my business is every bit as painful as an attack on my own self.

Someone is going to fucking pay for this.

But who? How? When? And most of all—why?

I force myself to swallow back those questions and more. There will be time for answers later. For now, I need to see the extent of the damage.

I keep walking, moving slowly so as to not leave behind any DNA for the police to find. Umberto and I have masks over our faces, gloves on our hands, and wrappings on our shoes. No need to add intrusive police investigators to my life. Lord knows I have enough to deal with already.

But it is my duty to come here and see what has been done to the Bianci empire.

My initial assessment is complete and total loss. Every step I take inward confirms that.

And when I round the corner and pass through the door that Roberto took me through earlier today, I see that I was correct.

The entire storeroom is a charred mess of melted plastic, destroyed computers, and crates still burning and emitting a foul-smelling smoke. The back wall is blown out completely. And the bodies ...

There are so many dead. Earlier this afternoon, they were all buzzing around, the efficient hands of my organization at work. Now, they are disfigured by gunfire and utter savagery. I want to look away so badly, but I cannot. This is my duty. This is what I was born to do.

So I survey the scene. As my eyes pass over each one of the dead, I force myself to look them in the eye—or what's left of the eye—and acknowledge their loss, thank them for their service, and bid them goodbye.

But when my eyes rest on the body propped up against the door just to my right, I freeze in place.

Roberto's chest is a yawning gap of blood and broken bone. He looks barely human, more like something out of a horror movie. His face is unmarred. I can see the firm set of resolve in his jaw. He went out like a fighter. I wonder grotesquely how long it took him to die. I pray he did not suffer. That—more than the dozens of other deaths in here, more than the millions of dollars of product lost to this attack—is what ignites me.

I turn to Umberto. "What happened?"

"We don't know yet. But whoever attacked knew exactly how to do it. None of our guard posts were alerted, and they chose the perfect point of entry. This had to be an inside job, sir."

I grind my teeth and point at Roberto. "That was a good fucking man, Umberto. He did not betray us." I sweep my hand around. "These were all good people. Don't tarnish their memories like that, you son of a bitch."

He holds up his hands in a mea culpa gesture. "I apologize, sir. I meant no offense. I intended only to relay you my analysis of the attack."

I realize that I have my fists clenched like I'm ready to strike him in the face. How many allies do I have left? I ought not to intimidate this man into abandoning me too. Forcing myself to breathe, I let my hand drop down by my side.

I turn towards Roberto and walk over to him. I feel stiff and robotic, like I have to consciously think, "Step forward with your left foot. Now, with your right. Bend down. Kneel. Breathe. Breathe."

I raise a hand and gently touch his cheek with a single leather-gloved finger. "I am sorry, old friend," I whisper to him. He can't hear me, but for some reason it feels massively important that I tell him this. "You didn't die for nothing. I'll find who did this to you."

"Sir?" Umberto's voice cuts through my haze. "I can hear sirens. We need to leave now."

I look at Roberto for one second longer. I want to memorize his face. Another loss in a sea of dead bodies, but this one hurts almost as bad as Sergio's did.

The sound of sirens in the distance floats through to me. Sighing, I rise to my feet. Then, Umberto and I slip out of the cavernous hole in the back of the facility and disappear into the night.

I as good as killed those men myself.

That's all I can think as I stumble back into the castle, leaving Umberto in the garage.

Their blood is on my hands. I let them down. I am the don and they are dead now; that makes it my fault.

I have to do something about it. I have to act—anything is better than nothing. *If you stop, you die.* That's what I told Audrey that night. That's what I've told myself every day since.

If I stop for even a moment—stop doing what my father bred me to do, stop moving forward—then the cumulative weight of everything I have been outrunning will kill me. My demons will kill me. The ghost of Audrey's memory will kill me. I was dreaming of her when Umberto awoke me, and now I cannot shake her.

She is gone, Vito, I tell myself. *You will never see her again.* I want to believe that.

But when I saw Milaya, it was like she had come back to me.

They have become one and the same in my eyes. Milaya is Audrey and Audrey is Milaya and both of them haunt me every time I slow down for even the briefest of pauses. I close my eyes and I see Milaya, I see Audrey, I see my father, I see Sergio, I see Roberto. All of those ghosts are crowding around me now, because at long last, I can't keep running.

I trip and keel over and strike my head against the cobblestones of the hallway. I can feel the skin break immediately and feel the hot burst of blood. I see stars. And I fall right back into the dream that I thought I had left behind.

Father opened the door and let it swing inwards. I saw the blood first. I heard the pained moans second.

My jaw threatened to drop, but I knew better than to display such weakness in front of my father. I turned to look at him and swallowed hard. I could feel my Adam's apple ride up and down in my throat with the effort. "What is this, Father?" I asked.

He nodded solemnly. "It's time for you to cut your weaknesses loose, Vito. Now step in and finish the job."

He put a crudely made shiv in my hand, pushed me forward, and shut the door behind me.

Audrey was tied to the chair with thick rope. Her mouth had been gagged, but her eyes spoke to me. She had the red imprint of a slap across her face and crusted blood drying at one corner of her mouth. Someone had backhanded her hard. I took one hesitant step forward, sweaty hand slipping on the taped grip of the razor-sharp shiv Father had handed me in the hallway, and saw the telltale imprint in the middle of the slap mark—the imprint of the ring Father always wore.

How many times had I seen that mark on my own face? If I was too slow in training, or too forgetful, or too soft—boom, a strike like lightning, and that brief delay between the shock of realizing I'd been hit and the pain setting in.

I was seventeen. Not yet a man, but no longer a boy. I was staring into the terrified eyes of the girl I loved, who was roped to a rickety chair in a dimly lit basement in a godforsaken castle run by a psychotic killer.

It was my job to end her life tonight.

"I'm sorry," I whispered to her. Her eyes bulged. I tried to adjust my grip, but it kept slipping. I was sweating like a pig, cold sweat, rivulets of it streaming down my face and neck like I'd just run a marathon. The sleep was still crusted in the corners of my eyes, but I was wide awake.

Audrey wailed wordlessly against the gag in her mouth. The sound broke my heart. I couldn't do this. Almost two decades of training for a moment like this and I was failing. I knew my father would be waiting upstairs for me to come back and show him her life's blood drenching my hands.

I reached forward to loosen the gag. Then I stopped.

If she said so much as a single word to me, I would shatter like glass. I couldn't let that happen.

I let my hand fall to my side. God, she looked beautiful, even in the flickering fluorescent lights overhead. Even with terror in her eyes. She was so precious to me, so flawless, so utterly unlike anything else in my dark and broken life.

Father knew that, of course. Why else would I be here? "Cut your weaknesses loose," *he'd said to me. What he meant was,* "Burn up the last of you that feels."

Time passed meaninglessly. Seconds, minutes, hours, days—it didn't matter. I stood there in that cramped little room and stared into the eyes of the only girl I'd ever loved and tried to will myself to do what had to be done.

But I couldn't do it. I didn't care that this was the final test, the only way forward. I didn't care that my destiny was one quick swipe of the knife away.

So, on that hideous, horrible night, I did the one good thing I'd ever done in my miserable life. I bent down in front of her and said in a frantic whisper, "Listen to me very closely: I'm going to get you out of here. When I do, you need to run. Run as far as you can go and never, ever come back. Get out of the state, out of the country. Change your name and cut your hair. I can't give you any money or any help and I can never talk to you again. Okay?"

She stared at me and said nothing. Her eyes burned with emotions I refused to decipher.

"Nod so I know you understand," I ordered.

She hesitated for a long moment before she nodded. She was crying. I didn't realize until much later that there were tears streaming down my face too.

I turned and pushed open the door. The hallway outside was empty and dark. Returning to Audrey, I cut the bonds that secured her to the chair, but I left the zip-tie handcuffs and gag in place. I didn't want to take the chance of hearing her voice again.

I grabbed her and pulled her in my wake as we raced silently down the hallway. There was a small service entrance that led to a rear driveway. Thirteen years later, I would bring Milaya's unconscious body down the same route.

We pushed open the door together. The night outside yawned like a chasm. I didn't cross the threshold. "Run," I told her once more. "And keep running. Never forget: if you stop, you die." Then I slammed the door shut before I could change my mind.

That was the last time I ever saw Audrey.

When she was gone, I cut open a careful slit in my thigh and let the blood spill over my hands. Then I went upstairs to tell Father that the job had been completed. I showed him my stained hands as proof.

He looked at them, nodded slowly, then looked into my eyes.

"You've done well, son," he told me.

I never wanted to hear those words from him ever again.

"Vito!" A voice cuts through the haze, slicing my dream open and revealing it as nothing more than ash on the wind.

I open my eyes blearily and take in my surroundings. I'm propped up against a wall in the hallway. There is a window at the end of the hall. I can see the first rays of dawn piercing through the indigo night sky. My head aches something fierce, and when I reach up to touch the source of the pain, my fingers come away tacky with blood.

Milaya's face swims into view. Her eyes are dense with concern. "Are you okay?" she asks again.

"I ... fell ..." I say thickly. My lips aren't working right, aren't responding to my commands, so those few stumbling words are the best I can manage.

I'm not sure what's real and what's fake right now. I know my head is throbbing and my past is threatening to consume me. My father's voice and Milaya's mingle horrifically in a cacophony of things that should never be woven together. I hear him telling me, *"If you stop, you die,"* just as I hear her say, "You're hurt; you need to sit and breathe."

I try to struggle to my feet, but she presses me back down. I'm so weak with exhaustion and grief that just the gentle pressure of her hand on my chest is enough to keep me rooted to the floor. She raises my head up and slips underneath me so I can rest on her soft lap. Her touch is heavenly. It's everything I've spent almost two weeks desperately avoiding. I knew from the very beginning that if I let her touch me, everything would come crashing down.

But things have come crashing down anyway. My empire is in shambles. I am a failure as don. My family is dead; my men are dead; Roberto is dead. And I cannot even stand on my own two feet without tumbling to the ground in my own home.

So what does it matter anymore? I have already lost the war. Luka Volkov will be here tomorrow, and though the plan all along has been for us to kill him then, I realize now that it might as well be his victory parade. Because, as I sit here with my head in his daughter's lap and gaze up blearily into her shimmering hazel eyes, I understand that I have come completely undone.

I reach up to touch her face. My fingertips are rough and calloused, but even then I can still tell that her cheek is smooth. When she turns and kisses the heel of my palm, I can feel the gentle heat of her lips.

"You have to sit and breathe," she whispers again.

"I can't ..." I murmur hazily. "If you stop, you die."

"What?"

I try to say it again, but my lips don't want to work anymore. She must realize how much effort it is costing me to talk, because she just shushes me when I keep trying to speak, pressing a long, pale finger over my lips. "Shh," she says. "Just rest here until you feel better. It's okay to stop."

What happens after that is a dream of its own. We lay there for some indeterminate amount of time. I drift in and out of this world and make no effort to steer the ship of my consciousness in any particular direction. After a while, I feel motion. I start to open my eyes, but

Milaya gently closes them with her fingertips. "No," she whispers. "Just feel it."

Her hand moves down and frees me from my pants, just as she straddles me. I see only darkness, but I gasp out loud when I feel the wet warmth of her surround my manhood.

I am glad she told me to keep my eyes closed. As long as I do, I can pretend this is a dream. And if it is a dream, I don't have to fight it. Because dreams mean nothing. If this were real, it would mean everything. So I cannot let it be real. That would be the final blow.

More motion. The gentle rise and fall of her tightness around me, squeezing the soul from me. One hand of hers presses against my chest. I want so badly to wrap my fingers around her wrist and feel her pulse. But that would be too real. I keep my palms flat against the flagstones of the floor as she rides me.

The only sound in the hallway is the short, sharp panting coming from both of us. Her hair tickles my face. The edges of this dream and my reality are blurred, erased.

I am suddenly aware of a subtext to this unreal moment. Like realizing that you've been eavesdropping on a conversation between strangers without ever intending it. She is coaxing me to stop, to let go. How many years have I spent raging against that very instinct? Every fiber in my being has been trained not to do that. I cannot stop. I cannot let go.

But that's exactly what she is telling me to do. With her body, with her touch, with her scent, she is urging me, pleading with me.

And when she delicately plucks my hand from the stones by my side and kisses it once more, I can no longer resist.

I burst into her, groaning and heaving. She slows down, dismounts, curls against my side. I do not open my eyes.

Not long afterwards, the dream finally subsumes reality, like a drawing in the sand at the beach washed away by the tide.

I don't remember what happens after that.

24

MILAYA

I feel like I've entered a dream world. At dawn this morning, I was cradling Vito's bleeding head in the dark hallway. By sunset, I am standing on one side of a door, preparing myself to walk through and talk my father out of a war. I don't even know how to process everything that has happened in the interim.

Just a little while ago, I was curled up in my bed, sleeping through the afternoon with weird and uncomfortable thoughts racing through my head. Mateo had knocked on my door and opened it. "Wake up," he'd said. "It is time for you to do something for us."

"Ugh," I'd snapped, "how many times are we going to do this stupid ritual? *'Get up, Milaya,' 'Wake up, Milaya,' 'Come with me, Milaya.'* Do you all draw straws for who gets to annoy me on any given day?" I knew I sounded childish and stupid. Petulant, even. I was acting as if I didn't remember anything that had transpired between me and these men since they first brought me back to this place. Mateo must have sensed that, because he didn't even acknowledge my petty whining. He just waited for me to get up and get dressed. When I'd done that—reluctantly—he'd led me through the great room and to a hall I hadn't yet explored. He turned to me just before we entered.

"Your father is in that room," he told me, pointing to an innocuous door off to my right.

My blood ran cold. "What?"

Again, he didn't repeat himself.

It felt like my heart was pounding a million beats per minute. Why hadn't they told me anything before now? What did they expect me to do?

I started to ask Mateo those questions—"What do you—I mean, how am I supposed to—" But for the third time, he stayed silent.

Because he knew damn well that I already knew the answers.

It had all become so crystal-clear last night, in the hallway with Vito. Vito must have fallen and hit his head or something like that, because when I rounded the corner on my way back to my room after the wine cellar encounter with Mateo, he was lying on the floor, bleeding and groaning like he was having a nightmare. He kept muttering again and again, "If you stop, you die." I don't know what the hell that meant, but it was obviously significant to him, because he wouldn't stop saying it.

We fell asleep there in the hallway after he finally calmed down. I was still drunk from the bottle of wine I shared with Mateo, so it was easy to slip off into a deep and dreamless sleep.

When I woke up, Vito was gone.

There was a trail of blood leading up the hallway and through the door of his bedroom. I thought for a long time about following it. I went up to it and rested my cheek against the wood. I imagined that I could hear his breathing on the other side, though the door was far too thick for that to actually be the case. I just wanted to know that he was alive. I wanted him to know that he could stop and breathe if he wanted to, if he needed to.

Of all the brothers, the darkness is coiled most tightly in Vito's heart. One by one, each of them has come to me and I've taken some of it from them. Vito has tried so hard to refuse that. He thinks he's a martyr. He thinks that he is the only one who has suffered, and he is ashamed of that, like it marks him as lesser- than. I want him to know that that's not true.

We've got sins. All of us. The blood that runs in my veins is its own kind of sin. I saw years ago what kind of man my father was, what kind of things he did. And I chose to ignore it. That's the sin I have to live with.

But now, as the sun dies in the window outside and my father waits on the other side of this door, I have a chance to fix it. I can save lives.

I grip the handle and push it open.

My father is facing away from me, looking through a window onto the garden below. He is wearing a suit—the dark navy one I like so much. He turns to face me when he hears the door open. When our eyes lock, he stiffens.

"*Lubimaya*," he breathes. "My love."

I want to do a million things at once in that moment. In all those dark days and nights in the dungeon cell, how badly did I dream of this: Daddy coming to rescue his little girl and save the day. He's been my hero for as long as I can remember, and I thought that this would be no different. *I can handle anything you need*, he told me during that phone call in the parking lot outside the boxing studio. That feels like lifetimes ago. I believed that he would handle this. It was only a matter of time.

And, sure enough, here he is. He hasn't changed. The lines in his face are as rigid and proud as they've always been. The steel in his eyes is exactly the same.

But I have changed.

I'm not the same girl who was dragged out of a hotel room two weeks ago. I'm not the same daughter he once knew. I am not Milly van der Graaf, nerdy college girl.

I am Milaya, princess of the Volkov Bratva. I mean something to the Bianci family too, though I have no idea what kind of title would be appropriate for that tangled, sordid little arrangement. I am a woman. I am an adult. I am myself.

And I need to make things right.

"Dad," I say back. He opens his arms to welcome me into a hug, but I stay rooted in place. He must see the set in my jaw or the look in my eye. He ought to know that look—he taught it to me, after all.

I feel a deep kind of sadness, to go along with the rest of the cocktail of emotions simmering inside my heart right now. Sadness for the loss of innocence, maybe. I think back to that spa party, how funny it was to put a mud face mask on my father. And then how heartbreaking it was to see those cucumbers lying forlorn on the concrete floor. I think of the night I saw him beating that man senseless in his office with Uncle Alexei.

I'm no longer a little girl who loves her father unconditionally. This isn't the rescue I dreamed of. This is something I never could have prepared for.

"What have they done to you?" he asks. He steps forward to cross the distance between us and raises one hand as if to stroke my cheek. But when I flinch, he freezes before letting his hand fall to his side. "What have they told you, my sweetness?"

It takes all the willpower I can muster to say, "We need to talk, Dad."

He nods slowly as he studies my face. "Okay," he says. "Let's sit."

We sit down at the table set before us. It's just two chairs and a small, ornate wooden tea table. The evening sky is gorgeous, and from this vantage point, we can see for miles. The sun's pinks and oranges are skewed into abstract pastels by the Los Angeles smog. I want to frame the sky and put it in a museum.

I have so much in my heart I want to say to him, but I don't know where to begin. He must sense my uncertainty, because he clears his throat and says, "I am sorry it took me so long to get to you, my daughter. I looked everywhere."

"I know," I say, tears threatening to crack at the edge of my voice. I don't doubt for a second that he did. I don't doubt for a second that he loves me. Those things have never been the issue. If anything, they're the problem.

Because it's what he does in order to safeguard that love that has brought us here. The lies. The blood. The bodies carried out under cover of darkness. It can't continue like that. One way or another, this has to come to an end.

He starts to say something else, but I hold up a hand to cut him off. "You killed so many people, Daddy," I whisper. I'm crying now. I can't hold them back anymore. Tears are streaming down my face and my voice is choked and pathetic. But I don't give a shit. Let him see me cry.

That's the problem with all these men—my father and the brothers alike. They're all broken, numb, shrouded in darkness. Somewhere along the way, someone told all of them that to feel anything is a failure. But *I* feel things. I feel enough for all of them.

And I'm sick of being the only one who does.

Dad doesn't say anything for a long time. My choked sobs quiet down as I regain control of myself. He looks out the window again, his face betraying nothing. "I did what I had to do for you and your mother," he whispers.

"No." I shake my head firmly. "We never asked you to kill for us. We never needed you to hurt people on our behalf. You didn't do anything for me and Mom. You did it because you wanted to."

It's so hard to read him. He's always had a great poker face. But as I watch with firm resolve despite my tears, I swear I can see the mask slipping a little bit. There is a human in him—somewhere deep down inside.

"You're not wrong," he admits finally. "But you're not quite right either. I think the truth is that I did what I've done because it's what I've always done. It's what my father did. It's what he raised me to do."

I blink. It's like I am seeing double. The Bianci brothers and my father are birds of a feather, men cut from the same cloth. They are broken men who are sons of broken men. And if something doesn't intervene to stop them, they will have sons and turn them into broken men too. I think of all the portraits lining the walls of the castle and I realize just how far back this chain stretches. I remember the dusty photo albums shoved in a deep corner of my father's office back home. His dad and grandfather and all the men in his family going back generations. I always wondered why those men looked so grim-faced and brooding. Now, as I see it in my own father and in the faces of the men I now belong to, I understand. It's all so clear. So wrong.

But it's not irreversible. I have to do what I stepped into this room to do.

"They're going to hurt you, Dad," I whisper. "Because of what you did."

He shakes his head. "I would never let that happen, *lubimaya.* I would never abandon you like that."

"It doesn't matter what you would let happen, Dad. You killed their family. They want revenge."

He scoffs. "I have troops waiting. If I don't come out, they will come in." He cups my face in his hands. "I will protect you, Milaya."

A lone tear chases after the others on my face. He doesn't understand. He doesn't see that their way of life will only lead to more bloodshed and more bodies. How many lives ruined is enough? I think of Anastasia, of the Frat Stars, of the other countless, faceless victims that the brothers and my father have alluded to over the years. War begets war. Blood begets blood. Broken men beget broken men. It's a vicious cycle, spinning endlessly into the future.

"I wish I could believe that," I tell him. "I really do. But I can't rely on you to keep me safe anymore."

I push back from the table and stand up. As I do, the door swings open to reveal Mateo, Leo, Dante, and Vito standing there. They file in one after the other. They really are beautiful, I notice, grim and stark like avenging angels. Their eyes burn in that rainbow of colors.

My father stands. "You never intended to negotiate," he says softly.

"No," Vito answers. "We intended to execute."

He nods. "That is a mistake, Bianci."

"It is inevitable, Volkov."

I'm crying freely now. The tears drip from my jaw onto my bare feet. Everything is so fucked up. I wanted so badly to fix it. Maybe I was wrong though. Maybe none of this is fixable at all. This is just how the world works, perhaps, and I'm powerless to do anything about it.

"Come with us," Mateo says. He steps out of the way of the door. My father marches through, head held high. Mateo, Leo, and Dante all follow him out.

Vito turns to look at me just before he leaves. "Are you coming?" he asks.

I wish I could say no. I wish I could stay here and cry by myself, the way I want to. I want to cry for innocence lost, for lies revealed, for the ugliness of the world being shoved into my face.

But I can't say no.

So I nod and follow the Bianci brothers to my father's execution, wondering the whole time: *how can I stop this?*

25

VITO

This is a moment ten years in the making.

Luka Volkov stands in front of the hearth in the great room. He is haughty and proud, as befits a man of his stature. But pride will do him no good now. He walked willingly into the lion's den. Surely he knew how this would end. How could he not? And yet he came anyway. Perhaps he is not the brilliant tactician that the legends made him out to be. Perhaps he is just like my father—overcome in the end by his own obstinacy.

I wonder if he has a trick yet to play though. The room in which he spoke with Milaya was bugged of course, and we heard what he said. *"I have troops waiting. If I don't come out, they will come in."* Does he know that we have soldiers stationed all in and around the castle, nestled amongst the trees and the turrets, standing at the ready should anything unexpected unfold? He must know. But all is quiet for now. All is still. There is only the crackling of the ever-present fire and the creak of a castle that has seen so much bloodshed and is about to see yet more.

Ten years have passed from the first seeds of this war until now, when they have matured into full bloom. Ten years since we found my uncle's body dumped like a cut of beef on the front steps of this very building. Ten years since I watched my father fall to his knees at his brother's side and cry to the heavens for mercy. It was the only time I saw his hardened shell crack.

And though I stand at the tail end of ten years of whispered knifings, surreptitious struggles in dark alleyways across the country—the normal tic and tac of power struggles between the men who seek to rule the underworld—one thought stands out above all the rest of the din in my mind:

I don't give a fuck.

I don't care about any of it. I don't care about being don or the boundaries of my empire or the politics of American crime lords. I don't care about my money, my status, my reputation.

All I care about is the memory of Milaya's lips pressing against the back of my hand. That hazy, half-remembered moment is the only thing that has made my heart stir since the night I set Audrey free and told her to run.

I haven't stopped since that night. I kept doing what I was told, training to become the man I am today. And what has it earned me? Nothing but pain. I close my eyes and see Roberto's dead, gaping face and I feel a clench of agony seize hold of my innards. Countless good men have died. As don, my throne rests upon that heap of bodies. They died for me, for what I represent. And as far as I am concerned, that means they died needlessly.

I wonder if Luka Volkov has ever had the thoughts I am having now. He has ruled his corner of the world with an iron fist for nearly twenty-five years. I search his face, but he betrays nothing. In fact, he hasn't said a word since we brought him in here. He shows no fear; he does not tremble or beg for mercy. Does that make him a fool or a hero? I can't fucking decide.

The time for that is long gone, however. Whether I did them enthusiastically or not, the things that brought us here on this collision course were done. There can be no turning back.

"Luka Volkov," I begin in the same formal tone that my father used to start council meetings for as long as I can remember. "You stand before us as an enemy. You wear the blood of my uncle, my father, and my brother on your hands. As payment for their deaths, it falls to me to claim your life as forfeit." My brothers are arranged on either side of me. None of them blink or say a word. Each of us has a hand on the guns tucked into the back of our pants or holstered at our sides. When I issue the command, Luka Volkov will perish like a dog.

This is the moment for him to ask for an alternative. We will not give it to him, of course. The laws of our family dictate what happens next. But he owes it to his daughter, to his wife, to his empire to ask, doesn't he?

And yet, he does not ask. He does not beg.

Instead, he laughs.

"You don't know what the fuck you're talking about," he snarls. "I didn't kill your family. I don't give a shit about your family." He points at Milaya, standing a few yards off to the side behind us and looking like this is the worst day of her life. "I came here to rescue my daughter. Not to pay for your imaginary accusations. If you kill me, you will all die too. You would be a fool not to realize that."

Mateo speaks up. "Do you think we would let that happen?"

Luka's eyes shift smoothly from my face to Mateo's as he answers, "I don't think you have a choice, Bianci."

"Enough of this!" Dante interrupts. He rips his gun out from the back of his pants and swivels it up to aim at Luka's head.

To his credit, Luka doesn't flinch. He stares calmly down the barrel of the gun. "That would be a very grave mistake," he says.

"Dante," I warn. My younger brother is fidgeting with rage and aggression like an angry dog held back only by a thin chain leash. He is moments away from snapping.

The tension is unbearable for all of us. Even Leo looks uncomfortable. As well-trained as we all are, some moments are too much to swallow with ease. It feels like we are all choking, suffocating on grief and rage and confusion.

Dante reluctantly lets his gun hand fall back down by his side and steps backwards to rejoin our semicircle pinning Luka against the fireplace.

Satisfied that we have not yet reached our boiling point, I turn my attention back to Luka. "How can you say you are not responsible for the deaths of my family?" I ask him.

"Your father was a sick man," he tells me. "Twisted and broken, long before you were old enough to realize that truth. But I did not kill him. I did not kill your uncle, either, though I wish I had. He came to me years ago to broker a deal betraying your father. I did what a good don should do: beat him and returned him to the man who raised you for punishment. I had no interest in a coup. I was content with my life. With my family. I did not want a war."

"Bullshit," I say. I meant for it to be a seething roar, but somewhere between my brain and my lips, the message was confused. It comes out instead as the disbelieving gasp of a man who is finally seeing things in a clear light for the first time. "I saw my father find his brother's body. I was there. We all were. We saw his grief."

Luka shakes his head sadly. "You saw the playacting of a psychopath. Your father was the one who killed his brother. I had nothing to do with it."

"Bullshit," I say again. "That's not right. That's not true."

The Volkov don shrugs. "It is the unvarnished truth. What you do with it is your choice. But," he continues, "if you are going to kill me, do it quickly. If not, I would like to return home with my daughter."

I can sense Milaya's presence in the corner, but internally, I am reeling. My world has been battered again and again over the last few days. The man standing in front of me does not seem to be lying. But if he truly came for nothing more than to retrieve his daughter, why would he attack my stash house? Why would he kill my father and brother to begin with? Why would he start a war he clearly has no interest in fighting?

It can't be true.

"No," I say. I raise my gun and point it at him. "You are lying. For that and for your other crimes, you will die now."

I unlock the safety and set my sights right between his eyes. Around me, my brothers do the same. Four guns aimed to kill the man who destroyed our family. At long last, we are united in purpose and intention. Brothers again.

My finger rests on the trigger. It takes five pounds of pressure to fire a bullet. I apply four. One pound separating Luka Volkov from the end of his life. "On my command," I tell my brothers. "Three. Two. One …"

Right then, the windows explode.

26

VITO

I learned long ago that it takes two hundred and fifty milliseconds for the average person to respond to visual stimulus, one hundred and seventy milliseconds to respond to auditory stimulus, and one hundred and fifty milliseconds to respond to tactile stimulus.

But my father and Antoni did not train us to be average.

All of which is to say that I am already moving less than a second after the explosion blows all the windows along the northeastern wall inwards in a hailstorm of deadly jagged glass shards. I spring forward, jam my gun into Luka's ribs, and yank him with me. Over my shoulder, I see Mateo doing the same with Milaya. Dante and Leo are providing covering fire, shooting at the men in tactical suits rappelling in through the gaps where the windows once were.

We move backwards as a unit towards the tapestry hanging on the southwestern wall, the one that leads to the dungeon. We clear the fifty-four yards between the hearth and the tapestry in less than a minute as all hell breaks loose around us. I feel a bullet graze my calf and I roar in pain but I do not stop.

If you stop, you die.

I once believed that to be true, the one true thing in a life full of shadows and lies. Milaya's kiss changed everything. It made me question things I never knew could be questioned.

But right now, it is as true as it ever was. If we stop, we die.

So we run.

We burst through the tapestry and do not stop. Mateo leads the way, Milaya behind him. I force Luka to run ahead of me, following in their footsteps, while Dante and Leo take the rear guard. The sound of gunfire, bursting flash bangs, and pounding boots doubles and triples in intensity in our wake. We're trying to stay ahead of the storm, descending the stairs five and six steps at a time, leaping down as far as we can manage again and again. I collide with the thin metal handrail dozens of times, but I do not feel that pain, nor the pain from the bloody furrow etched in my calf by the errant bullet.

Down we go, until at long last we reach the dungeon. Leo, the last one down, slams shut the door and locks it. "It won't hold for long," he says grimly. "I saw C4 on their belts."

"Your men came prepared," Dante remarks to Luka.

My blood runs cold when Luka draws in a deep, ragged breath, then straightens up and says, "Those were not my men."

We all fall silent at once. I think each of us had assumed the same thing—that the Volkov Bratva troops were making a last-ditch effort to rescue their leader from surefire death. How they got past our own defenses, I haven't the faintest fucking idea, not that it matters right now. But if they aren't Luka's soldiers ... then who the hell are they?

"What?"

"Those were not my men," he repeats. "My men were stationed primarily to the southeast, and told not to enter unless they received explicit instructions. Whoever attacked just now, it wasn't me."

I look to my brothers in turn. Even Mateo looks dumbstruck.

"He's lying," Dante declares boldly as the uncomfortable silence thickens.

"I have not lied since I set foot in your home," Luka answers quietly. "I see no reason to start doing it now."

"Fuck," Leo snarls. He glances up to Mateo. "So who is it?"

"I don't know," he replies grimly.

My thoughts drift elsewhere as they descend into a harried discussion about the various enemies who would have the balls to launch a full-scale attack on the heart of our turf. None of the answers seem plausible. The Albanians don't have the muscle; the Cubans don't have the balls; the Mexicans don't give a damn about what happens north of the border as long as they get their money. One by one, they cross off potential assailants.

The whole time they talk, I try to ignore the thought that's building in my brain like an underground geyser, threatening to erupt.

"The Irish wouldn't fucking *dare,*" Dante is arguing when I raise a hand to cut him off. Everyone looks to me.

"I know who it was," I say.

Everyone looks at me.

I clear my throat. "It was the biker."

"The bikers?" Mateo asks in disbelief. "Not a chance. We are on good terms with the Diablos MC. Umberto did a stint with them, remember?"

"Not the *bikers,*" I correct. "The biker. The violet-eyed one."

Quickly, I explain to them what happened yesterday. The pursuit, the encounter in the alley, how I thought my life was over, how it all ended not with a bang but with a whimper.

Only now as I explain it do I realize that the biker is what ties everything together. He knew my vehicle. He knew my route. He knew where I would go to hide from a pursuer. And if he knew all that—if he knew me down to my bones—surely he knew enough to attack our stash house and now, our castle.

"Who the fuck could he be working for?" Leo asks.

I shake my head. It's all so fucking clear now. The biker runs through it all like a violet-tinged thread.

"He is not working for anyone," I whisper. "They are working for him."

I glance up to my brothers, who all look slack-jawed. For the first time in weeks, since I took the throne, they see me as the don. The man in charge. It is too little, too late though. None of that matters anymore.

"Then who is he?"

They all know the answer before I say a word. But I have to say it anyway, though I don't want to. If I say it out loud, it will become true.

I wish I had another choice. Too bad I don't.

"It's Sergio," I say, my voice barely audible. "He's alive."

Dante staggers like he's been hit. He slumps against a wall for support. I feel his pain as if it were my own. Sergio was his twin, his shadow. If I feel like something essential has been scraped out of my soul, then I can only imagine how greatly Dante is suffering as it is all laid out clearly. The truth is unavoidable and it has wicked, jagged edges. In all my time as his brother, I have never seen the roiling fire in his eyes extinguished. But now, as I look at him, I swear that the lights go out. He is retreating inwards. I fear we will never bring him back from the chasm into which he is falling.

How could we have avoided this? I have never once believed in fate, not since the day I shut the door on Audrey and turned my face back towards the shadows of the life I was born into. In that moment, I had what felt like a choice. I chose wrong.

But fate believed in me, it seems. It brought us to Milaya. It brought her here. And like a poison, she has seeped into each of us. I know without having to ask that she has corrupted my brothers' minds the same way she has corrupted mine. Whether with a kiss or a fuck, she owns all of us now. She is an addiction. One that is killing us piece by piece.

This is all her fault.

She and her fucking father did this to us. They turned Sergio somehow. Luka might not have personally fired the bullet that killed my father, but he has played us all like marionettes from the beginning. We thought we were the ones making the aggressive move when we kidnapped his daughter, but it turns out that that too—like so many other tactical errors I've made—seems to have been merely part of his plan.

All of which leads to me to one inevitable conclusion: both of the Volkovs need to die.

Once upon a time, I would have killed them both right here and right now. Two quick squeezes of the trigger would end this chapter. What would happen after that, I don't know, but it would not matter.

That ending is not enough though. They need to suffer for what they've done. To suffer as I have suffered, as my brothers have suffered. I want each of them to watch the other one die. I want it to be slow and agonizing so they can feel what I feel—a pain that only death will ease.

But when we hear the clatter of boots coming down the spiral staircase, I know that I will have to delay our retribution a little longer.

"We have to move," I order.

Mateo points to a door on the far right-hand side of the torture chamber. "Into the catacombs," he says.

I nod, and we move.

Leo unlocks the door with the key around his neck and we all race in, with Luka and Milaya forced to the front. Mateo barks out directions —"Left! Straight! Down!"—and we venture deeper into the guts of the castle, as Sergio's troops batter at the door we locked behind us.

It gets colder and colder the further we go. The hallways shrink, until I'm running hunched over and praying I don't knock myself unconscious on a low overhang. Stone floors give way to dirt that muffles our footsteps, so that all I can hear is our labored breathing.

At long last, we emerge from the smallest corridor yet into a cavern. The stone in here is rough and unfinished. But we can stand now at least, underneath a ceiling that is perhaps fifteen or twenty feet tall.

These catacombs were made long ago as a refuge for an assault precisely like this one. There is a door on the other end of the rectangular-shaped room that will spit us out into the scrubby patch of wilderness on the steep back side of the hill on which our castle is perched. From there, we will find a way to one of the safe houses we keep around the city and decide our next move.

"There," I point towards the door. "Go that way." Luka hesitates until I point the gun at him. "Now."

Sighing, he turns and heads where I have indicated.

But we all freeze when the door opens before we are even halfway across the space ...

... and Sergio enters.

He looks exactly the same as the day he died. The shortest of us, though his facial features are much the same as my own. Same nose, same jaw, same dark hair swept backwards. His eyes are the violet I remember so well, the same violet I saw on the biker when he stared at me in the alley.

"Sergio," I say, still not really believing that all this is actually happening.

"Vito," he responds, inclining his head. Out of context, this would look like any other conversation between us. Innocuous, meaningless, nearly forgettable, were it not for the troops I can hear hurrying down the halls, headed for us.

"We need to run."

He laughs. "That would be wise, brother. But I'm afraid I cannot let you."

I nod slowly and wipe a drop of sweat from my forehead. A beat passes. "You followed me."

"You are very predictable," he answers. "Every move played out like you were reading from a script. It almost took the fun out of things, you know. And you—" he turns to face Luka. "You are just as easy to manipulate. You thought bringing troops here would save you? They died like dogs, Russian," he snarls. "I left their bodies in the woods to rot."

Luka's jaw tightens and I curse inwardly. I'd been holding out hope that the Volkov soldiers would intervene in whatever the fuck this is that is happening. No such luck.

I swivel my gaze back to Sergio. "This isn't you, Sergio."

His face folds into an ugly sneer, one I've never seen on him before. "What the fuck would you know about that?" he hisses.

I'm stunned. Where did this venom come from? This isn't my brother. I *know* Sergio. I grew up with him. I practically fucking raised him. This man is not him. The angry barbarian sneering at me is something else altogether.

It just doesn't add up. There is something missing here, an X-factor necessary to explain the most shocking betrayal of my life.

Except that it's not actually missing. It's standing right here in front of me, in the form of a pale, dark-haired girl and her father.

The soldiers are coming. I can hear them growing closer, their booted feet pounding into the stones. I'm not sure what I expect from Sergio, but he says nothing, merely looks at each of us with those vivid eyes.

"We need to run," I say again, more to myself than anyone else.

Sergio withdraws a gun from a holster on his belt and levels it at me. "Like I said, I'm afraid I cannot let you do that."

My own gun is still in my hand. I know I'm a faster shot than Sergio. I could get him if I wanted to. I could put a bullet between his eyes and end all this right now.

Or could I? Would killing my own brother end this?

No, I don't think so. He isn't the problem.

I turn my gun towards Luka.

"You poisoned him," I accuse.

Luka's eyes narrow. "What?"

"You poisoned my brother. You bribed him, hurt him, coerced him into this."

"What the hell are you talking about, son?"

I roar so loud that it shakes the walls, "I'm not your fucking son!"

Luka's hands are up in front of him as he backs slowly away. It's the first time he's looked afraid since he arrived at our doorstep, alone and unarmed. I savor that look. I was taught long ago to seek that look out wherever I could find it. It was how my father ruled, and it is how I intend to rule from now on too. I know fear when I see it. And right now, fear is stamped in Luka Volkov's face.

"Vito!" Milaya's voice cuts through the growing red tide of fury clouding my eyes. I keep my gun pointed at Luka, but I look at her. Off to my left, I'm dimly aware of Sergio watching proceedings with an expression of curiosity on his face. "Vito, stop!"

"Stay out of it," I snarl.

She closes the distance between us and tries to grab my arm. Before she can, I backhand her hard. The sound of flesh striking flesh rings out. She stumbles backwards, stunned, one hand holding her cheek. When she pulls it away, I see the imprint on her face—the same one I saw on Audrey's face that night. A red bloom, studded in the middle with the mark of the ring I wear.

The ring of the don.

The soldiers are almost here. Their footsteps sound like thunder. I feel their approach just as much as I hear it. *Boom boom boom.* We are running out of time.

But maybe escaping is not the right idea. Maybe this is as far as fate intended for me to get. Like meteors hurtling through space, perhaps the Volkovs and I have been charted on a collision course that was always meant to end violently. To end here and now in a fiery crash.

So be it.

If you stop, you die.

Maybe it is simply my time to stop then.

I close my eyes and squeeze off two shots.

27

MILAYA

Everything happens so fast.

Vito is pointing the gun at my dad. I'm screaming wordlessly, helplessly, my face still raw from where he slapped me. I close my eyes; I can't bear to look. The gun fires once, twice ...

... and two bodies hit the ground.

Then the door we came through bursts open and soldiers come pouring in. I open my eyes to see my father lying crumpled maybe fifteen feet away from me. And, up on the ledge leading out of this cavern into the Los Angeles night, I see the body of Sergio.

Vito shot both of them.

What the fuck is happening?

I don't have any time to think though, because there are bullets crisscrossing the air like deadly hornets. I run screaming over to my dad. There is a dark red rose in his upper left chest where the bullet hit him. He coughs. I scream again. My head is filled with the sound of my own horrified voice.

"Dad! Dad!"

His eyes flutter open.

He's alive. Barely, and maybe not for much longer, but somehow, he's alive.

I pick him up and loop an arm around him. His feet drag in the dirt, but somehow we manage to stumble towards the exit. The rectangle of night sky framed by the door is so beautiful. I never noticed before just how beautiful the sky is from up here. We're above the smog, so the stars are sparkling and brilliant.

I'm running as fast as we can, pulling my dad, using strength I never knew I had. Mateo, Leo, and Dante are all shooting back at the soldiers trying to enter. They have claimed a few lives already I see, judging by the pile of bodies at the mouth of the door.

But I don't care about that. I don't care about anything anymore. I just want to get the hell out of here.

Vito is standing stock-still. He hasn't moved since he fired the bullets that struck Sergio and my father. Sergio hasn't moved either. Maybe Vito's bullet found its intended target there. I don't plan on waiting around to find out.

We pass by Vito and for one brief moment, I almost think we're going to get away.

Then, he seizes my upper arm. "You're not going anywhere," he snarls.

"You have to let us go," I beg. "My dad's going to die."

"You're not going anywhere," he says again. An enemy bullet flies between our faces, but he doesn't seem to care.

"Vito!" comes Mateo's roar. The other three brothers have backed away through the escape route. They're calling for us to come. Vito looks at them, then back to me. With a grim set to his jaw, he drags me forward, keeping his grip on my arm.

We get through the door and push it shut behind us. Mateo and Leo immediately start stacking logs and rocks in front of it in the vain hope of buying us time. It won't do much, but I suppose it's better than nothing.

My father's breathing is ragged in my ear. The blood spilling from his wound is soaking my own shirt in grotesque torrents. I'm not even sure if he's conscious. But he's alive. That's what matters right now. That's the most important thing.

For at least a little while longer, I still have my father.

What we don't have is our freedom. Vito's eyes are burning coals in the night, like he's been possessed. Gone is the pain-stricken gentleness of the man in the hallway who let me kiss his hand and rest his head in my lap. In his place is a pure monster. There are no other words for him. He's still squeezing the shit out of my upper arm hard enough to bruise.

"You're hurting me!" I snap at him. I try to shake him loose, but he doesn't let go, doesn't say anything, just stares into the night.

"Let's go, Vito," Mateo says. He too has that thousand-yard stare on his face, though it looks less violent and more sorrowful than his older brother's. Dante is catatonic. Leo has retreated inwards.

The brothers are collapsing before my eyes. Maybe I would have cared about that a day ago. I was falling for them, I realize now. Funny how trauma can make me see things that were happening right in front of my face. But now, with everything I've seen, everything I've heard, I don't know what I feel for them. My body and heart both ache so badly. The thought of something like love or caring for another human being is so ridiculous compared to the pain I'm feeling. Not to mention the pain that lies ahead of us.

Everything is broken. I'm broken. They are broken. My father's body is broken. Whether we're all beyond repair is a question for another time. All I know is that, the longer we stay here, the fainter and fainter our hopes of a happy ending will become. We have to move. We have to go.

Most of all, I have to leave the Bianci brothers behind.

But Vito seems intent on keeping me ensnared. Even as the door explodes outwards, sending jagged shards of wood ricocheting into the night, and we all take off full-tilt running down the hill, he maintains his grip on my arm.

It's all a blur of motion and bullets, my father's ragged breathing in my ear, the spurting of his blood on my side. Through it all, the only constant is Vito's vise-like grip on my bicep. "Spread out," Vito orders, and the brothers disperse at once into the night, disappearing behind trees and turning to fire back at our pursuers.

It doesn't feel real. All of this is a bad dream, but I can't wake up. I've tried over and over again these last few weeks to wake up. I'm stuck here, caught between my dying father and the cold cruelty of a man I might have loved once. It's worse than a nightmare. It's hell on earth.

One thought runs through my mind for some inexplicable reason: did Vito intend to kill my father? It seems stupid on the face of it. Of course he did—why shoot someone in the chest if you don't intend to kill them?

But then I remember what Mateo told me about the decades of hardcore training the Bianci boys went through. Countless hours spent honing their crafts of killing and coercion. And it occurs to me that maybe Vito missed on purpose. I don't know what to make of that doubt. I choose to ignore it. My heart can't handle the implications.

It doesn't matter anymore, of course. We're all going to be dead soon. Sergio, newly risen from the dead, didn't seem interested in keeping any of us alive. These could be my last few breaths on earth. I can only hope that death will end this nightmare I've been trapped inside, but even that is uncertain just like everything else. The only thing that matters is to keep moving. Keep running. What was that thing Vito whispered to me in the hallway: *"If you stop, you die"*? It was perhaps the first honest thing he ever said to me. Not honest as in factual, but honest as in spoken from the heart. Something he truly believed. Not a lie or a con or a manipulation, but a fundamental credo, words from his soul.

Right now, it is my guiding light.

Vito is still holding me. Sergio's soldiers are still advancing. It all comes to a pinnacle, a moment where I have to act. If he keeps us trapped here, both my father and I are going to die. I have to move. I spy a rock on the ground. I reach down, scoop it up, and try to swallow the sorrow rising like a tsunami in my chest as I bring it crashing down on the back of Vito's head. He was in the middle of saying, "What are you—" before the blow landed. The words die on his lips. I feel a crunch. It takes everything in me not to puke immediately.

I feel like I'm sentencing him to death. But he made his choices. He chose to pull the trigger of his gun. He chose to pluck me out of that hotel room.

He made his bed, and now he has to lie in it.

"Come on, Dad," I say, re-shouldering his weight upon me and turning back down the hill. It's hard to fight the pull of gravity as we stumble and drag our way down. Fortunately, the moon is bright enough to light some of the path, but in the places where it's dark, I trip repeatedly over sticks, rocks, and roots, nearly crashing to the ground each time. By some miracle, I manage not to kill us both as we reach the bottom of the hill, near where it borders civilization.

The sounds of gunfire have softened and remain at the crest. I wonder if they've found the rest of the brothers or if they all escaped after parting ways. I have to force myself not to care. My feet are bleeding and bruised, each aching worse than the other, but I have to force myself not to care about that either. There is no time to stop and rest, to lick my wounds. I have to go. The only other choice is death.

Dad is slumping on me harder and harder. I don't know how much longer I can carry him. I glance over at his face and realize that he is ashen. I have to look at his wound.

Squatting down gingerly, I lean him up against the side of a building out of the light. He is soaked in blood and mumbling something nonsensical as his fingers feebly try to reach up and grab me.

"Shh, shh," I whisper to him, touching the side of his face. "Don't use your energy."

Opening his shirt with careful fingers, I peel back the fabric. When I see the bullet wound, I suck in a painful breath.

It's an ugly, ragged hole just below his collarbone. In my EMT prep course last semester, we covered gunshot wounds. This is as bad as anything we saw in a video or textbook. As best as I can tell, the bullet passed straight through, though the extent of the blood and messed-up tissue makes it hard to know for sure. If that's true, it'd be a miracle. But he's far from safe. He's lost so much blood. His lips are blue and he's having a hard time just keeping his eyes open.

He needs help. I can't help him without supplies, and even if I did have stuff, it would just be a temporary measure. He needs a hospital, surgery, a team of professionals. Not his frightened barefoot premed daughter performing slapdash surgery in some gross LA back alley.

"I'm gonna go get help, Dad, okay? Help," I repeat.

He nods, just barely, but it's enough.

I kiss him on the forehead. I've learned so much about him in the last few weeks, things no daughter ever wants to learn about her father. But he's still my dad. I still love him. I can't let him die.

Turning, I run into the city, hoping desperately that someone can hear my cries for help.

And hoping that I find a rescuer before the Bianci brothers find me.

I'm running for my life.

My lungs are screaming at me. They're filled with fire, acid, lightning. My body wants me to stop. It's practically begging at this point. I don't know how long I've been running. I don't know how much longer I'll have to run if I want to escape. I don't know if escape is even an option anymore.

The men pursuing me want me so they can break me.

They've come close to doing that already. All the days and nights I've been under lock and key in their fucked-up mansion of shadows and secrets have pushed me close to the edge. This is my last chance to get away before they finish what they've started.

They told me I'm their princess. They said that they serve me.

What a load of fucking bullshit.

For a while, they almost had me fooled. As whips turned to caresses and cruelty turned to kisses, I started to believe the lies they were feeding me. You're safer with us. We want what is best for you. We are on your side.

Lies, lies, and damned lies. I've been a pawn since the beginning.

I almost preferred the way things were at first, on those first few nights after they kidnapped me. Back then, I could understand their hatred for me. I could understand why they wanted to make me scream until my throat was raw and my voice gave out.

We were enemies, plain and simple.

But nothing is plain and simple anymore.

One thought runs through my head on repeat, a broken record: Don't stop. Don't stop. Don't stop. If I stop, I die. Simple as that. There are no second chances in this game I was born into. The men on my trail will kill me with their bare hands.

And the sickest thing of all is that part of me believes I deserve it.

Maybe I didn't choose to become an expendable piece on their chessboard. It was just my birthright. The blood in my veins is what brought me here.

But I've made all my own choices since then—that is, if choosing between death or captivity can even be considered a choice. So perhaps I've earned this ending. Perhaps I brought it all upon myself in some sick, twisted way.

The alley is long, damp with rain, cloaked with shadows. My feet pound the pavement. I don't have much longer before my body simply quits on me. It has been through so much already. I have been stretched and bent and broken during my nights in the Bianci Castle. Who knows how much fight I have left in my bones.

I can hear the breathing of the men behind me. Their footsteps are heavy and pounding. Four men, almost one thousand pounds of hot muscle and seething rage, have spread themselves out in the night to encircle and ensnare me.

Getting this far was a miracle.

And, as I'm beginning to realize, getting any farther will soon be an impossibility.

I go left, then right, winding through the labyrinth of interconnected alleyways. I run, run, run—until I'm aware that suddenly, I don't hear my pursuers anymore.

There is a rectangle of light at the end of the alleyway I've found myself in. I go towards it. My bare feet splash through puddles, crunch broken glass, step past rats and cockroaches skittering around the dark concrete. I'm bleeding, crying, sweating—but I can't slow down.

Don't stop. Don't stop. Don't stop.

I reach the mouth of the alley, burst out onto the street, and race halfway across without even bothering to check for oncoming traffic. I don't care anymore. If I die smeared across the grill of a taxi—well, so be it. Just another cruel twist of fate from an uncaring universe.

The night around me is silent and oppressive. It feels like the very air itself wants to suffocate me with its weight. Humidity and darkness combined are like a hand pressing against my chest, stopping me from drawing in a full breath. Time—brief, precious seconds—meanders past at the pace of a predatory shark trawling dark ocean waters.

I don't have much of it left.

I freeze in the middle of the road. There is a streetlight at the intersection fifty yards to my left. The lamp casts a cone of orange light that looks far too warm and friendly for what's happening to me right now. I think, with the same dark sarcasm that has stuck with me throughout this entire nightmare, that whoever designed this world fucked up. That light should be a cold, vicious blue. Fluorescent. The kind that exposes everything.

The first night I woke up in the castle, that was what greeted me. Harsh light. Illuminating faces that looked just as harsh and cruel, all sharp angles and deep shadows around the eyes—but God, those faces were beautiful, too. They made me understand why angels chose to follow Satan. Darkness can be beautiful. Tempting. It can swallow you whole and make you love every second of it.

The cone of light is empty. It reveals bare sidewalk, nothing more.

Then I blink.

A man steps into the light.

He is almost impossibly tall, with shoulders as wide as a doorframe. He is too far away to make out much of his face. But I don't need to be close to know what he looks like. I have seen it plenty. Up close and personal, just inches away from mine. How many nights have I seen that face? Too many to count. In real life, in my dreams—it won't leave me alone. That aquiline nose. Those verdant green eyes, like an ancient forest underneath the canopy of thick, dark eyebrows.

This can't be real. I'm dreaming. I have to wake up.

But I know I'm not.

How many times over the last few weeks have I tried to pretend I was Dorothy in Oz? How many times did I click my heels together and say, "There's no place like home"? Too many to count.

But here's the other thing I've learned:

Home isn't heaven, either.

Home might even be worse than this hell I've found myself in. At least, in this messed-up nightmare, the demons announce themselves as such. They don't hide who they are and what they want.

Home ... home is where the devils dress up as angels and say they're here to save you. Home is a thicket of lies. A hell of its own making, too.

Funny that I should be thinking of home right now. Because the man standing underneath the light is the one who ripped back the curtain and showed me the ugly underbelly of everything I once knew and loved.

He sees me now. I can tell he does, though he doesn't move or acknowledge me at all. He simply stands under the light, awash in orange. He's wearing a dark navy suit over a crisp white shirt. Both are torn to shreds and stained with blood. One of his hands is bloody, too. It drips from his fingertips and puddles on the sidewalk beneath him.

His other hand is holding a gun.

I freeze like a deer caught in the headlights. He won't fire. At least, I don't think he will. But there are no rules left to be followed. The game has been broken wide open. Up is down and left is right. The good guys are the bad guys and the bad guys are—fuck, I don't know what they are. Or who they are. Or what they want.

As I watch, another man materializes next to the first. Just as tall, just as broad. His hair is shaggier, hanging almost down to his shoulders. I can see the glint of an ear piercing. I know from firsthand experience that the rest of his body is similarly riddled with piercings and tattoos. The angle of the streetlight throws his five-o'clock shadow into sharp relief. He looks dirty, savage, like a wild beast merely pretending to be a man.

I didn't know it was possible, but at the sight of him, my heart sinks even lower.

I knew that he was with his brothers, of course. They were all after me, moving as one, as a pack of wolves, of hyenas. But somehow, seeing him here and now, in the dead of the night, is even more haunting than it was the first night I woke up.

He was the first one of them I saw. He sat in the corner of the room they held me in. I heard him before I saw him, actually. The sound of a blade sliding against a whetstone, again and again.

When I opened my drug-addled eyes, I saw him there, casually leaning backwards on a stool propped against the stone wall like this was no big deal. Like he did this all the fucking time. Like sharpening his knife and looking at a bound, captive girl was no big deal. Just another day in the life.

I knew instantly that he was unhinged. His eyes told the whole story. Pain swam in them like molten lava. He had honey-colored irises—if honey had a lethal aftertaste.

I see now that he is holding that same knife. His hands, like his brother's, are stained with blood.

I start to back away. I want to be anywhere but here.

As I watch, a third man steps into the light. He is jaw-droppingly beautiful. Even now, in the midst of all this whatever-you'd-call-it—chaos? nightmare? hellscape?—I sense his beauty and let out a soft sigh. His jaw is sharp enough to slice you wide open. His lips can say and do such beautiful things to me. I know this because he's said them. He's done them. Hell, I asked for it. I begged him to trace his lips down the curve of my neck, between my breasts, past the hollows in my hips, and down ... I wanted it so badly. And he gave it to me—in a manner of speaking. But like an evil genie, the wish he granted was somehow everything I wanted and nothing of the sort, all at the same time.

The third man's eyes are cold, blue, and clear. Right now, they betray nothing. A mountain lake, undisturbed by even the tiniest ripple. Like the first man, he is wearing a suit. The slacks, at least. The jacket must have been lost somewhere in the mayhem that all of us left behind. His white dress shirt is crisply ironed, the first few buttons rakishly undone. Somehow, he made it through everything with only one drop of blood staining the collar.

I count the men again. One, two, three. Green eyes, blue eyes, honey eyes.

But the fourth is missing.

The one who started it all.

The one whose voice, whose touch, whose very essence is seared into my soul like a cattle brand.

Where is Vito Bianci?

I turn and find out immediately.

Vito's chest is as solid as granite when I turn and collide into him. How he snuck up behind me without making a sound, I'll never know. There are many things I'll never know about Vito. He is like an ocean of oil, hiding so many secrets beneath his surface.

But I have seen some of them. There is a beating heart behind that chest. It is buried underneath pain, but I have seen it in one beautiful, unforgettable glimpse. He may regret showing it to me. In fact, I know he does. It makes what he has to do next so much harder.

I take a deep breath and swallow past the knot in my throat. It's over for me now. I am back in the brothers' possession. Perhaps it was foolish to think I ever had a chance of becoming free again. That shattered hope is stabbing me in the heart right now like shards of glass that once made up a delicate sculpture. I shouldn't have ever hoped. It will make the ending that much worse.

I look up at Vito. He is not as tall as his younger brothers, but he is the most muscular. He has the same nose that they all do. Strong, straight as an arrow, leading up into a proud forehead. Those eyes—I used to swear they were black all the way through, pupil and iris alike. I don't know anymore. I don't know anything anymore. What's real, what's fake, what's a lie, what's true?

Who the fuck knows?

"We have found you, Milaya Volkov," he growls in a voice deeper than sound, rasping like a metal edge on stone. "You cannot run anymore."

I don't say anything. There's nothing to say. He's right—I can't run anymore.

We stand there and stare at each other for a few long moments. My breath has slowed from short, sharp gasps to a soft inhale, exhale, inhale, exhale. He doesn't blink, doesn't move, doesn't say anything else.

Is it insane that I notice his smell? Blood and sweat and cologne all mixed together. It's as intoxicating as it was the very first time. I must be deranged. My time in their castle drove me mad. Stockholm Syndrome doesn't even begin to cover it.

Maybe I was wrong about being near the breaking point.

Maybe the truth is that I broke a long, long time ago.

I can sense the others drawing close around me. They step in and join me in a circle of darkness. I am surrounded now by a wall of men. They all have a similar smell. The same blood and sweat as Vito. But each of them bears a unique musk that is entirely their own.

Like a ballerina figurine in a toy box, I do a slow pivot and drink in the sight of them. Even now, I can see that my killers are gorgeous. Sculpted by the hands of angels.

Mateo, the wise one, green-eyed.

Leo, the beautiful, blue-eyed.

Dante, the wild, honey-eyed.

And back to the front, to the beginning, to Vito, the leader, black-eyed.

They're waiting for me to do something. To do anything.

I swallow again. It hurts. Christ, everything hurts, from the bottoms of my bleeding feet to the hair on my scalp, the same hair that each of these men has wound their hands through and tugged back on to make me moan and scream and beg in turns.

I didn't expect the end of my life to hurt this badly.

"Well?" I say with a voice cockier than I truly feel. I haven't made this easy on them since the night they took me. I don't plan on starting now. "You found me. Now what?"

"Now," Dante answers, "we are going to finish what we started."

But none of us are going to get the chance to finish what we started. Because, just then, Vito slumps over, dropping his full weight onto me. I catch him in surprise as his brothers rush to help me. Carefully, we all lower him to the ground. His head lolls forward, revealing a nasty crater where I struck him with the rock. I feel a surge of guilt, followed by defiance. I did what I had to do. He would've done the same if he were me.

"We need to move," murmurs Mateo for what feels like the thousandth time tonight. "They're not far behind us."

"Move where?" Leo asks bitterly. "How? In case you didn't notice, we're on foot. Do you want us to leave Vito behind?"

Dante says, "We're not losing another brother. Not again. Either he comes, or we all stay."

Mateo sighs. "So be it. Then I suppose it is time for us to die, brothers." He sits on the ground and buries his face in his hands.

They're all shells of what they were when they met me. No longer are they dark, avenging angels. Now, they are men who have lost everything again and again. My heart longs to break for them. But the truth is that my heart broke for good a long time ago. There isn't anything left to break.

So fuck it then. We're all going to die. I, the brothers, my father. I always thought I'd go down fighting. I thought for sure that they would too. But it turns out that in the end, we are going to tie the noose around our own throats and go out willingly.. Like motherfucking cowards.

Vito is mumbling under his breath, but no one even bothers to find out what he's saying. Why would it matter? We're rearranging deck chairs on the *Titanic*. All is lost. Nothing is salvageable.

None of us are surprised when a pair of dark-tinted SUVs pull up and troops issue forth from it like a plague. They bind each of us with plastic zip-ties and load us into the back seats. Gunmen keep their pistols pointed at us. No one says a word, except for Vito, who continues to mumble nonsense.

They take us back to the castle and throw us in a cell. My father is in there too. The life is draining from him one drop of blood at a time. I touch his hand and his fingers tighten around mine. It is the tiniest bit of comfort, but at least it is something. Maybe it is the last thing.

After that, the shock catches up to me, and all I know is darkness.

28

VITO

The only thing I know with certainty is that I am very badly hurt.

Everything else is hazy at best.

The woods ... We ran, my brothers and I, the Volkovs in tow, those fucking monsters ... Sergio, the cavern ... None of it makes sense; none of it adds up. My head aches so badly, white-hot intensity, a sun burning me up in the back of my skull.

I'm remembering things that happened fifteen years ago and things that never happened at all, and I don't even know where to start with deciphering fact from fiction. I see Audrey, I see Milaya, I see my father, I see my brother, and all of them whirl back and forth in my mind's eye like people dancing just outside the light cast by a huge bonfire. They flicker in and out of the darkness, looking different each and every time, and the shadows they cast on the ground behind them are monstrous and grotesque.

"He's going to die," I hear. I try to force my eyes open, but it doesn't work. Even the thin trickle of moonlight coming in from somewhere far above me is agony, like a needle piercing my eyeball. I grimace in pain and take a deep breath to try again.

"No, he's not."

"Yes, he fucking is."

"Not if I can help it."

I don't know whose voice is whose. It doesn't matter though. They're right—I am going to die. I can feel my life seeping out of me like water returning to the soil. Dust to dust, ashes to ashes, all that bullshit. I've never believed in anything but the here and now. But as I lie here, feeling the cold hardness of rock against my spine, I wonder if I was as wrong about heaven and hell as I was about everything else in my life. It turns out that I never understood anything at all. Too little, too late. Fuck it though. Fuck it all. Nothing matters anymore.

"Vito, can you hear me?"

This time, I know the pain awaiting me when I open my eyes. It hurts just as bad, but because I am ready for it, I manage to pry them open. Faces float above me. Dante, Leo, Mateo. My brothers. What is left of them. So much humanity has drained from their faces.

I failed them. It was my job to guide them, to protect them, and I did the exact opposite. I brought the hellhounds right to our fucking doorstep. I was the weakest link. Me, not them. At least I am the one bearing the brunt of the agony, or so it seems.

I want to talk. I want to tell them how sorry I am, that I understand all of this was my fault. But my lips don't want to work.

"He's losing it," Leo says.

"It's a traumatic brain injury," replies Mateo. "His brain is swelling. We have to find a way to relieve the pressure."

Leo grimaces. "How the fuck would we do that? We're trapped in our own goddamn cells. It's not going to work."

Dante says nothing. He looks utterly catatonic. A sleepwalking zombie. I try to reach out and touch him, but my hand doesn't cooperate any more than my lips did. I am like a circuit board that has been dunked in the ocean. Nothing works. Nothing makes sense.

Father used to joke that he wanted to die while balls-deep in the wives of his enemies. Even when I was a thirteen-year-old, I knew that was a crude request. But the truth was that I never thought about dying at all. I assumed that, when my time came, it would just be lights out immediately, as swift and sudden as a power outage. No time to prepare or to stage the scene. Just *Game Over* flashing across the screen. Then darkness.

This is painfully drawn-out though. That feeling of being pulled back towards the source that made me is uncanny and yet undeniable. I know that I am dying. Every cell of me knows. And it wants to rage against the dying of the light, like that old poem said to do. That's what I was trained to do. That's what I was taught.

But fighting has become so exhausting.

How many years have I spent raging already? Far too many. I raged against the loss of my mother, of Audrey, of my innocence. I raged against my father's cruelty. I raged against my own weaknesses. And as I lie here in this dungeon cell with my brothers arguing above me, I realize something:

I lost every one of those battles.

So why the hell would I think that I have any chance of winning this one?

I start to let my eyes flutter closed again. But before I do, I glance into the corner and see Milaya. She is hunched over the body of her father. I cannot tell whether or not he is alive. I wonder if my shot landed where I intended it to land. I wonder if I'll ever get the chance to find out. That doesn't matter either, I suppose, though I can't help but be curious.

She glances back at me and I see those green eyes flash in the moonlight and my heart seizes in my chest as painfully as the back of my head throbs. I've seen a look like that only once before: the night I shut Audrey out of the castle. It is hot love and cold fury swirling together. She hates me and yet she cannot bear to let me die.

I know the feeling.

I feel the same for her.

I look away and close my eyes. I don't want to be conscious anymore. Let the darkness come swallow me up again, perhaps for the last time. I don't intend to wake up on the other side of it. Too much has happened for that to be a reasonable expectation. I fucked up, I failed the ones I loved, and this is the price.

If you stop, you die.

I have finally stopped.

Now comes the second part.

"Wake him up."

The voice issuing the order is gritted and angry, seething with pain. I hear footsteps, then the shock of a bucket of ice-cold water being tossed into my face.

I roar wordlessly. Pain lances through the back of my head. I try to reach up a hand to touch the site of the injury, but I can't move my arm. When I open my eyes, I realize that's because I am strapped to a solid wooden chair. My arms, torso, and legs are all secured to the seat with thick leather straps cinched down tight enough that I can't budge my limbs an inch in any direction. I can only raise my chin from where I was slumped forward and look over to see something I never thought I'd see again.

Sergio is in an overstuffed leather armchair directly across from me. He is leaning awkwardly to one side to make room for the mass of bloodstained bandages wrapped around his upper left chest and shoulder. His left arm rests uselessly on his lap, while his right hand squeezes the arm of the chair as tight as he can to stay upright. His brows are furrowed in a furious downward-sloping V over those incandescent purple eyes. He looks at me, unblinking.

I open my mouth to speak. No words come out.

Sergio snaps his fingers at someone behind me. "Get him water to drink."

Rough hands appear from out of my field of vision, force my jaw open, and clumsily pour a water bottle down my throat. The sensation of water hitting my parched throat is indescribable. But I don't show any of that on my face.

"That's enough," Sergio says. The water bottle is wrenched away. "Leave us."

Footsteps retreat away from me. A door opens and closes.

"Now," Sergio adds, turning his attention back to me. "What were you going to say?"

With the water in my system, I can finally muster up the energy to speak. "Guess I hit my target after all," I rasp.

His eyes narrow further. "You have some fucking balls to say a thing like that, brother."

I merely shrug.

"I could kill you right now, you know."

I shrug again. "So be it." I was ready to die whenever it was that I last closed my eyes. If it turns out that I was only off by a little bit, then that is all well and good. "My life as I knew it is over. Might as well wrap everything up neatly."

"Hm."

"Hm?"

The corner of his mouth twitches up in a smile unexpectedly. "Do you think you can't suffer anymore, Vito?"

I laugh hollowly. "I have been suffering for thirty-two years, Sergio. How much more is even possible?"

His smile grows one sinister notch. "More than you could ever imagine."

The first inkling that he knows something I don't begins to stir in my broken brain. He is too self-assured for a man who was recently shot. I didn't shoot to kill, and that was intentional, but I did shoot to put him down for a long time.

And yet, there's a smugness in his face that does not compute. I'm having a hard time stringing thoughts together, but the pervasive underlying feeling is that uneasy anxiety of being on the wrong end of a surprise.

"Well?" he asks.

"What?"

"Don't you want to know?"

"Know what?"

"To know what I know, Vito. To know what has happened."

I sigh, long and slow. It's taking all of my willpower just to follow along with this conversation and the billion thoughts buzzing through my head like hornets. I don't have the mental capacity to play Sergio's guessing games. He wants badly for me to take the bait, judging by the grin playing at his thin lips.

"Tell me if you're going to tell me," I finally manage to say. "Or don't if you're not. I don't really give a damn one way or the other anymore."

Sergio's face twitches. He catches himself a moment later, but I saw the mask slip. For the briefest of seconds, I saw my little brother in him. It's gone as quickly as it came.

"Do you think you are brave for staring death in the face?" he asks me. "Do you think this makes you a man?"

"I don't think I'm anything," I reply flatly. The room is swimming in and out like a TV with a bad connection. One minute, the lines of the objects before me are clear and distinct. The next, everything fuzzes together and sound becomes muffled and the only clear thing I can see are Sergio's eyes, boring into me. My head is a lava pit of pain. The straps are compressing the veins in my forearms and calves, so I feel the staticky tingle of restricted blood flow in my extremities. All of it combines to make this feel less than real. I know I'm not dreaming—the pain in my head is far too intense for that—but it doesn't feel like reality either. Somewhere in between, neither here nor there.

"You are many things, Vito," Sergio purrs. It seems like he's switching gears, or at least trying to. He slides from anger and pain to the smooth acidity of a man who knows he holds all the advantages. I have been in his shoes before, with an enemy bound and helpless before me. "You are a fool. You are a coward. You are a pawn."

He wants me to argue back, or at least to deny the accusations. But he doesn't know that I agree with him. I fought it for so long. Why fight anymore? If I wasn't those things, I wouldn't be tied up in a chair in my own home, looking up at my supposedly dead brother and wondering when he is going to kill me.

"Why aren't you dead?" I ask finally, in a voice that sounds far too weak and timid to be mine. "I watched you die."

"Wrong!" he snarls with a sudden twist of anger. The knuckles of his right hand, the good one, turn white as he grips the armchair as hard as he can. "You didn't watch a fucking thing. You left me."

"We had no choice."

"You always had a choice, Vito. You chose wrong. If you were smart, you would've chosen to step aside a long time ago. You aren't cut out for this life."

I think of Milaya's kiss pressed into the back of my hand and I know at once that what Sergio is saying is true. If something so small and soft could split me in two, then it is obvious that I am not made up of don stuff. I am cast from weaker material. Tin, not steel. She broke me. Now my own brother is going to kill me. It all seems so inevitable.

"Perhaps not," I say, as much to myself as to Sergio.

"Oh, Vito," he murmurs. He scoots his chair closer to mine so that our knees are almost touching, and reaches out to force my chin up. His eyes find mine and lock on with what looks at first to be tenderness, but is actually the coldest malice I have ever seen in a human gaze. "You think that you are completely broken already. I want to tell you something: you are not even close to rock bottom yet. Listen to what I am about to tell you and listen very carefully. When it is all over, you will know what it is to be utterly ruined."

Then he starts to tell me, and by the time he finishes, I realize one thing:

He was right.

"Let me ask you, Vito: do you know what it feels like to watch your brothers leave you to die? I planned everything from the very beginning, and yet I still cannot describe to you how that moment hurt. Everything we suffered through as children was nothing compared to the sight of your car receding into the darkness. You left me to die at the hands of our enemies. But that is okay. It gave me resolve. I knew then that I was on the right course.

"You did not deserve what you had been given. By a mere accident of birth, a whole empire was destined to become yours. You were never made of the right stuff though, were you?" He slaps my cheek lightly. "Eh? Look at me. You are soft. You are weak. You are pathetic. Even now, you cannot hold your head up and look me in the eye."

Sergio's eyes sparkle in the firelight. "Father was weak too, though in a different way. He thought he could control me. Mother knew best. She was right to kill herself all those years ago. She was right when she thought that she had given birth to a devil. I am exactly that and more. But that is why *I* deserve what *you* have."

"I killed him, you know," he remarks casually.

I look up at him in shock.

"What?"

"Father. I killed him."

"No. We saw what happened. The Russians ..."

He laughs callously. "The Russians were working for me, idiot. Why do you think they knew we were coming? Why do you think they were ready for us?" He shakes his head sadly. "You really didn't figure that out? My God, you are even stupider than I thought."

"No." That's all I can manage to say. My vision is swimming, things in the room blurring and reconstituting and blurring again. I hurt so badly, from head to toe.

"Yes," Sergio purrs. "The Volkov don is as blind as you are. It was easy to lure his men out from under him. And it was easy to lure Father to me. You all were supposed to die with him. That didn't happen then, but it will happen tonight, so I suppose all is fair in the end."

"Why?"

He grabs my chin roughly in his hands and keeps my gaze locked on his. "Because it should have all been *mine*," he seethes with venom dripping from his voice. "Mine, not yours."

"Have it then," I whisper. "I don't want it."

Sergio laughs again, louder and more viciously than the first time. "Oh, don't you worry about that, brother. I will have it. I will rip it from your dead hands. I have already taken everything else from you. What is one more thing?"

At that, it is my turn to laugh. "What have you taken from me? I have never had anything worth saving."

Sergio smiles, slow and creepy. "Tut-tut, Vito. Think harder. You had something special, once upon a time, didn't you? In fact, I think you still have a picture of that something hidden in your nightstand."

My mouth falls open. Sergio's grin spreads wider.

"Ah yes," he murmurs, "now you know what I'm talking about."

"How do you know about her?"

"You think you could keep secrets? Oh, Vito, I overestimated you so very much. You are even weaker than I suspected. A broken heart for a servant's girl? It takes so little to hurt you. Hardly even worth the effort. And yet, I persevere, if for no other reason than because I simply want to watch you suffer."

"What did you do?" My voice is barely audible above Sergio's breath and the crackle of the fire in the hearth.

"Do you remember the night you let her go?" he asks me.

I say nothing. I can't. Maybe, if I don't hear what he's about to say, then it won't become real for me. The feeling of horror, like a subliminal droning noise growing louder and louder in the background, is pressing down upon me savagely. I can hardly breathe.

"You were supposed to kill her. Father gave you the blade and the room and the privacy. He thought you might even do it. But I knew better. I knew even back then that you didn't have the fucking balls."

"Stop."

"You took her downstairs, shut the door, and you thought that little act would save her? Oh, Vito. Oh, brother. You were so wrong."

"Stop it. Shut the fuck up."

"I followed her into the night. It wasn't hard. She didn't get very far. And she went down easily. Like a fawn, you know? Hardly even bleated before I cut her throat."

I realize suddenly that I'm roaring wordlessly and yanking at the straps as hard as I can. They don't budge. I can't move. Tears are streaming down my face and the world has narrowed down to Sergio's Cheshire Cat smile.

"The one good thing you ever did turned out to be for nothing. How does that feel? Does it hurt you, brother? Does it break your heart the last little bit? Picture it: that pale, pretty skin, stained with blood, left in the woods for the scavengers to find. She didn't get away. You didn't save her. She's dead. Remember that, Vito. Remember you failed her. I want it to be your last thought before you die."

I'm still roaring when soldiers come pouring in and drag me, screaming, out of the room. I'm still roaring when they strap me to a table in the great room and set upon me with blades and fists. I'm still roaring when they take my finger from my hand, when my blood splatters on the stones. My ancestors look down at me from the walls as I break, that last little bit of me left to be broken.

And then the darkness consumes me.

29

MILAYA

The cell door clangs open and wakes me up. It's too dark to see much, since the moon has gone behind the clouds, but I can hear the shuffling of heavy boots and the groaning of a dying man. Someone curses in Russian and then Vito comes stumbling in. He is trembling, slick with blood from head to toe, and there is a bloodied stump where his right pinky finger once was. He takes one step and collapses to the floor.

I rush over to him. Exhaustion has me swaddled, muffled. Nothing feels real, like I'm at the bottom of the ocean. All the sounds are dampened, the sights are vague, the emotions are hollow. I just have to keep doing the next thing, and the next, and the next, robotic and unthinking.

We'd been in here for a day or so, I believe, when men in ski masks and all black clothing came and grabbed Mateo, Dante, and Leo a few hours ago. I heard other doors opening and shutting outside of this one immediately afterwards, so I'm assuming they split us up and threw them each in their own holding cell for some reason, though I don't know anything for sure.

They took Vito around the same time. He was in bad shape when he left, but that was my fault.

Now that he's back, he's on death's doorstep.

And his own brother is to blame.

What am I supposed to feel as I look down at his bruised, battered body where he fell? Guilt? Longing? Fear? Pride? There's no rulebook in the world that could govern this moment. I couldn't possibly be ready for something like this.

A quick review of what has happened between me and the man at my feet: he kidnapped me, tortured me, made me fall for him, shot my father, broke my heart. And at the end of all that is a big fat question mark, a glaring *TO BE CONTINUED*. But I don't know what happens next in this story. I haven't known for a very, very long time.

I can hear my father breathing behind me. It's a nasty, pained, rattling noise, but it's miles better than no noise at all. I don't know how he's clinging to life. I'm just grateful that he is. I've done the best I can to keep his heart beating, though I have next to nothing to work with. I tore my T-shirt into shreds and tried to pad the bullet wound to slow the bleeding, with middling success.

He fell asleep just a few short minutes before Vito was thrown in here. Now, I'm standing between the two of them, wondering how the hell—or *if*—we will ever emerge from this cell alive.

Vito mumbles something. I crouch down and put my face next to his mouth, trying to understand what he's saying.

"Serg ... Sergio ..." he rasps in the voice of a dying man.

"Save your energy," I tell him. My own voice comes out strangled and desperate. So many things are warring inside of me that it's impossible to know how I'm supposed to sound. I hate this man; I love him; I blame him; I need him.

He grabs my hand and tries to squeeze, but there's no strength left in his grip. I remember how solid he felt escorting me from my bedroom to the great room on the first night I was brought up from the dungeon, the night I wore the gold dress. He felt so vibrant with strength that night. Unyielding, like a mountain. Now, he is a ghost of himself. His eyelids flutter open and shut, as if he's trying and failing to hold onto consciousness. He needs to sleep. I sweep my gaze down his body and note countless cuts, bruises, ragged clothes, torn flesh. They worked him over mercilessly. As with my father, it seems like a miracle that he's still alive.

Broken men do not die easily, it seems.

"No," Vito says with a sudden infusion of strength. He adjusts his grip on my hand and—slowly, agonizingly— pulls himself up into a seated position against the wall. His breath grows labored with the effort, but he seems satisfied. Like conquering one simple thing is giving him the bravery to look ahead to the next.

Sighing, I settle into a seat against the wall next to him. I sit there with bated breath until his eyes open again. I'm shivering, I realize—the cell is cold this time of night. I remember well just how cold it can get. But Vito is radiating heat. Consciously or unconsciously, I scoot closer to him and bask in his warmth. His hand has never left mine. Unlike in the woods, though, this is not a possessive grasp. It's the grasp of a man who doesn't want to lose the one thing he has left.

Vito lets loose a long, rattling exhalation, then turns to look at me. He's so pale and forlorn. Like that night in the hallway. I want to kiss his hand again, and I have to suppress the urge. *Remember what he's done. Remember who he is.* Somehow, I manage to resist it.

"Sergio told me everything," he whispers.

"What is everything?"

He takes long pauses between his sentences as he begins to explain in short, halting bursts what happened in the room upstairs with his brother. I don't know what all of it means, though I can put some of the puzzle pieces together. I don't suppose it actually matters. He's not telling me this because I need to know it. He's telling me because he needs to clear his slate before he dies. It's the confession of a man at the end of his life. That thought, even more than the cold, makes me shudder.

As he talks, a drop of blood trickles from his forehead down onto his chin. I stare at it as it clings there, catching the moonlight like a brilliant ruby. It is violently beautiful. Just like Vito himself.

Eventually, the story ends. I know everything now. Not that it matters.

"I'm sorry," he whispers to me. He reaches up a fragile hand to touch against my cheek. I almost turn away.

But I can't.

Because the truth staring me in the face can no longer be ignored: I love this man. Or rather, I *could* love him. There is the possibility for love between us. And not just him—I love Leo, too. And Mateo. And Dante. I love all of them as if they were all unique facets cut into the same gem. It doesn't make any sense and it's kind of breaking my brain just thinking about it, but it's so true that how could I deny it? They broke me in their castle, but when they cracked me wide open, they revealed a Milaya inside of me that could be anything she wanted to be.

I'm not just a Volkov princess anymore. I am what Dante called me as I rode him in the moonlight with a knife held against his throat—I am a queen. I am *their* queen.

I open my mouth to say those words to Vito. If he is going to die, I want him to die knowing that I am broken just like him, and that our jagged pieces fit together like a puzzle, and that if he dies, part of me will die too. I want to tell him that I forgive him and I want to take his pain away now and forever. I want him to lay his head in my lap and give me the back of his hand to kiss. He can't die without hearing those words. I can't let that happen.

But before I can find a place to begin, the cell door clangs open once more. Three men stride in with menace in their faces. They pick me up and drag me out as I scream.

Vito's eyes don't leave mine until the very last second. Then the door shuts in my face, and we are separated, and once again, I am alone in the hands of men who want to hurt me.

This time though, I don't think there will be a happy ending.

I'm still screaming and crying as they carry me through the dungeon space. I see Mateo, Dante, and Leo strung up from chains in the ceiling. Each of them is badly hurt. My tears thicken, my screams grow hoarser. Why is there so much blood at my feet? Why aren't they looking at me? What is going to happen to them?

There are no answers to be found. There is only pain down here, pain and darkness and hatred.

I assumed they were going to take me upstairs, but instead, they take me down the side hallway that Mateo once took me down. A familiar door is already open, waiting for me. When they hurl me inside and slam it shut, I know just where to turn.

To the confessional screen separating me from whoever is waiting on the other side.

"Hello, Milaya," seethes a menacing voice.

"You're Sergio."

He drawls, "They did mention that you were a smart little thing."

"I'm a spiteful little thing too, so you should let us all go before it backfires on you." I'm trying to sound bold, though judging by how hard Sergio starts laughing the moment the words are out of my lips, I'm not exactly convincing.

"That is a sight I would love to see. Unfortunately, not in the cards—but still, tempting."

"What comes next then?"

"Just a little more blood to be spilled. Then we can wrap things up, I think."

"Whose blood?"

"Oh, you know," Sergio says in a hand-wavey voice. "A little of yours, a little of your father's, a little of each of my brothers'. Or rather, to be clear—a lot of each."

"So this is it then."

"For you, yes, darling."

I flinch. "Don't call me that."

"Why ever not?" Sergio asks me. He sounds plaintive, almost like he's offended. "Are you not darling and precious to my brothers? And what is theirs is mine, no? Then you are my darling, certainly."

"I'm not anybody's anything," I fire back. "I am Milaya Volkov. That's all."

He chuckles. "Only for a little while longer. Then you will be nothing whatsoever. Hardly even a memory."

I pause. "Why are you doing this?"

"Because it is my time to make things right, Milaya Volkov. To correct the record."

I shudder at the way he says my full name so carefully. It's the same way Vito has always addressed me. Over time, it became something close to a term of endearment, though neither of us ever explicitly acknowledged the change in tone. But out of Sergio's mouth, it has the same sinister quality that Vito once imbued in it. And in this cramped, stuffy confessional, it sounds downright wicked.

"You're killing your own siblings because Daddy didn't love you enough?"

"I'm killing everyone who ever took what was rightfully mine," he snaps. "Do not confuse the two, Volkov whore."

I smile thinly, even though I know he can't see it in the darkness. "You went from darling to whore awfully fast."

"I don't think I like your tone anymore."

I can't help but giggle at that. How am I giggling at anything? That's how I know I'm really losing it. But giggle I must. He sounds like a disapproving teacher, trying to lecture a bad student into behaving. "Not the first time I've heard that," I fire back, "and probably not the last."

"Oh, I can guarantee it will be the last," Sergio growls. He pounds the flat of his hand on the wooden divider. It must be a signal to his guards, because at the sound, my door swings open and one of the men who brought me here steps in to retrieve me.

"Wait!" I cry out. The guard freezes. I turn back to the screen. I can just barely see Sergio's silhouette through it, courtesy of the dim light offered by the gas lamp set to low overhead. "I have a question for you."

"Yes?" he drones lazily.

"What color are your eyes?"

"My eyes?"

"Yes," I say, nodding. "Leo is blue. Dante is amber. Mateo is green. Vito is black. What are yours?"

I hold my breath, hoping beyond hope that he falls for the stupid little bait I have dangling for him. I hear him shifting around on the other side of the confessional.

And then, against all odds, he does exactly what I'd hoped. He presses his face against the screen. It's thin enough that I can see him now, though the valley of shadows cast by his proud nose obscures one half of it. He flutters his eyelashes playfully, like a movie starlet.

"My eyes are violet," he says.

"Really?" I ask. "Because they look more red to me."

I move as fast as I can. With one hand, I reach down to the waistband of my bloodstained, torn-to-pieces jean shorts and retrieve Dante's switchblade. It flicks open with a *shiiiiink* that brings me back to the night I woke up with him sharpening it beside the table I was tied to.

I remember what he told me that night. *You are the key to it all.* Maybe I am. But not in the way he expected.

I know one thing now: I can't fix these men. The Biancis, my father—they are broken in ways that can never be repaired. If they shape this world in their own image, then everyone else who lives under their rule will be forced to inhabit a nightmare. I've lived that nightmare for far too long now. I have to get out.

But just escaping from underneath the thumb of powerful men will not be enough. There has to be a better way. It's not just about me. It's about Audrey. It's about my mother. It's about everyone who has ever stared into the face of the devil and wondered if there is a way to rescue the angel that he once was. I've seen into the eyes of each of the men currently dying in the dungeon behind me.

I can't fix them.

But I can save them.

And it starts with this.

The blade flies through the air before the soldier in the doorway can stop me, before Sergio can pull his face back. As my parting words ring out— "*look more red to me ...*"—the knife slashes through the mesh partition and plunges straight into Sergio's right eye.

I feel the judder of the blade striking bone. Quick as a flash, I yank it out, feeling the hot gush of blood splash into my wrist, and turn to make another sweeping strike across the throat of the soldier lunging towards me. My swing finds its target. He hits the ground, gurgling.

I don't have time to stop and admire my handiwork or even to make sure that Sergio is dead. I have to keep moving.

I leap over the guard's thrashing body and run out of the confessional to check the hallway. The other two men who brought me here must have disappeared. They thought that one burly traitor could restrain a feeble little girl. Well, they thought fucking wrong.

I spy a walkie-talkie on the belt of the dying soldier. Grabbing it, I depress the button and cast my voice as low as I can to yell, "Intrusion on the main floor! All soldiers respond to the great room!"

I pray to the heavens this works.

30

MILAYA

I stand in the hallway and count to fifty under my breath. Both Sergio and the dying soldier in the confessional have stopped thrashing around, so all I can hear is my own labored breathing and the thunder of boots running up the spiral staircase. When the footsteps have receded, I can wait no longer. I have to go.

Bursting into the main dungeon area, I see Mateo, Dante, and Leo. Each of them is strung up on what looks like a giant wooden X. It's an eerie sight—part crucifixion, part horror movie. I don't have time to reflect on it though. I use the blood-slicked switchblade in my hand to saw Mateo free of his restrains.

He falls to his hands and knees, breathing hard. "We can't wait," I tell him. "I'm sorry, but we have to run." I turn to cut Leo loose. Behind me, I hear a clanking sound as Mateo finds a machete hanging on the wall and goes to do the same for Dante.

I try not to focus on their injuries. They're all dripping blood and breathing heavily, clearly in agonizing physical pain. God only knows what kind of pain they are going through on the inside. But there will be time to lick our wounds later. Right now, if we want to survive, we need to get the hell out of this castle.

"Where is Vito?" Leo asks when he's free. He's rubbing his wrists, which are chafed completely raw from tugging against his bonds while Sergio's men tortured him.

"In the cell, I think."

He goes to get Vito while I turn to help Mateo finish freeing Dante. When that is done, we all go to the cell. I grabbed the key from the dead soldier's neck, so I open it up.

Vito and my dad are inside. The floor is sticky with blood. Like so many other things, I force myself not to focus on that. If I let the horror of the moment overwhelm me, I'm going to die down here. We have to run like the freaking wind. I don't want to know what will happen when the troops realize the diversion I caused is a false alarm, or when Sergio's body is discovered. All hell is about to break loose.

Everyone is just standing around though. Am I the only one who realizes the urgency of the situation? "What are you doing?" I screech. "Help him up!" I push Dante forward towards Vito's prostrate body. He stumbles to catch himself, but stops again and looks up at me dumbly. He says nothing.

They need me, I'm realizing. They're all paralyzed by shock. I'm the only one left.

I wanted to be a queen? Fine then. I will be.

"Leo, Dante, get Vito. Mateo, you come here and help me with my dad." They all stare at me blankly for one long moment before I add, "Now!"

That seems to pierce through the haze surrounding each of them. Numbly, they step forward and do what I said. We help Vito and my dad up, both of them groaning softly under their breath. And then we make our way to the rear entrance like some hideous, bleeding, twelve-legged beast.

We're about five steps away from getting to the door and escaping into the night when I hear something.

Footsteps outside.

It's the pounding cacophony of armed men with violent intentions. We have to act quickly. I throw my dad's arm from around my shoulders, lunge forward, and grab the massive wooden chest of torture devices that stands right next to the door. I'm pulling with all my might, every muscle straining, but the thing won't budge.

Mateo joins me. He throws his weight into the furniture. Still, it won't go. "Help me!" I cry. The pain in my voice jolts everyone else into action. They add their strength until, with the splintering groan of wood breaking, the whole thing falls down in front of the door. It swings inward, so the toppled drawers will slow the entrance of the troops trying to come in from outside.

But it means that we have to find a new way out. We can't go upstairs—that's where I diverted the other soldiers to. That means one exit is left: back into the catacombs.

I turn and lead the ragtag band back through the dungeon, down the side hallway. I remember the path like it was seared into my brain. Down, left, right, down. The hallway shrinks around us like a birth canal. It's a gross analogy, but it seems fitting. We're being born into a new life. Part of each of us died back there. If we do in fact make it out of here, none of us will ever be the same. This is a clean slate. A fresh beginning.

We're so fucking close.

We burst out into the cavern where Sergio confronted us. The entrance is stacked with the bodies of the men that were shot during our escape attempt. At least half a dozen of them died here.

I look to the door we ran through out into the woods. It's still hanging partially open. I can feel the warm draft of Los Angeles night air wafting over to me. It's like a caress in the middle of a nightmare, so tender that I almost can't believe it's real. I wondered not too long ago if I'd ever smell fresh air again.

Something occurs to me. The freedom I've always wanted? It's right there for the taking. I can just run. I can leave behind these broken men. I don't have to be Luka Volkov's daughter anymore. I don't have to be anybody I don't want to be. I can just be me. I could run somewhere else and find a new name and start over completely. My father, the Bianci brothers—they carry shadows and pain everywhere they go. I don't have to keep them with me.

I turn and look at them. The five of them are all linked with their arms around each other's shoulders. I wonder if they understand the way I do how they are all the same. Broken men, the broken sons of broken fathers. The violent leaders of violent troops. The wicked purveyors of wicked deeds.

But there is good in them too. I have seen glimpses of it. I've seen the tears in my father's eyes when I unlocked myself from the closet and he was there waiting for me, begging my forgiveness, whispering, "I had to, I had to," again and again. I've felt Dante's hands clinging to me like a drowning man to a raft. I've savored Leo's lips between my legs, so desperate and longing. I've sat in the warm night with Mateo and watched the fireflies drift past. I've kissed Vito's hand in a dark hallway and stroked his hair until he fell asleep in my lap.

They are not all bad. None of us are. I can redeem them. I can take their pain away and fight back the darkness.

So I don't run. Instead, I look at them and tell them what has to happen next.

It doesn't take long to get everything set up. The dead soldiers had enough supplies on them to rig explosives throughout the yawning cavern. We've walked through the exit and are standing in the night, looking up at the castle. Leo is holding the switch.

"Are you ready?" I ask the brothers.

Vito has woken up, more or less. He fixes me with a pain-glazed look. "This can't be the only way," he murmurs.

"It is. This place can't stand. It's the only way to end everything."

He turns his gaze up to the castle. The highest turrets look almost like they're stabbing into the fabric of the night sky. It cuts an impressive silhouette. I wonder how many people have entered here and never left. How many of them walked in of their own accord, and how many of them—like me—were brought under cover of darkness against their will. The stones themselves are brimming over with pain.

The place must be destroyed.

"Do it," I tell Leo.

He presses the button.

And just like that, the C4 detonates.

There was enough of it to completely destroy the cavern. I hear one seismic boom, and then, just as I suspected, everything begins to crumble.

The catacombs collapse, and as they go, so, too, does the foundation of the castle. Layer by layer, it consumes itself. Clouds of dust erupt into the air. Soon, the stars are blotted out by it. I can feel the dirt stinging my throat.

It's time for us to leave. Most of the enemy troops—the Russian faction who betrayed my father to follow Sergio—will have died within the collapsing walls, but there is still a chance that some may escape. That is a problem for another day. For now, we need to get ourselves far away from here.

I grab my father's hand with my left and Vito's hand with my right. Mateo, Dante, and Leo fall in around us. Then, together, we begin to pick our way down the hillside, headed for an uncertain future.

But at least we are headed there together.

31

MILAYA

ONE YEAR LATER

For the first time in what feels like a freaking eternity, I'm finally alone. It's a little weird though. Like when you've been somewhere loud, a concert or a bar or whatever, for a long time, and then you leave and your ears are still ringing. No one else is in this small, sunny little room with me—I've checked half a dozen times already—and yet I still feel their presence as if they're hiding just out of sight.

Dad has barely left my side since we got back, and I've barely left his. He's getting a little too old to be taking bullet wounds like that. But Luka Volkov is a tough old bastard, as hard to kill as can be. It'd require more than one measly shot to take him down. He's been scowling at nurses and snapping at my mom's insistence that he take things easy. The first day they let him out of the hospital bed to give walking a shot, he tried to throw the walker they gave him through a nearby open window. "I don't need a fucking walker," he muttered. "Walkers are for babies and cripples. I'm neither. Now get out of my way and let me stretch my legs."

I just laughed at that. What else was there to do? Dad is Dad. Dad will always be Dad, for better or for worse. I think I'm finally learning to accept that. Can't have light without the darkness after all, right?

The Bianci brothers haven't left my side either. They've stuck to me like shadows, each in their own peculiar way. Leo lounges wherever he pleases, Mateo and Vito situate themselves like sentries in the corner of whatever room I'm currently occupying, and Dante just does Dante stuff in my vicinity. It's funny—in so many ways, they are completely different men than they were when I met them. And yet, like my dad, they are also completely the same. They have just become more themselves, if that makes any sense at all.

But as unique as the men in my life are from one another, they all have one thing in common: they won't leave me alone. I normally don't mind it. After years of being an only child and then a little bit of a studious loner at college, it's actually been a refreshing change of pace to have company all the time. Especially when they're pretty easy on the eyes.

Right now though, I'm savoring the rare moment of silence and stillness. None of Mateo's heavy sighs or Leo's absentminded murmuring fills the air. None of Vito's "hmms" or Dad's old-man grumbles. None of the clinking and clacking of the nunchucks that Dante bought for himself.

"Nunchuks?!" I asked in amazement. "Do you think you're a Ninja Turtle or something? Here, just take your knife back." But he refused to take it, the stubborn psychopath. He said it was mine now, that it had a new master. I corrected him and said I was actually a "mistress" and that he should call me by my proper title. In response, Dante just grinned wolfishly and tried to grab my ass while I skipped away, laughing.

They're all outside waiting for me. But I need a moment before I go out there. I look up into the mirror of the vanity at which I'm seated. It's still a strange sight to see makeup on my face and artfully woven braids in my hair. The makeup artists and hairdressers did a fabulous job, I gotta say. I look downright regal, with diamonds dripping from my ears and dark strokes of mascara making the luminescent greens of my eyes really shine.

Anastasia was mad that I didn't let her do my makeup, but I told her that this was a wedding, not a rave, so we'd better leave it to the professionals. It was a little hard at first to mend things with her. It took a lot of crying together before we found our footing again. But I'm glad we did. She may be a blonde bombshell party girl, but she's *my* blonde bombshell party girl, and my best friend. I know she'll feel guilty forever, though I really do hope she finds a way to move past it. Everything has worked out well for pretty much everyone. Besides, I understand why she did what she did. It was an impossible situation that she was forced into. Anyone else would have done the same. I've forgiven her. Mostly because I've learned that life is far too short and fragile to live with hatred held so close to your heart.

I turn this way and that in the mirror. It's nice to allow myself a little bit of narcissism. Lord knows everyone else in my life has that in spades. I caught Leo using my tweezers to pluck his eyebrows the other day, for crying out loud! He even had the gall to tell me to leave him alone while he finished. And Vito gets exceedingly grumpy if I interrupt his workout routine. Those men make me roll my eyes sometimes, I swear.

This moment is about me though. As soon as I pass through the doors behind me, I'll be rejoining the world. Out there, there are other people to care about, other people I love. But in here, I am all by myself. Just me, Milaya Volkov. No titles, no responsibilities, no burdens hefted on my shoulders. Just the faint smell of jasmine and soft peals of string music from the stereo system. I close my eyes and try to enjoy it. I breathe, I sit, I feel the warmth flowing throughout my body.

There was a time when I didn't think I'd ever find this peace again. During all those nights spent shivering in a cell, I almost forgot how it felt to be warm and safe and calm. I lived in fear, the fear of a mouse in the underbrush when he senses an owl overhead. So many times, I came close to giving up. But I held on. I made it out. I made things better.

I open my eyes. Once upon a time, I would have been critical of every tiny flaw in my appearance. Now though, all I see is what I am: a queen. A warrior. A survivor. A fighter. I know I can do anything, because I have already done everything. I went to hell and stabbed the devil in the eye. After that, what is left to frighten me? Not a damn thing, is the answer.

I'm proud of what I've done, even the parts that are drenched in blood and tears. Our scars are what mark us as unique, after all. I've come to think of my scars as the stitching that holds me together. I've got my stories on my skin; that's what makes me who I am. I like that this dress shows that. It's strapless and sleeveless, so that the paleness of my skin glows against the pure white of the fabric. I run my hand down the skirts, savoring how fine and delicate it feels against my fingertips. This, too, once seemed like an impossibility. And now, I am moments away from stepping out of my life and into a happily ever after that I never dreamed of.

A knock at the door startles me out of my reverie. "Yes?" I call.

"It's me," rumbles a deep voice.

I'd know that voice anywhere. Rising, I walk over to the door, turn the handle, and open it maybe just a quarter of an inch. "You, sir, are most definitely not supposed to be here," I reprimand playfully.

"I'm not coming in," Vito answers, "so no rules are being broken."

"Well, no peeking," I snap. "And don't let anyone else see either."

"About that ..." interjects Mateo's voice.

"You'll have to forgive us, princess," adds Dante.

Leo finishes, "We've never been much good with rules anyway."

I sigh and roll my eyes. So much for my peaceful solitude. "I'm still not opening the door, you know."

"We wouldn't dream of asking such a thing."

"Mhmm. Color me skeptical."

Dante chimes in, "Such little faith! Hey, I could still steal a car if you wanna ditch these guys and elope to Vegas or something."

I hear a rustle and the thump of one of the brothers punching the other in the arm.

"I've seen you drive," Leo scowls. "You wouldn't even make it to the end of the street without wrecking the damn thing."

"You couldn't outdrive me in your wildest dreams."

"Luckily for me, you never set so much as a goddamn *toe* in my wildest dreams. If you did, it'd be a nightmare."

"My nightmare is listening to the two of you bicker," Mateo cuts in.

I just laugh again. With the door closed and the voices somewhat muffled, it's hard to tell who is who, but I suppose it doesn't really matter.

Because they're all mine.

I'm not eloping with any of them; I'm marrying all of them.

It's still hard to wrap my head around. A year is a long time in certain regards, but it's not so long in a lot of other ways. And it's only been a year since these very same men came barging into a hotel room disguised as cops and dragged me out kicking and screaming. Couple that with all the horrors that happened from that point forward, and part of me thinks I'd have to be insane to go forward with the ceremony today.

But another part of me knows I'd have to be insane *not* to go forward with it, too.

Because the truth—a truth that we've only recently begun to actually acknowledge between us—is that I love the Bianci brothers. All of them. And they love me. They're my princes; I'm their queen.

Marrying them has another purpose too. It ends a war that has already cost far too many lives.

I still remember the night all this was decided.

Three days had passed since the Bianci Castle went up in a torrent of flames. Dad was seated at the kitchen table. He was still in pain, but thanks to the supplies in the Bianci safe house where we were all staying, he was stable for the time being. The plan was to get him to a hospital back on the East Coast as soon as the arrangements could be made to transport him safely. That would come soon, perhaps the next day. For right now, he was stable enough for what had to happen next—which had yet to be determined.

Seated across the table from him were the four brothers. Vito was in the worst shape, but like my dad, he was somehow finding a way to stay awake and alert. Mateo, Dante, and Leo each had some horrific-looking injuries of their own, though those too had already begun to heal.

So much had happened since we escaped by the skin of our teeth. The lies and betrayals Sergio had wrought had all been brought to light. He'd been planning his coup for a long time, driven by hatred for his father and envy of Vito's birthright. By convincing a faction of Russian troops to turn on my dad and follow his traitorous lead, he'd found himself a rogue army of men thirsty to inherit the wealth and power of two empires at once. Watching the brothers' faces as they figured out the ins and outs of Sergio's betrayals nearly broke my heart. But it had to be done. Like ripping a Band-Aid off, like blowing up the castle—some things are painful but necessary.

There was still one thing left to solve though, the question we'd all been thinking in one form or another: what happened next?

Too much had happened to simply return to the previous equilibrium. Were the Volkovs and Biancis supposed to simply part ways, each retreating to their old haunts, and pretend like none of this ever transpired? How could I *pretend like this never happened? The truth of the matter was that they had kidnapped me, twisted me, and come perilously close to permanently breaking me. My father could not easily forget that. Neither could I.*

And the brothers couldn't forgive decades of hatred towards my dad and his organization. They'd spent years believing that he had murdered their uncle in cold blood and thrown his body on the steps of their home like roadkill. Even if that turned out not to be true, it was proving awfully hard to let go of those feelings.

So we'd all come to sit at this kitchen table in this ratty LA apartment and try to answer the question of how our futures should look.

The conversation didn't start well. Clipped threats turned to angry yelling and before I knew it, blood was dripping on the table as my father and the brothers both reopened wounds they'd suffered during our captivity and escape.

"You fucking Russians always want—"

"As if you Italian cocksuckers could even hold a candle to—"

"Sit the fuck down!"

Everyone fell silent when I stood up and interrupted. I think part of the shock was that they weren't used to women interfering in business discussions. But if this was how they intended to conduct themselves, then they had another thing coming, because I wasn't about to sit idly by and let the two sides of my heart go to war with each other right in front of me. Their way was what caused all of this in the first place. So fuck their way. The time for that was gone.

It was time to do things my way now.

"I'm the only thing holding all this together," I began. "Don't you see that? And I'm the only thing stopping you from spending the rest of your lives

—whatever is left of them—going at each other's throats. But let me say this clearly, because I'm only going to say this once: that's not going to happen anymore. The old guard is gone. Your father is dead. And you, Dad—it's time for you to retire soon. That means I'm going to be in charge. And that means I'm deciding what happens next. So listen closely."

Five pairs of stunned eyes drank in my every word silently and obediently. I still don't know where the forcefulness of my manner came from. Maybe I had more of my dad in me all along than I'd ever suspected. Mom would disagree—she'd always had more fire than people realized when they first met her, so she'd probably argue that she was the source of this. But whether it came from my parents or from my time in the Bianci dungeon or somewhere else altogether, it was here to stay now.

"You, you, you, and you," I said, pointing at each of the brothers in turn. "Get on your knees."

"Why?" blurted Vito, but his voice died when I shot him a withering stare.

"Didn't I just tell you that I'm in charge now?" I snapped. "Do what I said."

The brothers looked back and forth at each other. Then, with a smile playing subtly at the corners of his lips, Mateo knelt down. Each of the others followed suit, and when they were down, I rose. "Look at my dad," I ordered. "And ask for his blessing."

It was Leo's turn to interrupt. "His blessing for what?"

I turned my gaze on him. Like Vito, he shrugged and fell silent.

Again, Mateo took the lead. "Mr. Volkov, sir," he said deferentially. "I humbly request your blessing."

"Good," I said approvingly. I looked at my dad. "Say yes."

"Lubimaya ..." *he started to say.*

"No!" I shake my head. "I am not your lubimaya *right now. I am Milaya Volkov, head of the Volkov Bratva, and I am telling you what I want you to*

do. I don't give a damn if you're my dad. It's my time to talk, and your time to listen."

Dad looked shocked for a moment, and I was struck again by how similar he and the Biancis were. But just like them, he smiled just the tiniest bit and nodded. "I grant you my blessing," he said.

"Good. Great. Thanks. Now," I said, turning back to look at the brothers kneeling in a row by the side of the table, "ask me to marry you."

Vito's jaw fell open. "You've gotta be kidding me."

I fixed him with my fiercest expression. "Do I look like I'm kidding you, Vito Bianci?" I asked in the venomous voice I'd heard my father use long ago. "Do I look like I'm in much of a kidding mood?"

He said nothing for a long beat, just looked around in amazement as if he couldn't believe this was happening. Finally, his stare settled on my dad, who was still seated on the other side of the table. "Luka, surely you can't ..."

Dad shrugged. "Did you not hear my daughter? I would advise you to do as she says, son."

I bit back a smile of my own. On the floor to my right, Mateo nudged Vito in the ribs with his elbow and nodded subtly. Dante and Leo looked at each other and both shrugged. They all turned their faces up to me. Vito still looked lost, until he coughed and blinked hard like he was clearing away cobwebs in his head. He looked down at the floor between his knees.

That moment was the one I remember most clearly. It was pregnant, full of promise and disaster alike. The question that hung in the air was, Could these broken men let go of their hate? It had clouded their hearts for as long as they'd been alive. They'd been steeped in it. It drove them and they sought it.

But it was poisonous, dirty fuel. It was consuming them alive, and if they kept along the path they'd charted for themselves, they wouldn't have much longer left. Surely they had to realize that. And surely they had to realize that there was an alternative. It was standing in front of them in the shape *of the prisoner who had become their queen. The hunted who had become the huntress. If they wanted out, they had to say yes now. They wouldn't have another chance.*

Vito looked up. "Milaya Volkov," he said in the way that only he could say it, the way that inevitably sent shivers racing down my spine. "Will you marry us?"

"Getting cold feet?" Dante teases. I hear a second thump. Someone has punched him again. "Ow! Motherfucker. You're lucky I don't have my 'chucks."

"*You're* the lucky one. I'd wrap them around your throat if I could."

"That'd be the day."

"Enough, both of you," I scold, though I'm still laughing inwardly. "It's our wedding day. You're supposed to be on your best behavior."

"Tell it to the runt of the family here," Mateo mumbles.

I can picture Dante getting worked up on the other side of the door as they all tease each other back and forth. It never stops with them. But it makes me smile, so I allow it.

It's crazy to think of spending a lifetime with them. When I first proposed the union that night in the LA safe house apartment, I was careful to pitch it as a peace offering. Nothing more, nothing less. Mostly because I was scared of what it would mean if I confessed that I wanted it for more reasons than that. And also because I was downright terrified of what it would mean if they confessed that they did, too.

Can a girl love four men? Can four men love one girl? Can my father let me go? Can my enemies become my lovers, my guardians, my husbands, my kings? I still don't know. I won't know for sure until we all take our last breath, I suppose. I've learned that nothing in this world is for certain. Nothing can be taken for granted. At any moment, it could all go up in flames. You can think your life is headed one way, but all it takes is a few men in ill-fitting cop uniforms to yank you down another path altogether. So I'm slowly figuring out how to take things one day at a time.

That's not to say that the questions don't overwhelm me though. Because they definitely do. Like a swarm of hornets I can't get away from, buzzing around on the inside of my skull. They keep me up at night sometimes. Often, actually, if I'm being honest with myself. The things I'm doing have never been done before, at least as far as I'm aware. I'm trying to build bridges between worlds that were never meant to be joined together. Every now and then, I feel like I'm the last little thread keeping it all from tearing in two. But then other times, I feel so lucky to be able to straddle these universes. To be the glue that keeps it all connected. That's a unique power, a unique privilege, a unique calling. And it's all mine. I try to remind myself of that when I'm feeling overwhelmed—that I'm doing what I was always meant to do.

Right now is more like one of the "feeling overwhelmed" moments than a "feeling like queen of the world" moment. I catch sight of myself in the mirror across the room and feel for a second like I'm a little girl playing dress-up in her mother's closet. What is this dress? What are these heels? Who is this girl in fancy makeup and an absurdly elaborate up-do? I want so badly to feel beautiful, and part of me definitely does. But another part of me feels like I should stop pretending and instead go join a nunnery or something. Who do I think I am?

I need reassurance. I am the queen of my men, aren't I? Yes. But I most certainly am not feeling that way at the moment. And even a queen needs to feel the weight of her crown every now and then to be reminded of her station.

I don't know when it happened, but somewhere along the line, the Bianci brothers became my crown jewels. I keep them together, but they lift me up. We need each other.

They need me. I need them. More now than ever.

I take a deep breath, then pull the door all the way open.

"I know this is completely against the rules," I begin, "but I decided: fuck the rules. I, uh—I could use a little confidence right now."

Vito, Mateo, Leo, and Dante are arranged in a row standing in front of me. They're each wearing tuxedos, and the white pocket square tucked into each of their breast pockets has their initials embroidered in thread that matches their eyes. The white rose pinned against their lapels is the exact same cream color as my dress.

As with the first time I saw them, my first thought is how gorgeous they are. My angels and my devils bundled into one. Jawlines sharp as razors, hair dark and thick, and those eyes—the first and last thing I notice about them every time I look. It's insane how their personalities are perfectly reflected in their irises. Dante's roiling amber, Leo's placid blue, Mateo's deep green, and last of all, Vito's surge of black.

The Bianci men have never been particularly expressive. Not even Dante. But as they look at me, their jaws drop one by one.

Dante is the first to talk, as always. "Princess, you look ..."

"Incredible," Mateo finishes in a hushed voice.

"Come inside, before someone sees you," I say. I'm blushing like a stoplight, and I don't want anyone else to accidentally wander past the bridal prep room and witness me flagrantly flouting wedding custom.

They file in, then fan out again. I shut the door once they've entered, but I hesitate for a moment and stay there with my forehead resting against the closed door. I close my eyes. The first thing I notice is that

I smell them now. Against the backdrop of jasmine and lilies floating from the floral display in one corner, I am buried beneath their combined odor of sandalwood, citrus, and a kind of cool, musky darkness, like a panther would find between the roots of a tree on a warm summer night. It does to me what it always does: sends heat rushing through my face and between my legs. My lips part, my thighs tremble, my breath quickens. Beneath my dress, I feel my nipples pebble against the soft fabric. If I were wearing any underwear, I would feel wetness against my panties, too. As it is, I feel only the cool draft of the air conditioning.

I keep my forehead against the door. It feels solid and reassuring. But the touch I really need is behind me. I take a long breath, steel myself, then pivot slowly to face them once more.

I immediately notice the hardness of their manhoods straining at the zippers of their tuxedo pants. I hurriedly force myself to glance away. I have to crane my neck to look up into their faces. They're each at least a foot taller than me, Mateo most of all. When I'm this close to them, they're all I can see. Just an ocean of Bianci men in tuxedos, stretching from edge to edge of my vision.

They gaze back at me, unblinking, unmoving. We stay like that for a beat too long. Suddenly, I feel overwhelmed. It's hard to breath, and I have to look away, down to the floor, or else I feel like I might faint.

"I'm sorry," I whisper. "Maybe this was a bad idea."

"Milaya Volkov," says the one man I was most afraid would speak up. Vito reaches his hand forward and gently forces my chin up so I am looking him directly in the eyes again. How much I hated that face once upon a time! That Bianci nose, so cruel and proud. Those eyes, so dark and angry.

Not now though. Not anymore. Vito's eyes are as dark as ever, but the black hellfire that used to burn in them has cooled to something else now. It's the darkness of space, of eternity, of endless possibility. I could tumble head over heels forever in those eyes and never find ground again, and for some reason, I'm perfectly okay with that.

"We were broken when you met us. I most of all. Look at me now, though. Do you see a broken man?"

He waits for me to answer. I shake my head imperceptibly. I don't trust myself to speak out loud.

"You fixed me," he continues. "You saved me. All of us. You don't have a damn thing in the world to apologize for. Not a rule can bind you anymore. We want to give you the universe on a platter. Will you let us?"

He waits for me again. I hesitate for the longest time, mostly because I'm trying as hard as I possibly can not to cry.

Finally, I nod. "Can I ask you all a favor?"

"Anything," Dante answers without hesitation.

"Can you go ahead and kiss me now?"

An identical grin spreads across each of their faces. Then they move towards me, and the moment I've been dying for since dawn finally sweeps me up, and I can let go of anxiety I've been holding onto for far longer than I realized.

Mateo's mouth finds my left earlobe and suckles gently, while Leo comes around and presses into me from behind as his hands grip my hips and pull me back towards him. Dante gently caresses my abdomen. Vito steps up, leans forward, and claims me with a greedy, open kiss.

Things happen fast. Leo undoes the clasps at the back of my dress, then Dante and Mateo slide it down gently. We're breaking every rule in the entire wedding book, but I stopped caring about that a long time ago. I want this, I need this, I deserve this, and so do they. We've never done things the conventional way anyhow. Why start now?

Before I know it, I'm standing naked between the four of them. There are hands tweaking my nipples and hands tugging dominantly on the roots of my hair and hands finding the hot slash between my legs and starting to coax moans out of me like the rippling of an incoming tide. I just close my eyes and let it all happen. Why differentiate between the men? To me, they're different sides of the same beautiful diamond. I turn in the light and see how they each catch and refract it differently. But at the end of the day, they're all bound together by my love. By *our* love. By what we've seen and done to each other, by what we've fought and survived together. That's the only thing that matters. Everything else is just a footnote at best.

There's no bed in here, so we end up on the floor, with clothes strewn around us on all sides. I want—no, I *need*—to see their nakedness and to feel them in my hands, in my mouth. They don't hesitate to give me what I need either. It takes only moments before Dante is plunging himself into my aching, needy pussy from behind while I lick up and down along Vito's length and fondle Leo and Mateo, who are kneeling to my left and my right.

The feeling of Dante filling me up is indescribable. There's the naughty edge of fucking when we aren't even supposed to be seeing each other, that illicit thrill of breaking the rules. There's the raw physical sensation of his wickedly curved cock finding that place in me that only he can reach. And layered on top of that is that dangerous, wild love that he and I share, the love that's uniquely ours.

In my mouth, I taste pure Vito. The tang, the salt, the sweat, the raw masculine essence that only he has. He's already bucking and writhing as I take him past my lips and lave my tongue around his shaft. More than any of his brothers, he's the one who has the hardest time stopping himself from loosing his seed into me at the merest touch. I touch something in him that only I can touch. I am the one who tells him it is okay to stop. The world will not go on without him. He can breathe.

Mateo and Leo are patiently waiting for their turns, so I go back and forth between them. Mateo rumbles like a mountain the way he always does. His eyes are closed and his hand rests gently on the back of my head. He's not pushing me farther down on his length, but I want to go farther. I want those rumbling sighs to reverberate through me and make my cells come alive. Sure enough, as I groan and strain to swallow all of him, his deep moans intensify, and with it, so too does the burgeoning orgasm taking root deep in my core.

Dante keeps fucking me relentlessly from behind while I switch my mouth over to Leo. I cradle his balls as I lick with just the tip of my tongue teasingly from base to tip and back again. "Oh, you cruel girl," he mutters. His blue eyes flash in the chandelier light overhead. Unlike Mateo, he doesn't let me choose my own pace. Instead, he shoves his hips forward and fills my mouth like a battering ram. It's a game of give and take with him, each of us alternately wrestling for control or letting the other one torture us mercilessly. We both savor the pain that gives pleasure its shape. What's sweetness without bitterness after all? What's a sunrise without the dark that precedes it? We need the broken edges to show us where the light begins. He taught me that. They all did, actually.

After one particularly savage thrust, Dante uses the leverage of my hips to flip me over. I'm lying back to front on top of Vito while Dante shuffles around to one side and trades places with Mateo.

I gasp out loud as Vito takes the head of his cock and starts to trace delicately at my other entrance. "Easy, darling," Leo whispers in my ear when he senses my fright. "Just relax."

It takes me a moment, but Leo's gentle touch on my abdomen helps bring me back down. Slowly, I unclench and feel myself begin to open. I grip onto Dante's cock and stroke while Vito keeps probing gently, giving me the time I need.

I look up at Mateo, who is crouched on top of me. His cock is tapping at the wet slick between my legs. He arches one eyebrow in a silent question. When I nod, he slides into me without hesitation. That breaks the dam, and my first orgasm comes tumbling through me. I twitch and writhe while Mateo takes long, slow strokes in and out. At the very farthest part of his withdrawal, my body is insanely hungry for him to return to me. Only the sounds of my wetness and our mingled breathing fill the room, plus the smell of sweaty bodies colliding blissfully. Dante finds my clit and begins to work it as his teeth nip at the peak of my breast.

I'm awash in everything, overwhelmed by the quartet of cocks and mouths finding purchase along every nook and cranny of me that can be explored. The heat of breath on my skin combines with the electricity of nerves on fire. *The only way out is through*, right? In this case, that means I can't keep holding onto these orgasms. If I do, they'll tear me apart from the inside out. I have to let go. I have to breathe.

As I do, Vito finally delves into me. I've never been so full. There is a cock in my hand, a cock in my mouth, a cock in my pussy, a cock in my ass, and all I can think is that I want *more.* More of them, closer to me. More of their heat, their smell, their touch, their kiss.

The one thing I don't need more of is their love. I am rich with their love already. They've given me all that can be given. And I've given mine to them.

We own each other, the Biancis and me. I'm no longer fully Volkov. Part of me belongs to them, and it always will. But maybe that's how we fix broken things. We have to take a little bit of something else to bind it all up and make it whole again.

The time eventually comes for each of the brothers to find their own release. I want it all to be in me. Not a drop spilled—it's all mine. *They* are all mine.

One at a time, they lie down and let me straddle them and ride until they burst. I stare each of them in the eyes and plant a soft kiss on their lips as the tremors coarse through their bodies. Only when Vito has finally loosed himself do I slump over between them and let them rain kisses down my naked, sweaty, trembling body.

I'm not sure how long we lie there before I remember that there is a wedding meant to take place today, and it is sort of important for us to be there. We get up, bantering and laughing and smiling, as they get dressed and help me get back into my dress. Then they leave with a kiss on the cheek, and I'm alone once more.

Except, not actually alone. I'll never be truly alone again.

EPILOGUE: VITO

I'm standing at the altar with my brothers next to me. How we ended up here, I may never know. It doesn't matter. We have what we wanted, the thing we never knew we needed. At the chiming of a bell, I look down to the end of the garden and see exactly that thing.

Milaya looks radiant. After our forbidden romp in the bridal room, her hair was mussed. She fretted about it, so I told her what to do. *Leave it down. Show them you are wild. Show them a queen does whatever she likes.*

She took my suggestion. I am glad she did, because the sight of her long, dark hair tumbling down over those pale cream shoulders is one I will never forget as long as I live. This moment is seared into my brain. There is no sound, no smell, no taste, no touch associated with it. I know immediately that all I will have to do for the rest of my life is close my eyes to envision our bride under a floral arch, with her green eyes shimmering as if she sees things that no other being alive could have seen in us.

I do not remember what is said during the ceremony. Perhaps one of my brothers will be able to recount it to me one day, or Milaya herself. I repeat what I am told, and when it is my turn to kiss her, I keep my eyes open so that I can see her flawless beauty while my lips press into hers.

The record that has played in the back of my mind for my entire life sounds its message once more: *if you stop, you die.*

I'm stopping here, surrounded by my brothers and our bride. But it turns out that my father was wrong. I am not dying after all.

I am being reborn.

And in the distance, there's a whole new life waiting for us to find it.

Together.

THE END

SNEAK PREVIEW (BROKEN VOWS)

Keep reading for a sneak preview of my bestselling mafia romance novel, BROKEN VOWS!

She's my fake wife, my property... and my last chance at redemption.

She's beautiful. An angel.

I'm dangerous. A killer.

She's my fake bride for a single reason – so I can crush her father's resistance.

But marrying Eve brings me far more than I bargained for.

She's fiery. Feisty. Won't take no for an answer.

She makes me believe that I might be worth redemption.

Until I discover a past she's been hiding from me.

One that threatens everything.

Now, I know that our wedding vows are not enough.

I need to make sure she's mine for good.

A baby in her belly is the only way to seal the deal.

In the end, the Bratva always gets what it wants.

Luka

Their fear tingles against my skin like a whisper. As my leather-soled shoes tap against the concrete floor, I can sense it in the way their eyes dart towards and away from me. In the way they scurry around the production floor like mice, meek and unseen in the shadows. I enjoy it.

Even before I rose through the ranks of my family, I could inspire fear. Being a large man made that simple. But now, with brawn and power behind me, people cower. These people—the employees at the soda factory—don't even know why they fear me. Other than me being the owner's son, they have no real reason to be afraid of me, and yet, like prey in the grasslands, they sense the lion is near. I observe each of them as I weave my way around conveyors filled with plastic bottles and aluminum cans, carbonated soda being pumped into them, filling the room with a syrupy sweet smell.

I recognize their faces, though not their names. The people upstairs don't concern me. Or, at least, they shouldn't. The soda factory is a cover for the real operation downstairs, which must be protected at all costs. It's why I'm here on a Friday evening sniffing around for rats. For anyone who looks unfamiliar or out of place.

The floor manager—a Hispanic woman with a severe braid running down her back—calls out orders to the employees on the floor below in both English and Spanish, directing attention where necessary. She doesn't look at me once.

Noise permeates the metal shell of the building. The whirr of conveyor belts and grinding of gears makes the concrete floors feel like they are vibrating from the sheer power of the sound waves. A lot of people find the sights and smells overwhelming, but I've never minded. You don't become a mob underboss by shrinking in the face of chaos.

A group of employees in blue polos gather around a conveyor belt, smoothing out some kink in the production line. They pull a few aluminum cans from the line and drop them in a recycling bin, jockeying the rest of the cans back into a smooth line. The larger of the three men—a bald man with a doughy face and no obvious chin—flips a red switch. An alarm sounds and the cans begin moving again. He gives the floor manager a thumbs up and then turns to me, his hand flattening into a small wave. I raise an eyebrow in response. His face reddens, and he turns back to his work.

I don't recognize him, but he can't be in law enforcement. Undercover cops are more fit than he could ever dream to be. Plus, he wouldn't have drawn attention to himself. Likely, he is just a new hire, unaware of my position in the company. I resolve to go over new hires with the site manager and find out the man's name.

When I make it to the back of the production floor, the lights are dimmed—the back half of the factory not being utilized overnight—and I fumble with my keys for a moment before finding the right one to unlock the basement door. The stairway down is dark, and as soon as the metal door slams shut behind me, I'm left in blackness, my other senses heightening. The sounds of the production floor are but a whisper behind me, but the most pressing difference is the smell. Rather than the syrupy sweetness of the factory, there is an ether, chemical-like smell that makes my nose itch.

"That you, Luka?" Simon Oakley, the main chemist, doesn't wait for me to answer. "I've got a line here for you. We've perfected the chemistry. Best coke you'll ever try."

I pull back a thick curtain at the base of the stairs and step into the bright white light of the real production floor. I blink as my eyes adjust, and see Simon alone at the first metal table, three other men working in the back of the room. Like the employees upstairs, they don't look up as I enter. Simon, however, smiles and points to the line.

"I don't need to try it," I say flatly. "I'll know whether it's good or not when I see how much our profits increase."

"Well," Simon balks. "It can take time for word to spread. We may not see a rise in income until—"

"I'm not here to chat." I walk around the end of the table and stand next to Simon. He is an entire head shorter than me, his skin pale from spending so much time in the basement. "There have been nasty rumors going around among my men."

His bushy brows furrow in concern. "Rumors about what? You know we basement dwellers are often the last to hear just about everything." He tries to chuckle, but it dies as soon as he sees that I'm not here to fuck around.

"Disloyalty." I purse my lips and run my tongue over my top teeth. "The rumbling is that someone has turned their back on the family."

Fear dilates his pupils, and his fingers drum against the metal tabletop. "See? That is what I'm saying. I haven't heard a single thing about any of that."

"You haven't?" I hum in thought, taking a step closer. I can tell Simon wants to back away, but he stays put. I commend him for his bravery even as I loath him for it. "That is interesting."

His Adam's apple bobs in his throat. "Why is that interesting?"

Before he can even finish the sentence, my hand is around his neck. I strike like a snake, squeezing his windpipe in my hand and walking him back towards the stone wall. I hear the men in the back of the room jump and murmur, but they make no move to help their boss. Because I outrank Simon by a mile.

"It's interesting, Simon, because I have reliable information that says you met with members of the Furino mafia." I slam his head against the wall once, twice. "Is it true?"

His face is turning red, eyeballs beginning to bulge out, and he claws at my hand for air. I don't give him any.

"Why would you go behind my back and meet with another family? Have I not welcomed you into our fold? Have I not made your life here comfortable?"

Simon's eyes are rolling back in his head, his fingers becoming limp noodles on my wrist, weak and ineffective. Just before his body can sag into unconsciousness, I release him. He drops to the floor, falling onto his hands and knees and gasping for air. I let him get two breaths before I kick him in the ribs.

"I didn't meet with them," he rasps. When he looks up at me, I can already see the beginnings of bruises wrapping around his neck.

I kick him again. The force knocks the air out of him, and he collapses on his face, forehead pressed to the cement floor.

"Okay," he says, voice muffled. "I talked with them. Once."

I pressed the sole of my shoe into his ribs, rolling him onto his back. "Speak up."

"I met with them once," he admits, tears streaming down his face from the pain. "They reached out to me."

"Yet you did not tell me?"

"I didn't know what they wanted," he says, sitting up and leaning against the wall.

"All the more reason you should have told me." I reach down and grab his shirt, hauling him to his feet and pinning him against the wall. "Men who are loyal to me do not meet with my enemies."

"They offered me money," he says, wincing in preparation for the next blow. "They offered me a larger cut of the profits. I shouldn't have gone, but I have a family, and—"

I was raised to be an observer of people. To spot their weaknesses and know when I am being deceived. So, I know immediately Simon is not telling me the entire story. The Furinos would not reach out to our chemist and offer him more money unless there had been communication between them prior, unless they had some connection Simon is not telling me about. He thinks I am a fool. He thinks I will forgive him because of his wife and child, but he does not know the depths of my apathy. Simon thinks he can appeal to my humanity, but he does not realize I do not have any.

I press my hand into the bruises around his neck. Simon grabs my wrist, trying to pull me away, but I squeeze again, enjoying the feeling of his life in my hands. I like knowing that with one blow to the neck, I could break his trachea and watch him suffocate on the floor. I am in complete control.

"And your family will be dead before dawn unless you tell me why you met with the Furinos," I spit. I want nothing more than to kill Simon for being disloyal. I can figure out the truth without him. But it is not why I was sent here. Killing indiscriminately does not create the kind of controlled fear we need to keep our family standing. It only creates anarchy. So, reluctantly, I let Simon go. Once again, he falls to the floor, gasping, and I step away so I won't be tempted to beat him.

"I'll tell you," he says, his voice high-pitched, like the words are being released slowly from a balloon. "I'll tell you anything, just don't hurt my family."

I nod for him to continue. This is his only chance to come clean. If he lies to me again, I'll kill him.

Simon opens his mouth, but before he can say anything, I hear a loud bang upstairs and a scream. Just as I turn around, the door at the top of the stairs opens, and I know immediately something is wrong. Forgetting all about Simon, I grab the nearest table and tip it over, not worrying about the potential lost profits. Footsteps pound down the stairs and no sooner have I crouched down, the room erupts in bullets.

I see one of the men in the back of the room drop, clutching his stomach. The other two follow my lead and dive behind tables. Simon crawls over to lay on the floor next to me, his lips purple.

The room is filled with the pounding of footsteps, the ring of bullets, and the moans of the fallen man. It is chaos, but I am steady. My heart rate is even as I grab my phone, turn on the front facing camera, and lift it over the table. There are eight shoulders spread out around the room, guns at the ready. Two of them are at the base of the stairs, the other six are spread out in three-foot increments, forming a barrier in front of the stairs. No one here is supposed to get out alive.

But they do not know who is hiding behind the table. If they did, they'd be running.

I look over at one of the chemists. They are not our family's soldiers, but they are trained like anyone else. He has his gun at the ready, waiting for my order. I nod my head once, twice, and on three, we both turn and fire.

One man falls immediately, my bullet striking him in the neck, blood spraying against the wall like splattered paint. It is a kind of artwork, shooting a man. Years of training, placing the bullet just so. Art is meant to incite a reaction and a bullet certainly does that. The man drops his weapon, his hand flying to his neck. Before he can experience too much pain, I place another bullet in his forehead. He drops to his knees, but before he falls flat on his face, I shoot his friend.

The men expected this ambush to be simple, so they are still in shock, still scrambling to collect themselves. It makes it easy for my men to knock them off. Another two men drop as I chase my second target around the room, firing shot after shot at him. He ducks behind a table, and I wait, gun aimed. It is a deadly game of Whack-a-mole, and it requires patience. His gun pops up first, followed shortly by his head, which I blow off with one shot. His scream dies on his lips as he bleeds out, red seeping out from under the table and spreading across the floor.

There are three men left, and I'm out of bullets. I stash my gun in my pocket and pull out my KA-BAR knife. The blade feels like an old friend in my hand. I crawl past a shivering Simon, wishing I'd killed him just so I wouldn't have to see him looking so pathetic, and out from behind the table. I slide my feet under me, moving into a crouch. The remaining men are wounded, and they are focused on the back corner where shots are still coming from my men. They do not see me approaching from the side.

I lunge at the first man—a young kid with golden brown hair and a tattoo on his neck. It is half-hidden under the collar of his shirt, so I cannot make it out. When my knife cuts into his side, he spins to fight me off, but I knock his gun from his hand with my left arm and then drive the knife in under his ribs and upward. He freezes for a moment before blood leaks from his mouth.

The man next to him falls from multiple bullets in the chest and stomach. I kick his gun away from him as he falls to the floor, and advance on the last attacker. He is hiding behind a metal table, palm pressing into a wound on his shoulder. He scrambles to lift his gun as I approach, but I drop to my knees and slide next to him, knife pressed to his neck. His eyes go wide, and then they squeeze shut as he drops his weapon.

The blade of my knife is biting into his skin, and I see the same tattoo creeping up from beneath his collar. I slide the blade down, pushing his shirt aside, and I recognize it at once.

"You are with the Furinos?" I ask.

The man answers by squeezing his eyes shut even tighter.

"You should know who is in a room before you attack," I hiss. "I am Luka Volkov, and I could slit your throat right now."

His entire body is trembling, blood from his shoulder wound leaking through his clothes and onto the floor. Every ounce of me wants this kill. I feel like a dog who has not been fed, desperate for a hunk of flesh, but warfare is not endless bloodshed. It is tactical.

"But I will not," I say, pulling the blade back. The man blinks, unbelieving. "Get out of here and tell your boss what happened. Tell him this attack is a declaration of war, and the Volkov family will live up to our merciless reputation."

He hesitates, and I slash the blade across his cheek, drawing a thin line of blood from the corner of his mouth to his ear. "Go!" I roar.

The man scrambles to his feet and towards the stairs, blood dripping in his wake. As soon as he is gone, I clean my knife with the hem of my shirt and slide it back into place on my hip.

This will not end well.

Eve

I hold up a bag of raisins and a bag of prunes a few inches from the cook's face.

"Do you see the difference?" I ask. The question is rhetorical. Anyone with eyes could see the difference. And a cook—a properly trained cook—should be able to smell, feel, and sense the difference, as well.

Still, Felix wrinkles his forehead and studies the bags like it is a pop quiz.

"Raisins are small, Felix!" My shouting makes him jump, but I'm far too stressed out to care. "Prunes are huge. As big as a baby's fist. Raisins are tiny. They taste very different because they start out as different fruits. Do you see the problem?"

He stares at me blankly, and I wonder if being sous chef gives me the authority to fire someone. Because this man has got to go.

"You've ruined an entire roast duck, Felix." I drop the bags on the counter and run a hand down my sweaty face. I grab the towel from my back pocket and towel off. "Throw it out and start again, but use *prunes* this time."

He smiles and nods, and I wonder how many times he must have hit his head to be so slow. I motion for another cook to come talk to me. He moves quickly, hands folded behind his back, waiting for my order.

"Chop up the duck and make a confit salad. We can toss it with more raisins, fennel—that kind of thing—and make it work."

He nods and shuffles away, and I mop my forehead again.

At the start of my shift, I strode into the kitchen like I owned the place. I was finally sous chef to Cal Higgs, genius chef in charge at The Floating Crown. After graduating culinary school, I didn't know where I'd get a job or where I'd be on the totem pole, and I certainly never imagined I'd be a sous chef so soon, but here I am. And now that I'm here, I can't help but wonder if it wasn't some sort of trick. Did Cal give into my father's wishes easily and give me this job because he needed a break from the insanity?

I've been assured by several members of staff that the dishwasher, whose name I can't remember, has been working at the kitchen for over a year, but he seems to be stuck on slow motion tonight. He is washing and drying plates seconds before the cooks are plating them up and sending them back out to the dining room. And two of the cooks, who were apparently dating, decided that the middle of dinner rush would be the perfect time to discuss their relationship, and they broke up. Dylan stormed out without a word, and Sarah, who should be okay since she was the dumper, not the dumpee, is hiding in the bathroom bawling her eyes out. I've knocked on the door once every ten minutes for an hour, but she refuses to let me in. Cal has a key, but he has been shut away in his office all night, and I don't want to go explain what a shitshow the kitchen is, so we are making do. Barely.

"Sarah?" I knock on the door. "If you don't come out in five minutes, you're fired."

For the first time, there is a break in the crying. "You can't do that."

"Yes, I can," I lie. "You'll leave here tonight without your apron. Single and jobless. Just imagine that shame."

I feel bad rubbing salt in her wound, threatening her, but I'm out of options. I tried comforting her and offering her some of the dark chocolate from the dessert pantry, but she refused to budge. Threats are my last recourse.

There is a long pause, and I wonder if I'm going to have to admit that I actually can't fire her—I don't think—and tell the staff to start using the bathrooms on the customer side, when finally, Sarah emerges. Mascara is smeared down her cheeks, and her eyes are red and puffy from crying, but she is out of the bathroom. As soon as she steps through the doorway, one of the waitresses darts in after her and slams the door shut.

"I'm sorry, Eve," she blubbers, covering her face with her hands.

I grab her wrists and pry her palms from her eyes. When she looks up, her eyes are still closed, tears leaking from the corners.

"Go to the sinks and help with the dishes," I say firmly. "You're in no state to cook right now. Just focus on cleaning plates, okay?"

Sarah nods, her lower lip wobbling.

"Everything is fine," I say, speaking to her like she is a wild animal who might attack. "You won't lose your job. Cal never needs to know, okay? Just go wash dishes. Now."

She turns away from me in a daze and heads back to help the dishwasher whose name I can't for the life of me remember, and I take a deep breath. I've finally put out all the fires, and I lean against the counter and watch the kitchen move around me. It is like a living, breathing machine. Each person has to play their part or everything falls apart. And tonight, I'm barely holding them together.

When the kitchen door swings open, I hope it is Makayla. She has been a waitress at The Floating Crown for five years, and while she has no formal culinary training, she knows this kitchen better than anyone. I've asked her for help tonight more times than I'm comfortable with, but at this point, just seeing one, capable, smiling face would be enough to keep me from crying. But when I turn and instead see a man in a suit, the tie loose and askew around his neck, and his eyes glassy, I almost sag to the floor.

"You can't be back here, sir," I say, moving forward to block his access to the rest of the kitchen. "We have hot stoves and fire and sharp knives, and you are already unstable on your feet."

Makayla told me a businessman at the bar had been demanding macaroni and cheese all night between shots. Apparently, he would not take 'no' for an answer.

"Macaroni and cheese," he mutters, falling against my palms, his feet sliding out from underneath him. "I need macaroni and cheese to soak up the alcohol."

I turn to the nearest person for help, but Felix is still looking at the bags of raisins and prunes like he might seriously still be confused which is which, and I don't want to distract him lest he ruin another duck. I could call out for help from someone else or call the police, but I don't want to cause a scene. Cal is just in the next room. He may have hired me because my father is Don of the Furino family, but even my father can't be angry if Cal fires me for sheer incompetence. I have to prove that I'm capable.

"Sir, we don't have macaroni and cheese, but may I recommend our scoglio?"

"What is that?" he asks, top lip curled back.

"A delicious seafood pasta. Mussels, clams, shrimp, and scallops in a tomato sauce with herbs and spices. Truly delicious. One of my favorite meals on the menu."

"No cheese?"

I sigh. "No. No cheese."

He shakes his head and pushes past me, running his hands along the counters like he might stumble upon a prepared bowl of cheesy pasta.

"Sir, you can't be back here."

"I can be wherever I like," he shouts. "This is America, isn't it?"

"It is, but this is a private restaurant and our insurance does not cover diners being back in the kitchen, so I have to ask you—"

"Oh, say can you see by the dawn's early light!"

"Is that 'The Star-Spangled Banner'?" I ask, looking around to see whether anyone else can see this man or whether I'm having some sort of exhausted fever dream.

"What so proudly we hailed at the twilight's last gleaming?"

This is absurd. Truly absurd. Beyond calling the police, the easiest thing to do seems to be to give in to his demands, so I lay a hand on his shoulder and lead him to the corner of the kitchen. I pat the counter, and he jumps up like he is a child.

I listen to the National Anthem six times before I hand the man a bowl of whole grain linguini with a sharp cheddar cheese sauce on top. "Can you please take this back to the bar and leave me alone?"

He grabs the bowl from my hands, takes a bite, and then breaks into yet another rousing rendition of "The Star-Spangled Banner." This time in falsetto with accompanying dance moves.

I sigh and push him towards the door. "Come on, man."

The dining room is loud enough that no one pays the man too much attention. Plus, he has been drunk out here for an hour before ambushing the kitchen. A few guests shake their heads at the man and then smile at me, giving me the understanding and recognition I sought from the kitchen staff. I lead the man back to the bar, tell the bartender to get rid of him as soon as the pasta is gone, and then make my way back through the dining room.

"She isn't the chef," says a deep voice at normal volume. "Chefs don't look like *that*."

I don't turn towards the table because I don't want to give them the satisfaction of knowing I heard them, of knowing they had any kind of power over me.

"Whatever she makes, it can't taste half as good as her muffin," another man says to raucous laughter.

I roll my eyes and speed up. I'm used to the comments and the cat calls. I've been dealing with it since I sprouted boobs. Even my father's men would whisper things about me. It is part of the reason I chose a path outside the scope of the family business. I couldn't imagine working with the kind of men my father employed. They were crass and mean and treated women like possessions. Unfortunately, the more I learn of the world beyond the Bratva, the more I realize men everywhere are like that. It is the reason I'll never get married. I won't belong to anyone.

I hear the men's deep voices as I walk back towards the kitchen, but I don't listen. I let the words roll off of me like water on a windowpane and step back into the safe chaos of the kitchen.

The kitchen seems to calm down as dinner service goes on, and I'm able to take a step back from micro-managing everything to work on an order of chicken tikka masala. While letting the tomato puree and spices simmer, I realize my stomach is growling. I was too nervous before shift to eat anything, and now that things have finally settled into an easy rhythm, my body is about to absorb itself. So, I casually walk over to where two giant stock pots are simmering with the starter soups for the day and scoop myself out a hearty ladle of lobster and bacon soup. Cal doesn't like for anyone to eat while on service, but he has been in his office all evening, and based on the smell slipping out from under his door, he will be far too stoned to notice or care.

The soup is warm and filling, and I close my eyes as I eat, enjoying the blissful moment of peace before more chaos ensues.

The kitchen door opens, and this time it really is Makayla. I wave her over, eager to see how everyone is enjoying the food and whether the drunk patriot finally left the restaurant, but she doesn't see me and walks with purpose through the kitchen and straight to Cal's office door. She opens it and steps inside, and I wonder what she needed Cal for and why she couldn't come to me. Lord knows I've handled every other situation that arose all night.

I'm just finished the last bite of my soup when Cal's office door slams open, bouncing off the wall, and he stomps his way across the kitchen.

"Eve!"

I shove the bowl to the back of the counter, throwing a dish towel over top to hide the evidence, and then wipe my mouth quickly.

"Yes, chef?"

"Front and center," he barks like we are in the military rather than a kitchen.

Despite the offense I take with his tone—especially after everything I've done to keep the place running all night—I move quickly to follow his order. Because that is what a good sous chef does. I follow the chef's orders, no matter how demeaning.

Cal Higgs is a large man in every sense of the word. He is tall, round, and thick. His head sits on top of his shoulders with no neck in sight, and just walking across the room looks like a chore. I imagine being in his body would be like wearing a winter coat and scarf all the time.

"What is the problem, Chef?"

He hitches a thumb over his shoulder, and Makayla gives me an apologetic wince. "Someone complained about the food, and they want to see the chef."

I wrinkled my forehead. I'd personally tasted every dish that went out. Unless Felix managed to slide another dish past me with raisins in it instead of prunes, I'm not sure what the complaint could be. "Was there something wrong with the dish or did they simply not like it?"

"Does it matter?" he snaps. His eyes are bloodshot and glassy, yet his temper is as sharp as ever. "I don't like unhappy customers, and you need to fix it."

"But you're the chef," I say, realizing too late I should have stayed quiet.

Cal steps forward, and I swear I can feel the floor quake under his weight. "But you made the food. Should I go out there and apologize on your behalf? No, this is your mess, and you will take care of it."

"Of course," I say, looking down at the ground. "You're right. I'll go out there and make this right."

Before Cal can find another reason to yell at me, I retie my apron around my waist, straighten my white jacket, and march through the swinging kitchen doors.

The dining room is quieter than before. The drunk man is no longer singing the National Anthem at the bar and several of the tables are empty, the bussers clearing away empty plates. Happy plates, I might add. Clearly, they didn't have an issue with the food.

I didn't ask Makayla who complained about the food, but as soon as I walk into the main dining area, it is obvious. There is a small gathering at the corner booth, and a salt and pepper-haired man in his late fifties or early sixties raising a hand in the air and waves me over without looking directly at me. I haven't even spoken to the man yet, and I already hate him.

I'm standing at their table, staring at the man, but he doesn't speak to me until I announce my presence.

"I heard someone wanted to speak with the chef," I say.

He turns to me, one eyebrow raised. "You are the chef?"

I recognize a Russian accent when I hear one, and this man is Russian without a doubt. I wonder if I know him. Or if my father does. Would he be complaining to me if he knew my father was head of the Furino family? I would never throw my family name around in order to scare people, but for just a second, I have the inclination.

"Sous chef," I say with as much confidence as I can muster. "I ran the kitchen tonight, so I'll be hearing the complaints."

His eyes move down my body slowly like he is inspecting a cut of meat in a butcher shop. I cross my arms over my chest and spread my feet hip-width apart. "So, was there an issue with the food? I'd love to correct any problems."

"Soup was cold." He nudges his empty bowl to the center of the table with three fingers. "The portions were too small, and I ordered my steak medium-rare, not raw."

Every plate on the table is empty. Not a single crumb in sight. Apparently, the issues were not bad enough he couldn't finish his meal.

"Do you have any of the steak left?" I ask, making a show of looking around the table. "If one of my cooks undercooked the meat, I'd like to be able to inform them."

"If? I just told you the meet was undercooked. Are you doubting me?"

"Of course not," I say. *Yes, absolutely I am.* "It is just that if the meat was undercooked, I do not understand why you waited until you'd eaten everything to inform me of the problem?"

The man looks around the table at his companions. They are all smiling, and I can practically see them sharpening their teeth, preparing to rip me to shreds. When he turns back to me, his smile is acidic, deadly. "How did you get this position—sous chef? Surely not by skill. You are pretty, which I'm sure did you a favor. Did you sleep with the chef? Maybe—" he moves his hand in an obscene gesture—"'service' the boss to earn your place in the kitchen? Surely your 'talent' didn't get you the job, seeing as how you have none."

I physically bite my tongue and then take a deep breath. "If you'd like me to remake anything for you or bring out a complimentary dessert, I'm happy to do that. If not, I apologize for the issues and hope you will not hold it against us. We'd love to have you again."

Lies. Lies. Lies. I'm smiling and being friendly the way I was taught in culinary school. I actually took a class on dealing with customers, and this man is being even more outrageous than the overexaggerated angry customer played by my professor.

"Why would I want more food from you if the things you already sent out were terrible?" He snorts and shakes his head. "I see you do not have a ring on. That is no surprise. Men like a woman who can cook. Men don't care if you know your way around a professional kitchen if you don't know your way around a dinner plate."

The older gentleman is speaking, but I hear my father's words in my head. *You do not need to go to culinary school to find a husband, Eve. Your aunties can teach you to cook good food for your man.*

My entire life has been preparation for finding a husband. The validity of every hobby is judged by whether it will fetch me a suitor or not. My father wants me to be happy, but he mostly wants me to be married. Single, I'm a disappointment. Married, I'm a vessel for future Furino mafia members.

Years of anger and resentment begin to bubble and hiss inside of me until I'm boiling. My hands are shaking, and I can feel adrenaline pulsing through me, lighting every inch of me on fire. This time, I don't bite my tongue.

"I'd rather die alone than spent another minute near a man like you," I spit, stepping forward and laying my palms flat on the table. "The fact that you ate all of the food you apparently hated shows you are a pig in more ways than one."

In the back of my mind, I recognize that my voice is echoing around the restaurant and the chatter in the rest of the room has gone quiet, but blood is whirring in my ears, and I can't stop. I've stayed quiet and docile for too long. Now, it is my turn to speak my mind.

"You and your friends may be wealthy and respected, but I see you for what you are—spineless, cowardly assholes who are so insecure they have to take their rage out on everybody else."

I want to spin on my heel and storm away, making a grand exit, but in classic Eve fashion, my heel catches on the tablecloth, and I nearly trip. I fall sideways and throw an arm out to catch myself, knocking a nearly full bottle of wine on the table over. The glass shatters and red wine splashes across the tablecloth and onto the guests in the booth like a river of blood.

I pause long enough to note the old Russian man's shirt is splattered like he has been shot before I continue my exit and head straight for the doors.

I suck in the night air. The evening is warm and humid, summer strangling the city in its hold, and I want to rip off my clothes for some relief. I feel like I'm being strangled. Like there is a hand around my neck, squeezing the life out of me.

Breathing in and out slowly helps, but as the physical panic begins to ebb away, emotional panic flows in.

What have I done? Cal Higgs is going to find out about the altercation any minute, and then what? Will he fire me? And if he does, will I ever be able to get another chef position? I was only offered this position because of my father, and I doubt he will help me earn another kitchen position, especially since I'm no closer to finding a boyfriend (or husband) since I left for culinary school.

Despite it all, I want to call my dad. He has always made it clear he will move heaven and earth to take care of me, to make sure no one is mean to me, and I want his support right now. But the support he offered me when a girl tripped me during soccer practice and made me miss the net won't apply here. He will tell me to come home. To put down my apron and knife and focus on more meaningful pursuits. And that is the last thing I want to hear right now.

I pull out my phone and scroll through my contacts list, hoping to see a spark of hope amidst the names, but there is nothing. I've lost touch with everyone since I started culinary school. There hasn't been time for friends.

This is probably the kind of situation where most girls would turn to their moms, but she hasn't been in the picture since I was six years old. Even if I had her number, I wouldn't call her. Dad hasn't always been perfect, but at least he was there. At least he cared enough to stay.

I untie my apron and pull it over my head, leaning back against the brick side of the restaurant.

"Take it off, baby!"

I look up and see a man on a motorcycle with his hair in a bun parked along the curb. He is waggling his eyebrows at me like I'm supposed to fall in love with him for harassing me on the street, and the fire that filled my veins inside hasn't died out yet. The embers are still there, burning under the skin, and I step towards him, lips pulled back in a smile.

He looks surprised, and I'm sure he is. That move has probably never worked for him before. He smiles back at me, his tongue darting out to lick his lower lip.

"Is that your bike?" I purr.

He nods. "Want a ride?"

My voice is still sticky sweet as I respond, "So sweet of you to offer. I'd rather choke and die on that grease ball you call a man bun, but thanks anyway, hon."

It takes him a second to realize my words don't match the tone. When it hits him, he snarls, "Bitch."

"Asshole." I flip him the bird over my shoulder and start the long walk home.

Click here to keep reading BROKEN VOWS.

ALSO BY NICOLE FOX

Belluci Mafia Trilogy

Corrupted Angel (Book 1)

Corrupted Queen (Book 2)

Corrupted Empire (Book 3)

De Maggio Mafia Duet

Devil in a Suit (Book 1)

Devil at the Altar (Book 2)

Kornilov Bratva Duet

Married to the Don (Book 1)

Til Death Do Us Part (Book 2)

Heirs to the Bratva Empire

**Can be read in any order*

Kostya

Maksim

Andrei

Tsezar Bratva

Nightfall (Book 1)

Daybreak (Book 2)

Russian Crime Brotherhood

**Can be read in any order*

Owned by the Mob Boss

Unprotected with the Mob Boss

Knocked Up by the Mob Boss

Sold to the Mob Boss

Stolen by the Mob Boss

Trapped with the Mob Boss

Volkov Bratva

Broken Vows (Book 1)

Broken Hope (Book 2)

Broken Sins *(standalone)*

Other Standalones

Vin: A Mafia Romance

Box Sets

Bratva Mob Bosses (Russian Crime Brotherhood Books 1-6)

Tsezar Bratva (Tsezar Bratva Duet Books 1-2)

Heirs to the Bratva Empire

MAILING LIST

Sign up to my mailing list!
New subscribers receive a FREE steamy bad boy romance novel.

Click the link below to join.
https://sendfox.com/nicolefox

Printed in Great Britain
by Amazon

36981493R00225